ABORT
(TERMINATE PREMATURELY)

ABORT

(TERMINATE PREMATURELY)

RANDY HUDSON

ReadersMagnet, LLC

TABLE OF CONTENTS

INTRODUCTION

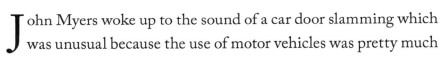

J ohn Myers woke up to the sound of a car door slamming which was unusual because the use of motor vehicles was pretty much prohibited in the neighborhood. He rolled over to see his partner Mary already having a cup of coffee and checking the link.

John and Mary were a team of assassins. They worked for an outfit subsidized by the government. They preferred not to be called assassins. They were the cleaners or the trash crew or even the environmentalists. Since the democrats took control and voted to ensure that it was okay to let a human baby die after birth (infanticide), some of the older persons in power formed this assassin group to clean up the evil, radical, and mental cases whose brains are focused merely on wrong doing. The assassins refer to their eradication of these individuals as really late term abortion.

They never knew who their target would be, but it had become a day-to-day mission. From the link they would get a photo ID and last known GPS position which would be updated on the server every thirty minutes. John and Mary would go out into the throngs of people in the streets to search out their target. They would work both sides of the street at the same time. They each had GPS display in their proximity sunglasses so they would know where the other was at all times in the large crowded streets so they would not accidently shoot each other in crossfire.

John was an exceptional shootist. Whenever he could he would go out to the Rock and meet up with Bobby. Bobby would take John out to compete in some good old fashioned Pistol shoots. Whereas you would race through a mock up western town on horseback through various stations along the street shooting at balloon targets making sure you shoot bad balloons as intended targets and not shoot the good balloons. This practice kept John on top of his game while having to shoot on the move in the city. This greatly improved his accuracy. The last new recruits in Johns group had already been taken out because of bad training. They would move, stop, stance and shoot, move, stop, stance and shoot. They may have aced on the firing range but it was the stop and stance that got them killed. In the real-world people shoot back.

CHAPTER ONE

A s John worked his way down the street a gunshot could be heard as he went down in instant pain. The bullet went through the meaty part of his leg. He expected the kill shot to come at any second, but it did not. Mary fought the crowd to get to him and was so relieved that he was still alive. John was just about to use Mary's scarf to wrap around his leg to cover the entry and exit wounds and stop the bleeding when just at that moment the company doctor showed up with a gel patch. John thought to himself, this is odd! The doctor gel patched the holes and wrapped Mary's scarf around to hold them in place and tied it just tight enough to do the job. The doctor then helped Mary get John back to their little cubby hole in a side alley that they called home for now. The doctor gave John some pain meds and instructed him to stay off the streets for a while.

After the doctor had left, John and Mary just could not figure out what the company doctor was doing in this outlying neighborhood when his office was centrally located in midtown. Albeit John was glad that the doctor was Johnney on the spot with gel patches in hand that kept him from bleeding out if a major artery had been hit. As John lay up trying to figure out just what had happened, what had he missed, Mary tried to comfort him and suggested that just maybe it was a fluke.

Someone in the crowd may have had an itchy finger and someone else bumped into them and caused the gun to go off.

John considered this but did not notice anyone turn and run when he was shot. He remembered as he went down all eyes were on him and when the bullet passed through, it did not hit anyone behind him. John decided it was a well-placed shot meant for him only and now he needed to find out who was behind it.

After a couple of weeks of mainly laying around with his leg elevated to keep the swelling down, John was getting pretty antsy. He had been limping around the small living area the last couple of days so he figured he needed some fresh air and a longer walk would help take the stiffness out and improve the healing process. Mary was sent to work in another part of the city to train a new company recruit while John was recuperating, so that left John alone in their small cubby hole with lots of time to think. Finally, John decided he had enough strength in his sore leg to make a trip around the block. He was about to walk out the door when he had second thoughts. Why was he the target? Was someone striking back against the environmentalists? These thoughts caused John to regroup and dress out in his full body armor which was more weight to bare on his wounded leg. Better safe than sorry he thought to himself as he walked out the door pulling it closed behind him.

It was another non spectacular day as John hobbled down the street favoring his good leg. There was nothing unusual in the air and scanning the crowds, John did not notice any person acting out of the ordinary. Just as John rounded the corner, the bullet hit him like a pile driver in his heart. The body armor stopped the bullet but the impact of it knocked him back and he fell beside a bench. Catching his breath at the surprise of the impact knocking the wind out of him he scanned the area in the direction he had just turned. Peeking through the cracks in the bench so as not to raise his head up, he saw the glint off the optics system the shooter was using in a shallow alley way, but out of sight.

John reached under his armpit and pulled out his long-barreled Ruger super Blackhawk which he had named AT&T because it had the ability to reach out and touch someone. He didn't particularly like to use this specific weapon because it had a noise all its own. If it did not hit you the noise might just scare you to death. At any rate John aimed AT&T just above and to the left of where he caught a glimpse of optics of the shooter. Two quick thunderous bursts from AT&T and John saw a red mist come out of the area of his target. John put AT&T away and clambered back to his feet using the bench for all the help he could get from it. He hobbled across the street to see who was trying to kill him. He arrived about the same time as security. His would be assassin was a young fellow with a mohawk haircut which is usually associated with one radical group or another. John was not sure. He never hunted radical groups, only individuals that were sent to him via the link. He still had no clue who wanted him dead.

John showed security the slug still stuck in his armor over his heart and where he was at the time of the shooting. When security saw John had used AT&T in his defense, he let out a low whistle. Security turned back to where the shooter was standing and looking the wind out of him he scanned the area in the direction he had just turned. Peeking through the cracks in the bench so as not to raise his head up, he saw the glint off the optics system the shooter was using in a shallow alley way, but out of sight.

John reached under his armpit and pulled out his long-barreled Ruger super Blackhawk which he had named AT&T because it had the ability to reach out and touch someone. He didn't particularly like to use this specific weapon because it had a noise all its own. If it did not hit you the noise might just scare you to death. At any rate John aimed AT&T just above and to the left of where he caught a glimpse of optics of the shooter. Two quick thunderous bursts from AT&T and John saw a red mist come out of the area of his target. John put AT&T away and clambered back to his feet using the bench for all the help he could get from it. He hobbled across the street to see who was trying to kill him. He arrived about the same time as security. His would be assassin was a young fellow with a mohawk haircut which is usually associated with one radical group or another. John was not sure. He never hunted radical groups, only individuals that were sent to him via the link. He still had no clue who wanted him dead.

John showed security the slug still stuck in his armor over his heart and where he was at the time of the shooting. When security saw John had used AT&T in his defense, he let out a low whistle. Security turned back to where the shooter was standing and looking at the two big forty-four magnum holes in the wall, they decided to look on the other side. When they opened the door, they were surprised to find another dead body on the inside. This one too had a huge hole in her head. Security whistled again. The female had a gun in her hand also so it was concluded that this was some sort of radical assassin team. Now the environmentalist commission had to call a meeting to discuss procedures going forward. John was alone and incredibly lucky it was a heart shot and not a head shot. He thought to himself just how lucky as he almost left the house without armoring up. That will not ever happen now, even if he is just going out to pick up take out.

When Mary heard what had occurred, she came rushing back to their little cubby hole to be with John. At first, she was angry with him, then seeing that he was okay and only got a fist sized bruise on the left side of his chest, she eased up. "Who were these people, and why were they targeting you?" Mary asked.

John replied "I have no clue, but I certainly intend to find out." He continued "Man with all this excitement, I sure am hungry. Why don't we order a huge 18" super-duper acropolis pizza from down on the bayou."

"Yeah, Bibba's Pizza sounds good to me, it's the best Greek pizza in the city." Mary replied. And so it was.

Early the next morning John received a message via the link from the environmentalist commission. It turns out the fellow's name was Todd Rez and the females name was Teresa Wrob. Both were involved in the porn industry. Not just any porn, filming children in bathing situations as they performed sex so the kids could watch. They were up and coming business associates making money off this filth until John put them out of business permanently. The question remains, why was John their target? John replied "Maybe some of those in the underworld are thinking that their face is going to show up on my screen one day. My question is who in the commission may have leaked my identity. It's not like I report to an office building every day. I am incognito with no physical contact with the commission. If someone on your end leaked out my name then how many other environmentalists have been made public. This kind of leak could be bad, and I mean very bad for all concerned."

The commissioners gave their apologies and thanked John for all the good work he has done for the commission as well as his country. They said "We will look into it." And disconnected the link.

A couple of days later John woke up, sat up in bed grabbing the hand mirror and looked over the still yellowish green bruise on his left breast. Lucky no ribs or sternum were broken. Still, it was very sore. He looked over to the table and Mary was in her usual spot with her cup of coffee reading some updates posted on the link. When she noticed John was gazing at her she smiled and said "Good morning, John. Are we feeling well today?"

He smiled back and said "As near as I can tell the bruise on my chest hurts more than the hole in my leg so my leg must be getting better." They both laughed. He got up and wobbled over to the table in his boxers and sat down to have a cup of coffee with Mary. He didn't say much at first during his downtime, he had had more time to think about his world around him. His relationship with Mary was that of a Friend. They were working partners in a dangerous line of work. Lately though he had been having thoughts that he did not know how to tell Mary. Things like how she was pleasant to see out on the streets in a crowd of people, but to tell the truth he would much more like to just see her alone in front of him wearing nothing but a thong. Just the thought of that made him blush.

Mary looked curiously at him as he was blushing but not wanting to embarrass him, she said nothing. Mary liked John as a partner and even thought about what it would be like to have him as a relationship partner. They got along great even though they had never shared a bed. She wondered to herself at times how long she could keep their relationship with him on a professional level going. Sometimes it seemed the ice was melting fast. There was no company policy yet that environmentalist could not have an ongoing relationship as long as it did not interfere with the job at hand. Having finished his coffee, John had a shower, shaved and got dressed for the day. When he returned Mary said "Well don't you look refreshed."

John smiled at her and replied "I feel it too". John still recovering from his wounds was still off the work roster. After the second incident the commission decided it may be better to leave Mary to watch over him for the time being. This basically gave them both paid vacation time. John asked Mary "Do you feel like getting out of the city for a few days?" As Mary was starting to feel cooped up in the little cubby hole she jumped at the chance for a change of scenery.

First on the list John took Mary to meet Bobby, his shootist friend. As it turns out when Mary was young, she had taken some riding lessons at some stables south of the city. This pleased John greatly. It did not take but a few hours of riding for her to get back used to being in the saddle.

John asked her, "Do you think you can ride and shoot?"

Mary laughed and said "Probably more proficiently than riding and roping." Everyone laughed at that one.

Bobby and John loaded up the six shooters with rat shot and staked out the good and bad balloons. Mary found out quick what it was like shooting balloons from the saddle of a galloping horse. Out of six shots she only hit two and one of those was a good balloon. 'Oops'. Mary felt bad and asked "where's the rope?"

Again, everyone laughed. Mary sat back and watched the guys run through shooting six shots hitting six balloons with amazement. She set about getting her rhythm down with the horse and soon she was hitting four or five and one time even six. She was incredibly happy. Now she understood John's meaning when he would say "shoot on the move and live longer."

After a couple of days of horsing around and shooting balloons, John asked Mary if she would mind going to church with him.

Mary replied, "I would be delighted, it's been a while."

They went to church in the Rock where Bobby lived. It was an old-fashioned Pentecostal church. (Full Gospel) These were of these were the kind of people John and Mary enjoyed being around. While they were there, Bobby introduced them to one of his brother-in-law Pearl. Pearl had a huge exotic game ranch which he invited John and Mary out to for a few days. They agreed and said "It sounds like fun."

When they arrived, they passed these big iron gates over the cattle guard. Driving through the coded gates, the gates automatically closed behind them. Miles of blacktop road to the main house, passing a couple of small lakes off on the left, they saw some Eland antelope. A little later an Aoudad was looking out of the brush at them not to mention the herd of whitetail deer that ran across the road in front of them.

When they arrived at the main house they were in awe. Compared to the six hundred square foot of their cubby hole in the city, they were looking at a ten thousand square foot home with Mexican tile shingles sitting next to a five-acre lake with an island, palm trees and a dock. From the house you can sit and watch all sorts of animals come down to the lake for water. John and Mary thought they had died and gone to heaven. When Pearl assigned accommodations, he put John and Mary in a single room with a single queen size bed. Pearl did not know that they were merely work partners and not a couple. Not wanting to be rude, John and Mary just smiled at Pearl and thanked him. Who would have guessed, it turned out to be a night of heaven.

The next morning Pearl woke John and Mary and asked them if they were in the mood to shoot something to put some meat in their freezer. There was no hesitation. They happily accepted Pearl's invitation. Pearl buzzed the hired hand Pat to go and sit with John and Mary in the stand and show them what to shoot. Since it was a freebee, he did not want them shooting any trophies. They had been sitting in the stand now for a couple of hours and Mary was starting to get antsy. It was cold and wet out and just when they were about to climb out of the stand John said, "what's that thing?"

Pat looked over to the left and replied, "That's a good size Nilgai coming your way."

John looked at Pat and asked, "Good eating?" Pat nodded in reply and Mary's eyes got big.

Pat asked John, "you want him?" John whispered, "hell yeah."

Pat said "slow and easy, get ready."

John chambered the 270 slowly got the barrel out the slot, clicked off the safety, put the butt tight into his shoulder and laid his cheek over stock centered the crosshairs mid-mass just behind the front shoulder blade. Boom.

Mary about wet herself. The Nilgai bolted. John thinking to himself, oh crap, I blew it. Just as the Nilgai was getting back into the brush it dropped in its tracks. Pat went and got the front-end loader to carry the Nilgai back to the barn to skin and gut out. This

Nilgai was a little over five hundred pounds. Pat told John, "I hope you have a big freezer." Pat was then trimming the back strap off and quartering the beast to hang in the cooler. By the time they got back to the big house John was still running on adrenaline. All the excitement took all his pain away making him forget about his recent injuries. He felt good.

Pearl was happy for John. Peg, Pearls wife took some of the fresh back strap in thin half inch slices and battered and fried it up. Along with a Salad, mashed potatoes, cookies, and key lime pie all home made from scratch, John and Mary were in heaven all over again. Later they could not help but ask themselves, why does the food taste so much better out in the country? After supper, the four of them sat around kind of getting to know each other a little better Somewhere during the discussion the subject of Johns limp came up. He mentioned how he mysteriously got shot and even that the company doctor was Johnney on the spot to fix him right up when it happened.

Pearl inquisitively turned and asked John, "you say this doctor works for the government?"

John replied, "yes." Pearl asked him to follow him into the other room.

John followed Pearl into what turned out to be a huge trophy room off to the left of the living room fireplace. Bears, goats, elks, monkeys, foxes, pheasants, and so much more. John was enamored by it all. Pearl was digging in a drawer that contained stacks of photo albums when he pulled one out and opened it. He flipped a couple of pages in and laid the album open on the class case holding the fox and the pheasant.

As John was still admiring the room and all of its inhabitants, he noticed Pearl just standing there and said "oh sorry, this is just too amazing in here."

Pearl just grinned. John walked over to Pearl and Pearl pointed to a picture of several people standing over a huge Pere David deer with an enormous rack. Pearl told him, "That one was close to four hundred pounds." Then John saw the smiling man holding the rifle. It was the commissions doctor. That was not as surprising as seeing the other fellows in the picture who he knew to be pure evil people. What were they doing on a hunting trip with the commissions doctor or vice versa? John did not like what he was seeing. About that time Pearl spoke up and said, "They come out a couple of times a year to get away from the city and talk business."

John asked Pearl if he could make a printout copy of the photo for him. Pearl hesitated for a moment and then agreed. He took the photo to Peg's office and ran off a color copy. Handing the photo over to John, Pearl asked that he not let anyone know how he got the photo for everyone's safety. John agreed.

Later that afternoon John and Mary were in their quarters and John showed the photo to Mary. She exclaimed, "Oh my God, what the hell is that doctor doing with those people? Could this be the commissions leak?"

John replied, "I haven't even had time to think about that, but you can bet your sweet bottom that we will find out." The next morning not wanting to wear out their welcome, John and Mary decided to head back into the city. Upon driving out of the massive gates to the ranch, they both had a sense of remorse. John exclaimed, "Man, in a different life the should of, could of, and would of."

Mary just sighed and responded "I know." A couple hours later they were back in their cubby hole they consider home in the city. They would have to make another trip back to the ranch to pick up the rest of their meat when they make room for it. Mary sat down and blew up the photo they had retrieved and photo shopped the doctor out of it. She then separated the other two fellows and cut out head shots of each of them. She sent the individual headshots of them to a friend in another agency to run a facial recognition to try to get a positive ID on these guys. That would help them find out what kind of business these fellows are in and how they are connected to the doctor. The next morning would tell the tale.

Meanwhile over supper reminiscing over sharing a room with Mary over the weekend John asked, "What do we do now?"

"About what?" replies Mary. John just put his hands to his face and grinned. "What?" Mary asked again with a smirk on her face. John sheepishly said "What should we do about our sleeping arrangements?"

She laughed and replied, "You are going to buy a bigger bed and put it in my room, unless you like sleeping in the street." John jumped up excitedly and exclaimed "Really." Before the pain in his leg and chest hit him. Mary just laughed at him and said, "Yep."

John was on the phone to Mattress Mack's and a new bed was delivered, set up, and the old one's hauled off in a matter of a couple of hours. Mary laughed at how John had that possum eating grin on his face. Mary looked at that proud look on John's face then she said, "You forgot to order bigger sheets."

"Oh crap!" John said. That response had them both cracking up. They survived the blissful night. The next morning John walked into the main room where Mary was in her spot with her coffee checking the link. John poured himself a cup and sat down across from her. "Is the doctor in the same building as the commission?" John asked.

Mary shrugged her shoulders and replied, "Don't know, I've never been there."

"Neither have I," said John. "Maybe I should go find our good doctor who makes house calls and let him check me out, while I do the same to him." A moment later, Mary's device pinged. She clicked it and said, "Oh look here. This is the butcher; he deals in meat. The live one's with two legs."

John said, "Well that's not good. He looks like the ring leader of an international sex slave trade. What about the other fellow?" "Hold on, worse. He is an undertaker. He makes people disappear for good." Mary told him.

John says, "My question is why have these two bottom feeder, whale shit, scum suckers not ever been put on our list of targets to Abort?"

Mary says, "That's beginning to look like a very good question to ask. But who do we ask? Do you think those two you shot down on the corner were associated with the Butcher or Undertaker?"

John thought on this a few minutes and agreed it could have very well been. What has the Doctor got to do with it is still the question. As they both sat there sipping their coffee in silent thought, a ding went off on Mary's device bringing them both back to the here and now. John looks at Mary as she looks up and says, "Looks like we have an abortion to perform. It's time to get back to work."

John said, "Ugh, back to the routine. I was starting to like my quiet time with you Mary."

"Ditto that," she replied with a smile on her face. It's been a while since they armored up so they had to take extra time to make sure all was as it should be. Satisfied Mary unplugged the coffee pot and looked back once more before pulling the door closed behind them.

They walked together on the way to the destination point and amongst the throng of people. The throng made John think of the thong, so he looked at Mary and smiled and walked on. As they neared the destination, they both pulled down their optical shades and split up to run both sides of the street. They had multiple ways to cause one's death without the use of a noisy firearm. If done properly the person would not know they were dying until Mary or John were already some distance away from them. A quick search of the last pinged location came up empty. They would have to wait another five minutes for the next location ping update.

At the ping it showed their target another block up and over from their present location. Mary crossed over to join up with John as they walked the next block over. They separated again to go up the next block ahead. As they were working their way up Mary spotted the target. She let John know she had a visual. This was a scruffy looking guy who seemed to be just trolling along with no destination. Then Mary saw the child that old scruffy was following. Mary signaled to John that she was using the yellow jacket. John nodded. That's when Mary saw old scruffy reach out and grab the young girl, cover her mouth with his hand, and pulled her back against the flow of pedestrians. Mary in that moment hit the man in the back of his calf with the yellow jacket stinger injection. A super concentrated serum of bee poison. Old scruffy was suddenly unable to move his leg at that point, it was like it was planted and he could feel the poison racing up his leg killing all the nerves on contact. His leg could have just as well been a log hanging off his hip.

He lost his grip of the girl and she screamed and ran back in the direction of her mother who was just bursting through the crowd frantic in search for her daughter. At this point Mary turned and moved on just as old scruffy keeled over and died on the spot. When John caught up with Mary he had to hold her for a minute. She turned to John and said, "If we would have been a minute later that bastard would have had that young girl taken who knows where."

John smiled at her and replied, "You did good Mary. You got a twofer."

She exclaimed, "What do you mean I got a twofer?"

"You not only took out our intended target, you rescued a little girl in the process. That's a huge kudos to you my dear lady". She looked back up at him and replied, "That's the first time you called me dear." Hugging him a little bit tighter as they laughed together.

The walk back home to their little cubby hole was uneventful. As soon as they opened the door Mary took John by the arm and said, "Someone has been in here, the coffee pot is plugged back in."

John thinking maybe she was mistaken started looking around. Mary was more adamant telling him, "I know I unplugged the coffee pot and when we were leaving, I looked back to make sure. I double checked and now it is plugged in."

"Well now, ain't that like another burr under the saddle?" John says. Looking at the coffee pot it was half full. The real question is half full of what? Mary got on the link and contacted the commission who in turn sent a man from the lab with a brand new coffee pot and retrieved the old pot with its contents to run it through toxicology just to see what more was in the pot besides coffee and water. The commission also sent a tech to install an alarm and outside cameras for twenty-four-hour monitoring.

John says, "Now don't that make us all feel homey and secure." Mary just grinned at his sarcasm. When all was said and done and they were finally left alone, John turned to Mary and suggested "Why don't I make a big tub of popcorn and we sit down and watch a movie."

"I second that." Mary replied. They spent the rest of the evening cozied up, just the two of them, watching The Life of Pi.

When the sun came up the next morning both John and Mary were making faces over coffee. It seems the new pot just didn't have the flavor the old pot had to develop. John sighed and said, "How long does it take to break these things in?"

"I hope not too long." Mary responded. Ping. Mary looked down at her device and saw that it was a message from the commission. John raised his eyebrow. No strange prints on the old coffee pot but enough Oxycodone to kill a couple of horses. John says, "It seems I am still a target. I think this morning is a good time to go visit the doctor." As he was getting dressed to leave, Ping. "We got another abortion to make." Mary tells him. John smiled, "Early bird gets something I reckon." After checking all their equipment and armoring up they walked out the door not forgetting to set the new alarm system. This time their target was a little more off the main traffic area. It was in a more rundown neighborhood. No big crowds so John and Mary stayed together. A couple walking through a neighborhood is less likely to draw attention than two strangers on each side of thestreet. There was a little foot traffic. Not much. "Well this is going to be different." said John.

Still no sign of the target, but it has been a while. The next ping should be any minute now. John looked ahead at the ice cream truck with some little kids trying to buy ice cream. The older kids were trying to shoo the younger ones away. John asked Mary, "Would you like an ice cream cone?"

"Why not?" she replied. They went towards the truck. Just before getting there, John observed the driver give a kid a couple of bags of white powder and it sure as hell was not powdered sugar. John stepped up to the window and who was serving drugs, ice cream and whatever else but their target. Mary pulled her silenced 9mm at the young man with the two packs of powder. He dropped the packs and ran. The driver which happens to be their mark, reached for something but John had already aborted him between the eyes. Then John and Mary closed all the doors and locked them and strolled on down the street.

On the way home, John called a tip line reporting a drug deal gone bad in an ice cream truck and hung up the phone. A couple of minutes later, security passed them in a rush. John looked at Mary and said, "Yep, another late term abortion completed successfully." They gave each other a high five and finished the walk home by lunch time.

"What's for lunch?" He asked Mary. "I don't know, I haven't thought about it."

"What if I cook up a couple of those Nilgai steaks on the grill?" With a smile Mary replied, "Well aren't you turning into a regular homemaker." John grinned and blushed at that remark. He soon had the grill going and sizzled a couple of steaks. At first taste it was different than what they were used to. A little gamey but after all the Nilgai happens to be a member of the antelope family. It was different but it was enjoyed. John told Mary, "I hope you liked it because we still have about four hundred more pounds to eat". They both busted out laughing.

John said, "I have an idea. Why don't we invite out three units for some talking and grilling?"

"That would be wonderful." Mary replied, "We haven't had a get together in ages."

"Good" said John. "See if you can arrange for Lacy and Lloyde and Rochelle and Randy to meet up as well as invite Kathy and Jay also. We got some catching up to do. Don't forget to find out what any of them know about who our doctor is associating with."

"Sounds good to me, I wander if any of them have been targeted like you have" says Mary.

"Oh crap! We can't invite them over here right now. Whoever is after us doesn't need to know about them. We'll have to come up with a better plan." Mary agreed.

Mary said, "You reckon Bobby would mind if we invaded the Rock? It's such a small town and would be fun.

The next day Mary set about making some calls to set things up with the others. John came in and Mary exclaimed, "You are not going to believe this. Everyone is all in, and guess what. Randy owns a little piece of property there. We can set up camp at no cost. Can you believe the luck?"

"For real? That's great! Who would have thought?" he replied. About that time, Ping.

"You have got to be kidding me. Another Abort. We used to go for days and never get pinged, and now it's like every day. What's up with that?" Mary asked.

Again, John and Mary checked their gear and armored up. Checked the house, set the alarm and walked out. Mary said, "I hope it's not another kid snatcher." Before they arrived at the last known location, they split up as usual. As John approached what appeared to be a broken down van with oil all over the asphalt underneath it, John thought to himself what tough luck of this poor fool who threw a rod. As he neared the van John witnessed this big burly dude slapping around on a teen age girl. John lowered his head walking around the van. The side door was open and John was aghast. There were at least six to ten teenage girls handcuffed to a bar along the wall. John immediately froze. The big burly dude said, "What you looking at puto? You want some of that stuff?" John shook his head in disgust.

John asked, "Are you allergic to yellow Jackets?" Loud enough for Mary to hear him. The burly dude replied, "Them stinking yellow jackets don't bother me. I swat them away like gnats." At that moment Mary hit him in the calf with her deadly stinger. Instantly his leg froze up as he turned and looked at Mary and said, "What the fu…"

Mary smiled at him and said, "Yellow Jacket." That's when the fear appeared in his eyes. He wasn't so tough now. Within a minute he keeled over. John called the tip line and reported that it appeared as if someone broke down on the side of the road and must have had a heart attack and that it appears he has a group of girls handcuffed in his van.

Within minutes security was on site. As John and Mary walked away, they looked back in time to see the tears of fear turn into tears of joy on the girls. Maybe some of them would make it back home. At least that is what John hoped for.

All this walking was doing John's leg wonders. Only when he squatted and stretched his leg muscles did he still have a tender spot. As they proceeded down the street, John's eye caught sight of a Blue Bell sign. "Don't I still owe you an ice cream from the other day?"

"That's right! I never did collect that cone, you sure do." Once in the shop it was so hard to pick a flavor. Blue Bell being locally made had so many choices. John settled on two scoops of chocolate ripple and Mary went with strawberry delight. Once back out on the street they were both laughing and licking their ice cream like a couple of little kids, sticky chins and all.

Back at the cubby hole having both faces and hands washed, they took their places at the table. "I guess we should pack up the things needed for the camp out this weekend" he told her.

"I can't wait to catch up with the other crews. This is going to be so much fun."

John bolted up right, "Oh crap, tomorrow is already Friday. Where the hell are the days going?"

Mary laughed at his outburst. "Calm down John, we have been a little busier than usual as of late."

"Your right. I think I really need this weekend." Friday morning Mary linked up to the commission to let them know they would be out of pocket for the weekend. Mainly just as a professional courtesy. They set about tying up all the loose ends around the house, ate lunch, then loaded up and burned off out of the city.

CHAPTER TWO

In C-Town they stopped off at Walmart for supplies. Walking into the store they ran smack dab into Randy and Rochelle coming out. "Kapaso Amigo" Everyone was smiling as they all high fived each other. Randy gave John directions to find his place in the Rock. Not that it was really needed. The Rock is only about eight blocks wide. It would be kind of hard to get lost in a place like that. Although a few people have found their way to the Rock, some have yet to find their way back out. Kind of like the song Hotel California. As Randy and Rochelle headed to their cars, John and Mary continued on into the store.

About an hour later John and Mary caught up at Randy's place. Boy has nature taken over. Foundation of an old structure. Plants gone wild. Pecan, Walnut, Crepe Myrtle, Yeppoon Japanese rain tree, an ancient Mulberry, Hackberry and a stand of Yucca, Bamboo and China Berry. All of this on a quarter of a block of property.

"Man, this will be like camping in the Wilderness," exclaimed John as he looked around.

Randy had a good stash of fire wood stacked up on the old slab just for such occasions. Randy told John "Clear a spot and pitch your tent wherever you want."

John not wanting to be too intrusive asked "Where's your spot?"

"Follow me, I'll show you." Just north of the slab, hidden by the brush was what appeared to be an old Scooby Doo looking van. As Randy smiled motioning towards the van John couldn't help but shake his head and laugh. He then turned back to seek out a spot for himself.

About forty-five minutes later Jay and Kathy showed up. By now Randy had a little fire going. John already had his tent up under the Mulberry tree. Everyone greeted with high fives and hugs. Jay and Kathy set their tent up under the Hackberry tree a little further south of the slab giving John and Mary plenty of privacy as well. "You know tent walls aren't soundproof." Jay commented. Everyone laughed.

The Girls kind of got themselves off to the side trying to catch up on all the goings on and gossip in their lives. The Guys cleaned off a good part of the slab that was going to more or less be a social area. Since Randy had built the fire right in the middle of it, it worked out where everyone could scatter chairs around and watch the fire and visit.

It was soon to be dark and Randy pulled out this eighteen-by-eighteen steel grate with one inch rebar legs welded to it and set it over the fire. Rochelle took it from there. As it turns out, she is a campfire girl extraordinaire. She came out with that huge cast iron skillet and commenced to frying hamburger patties and fries after. She was just finishing up when Lloyde and Lacy arrived.

"It's about damn time!" yelled John grinning. Everyone greeted them.

"You would not believe the traffic leaving the city." Lloyd replied.

Randy said, "Yeppers, happens every weekend."

"Do you know how many years it has been since I had any reason to leave the City?" asked Lloyd.

In which Lacy quipped, "Yeah, He's a real homeboy. He don't even like to leave his own neighborhood."

"Two wrecks and a damn bottle neck at that bridge construction" Lloyd told them.

Randy replied, "You should have called me. I could have guided you down a few back roads to get you around that mess."

"You bet your ass I will next time."

John looked up and said, "So Lloyd, it's getting dark fast. You had better pop up your tent somewhere, then get back over here for these morsels of burgers before I eat them all." Jay stood up and volunteered to help Lloyd get set up. Lloyd chose his spot in the North West section by what at one time was a garden shed.

When they returned back to the group around the fire Lloyd exclaimed, "It's time to pop a top."

"I'll go for that." Lloyd pulled out his cooler and handed Jay a frosted can. After everyone was settled in hypnotized by the flickering flames Randy stood up and handed everyone a stick.

"Don't throw it in the fire." He told them. About that time Rochelle busted out the big bag of jumbo marshmallows and a pack of girl scout chocolate thin mint cookies. It dawned on everyone at the same time. Smores.

"Oh my God," Lacy said. "Do you know how long it's been since I have had real campfire smores?"

Randy winked at her and replied, "Well that is too long."

Between the laughter and the chewing and the blazing marshmallows, this group of assassins turned into little children.

John sat back thinking to himself that this was something that they all had needed. Just to let go and relax. The best kind of therapy money could not buy.

About that time Bobby showed up with a grin and a six pack in hand. He held out the six pack like a peace offering. Jay and Lloyde each helped their selves to one. Since Lloyd and Lacey were the only ones in the group that Bobby had not been acquainted with introductions were made. Bobby pulled up an unsplit log to sit on by the fire as a chair. It didn't take long for Mary to tell the other girls of her rather poor shooting skills on horseback. Mary said, "It looks easy, but looks are deceiving."

Bobby asked them If they wanted to give it a whirl tomorrow then? They all exclaimed, "Heck Yeah!" Then the girls started chattering together in excitement for the coming day.

Randy asked, "While the girls are playing giddy up, any of you guys want to canoe down the river?"

"I'm game." says John.

"Short version or long version?" asked Jay.

Randy said, "It's up to you guys, as you and I have already done multiple runs on both."

"What the hell, why not? Something else to scratch off my bucket list," said Lloyd.

Jay laughed, "What's that? How many times you can fall out of a canoe?" Everyone busted out laughing at that one. The day trip was decided. Randy and Jay had canoes available. After plans were made, the teams started drifting to their tents for the night. Randy and Rochelle to the old van.

At daylight Randy was kicking coals throwing more twigs and logs on the fire to get it going. Once it was going pretty well, he set the old ceramic pot of water on the corner of the grate kind of centered over the fire. He then diced up a pack of bacon and threw it into the skillet. As the bacon cooked, he chopped up a couple of potatoes and an onion. When the bacon was ready, he took it out of the skillet and added the potatoes and onion in to the hot bacon grease. While browning the ingredients, he scrambled about eight eggs in a bowl. Then he threw the bacon back into the skillet poured the eggs in and stirred until the eggs were done. By this time everyone started waking up and migrating towards the hot water pot for instant coffee. Randy pulled the skillet off the grate and opened a bag of extra-large tortillas. He took the first tortilla and flopped it on the hot grate. He got a look from a couple in attendance as it was just starting to brown in spots, so he flipped it over. After a minute he snatched it off of the grill, scooped in some bacon, potato, eggs, onions and a shot of picante and wrapped it up before taking a bite. He looked up at everyone and said this one is mine, make your own. Then it was a scramble to see who could get to the tortillas first.

After everyone had their fill and was drinking coffee, John spoke up. "Man, I can't understand why food tastes so good out in the country." Everyone nodded in agreement. Randy and Jay rounded up the canoes and the girls were getting antsy about going to play shoot- 'em-up on horseback. They just had to wait for Bobby to drop the guys off up river and come back.

The guys had an uneventful day on the river. Jay and Randy were at the rear station on canoes paddling and steering. John and Lloyd were in the front station with their paddles and fishing poles. John managed to snag an alligator gar about thirty-six inches in length. When he reeled it in and saw all those rows of pointed teeth, he just wanted it off his hook. Watching him retrieve his hook from all those rows of teeth was quite entertaining. "Man, I never knew a fish like that even existed." John said. Jay and Randy laughed out loud.

About that time Lloyd jerked his pole. "I got something." He said all excited. He reeled in his line and came up with about a nine-inch channel cat.

"Come on now," Jay said, "That's not enough for a meal."

As Lloyd fought the hook Randy told him, "You keep piddling with that all day and the poor thing is going to smother to death out in this air."

Everyone cracked up at that remark, and soon the channel cat was free of the hook to swim in the river again. They went around a bend and witnessed about thirty white tail deer midstream crossing the river. With the appearance of the canoes, it didn't take long for the deer to abscond. By the end of the day, they managed to see a pair of Bald Eagles. They spotted and picked up a couple of pieces of petrified wood off of a gravel bar and got plenty of sunshine. By the time they rounded the last bend and crossed under the suspended pipeline it was time to call Bobby. By the time they made it to the ramp Bobby was coming down the drive with perfect timing.

When they made it back to camp the girls had already stoked the coals and had a fire going. The guys were a little sunburned, but no worse for the wear Now the girl's day was a little different story. They not only were a little sunburned and tired from all that riding, they were a little saddle sore to boot. Ah the pain of having fun.

Lloyd said, "I need a beer."

"I second that," said Jay as he headed over to the cooler.

Someone asked, "What's on the menu for supper?"

Rochelle replied, "Peanut Butter and Jelly sandwiches."

"Really?" asked Lloyd.

"No silly," replied Rochelle, "Looks like grilled T-bone tonight." That definitely cheered everyone up. Randy proceeded to wire brush the grill and Rochelle laid out eight magnificent specimens on one-inch-thick cuts of T-bone. All eyes were on the grill, open flame fire cooking. There's got to be an art to it. Kathy, Lacy, and Mary chopped up a huge bowl of garden salad. Kathy wrapped two rolls of garlic bread in aluminum foil and set them down by the coals and turned them often. When all was said and done, they had to admit, it could not get any better than this.

After the meal, everyone was once again kicked back around the fire, hypnotized by the flickering flame. Finally, John spoke up. "What do any of you know about the commissions doctor?" No one had anything to say. John explained how he had been shot clean through his leg and out of nowhere the commission doctor shows up and he just so happened to have on him the gel packs needed to seal his wound. Then he asked them, "Now does this sound weird to any of you or is my imagination running away with me?"

The rest of the group agreed that it just sounded too weird to be a coincidence. After that John told them "Then I got Lucky and some low life assassins took a heart shot and not a head shot, otherwise I would not be talking to you all right now."

Lloyd said, "I thought you looked like you had a sort of bruise when we were cooling off down on the river, but I didn't want to stick my nose in your business."

Kathy said, "What the heck? Why would someone want to take you out?"

"Good question." Mary said. "It may be an us thing."

"What?" exclaimed Rochelle. "What to you mean an us thing?"

Mary explained about the tampering with the coffee pot while they were out aborting a target to which Jay replied, "You mean to tell me someone came in to your home while you were out on a mission?" John and Mary both nodded their heads in unison. "Something is not right here."

Kathy said, "I don't think we are in Kansas anymore Toto."

Lloyd asked John, "What the hell does the commissions doctor have to do with any of this?

"I really wish I knew, but I aim to find out."

Mary told them that she thinks there is a leak in the commission and explained that this was the reason they called everyone together out here. "Our home may not be safe for you all to stop by. I think we are being watched. Our house may also be bugged. We just don't know."

Lacy asked, "Why would you think that?"

Mary looked over at John and continued, "Everytime John mentions going to have a talk with the doctor we instantly get an abortion order."

At this John had a look of surprise come over his face. "Come to think of it, that is right. Every time I have told her I am going to see the doctor we get a ping."

Concerned faces all around as John tells them that they were called out every day of the last week. "Really?" asked Jay. "We only had one call out."

"Us to." says Lacy.

"Same." Randy chimed in.

Mary said, "I don't know what is going on, but it sure looks like big trouble in little China." Everyone agreed.

A collective silence fell on the group as they all sat staring into the fire, each of them wondering what the hell is going on? John broke the silence by asking, "Do any of you know of a man called the Butcher?" Only raised eyebrows. "How about a man called the Undertaker?" Still no spark. "The Butcher deals in international sex slave trade and the Undertaker makes people disappear."

Rochelle asked, "What have these two low lives have to do with anything?"

Mary told her, "We have a witness and a photo of these two on a hunting trip with our fine doctor."

"Holy Shit! This is crazy." Lloyd told them.

In unison John and Mary replied, "Our thoughts exactly."

Contemplating all that he heard Jay said to the group, "At the moment the focus seems to be on John and Mary we presume."

Kathy replied, "Yeah, but we can't be sure can we."

"If there is a leak, we sure as hell can't talk to anyone at the commission."

Lloyd asked, "Well what the hell can we do?"

John told him, "I know an old associate of mine who might be able to snoop around for us. He's been known to work both sides of the street."

Lloyd asked, "Can you trust him?"

"With my life, which is more than I can say about the commission at this point of time. I think we are going to need all the help we can get to get to the bottom of this mess." Now the mood around the campfire was solemn. "I'll see if I can look him up next week when we are back in the city."

"I need another beer." said Lloyd.

Lacy looked at him and said, "That stuff is going to kill you one of these days Lloyd."

He grinned at her and said, "There's worse ways to die you know." She just shook her head. She was a master at the art of death.

Rochelle once again pulled out the makings for smores, perking everyone up. Randy got up to go find new sticks to roast the marshmallows on. Jay threw another log on the fire and the mood around the fire changed. The group spent the rest of the evening talking about everything except work. The guys told the girls their stories from fishing and the one that got away. Told them about the Eagles and Deer and just the simple calmness to just follow the current. The girls started laughing and talking about their shooting skills and who killed the most balloons and who almost shot herself in the foot. All in all, they had a great time.

As the evening wound down, John asked if anybody was up for church the next morning. The little Full Gospel Church in the Rock was very welcoming to him and Mary before. Actually, the only real strangers to the church would be Lacy and Lloyd. It was a unanimous decision. Pastor Cal would have eight more souls to speak to tomorrow morning.

At the crack of dawn Sunday morning Randy and John already had the fire stoked and the water getting hot. Breakfast would be the same as yesterday, but with much more help preparing it. Everyone kind of fell into a chore of choice and in no time, breakfast was served. Two or three tortillas at a time on the grill. Randy said, "Now you're cooking. It's amazing how smooth things work out with teamwork."

"If you don't mind Randy, so as not to have to deal with Sunday traffic, Mary and I would like to stay another night and drive back after the morning rush.:

"I was just thinking the very same thought. We don't have normal office hours. You are all welcome to stay here anytime you feel like or need to without a problem."

Lacy and Kathy both agreed they will probably do likewise. John went over to Bobby's place to bum a five-gallon bucket of warm water and brought it back to the camp. Lloyd asked, "What's that for?"

"Well first, the girls might want to take a bird bath before going to church. After they are done maybe you should too."

"I didn't think of that," replied Lloyd. "Good idea."

Come Ten o'clock everyone was ready for church. The group decided to walk on over since after all at three blocks away. That's considered half way across town in the Rock. Lloyd commented, "I forgot they made towns this small." Everyone was laughing at that. With it being such a small town, they were surprised to see around forty attendees plus themselves. Pastor Cal had himself a decent-sized crowd today. After the choir sang a round of songs, the sermon was about relationships. Both personal relationships as well as the relationship with God.

After the Services there was a lot of fellowship and visiting. Lacy and Lloyd found that they fit right in with the congregation like a glove. After a bit the group headed back over to Randy's to just hang out. Lloyd walked over to grab himself a beer out of the cooler and Lacy told him, "You just walked out of church!"

"I'm still thirsty" he told her.

"I don't know about you sometimes Lloyd."

"What's to know?" They just stared at each other for a long minute before they both busted out laughing.

Rochelle asked Mary, "Why do they do that?"

Mary replied, "It must be their strange way of showing affection towards each other."

Rochelle shook her head, "I don't know." Randy and John already had the fire stirred back up with coffee water on when Pearl pulled up. He motioned for John. John walked over to his truck and they talked for a few minutes before Pearl reached back into a cooler and handed John a package.

"What's this?" John asked him.

"I heard you have been over here for a few days so I thought you would want some of your Nilgai steaks."

"Oh man, you sure got that right. I just didn't want to show up at your place unannounced to pick any up."

"I kind of figured that." Pearl told him. John expressed his thanks and Pearl went on his way. John was still standing next to the road holding the package of meat as he turned around and noticed everyone staring at him.

"What?" He asked holding up the package of steaks. "I have supper."

Jay asked, "What's for supper?" "Nilgai."

"Nil what?" asked Lloyd.

"You will see." John told him as he put the package on ice in the cooler.

Lacy asked, "Nilgai, what the heck is that?"

"It's a type of antelope." Kathy told her.

"Why didn't he just say antelope then?" "Because it's a Nilgai."

"Never mind." Lacy replied.

John got Mary's attention and motioned for her to follow him over by Randy's old van to talk to her for a minute. Mary asked him, "What's up?"

"Pearl just informed me that our good doctor was trying to schedule a time when he and his friends could come out for a hunt and do some business."

"Oh really? What kind of business do you think that might be?"

"I have no idea but it can't be anything good. Pearl didn't want to speak up in front of the others yet. No need to get them excited until we know more about what's going on." Mary agreed.

As they walked back to the group Lloyd said to them, "Oh here comes the lovebirds." They both blushed.

"Where did that come from Lloyd?" Mary asked.

"Well, it's kind of obvious." Rochelle said.

John replied, "Really?" Everyone busted out laughing and in unison all you could hear from everyone was "Yes really!"

Mary said, "Get over it." and received more chuckles all around.

John walked back over to the cooler, pulled out the package of Nilgai and handed it to Rochelle. "Work your magic." The group took the hint. It was time to change the subject. The girls grouped off and started to make preparations for the evening meal. The guys cleaned up around the social area and fed the fire. Jay and Lloyd grabbed themselves a beer and they all sat around in the afternoon shade. John then asked, "Hey Randy, I've been meaning to ask you. What's the story on that old two-story building across the street? The one with all the boarded-up windows."

"Oh, that one?" Looking over at the big silver structure. "I guess in its glory days it was a bank, a grocery store, dry goods and such. The upstairs functioned as a hotel of sorts and a meeting hall."

"What makes you say it was a bank?" John asked.

"I have been in the vault. It's made of concrete walls, with a big iron door with a dial with numbers on it and an eight-inch lever handle. I think it would be correct to call that a vault, wouldn't you?" Heads nodded all around.

John pointed towards the top of the building and said, "Way up there on that squared off false fascia it has those four letters. IOOF. What the heck does that stand for?"

"International Order Odd Fellows fraternity."

"I've never heard of them." said Lloyd. "What did they do?"

"It must have been something kind of like what is around today. Knights of Columbus and the Free Mason lodges you see everywhere. Who knows? There may still be Odd Fellows groups in other parts of the country, I just never looked into it. At the end of the block there used to be another big two-story hotel with about thirteen bedrooms in it. On a really cold night back in the sixties it caught fire and burned down. One of the boys living there at the time was more upset that his treehouse burned down, than he was about the hotel building. The sad thing is they had this almost famous dog."

Jay said, "Hold up Randy. What do you mean almost famous dog?"

"Well, it is believed to have been like the great grand-daughter of the original Rintintin."

"Well, what happened?" asked Lloyd.

"The dog ran back into the owner's bedroom and got trapped. Burned with the house."

"What about the fire department?"

"There wasn't one back then, not even the old ball water tower. No public water at all. Everyone had their own wells."

"Man, I bet that really sucked." They all nodded in agreement.

Mary yelled, "Hey you guys. If Ya'll are about done gossiping over there, we could use one of you kind men to stoke the fire. Rochelle is about ready with those Nilgai steaks." John and Randy were the first to jump up. Duty calls. They glanced back over at Jay and Lloyd still studying that old historical building across the street.

After Rochelle served up the grilled steaks, everyone dove in. After having eaten a few bites, Lloyd said, "I'm not sure if I like this Nilgai meat."

"Good, more for me." Jay told him.

"Hold on that was quick."

Lacy told Lloyd, "You have been eating the same stuff over and over for years in the city, your taste buds don't know how to react." Everyone chuckled.

"Maybe my taste buds need more practice with new flavors." Lloyd told her as he finished up his steak."

"Well?" Lacy asked him.

"Well, what?" She pointed at his empty plate. "Oh, not bad, not bad at all." Everyone cracked up. Lloyd got up for another beer and Lacy just rolled her eyes at him.

As they sat around the fire John was thinking about what Pearl had told him earlier about the doctor and his friends. He needed to make it a point to look up J-Lee as soon as he made it back into the city tomorrow. He looked around at the group and gave silent thanks to God for putting all these people in his life. Mary touched his shoulder. "Hey, are you alright?"

"He looked into her beautiful eyes and said, "could not be better." He meant it.

Jay asked, "What time are you heading back into the city John?"

"I'd say around eight-thirty, quarter till nine. That way we roll into the city between the morning rush and lunch hour."

"Sounds like a plan." Lloyd said.

About that time Bobby showed up holding out a six pack. Without comment, Jay and Lloyd grabbed one. "So, it's back to the grind tomorrow huh?" Heads bobbing all around. "If any of you feel the need to practice horseback pistol work, come on back, anytime."

"That would be great." Lacy said, "I would like to see if I could get Lloyd on a horse. He might fall off."

"What? Fall off a horse? No way. I didn't fall out of the canoe, did I?"

Randy stated, "As I said before, all of you are welcome to set up camp any time you feel the need and besides that, Bobby might need a little company every now and then."

"It doesn't hurt." Bobby replied.

Early Monday morning after breakfast, everyone started packing up reluctantly. The weekend flew by for all of them. It seemed as if none of them were really quite ready to return back to the city. It took Lloyd years to get out this time, and he sure didn't want to fall into the trap of city life again. He turned to Randy and said, "You don't mind if I pop out here like once a month or so do you?"

"I told you anytime is fine." Lloyd reached out and shook Randy's hand firmly.

"Thanks. That really means a lot." Lacy had a big smile. She spotted some good change going on with Lloyd during this trip and she liked it.

All packed up, with the social area all squared away and the fire put out, Randy announced, "I'll tell you all what. I will leave the grate grill over in that old garden shed so it is here for anyone to use. It just takes up space in the city. I can't build a fire there anyways unless I want to socialize with the fire police." Everyone laughed at that, knowing it is true.

John and Mary burned off first. John was on a mission to look up his old friend J-Lee and put him to work. Traffic was light as anticipated this time of morning as they pulled into the city around ten a.m. "Perfect timing honey." Mary told him. John looked over at her a moment until she said, "Watch the road John, what's the matter with you?"

John grinned that grin and told her, "That's the first time you called me honey."

"Oh, is that a problem?"

"No, no problem at all." He reached over and squeezed her hand. "Mary, could you look on your device and see if you can locate my old friend J-Lee? It's been some years since we last worked together."

"Sure," she said, and hooked up to the link. After about five minutes of clicking around, she said, "I think I found him."

"You got an address?"

"Yes."

"Okay, GPS the address."

"No Problem. Oh crap, exit the freeway now." John startled almost hit the vehicle next to him taking the first exit. "Turn right at the light." John did so. "Go one mile then turn left. After five hundred more feet, turn right." John realized he was in a huge parking lot. "You have reached your destination." John looked at the huge book store directly in front of him in the strip-mall.

"What the hell?" John looked at Mary who just shrugged her shoulders at him.

"I guess we will have to go in and find out." John found a parking spot and he and Mary approached the book store.

"This thing is huge!" John told her. Mary said nothing as they entered the store. John looked down the rows and rows and aisles and aisles of books. He noticed very quickly all the security cameras thinking to himself what an expensive theft deterrent. About halfway across the store the over-head speaker crackled and a mechanical voice come over the P.A. System.

"John Myer, please report to the main desk. I repeat, John Myer, please report to the main desk."

"What the hell?" John said out loud. "I've never been here in my whole life." Mary pointed to the left towards the main counter. A couple of cashiers were on post just as John and Mary arrived at the main counter. An office door opened and a familiar face stepped out. "J-Lee, what the hell?"

Grinning J-Lee said, "Come on around and step into my office." John and Mary did as they were told and when the office door closed behind them J-Lee grabbed John in a big bear hug. "Man, where have you been John? I haven't seen you in a couple of coon ages."

"I'm in a new line of work now." John tells him.

"Well, are you going to introduce me to this pretty lady right here?" J-Lee asked.

"Oh yeah, J-Lee this is Mary, Mary this is J-Lee." Mary put her hand out and J-Lee lightly grasped it, bent down and kissed it, and stood back up blushing.

"Mary, nice to meet you ma'am. So, what's the story John?"

"She is my partner."

J-Lee quick to speak, "Work, or otherwise?"

John smiled, "Both."

"Lucky you!"

"What the hell is all this you have going on?" John waving his arms around the whole office particularly towards the wall full of monitors on one side.

"It's all mine." J-Lee told him.

"No way."

"Yes way, but it's a long story. What brings you here to my neck of the woods John?"

"I need your expertise to look into a matter for me." John told him.

"Just like old times."

"Not quite," John replied. J-Lee raised an eyebrow. "It's sort of a life and death situation."

"Whose life?" asked J-Lee.

"Mine."

"Wow. Okay, fill me in."

"You don't know how much this means to me." John tells him. "After all that we have been through, how could I not help a friend in need. Let's sit down and get started. Just don't go all the way back to when God created light, Okay?" They all laughed at that. "Hey, before you start, would either of you like coffee, tea, or a soft drink?"

John said, "You know, it has been a while. Do you have a Dr Pepper in there somewhere?"

Mary raised surprised eyebrows looking at John smiling and said, "I will have the same."

"Good." J-Lee pushed a button and handed the cashier a piece of paper when he came into the room. The cashier did an about face and left the office. As J-Lee was scribbling on another piece of paper, John was still looking around taking in the office. The cashier returned with three glasses of ice and three Dr Peppers. J-Lee handed the other note to the cashier, and the cashier left the room. "Now, let's get started." J-Lee said.

John started explaining how he got shot in the leg and how the company doctor just happened to be Johnny on the spot. J-Lee raised an eyebrow and said, "weird." Mary nodded in agreement. John continued the story getting to the part about later turning the corner and walking into a bullet. "Wow, this is some serious shit." Then John had to tell him about their true line of work, and who for. He also told him about the doctor's strange hunting/business associates. J-Lee was about to say something when a green light lit up on his desk. He turned and pushed a button and a moment later the cashier came in carrying two huge pizza boxes and sat them on the desk and walked back out of the room. John looked down and read Bibba's on the box.

"No way." John said.

"Yes way." J-Lee told him, "I remembered it was your favorite. Was not sure if they were still open but apparently so." Pointing at the two boxes. "Let's dive in, after all, it is lunch time."

After the pizza, John continued to fill J-Lee in about recent goings on. How someone tried to kill them both by putting drugs into the coffee pot, and how it seemed every time John tried to go see the doctor, they mysteriously, coincidently got sent out to abort someone. J-Lee let out a low whistle. "Either you are one lucky fool or your guardian angel is watching out for you."

"I choose all of the above." Mary said. John nodded. "Wow." J-Lee said. "So, you think your house is bugged?"

"It's beginning to appear that way." John told him. "Our company techies came and installed an alarm system and outside monitoring."

"I have a friend, let me reach out to him. No, better yet..." he grabbed the phone and punched speed dial. "Hey Boston, you got a minute? I have a situation and I know you like to play with your toys. Are you interested?"

"When and where?" asked Boston on the other end of the line.

"My office, now." J-Lee said then hung up the phone. John and Mary just sat there looking at J-Lee and he just sat there looking back at them smiling. Just as John was about to speak up again the green light on the desk lit up again. J-Lee pushed the button and the office door opened and in came a fellow of about six feet with a New England accent.

"What's going on J-Lee?" He asked as he was looking over and studying John and Mary.

"Wow, that was fast." Mary told him.

J-Lee started laughing, "Yeah well, he happens to own the electronic store next door."

John replied, "I didn't even notice an electronic store next door when we came in."

Mary said, "How could you? The way you were google eyeing the big book store in from of you."

John laughed, "yeah well, I was looking for a friend, not a book store."

"Well, you found me, didn't you." J-Lee told him. "Damn right, and glad that I did."

"Me too. Boston, my friend here thinks there is a listening device in his house."

Boston said, "That's easy enough to take care of." "How so?" John asked.

"You have two choices. You can block it, or you can locate it and remove it."

"Block it?" asked John. "How can you block it?"

"Well, there is this device some smart college techies came up with called a ring of silence."

"How does it work?" Mary asked.

"Simple, really. You put it wherever you want to have a private conversation and it emits ultrasonic signals imperceptible to most ears other than dogs, but the high frequency sound jams any micro phones in the vicinity."

"Wow, that's cool." Mary replied, "But how long do the batteries last?"

"Oh, kind of like cell phones. So, if per chance you forget to charge it or turn it off, you run the chance of getting listened to and possibly recorded."

"So that application is meant for more business type meetings instead of fulltime use." John said.

"Well, I do have another trick up my sleeve." Boston told him. "How so?" Asked John.

"I can't explain it. You would have to see it."

"Fine." John said. "Let us think about it and we will get back to you."

"Fair enough." Boston said. "If J-Lee says your good, then your good."

J-Lee spoke up, "I will personally guarantee John is good. Period."

"That's all I need." Boston said handing John a card. He turned and grabbed a leftover slice of pizza and took a bite. "Damn, this is good." He looked at the box top. "Bibba's, I've never heard of them." Then he walked out the door.

John and Mary spent a few more hours sitting with J-Lee catching up on everything. Mary sat back just taking it all in. John looked at his watch. "Crap, we need to beat the five o'clock rush. Sorry J-Lee but we have got to get going. Thanks for your hospitality. We will meet up soon so we can point you in the right direction on our investigation part of this drama."

"Sounds good." J-Lee said. They all rose up and J-Lee gave John another bear hug and told him, "It's been good." Then he shook Mary's hand and guided them toward the door.

Once back out on the main floor, they waved their goodbyes and headed for the door. Finding their way back to the freeway and heading home. Mary said, "That was awesome."

"Yes, it was. I got a plan in the morning. I am going to talk about going to see the doctor. I want you to insist. Then let's see what happens.

CHAPTER THREE

—◦◦⌒◦◦—

Back at the cubby hole with everything unpacked and put away from their weekend camping trip John turned to Mary. "I really need a hot shower."

Mary replied, "I second that." John was just lathering up his hair and had soap in his eyes when the shower slider opened. He felt the draft of air hit him and tried to open his soapy eyes to see Mary standing naked in front of him. "Scoot over, I'm coming in." John obeyed. There was something about the hot water, soap and smooth curves that started affecting John.

He said, "I think we need a bigger shower."

"I think we need to rinse off and go to bed." She told him.

And so it was.

Daylight came early. John and Mary were both slow to get out of bed for obvious reasons, but they survived. Mary made it to the coffee pot, filled it with coffee grounds and started to brew. John came in dressed and smelled the brewing coffee. "Man, that smells so good." She agreed and poured them each a cup. John took a sip and smiled saying, "Boy, this sure beats instant campfire coffee, but why does the food in the country taste so damn good?" Mary just smiled.

After their second cup of coffee and some scrambled eggs, John caught Mary's attention motioning the shush with his finger over his mouth. Then John spoke up, "says Mary, I think I am going to go see the good doctor that patched me up. I think I have time this morning."

"It's about time. I was starting to worry about you." She told him.

"I'll probably head out in about ten minutes." John said.

"Fine, I will go restock our groceries." She told him.

"Sounds like a plan." he replied.

About four minutes later, Ping. Mary looked at her device. "Can you believe we have an abortion to go take care of?"

"Time to armor up then." John had to almost bite his tongue to keep from speaking out in anger. They checked out their gear to insure all was as it should be, armored up, and set the alarm as they walked out the door. They made it about half a block down the street when John burst out. "Damn, I'm pissed."

"That makes two of us." Mary replied.

"How come we did not notice this going on when someone ventilated my leg?" he asked her.

Mary still had that look of anger on her face and could only reply, "Well, who would have thought?" John just nodded in agreement.

"You would not believe all the scenarios running through my mind right now." He told her.

"I can only imagine." Was her reply.

"Well evidently, we know somehow the doctor is mixed up in all this. We don't know how, or who all is involved. Who is pulling the strings that has us dancing for them like puppets? Are they the bad guys working for the doctor or is it the other way around? Is the doctor on someone's payroll to keep us from interfering with their business? Better yet is someone higher up in the commission involved in this, that may be pulling the strings?"

"Oh shit." Said Mary, "I haven't even thought about that."

"That's why we have got to get J-Lee started on his new research project. This shit just boggles my mind." He told her as they continued their way up the street.

After a few more minutes of walking John said, "Okay, who are we aborting?" That's when Mary realized in all his anger, John did not even look at the information on the target yet.

She spotted a little side-walk café just ahead and told him, "Let's grab a table and get a cup of coffee and get our shit together, Okay?" John looked at her and knew she was on point. They sat down and Mary grabbed John's hand to calm him down a bit. "John, you and I both know we can't be walking into a mission blind. Are you trying to get yourself killed or what?"

"Or what." John repeated realizing that Mary was right. They ordered coffee to the sound of the ping, giving them their thirty-minute update on the location of their target. John was reading on his device when the coffee arrived, he did not even bother to look up. When he did look up at Mary, he told her, "Woo doggies, this is going to be interesting."

"How so?" Mary asked.

Pointing at his screen he told her, "Seems our Lezzy friend here is the owner operator of a type of elderly care place. You know the last stop before hospice at the end of the road."

"Okay, What's the catch. That sounds like a good service. Why are we here?" Mary asked.

"It's not the Lezzy part, it's the part that this fine lady is keeping these old folks drugged up with no known next of kin. She has got them writing, or should I say, she writes and gets them to sign checks all the while they don't even know what's going on."

"Well, what gave her away?" Mary asked him.

"I guess it was this enormous bank account that was growing exponentially compared to the type of care giving services average income."

"So basically, she is robbing these poor souls blind."

John replied, "Precisely. We have to formulate a plan. We just can't walk in there and plant a chunk of lead between the eyes now, can we? This has got to be a little different." They sat there thinking and sipping on their coffee and John watched a florist service vehicle drive by on the street. He contemplated for a moment and explained his plan to Mary.

She leaned back looking a John in the eyes and said, "You know John, that just might work." They finished off their coffee.

He stood up and said, "The next stop is the flower shop." They were off with a plan. They found a flower shop about a block out of the way of where they were going and went inside. Since this was more up Mary's alley, John just followed her around. She picked up one of these and a couple of those, added two or three of another. To John, flowers were just flowers, but Mary had that woman's touch and her little gathering made a colorful bouquet.

She turned to look at John and asked him, "What do you think?"

"That ought to work out just fine." He told her." We don't want it too big. We need to keep it fairly small for the aromatic advantage. I like what you put together." They headed for the cashier. Once out on the street he asked her, "Do you think the commission will reimburse us for the flowers?"

"Why?" She asked him.

"Heck, fourteen ninety-five seems a little steep for some colored weeds don't you think?" Mary just laughed at him as he continued, "Just kidding." With that they got back on track towards the target at hand. John had pulled a special little packet out of his stash of goodies. Checking the color bar to make sure it was still sealed one hundred percent; it was sealed in a double packet. The inner packet contained the active ingredients, while the outer packet had chemical strips in it to notify you if the integrity of the inner packet was breached. A safety precaution for what is inside.

Mary looked at him and said, "I'm amazed at all the ways the lab guys can figure out how to kill so easily.

"Yeah, I know." John replied. At that moment John was recalling just how deadly this little package called evergreen actually was. It was like some deranged chemist came up with the idea and to his surprise it worked. John was remembering how it was explained. How this guy managed to sort of freeze dry H25 better known as Hydrogen Disulfide in the oil field and managed to roll it into flower longevity granules. It is a super deadly gas. It is said that it smells like rotten eggs, but that is not quite the truth. It is colorless and odorless in its pure form. Back in the day a few oilfield workers died by rig drilling into pockets of gas. Some H25 escaped and all it took was one breath and it was lights out. It instantly shuts down the central nervous system on contact with the lungs.

Mary and John worked on their spiel just before arriving at the target's location. They went in and found the owner/operator and explained that they were looking for an affordable nursing home to put John's father in. For a good gesture Mary handed the owner the bouquet. "Oh, how beautiful." She exclaimed. "I must put these in some water."

As she got up to leave the room, John told her. "Hold on, here is a packet of evergreen." Digging into his pocket knowing he had already taken it out of the safety packet, he handed the inner packet to her and told her, "After you get the flowers and water into the vase, pour this packet in. Rumor is it will make these flowers last the rest of your life." They laughed at that one.

The owner then took the flowers into the bathroom with the automatic fart fan active while the lights were on, she reached under the sink cabinet and pulled out a vase, which she half filled with water. She then added the flowers and tore open the evergreen package and poured it into the water. It kind of reacted like instant coffee does in hot water except this stuff stayed clear. After wiggling the flowers around to stir the water a little she arranged the flowers, picked up the vase and put the flowers up to her nose and inhaled deeply.

Something started happening, actually a lot of things started happening in her all at once. She grabbed her chest and dropped the vase with a crash. She didn't even reach the door knob and she was down and out. John and Mary sat there for a while giving the gas some time to dissipate before catching the attention and waving over a member of the staff. She came over and asked, "May I help you?"

Mary told her, "We are waiting on your boss to come back out of the bathroom. She went in to put some flowers in some water and never came back out."

The staffer responded, "Maybe I better go check on her." She headed for the bathroom door. At first, she knocked a few times getting no answer. Then she cracked the door open and peaked in. "Oh my God, are you alright?" She screamed.

John and Mary walked up behind her at the door and suggested that the staff member call 911. She ran to the nearest phone and did just that. John reached into the room and grabbed the empty evergreen packet and slipped it back into its previous pouch and pocketed it. Mary was bent down by the corpse when the staff member returned stating, "An ambulance is on the way."

Mary looked up at her and replied, "She won't be needing it." At that the staff member broke down in tears so John and Mary comforted her until the medics showed up for the body. Someone mentioned that it must have been a heart attack and everyone around seemed to all agree that must be what happened. John and Mary took their leave.

John told Mary, "We have to go get the car. We need to go and talk to J-Lee and Boston." Mary agreed. This mission was accomplished. Another abortion was complete, yet there were no high fives this time. John had other things on his mind. On the way across town, he told her; "This damn doctor situation is driving me crazy. You saw what happened this morning. At the mention of me visiting, we got sent on a sudden abortion job. Are they giving us all the other teams jobs or what?"

Mary said, "I will go with the or what option."

"I just can't wrap my head around this mess, you know?" Said John.

"I know very well, John. We will figure this mess out.

As they pulled into the parking lot they parked in the front of J-Lee's bookstore. As they got out of the car, John steered Mary to the left and said, "I want to check out Boston first."

"Okay." Mary said nonchalantly. Boston's electronics was what the neon sign said. "I didn't even know they still made these types of signs anymore." said Mary.

"Well, the glass blowers need to have something to do, besides just making figurines." John told her.

She laughed and replied, "I guess you're right." Now Boston's store was not nearly as wide as J-Lee's book store, but it was just as deep. It had that Grand Canyon effect. Once inside it didn't take long to locate Boston. It was that accent of his that made it so easy to locate him. He was showing a customer some type of range finder, depth gauge, fish finder device. So, John and Mary just grazed around the store like a cow in a pasture. It wasn't long before Boston caught up with them.

"Back so soon?" He asked them.

"Yes," John replied. "We are now positive that we have some electronics problems."

"Step into my office." Boston pointed to the door over to the left. After closing the door behind them, Boston reached into what appeared to be a broom closet and pulled out what looked like a worn out, beat up, upright vacuum cleaner. He set it on his desk.

"What is that?" Asked John.

"Well, this is my Q45 Quantum proton ultrasonic phaser catcher." Boston told him.

"Do what?" John laughed.

Boston started laughing too and said, "I'm just kidding. Look here." Pointing to where the rubber bumper should have been wrapped completely around the sweeper portion of the vacuum. Now there was a clear thin window neatly wrapping the whole base. "This is a 360-degree laser distance finder. I can sit this on the floor in any room, no matter how large or small, and turn it on. The laser shoots us in all directions bouncing off the walls and gives me an exact dimension of whatever room it may be in."

"Wow." John said. "I'm impressed."

"That's nothing. You see this cylinder inside the dust container?" John nodded. "That is a micro sized two terabyte computer. It's kind of like faster than a speeding bullet. Stronger than a locomotive, so to speak."

"Why do you need all that power?" Mary asked.

"To drive the lasers for one." replied Boston. "That's not all. You see these four antennae like things hanging out of all four corners kind of like cat whiskers? That's my electronics sniffer. It can locate any type of device that even uses the minimum of microvolts of power. You see where that plastic headlight is? Watch this." He snaps up the headlight cover and there is a small flat screen in there about the size of one of those electronic book readers. "Do you see the grooves cut in the handle up here? Those are the cooling vents. When I turn on the vacuum, it runs like a vacuum. The sweeper sweeps, the suction is diverted down through the handle and back up through the dust bin to keep the computer cool. All the while, it is sizing up the room and pin pointing precisely the exact spot of any electronic devices and creates a three dimensional photo of the room. This can be seen on the flat screen as well as can be sent to your device or computer for your personal use to do whatever you wish with the objects you find."

"No wonder you told us yesterday at J-Lee's that you would not be able to explain it without us seeing it. Now I understand. Where did you find this magic clunker? Some government lab?"

"No," Boston replied. "I built it. There's not another one out there like it that I know of."

"When can you put it to work?" Asked Mary.

"Anytime. If I have anybody watching when I come over to clean a carpet, the sweeper gives impression in the carpet like the vacuum is doing what it is supposed to be doing. In reality, I am doing a clean sweep right under their eyes."

"How did you come up with an idea like this?" John asked him.

"I always have stuff laying around and like to tinker." He replied with a huge smile on his face.

"When do you open?" John asked.

"Around ten a.m."

"Do you think you can make it over to our place around eight in the morning?"

"I will be glad to." Boston replied.

"Great!" Mary exclaimed. "Do you like omelets?"

Boston smiled, "I've never turned one down yet." "Then it is settled then."

As they got up to leave Boston said, "When I come by in the morning, strictly speaking, it's about carpet cleaning and nothing else. We don't want to raise any eyebrows."

"Gotcha." John replied as Mary nodded in agreement. As they made their way out of Boston's electronic store John joked, "I didn't know they made geeks that smart." Mary slapped his arm and busted out laughing. They walked back down to J-Lee's book store in a much better mood. As they entered J-Lee motioned them back into his office and they settled in. "We are putting your neighbor to work in the morning." John told him.

"That's great. I'm glad he was able able to work something out with you." J-Lee replied.

"Now it's time to put you to work too." John told him.

J-Lee leaned back in his chair crossing his arms. "I'm listening."

"You still dabble in doing a little research every now and then?" John asked him.

"Yes, Indeed I do. What are you looking for?" "It's not a what, but a who." John said.

"Shoot." replied J-Lee. John started telling J-Lee about the butcher and the undertaker. "What do you have on them?" asked J-Lee.

"Nothing really. Just a line on their line of work is all. Mary has their photos."

"Photos would help a lot." J-Lee told him.

Mary asked, "What's your email? I can send them to you." J-Lee told her his email and after just a few clicks on her device she looked back up and said, "You've got mail."

J-Lee turned to his desktop and clicked a few times and said, "Wow. Those are some rough looking dudes. The one you call the butcher looks like he may have some Russian blood in him and the other fellow, European maybe, or French. No worries. I will find out."

Mary asked, "How can you deduct a person's origins?"

"Because J-Lee has already been around the block a few times." John told her.

J-Lee looked at John and said, "I have a street runner who might fit right in on this. He's a short chubby Mexican with squinty eyes and tattoos all over. He's really good at rooting around in the dirty side of the street and coming up with gold. His name is Moe."

"Why not?" John said. "I need all the help I can get."

J-Lee reached for the phone hit a speed dial button and after a few seconds said, "Hey Moe. J-Lee. You working? Well, you are now." Then he hung up the phone. "Good timing. We caught him in between jobs."

"Great." John said. The pieces were starting to fall into place.

Mary said to J-Lee, "I will see if I can fish any other leads on those two scumbags out of the sewer for you.

"Thanks." He replied as they all stood and said their goodbyes. On the way out the door, John asked Mary, "What was that show where that guy with a cigar would say, I love it when a plan comes together.?"

"I don't know." Mary replied.

"Come on." John said. "They rode around in that black van. A big guy with a Mohawk back when Mohawks were cool and he wore have a ton of gold around his neck." Mary just blankly looked at him like a deer in the headlights. He just smiled and repeated the line, "I love it when a plan comes together. Let's go home Mary."

"Now that sounds like a plan." She said as they both laughed. Back in the cubby hole John was contemplating all the gears that had recently set into motion, knowing he could not speak his thoughts out loud, which greatly frustrated him. He was used to speaking his thoughts out loud because sometimes when he heard what he said, he had answers for his own questions. Something about hearing it out loud. He would have to stay bottled up a while longer until Boston came by the next morning. Hopefully Boston would be able to cure some of his and Mary's ailments.

As John sank back in thought to the mornings work, he started asking himself questions. How could there be those greedy people who cared more for money than the welfare of the people they were charged to care for? What put evil into a person's heart and turned them into child snatchers? What sick need did they have? How could a human become a human trafficker? Buying, selling, and stealing young girls and boys as if they were goats, cattle, or whatever livestock. Auction them off as if they were just a piece of meat. How could the drug dealers get those young kids into the trade having them do the moving and the selling for the adults? He continued to think how he could understand theft to an extent, if someone wants what they have no means of achieving, but it still all boils down to greed. Most all of the crimes are in some way connected to greed. Now if you look at murder, that comes under a whole umbrella of a thing. Revenge, love, hate, self-defense, and on and on and on. Pretty sure greed could slip somewhere in there too. At this point John just started rubbing his eyes.

"Are you Okay?" Mary asked him, snapping him out of his thoughts.

He sat forward and could only reply, "I need a beer." Mary got bug eyed looking at him and he busted out laughing and said, "No, not really. I wonder how Lloyd and Lacy are doing?" Then it was Mary's turn to chuckle.

Mary had sent a message to her contact person asking for any help with more information on the butcher and the undertaker. They seriously had to find the strings that tied those two low lives to the commissions doctor and find out if it stopped there or went up into the very heart of the commission. Mary thought, now wouldn't that just be a kick in the pants if one or some of them were involved and the doctor was just a middle man, so to speak. This is another angle they have not thought of, so she decided to wait so she could speak freely without invisible ears listening. They might have to get the gang together at the park or some other safe location.

The afternoon crept by at a snail's pace. Mary was tending to the house chores and John was cleaning up and checking out both his and Mary's tools of the trade. He cleaned and oiled their firearms. Inspected the condition of the under armor. His still had a trace of lead where the hitman's bullet had struck him. He used a brush to try to rub those remnants away and swore to himself silently how thankful he was that this particular piece of equipment had saved his life. Again, he thanked God for the hitman choosing to target his heart and not his head.

Mary called from the kitchen, "Hey John, are you hungry?"

"Now that you mention it, I guess I am."

"You want a couple of cold cut sandwiches on wheat bread?"

"That sounds good." He told her as he joined her in the kitchen. He was leaning on the counter watching her stack the ingredients into the sandwiches when his device unexpectantly started to ring. "This is John." The voice on the other end was Pat from out at the ranch. "Hey Pat, I wasn't expecting to be hearing from you." Pat told him that Pearl wanted him to give a shout since he planned on making a run over to their favorite meat processers over in High Hill. "Where the heck is High Hill?" John asked him. Pat told him it was located outside of Shoeburg down the freeway about thirty miles from C-Town. He went on to explain to John that they would cut his meat into quality cut steaks, roast, ground breakfast sausage patties, full size link sausage with a blend of pork or beef added in and commented that his personal favorite was the smoked pencil sausages. "Wow, they do all that?" John asked him. "They do all that and more." Pat told him.

John considered for a minute and then told Pat, "Heck yea, I had not even considered all that. We need to get that meat out of Pearl's meat locker before it just dries up and turns into one big chunk of jerky."

"They do that to." Pat told him. "Just tell me how many pounds of regular links and breakfast patties you want, and how many pounds of pencil links and jerky you want and the rest will be basically steaks and roast."

"Since I don't know how many pounds in total we are working with, I'll keep it simple. Give me a quarter of it in regular links and patties. A quarter of it in pencel links and jerky and the rest of it in steaks and roast."

"Sounds good." Pat replied as he made notes of the portions of each. He then told John that he would call him in a week or so depending on the meat processor's schedule. "When you come to pick up the meat, Pearl said to tell you that he needs to talk to you."

"About what?" John asked.

"He didn't tell me. I was just asked to relay that message." "Consider it done." John told him. They said their farewells and hung up. As Mary was holding a half-eaten sandwich looking at him inquisitively wonder what that was all about, John told her, "It seems that sometime next week we need to buy a freezer."

"A freezer?" She asked.

"Yeah, I don't think we will be able to stuff three or four hundred pounds of meat in the overhead of ours, do you?"

"Oh crap, with everything going on I totally forgot about that. Your right." John then repeated the discussion he had with Pat so she had more details. "That sounds wonderful."

He didn't repeat the part about Pearl wanting to talk, so as not to let those invisible ears to listen. He would tell Mary tomorrow after all the sweeper was coming and the thought of that made John smile. After munching down on his cold cut sandwiches and cleaning up and putting everything away he suggested to Mary they should watch a movie.

"What do you have in mind?" she asked.

"Let's see," he said as he roamed around the list of titles. "How about 'The Gift'?"

"Is it any good?"

"I guess we will just have to watch and judge for ourselves as I don't always agree with those rotten tomato ratings."

"Me neither." Mary told him.

After the movie John told her, "You know that was a pretty awesome movie."

"It made me cry a few times." She told him.

"That's what good movies are supposed to do. They reach right inside of you and tickle your emotions."

"That it did."

It was getting late and Boston was supposed to be there first thing in the morning, so they decided to go and test the springs in their new mattress. After about half an hour of wrestling around on the bed so to speak, John set up with his back against the head board. He started picking his hand up with two fingers extended then put them to his mouth and then back down again. He repeated the process three or four more times and Mary said, "John, what are you doing?"

"Well, I have seen on movies and heard of people having after sex cigarettes. So, I am trying to figure out the point of it. There's no way a cigarette is the icing on the cake. I say sex is tops, period."

"You are crazy! But it's crazy in a good way. Maybe that's why I love you."

"Whoa," said John. "I thought I could have sworn I just heard a four-letter word." Mary started blushing as a result of the slip of the tongue and John started laughing and reached around Mary to give her a hug as he whispered in her ear, "I second that."

Mary looked into his eyes and asked, "Are you ready for round two?" And so it went.

CHAPTER FOUR

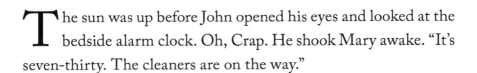

T he sun was up before John opened his eyes and looked at the bedside alarm clock. Oh, Crap. He shook Mary awake. "It's seven-thirty. The cleaners are on the way."

Mary rolled out of bed naked and headed straight to the shower. John just stared as she went, admiring the awesome beauty of all those curves in motion. He thought to himself that he was a very lucky man reflecting on last night's activities. She was freshly stepping out of the shower leaving the water running as John stepped in to take her place. She headed into the kitchen and put on the coffee before returning to get dressed.

By the time John got out of the shower and entered the kitchen, Mary was pouring them each a cup of coffee. There was a knock on the door. Perfect timing, John thought to himself as he walked to the front door. He opened the door expecting to see Boston, but instead it took his brain a second to register what his eyes were actually seeing. Standing in front of him in all his glory was the commission's Doctor. "Hello John."

His brain finally catching up, he turned to Mary with a surprised look. "It's the doctor," he exclaimed. Mary paled and quickly left the room to get her device and find Boston's number. She quickly typed two words, 'Stand by'.

Meanwhile the doctor was telling John, "I haven't seen you since the shooting so I figured I had better check in on you."

"I'm good." John told him. "The leg burns when I do really deep squats then stand back up."

"May I?" The doctor asked pointing to John's leg. John looked at the doctor, then at his leg, then back at the doctor before he unbuckled his belt buckle and dropped his pants down to his ankles. The doctor squatted down and inspected both the enter and exit scars, stood up before saying, "Well, that's better than what I expected. Very well, I won't take up any more of your time." John followed him to the door as he let himself out.

John turned to Mary, "What the hell was that?" Mary put a finger over her mouth to shush him and pointed at the ceiling. John's eyes got big as he covered his mouth.

"The cleaners are going to be late." Mary told him. Damn this girl is quick he thought to himself. Relieved he looked at Mary as she told him, "Coffee is ready." John sat down still recovering from what had just transpired. Thinking to himself he wondered why the doctor didn't even mention the heart shot bruise that had not yet gone fully away. He knew the commission had a meeting after his attempted assassination. How could the doctor not know and not question him about that wound as well? Damn, it seems every question is answered with more questions. Like killing snakes on Medusa's head.

"Earth to John." Mary said. "Earth to John." As he snapped out of his thoughts, he looked at her. "You want to get the door?"

"I didn't even hear anything."

"That's why I was calling earth to John, you must have been out there."

"I will tell you about it later," he told her motioning to the ceiling. When John opened the door, standing there was the cleaning crew.

"Did we miss breakfast?" Boston asked.

"If you did, then I did too. So, your answer is nope."

"Good," Boston said as he held up the modified vacuum and asked, "Before or after?" "How long does it take?" "About ten minutes."

"That's about how long it will take Mary to whip up them omelets, right dear?" She just smiled at him and set about her task. "Nothing like killing two birds with one stone." John said as he had a quick memory of the would-be assassins that he took out making him smile.

Boston came in with a helper and went to work unspooling the power cord and plugged it in to the wall outlet. John leaned against the counter that separated the kitchen and living room with his head on a swivel watching both Mary and Boston do their things. Boston was methodically sweeping the carpet around the room, stopping occasionally as he pushed some keys on a keypad. John hadn't even noticed there was a keypad and not a typical slide on/off switch. Interesting he thought. Boston would move over here, stop. Push some keys as his helper would move some furniture and Boston would sweep over there and stop, and push a few keys and so on. John was just amazed with it all. Finally, Boston said "Done, keep it or kill it?"

John said, "Kill it." John watched as Boston pushed a few more keys, then the old vacuum sounded like a turbine winding up when suddenly there was a pulse of light and the turbine sound wound down. "What the hell was that?"

"Trade Secret." Boston said with a smile. "The device was located, so my computer focused a straight-lined electromagnetic pulse. EMP for short. Your bug is dead, guaranteed." Boston reached over and popped open the light cover exposing the little monitor. "Look here. These lines are your walls. This dot is the location of the bug."

John looked at the diagram like a miniature blue print. He looked up at the ceiling judging from the scale and said, "Damn, you mean to tell me it's been in the smoke detector all this time?" "Yeah, looks that way. Yours is the type that is hard wired in, so you are not popping it down every couple of months to replace the batteries. It's a perfect place to plant a bug or even a camera as it's a continuous source of power." Boston explained to him.

"I would have never thought of that."

"What about the rest of the house? Sweep?"

"Go for it." John told him. "I will get a ladder and pop that damn thing open and have a look."

The rest of the house came up clean, so everyone gathered in the living room around the table and commenced to digging in on their huge ham and cheese with chopped shallot omelets. After a period of mass consumption leaving everyone satisfied, Boston said "Let me step up that ladder and have a look at what you got here." He popped the little microphone transceiver off of the smoke detector. "Well now, this is interesting."

"How so?" asked John.

Boston standing beside John rolling the device around in his hand, "No batteries, no power plug."

John said, "Well how does it work with no power?"

"Well, you foot the bill for the power so to speak." Boston told him.

"Do what?" John said.

Boston asked, "Do you know anyone who has an above ground swimming pool? You know the kind made of fabric with a pipe frame?"

John said, "Yeah, we had one when I was in high school."

"Ok." Boston said, "Did you have any lights in it?"

"Yes."

"Do you remember how you put those lights in?" Boston asked.

"Yeah, we held the power source on the outside of the pool and the light fixture itself had a magnet in it and you just stuck it to the fixture on the outside of the pool and you could move it anywhere you wanted without cutting holes in the fabric."

"Right." Boston said, "So how did the light work?"

John replied, "Well, I guess the power went from the outside base through the pool wall into the fixture. Shit. You mean to tell me that all these people have to do is find a power source such as house wiring and mount this bug and it's up and running?"

"That is the gist of it." Boston said.

"That is so easy, it is just plum scary." John replied.

"That is why I have my vacuum and will travel." Boston told him as he pointed at the contraption sitting in the middle of the room.

John said, "Can you tell or should I say, identify the owner of the thing?"

"I will have to get closer look back at the shop." Boston told him. Mary said, "I want to know one thing. Can we speak freely now with no worries about who may be listening in?"

"For now, yes. But whoever put this thing in here may come back." Boston told them.

"In that case, we may have to set up some kind of schedule for your house cleaning service."

"No problem, I would be glad to." Boston told them.

"So now, who is this silent partner you have with you Boston?"

"Oh, you mean this short fellow grinning? This is Moe." Boston said.

"Really?" John asked. "J-Lee said something about a fellow named Moe the other day."

Boston said, "He's the one and the same."

Moe spoke up, "Nice to meet you John," and he nodded at Mary. "We figured we better not speak or mention names until business was taken care of."

"We were half a block away when we got the stand by message from Mary. What was up with that?" Boston asked.

Mary said, "Now if we knew that, would you and Moe be standing here?"

"I guess not." Boston replied.

Moe asked, "Can anyone please fill me in?"

Mary and John both started to speak and then stopped. Boston then said, "I'll tell you what, I will leave Moe here so you guys can bring him up to date. I have a store to open and anyways I want to take a look at this little critter."

"Sounds good." Said John. "We will get Moe back to where he needs to be."

"Now," said Boston, "If you don't mind, I will grab my wonder vacuum and be on my way."

"Tell J-Lee thanks for the surprise."

"What surprise?" Boston asked. "This one standing right next to you."

"Oh, Moe? Sure thing." They all laughed. John shook hands with Boston and walked him to the door. Just as he was about to walk out, he turned to face Mary. "Thank you for the excellent omelet. I may have to come back for a repeat."

"Anytime." Mary said waving as he turned and vanished out the door.

John turned to face Moe and said, "I would not have guessed." Moe replied, "would not have guessed what?"

"J-Lee said you were a short chubby fellow." John told him. "Your more stocky than chubby."

Moe laughed and said, "I work at that. When I was in my young teens, I admit I may have looked like a walking butterball." He was holding his arms out like a huge circle. Everyone laughed.

Mary said, "Well whatever you are doing, keep doing it."

Smiling Moe said, "that's the plan." Then he turned to John open handed and said, "What do you got?"

John replied, "I like that. To the point and down to business at hand." Moe grinned.

Mary poured them all a fresh cup of coffee and they sat down at the table and Moe pulled out a pocket tablet so he could take notes and said, "Let the journey begin."

Mary laughed and said, "It's been a journey all right with no end in sight."

John frowned and said, "In the beginning." He paused and Mary glanced at him as he then let out his breath and said, "I was shot!" And so, the story began.

John and Mary took turns speaking and each picked up where the other left off. Moe, meanwhile was picking out pieces of information and entering them into his tablet occasionally raising an eyebrow while marking that note to come back to. After a few cups of coffee and trips to the restroom by all, Moe was pretty well up to date. He finally spoke up and said, "man this is some serious stuff."

"You sure got that right." John said as his and Mary's heads were bobbing up and down in agreement.

Mary interjected, "I didn't speak up to John because of the invisible ears, but I had a scary thought yesterday."

"What's that?" John asked her.

"You know that the majority of the commission is made up of senators and congressman. You know, the ones who find the funding for our little organization. The same ones who give the go, and the no go orders to our administration dispatchers. I'm just thinking out loud here, what if, and I'm saying what if our good doctor is some sort of middle man for one of them?"

"Shit" John exclaimed.

"And the plot thickens." Moe said.

Mary continued, "It is plausible. You know how those in power seem to always be in somebodies' pocket, right?" As the heads nodded around the table she went on, "so how much money would it take to protect an illicit business such as sex trafficking or making people disappear?" Silence filled the room as each individual fell into their own thoughts.

John spoke up, "Hell, maybe one of them got caught up in a sex trap or caused a disappearance and are now held hostage to blackmail. Crap, crap, crap. Why are there always more questions than what we started with?" As he sarcastically looked over at Mary he said, "Thanks a lot!"

Mary grinned and said, "Leave no stone unturned right!"

Moe and John both said "right" in unison.

John spoke up saying, "That call last night about the meat processors." Mary nodded and Moe looked up from his tablet quizzically. "Well, it turns out, Pearl has the need to have a chat."

"When?" Mary asked.

"After we buy that freezer, we talked about and go out and pick up the rest of that Nilgai."

Moe said, "a what?"

"It is a sort of antelope that John shot the other day." Mary explained to him.

Moe said, "I didn't know we had antelope around here."

John told him, "It was on an exotic animal ranch."

"Really?" Moe asked. "Kind of like a zoo?"

"Sort of." John said. "If you want it, and the price is right, you can shoot it."

Moe pondered this and asked John, "when are you going back out there?"

"In around a week or so." John told him. "Mind if I tag along?" Moe asked.

"I don't see why not." John replied.

"Great." Moe said. "I can't wait." John and Mary laughed.

Moe finished up with his intel gathering and said he would start by looking into those men called the Butcher and the Undertaker. He told them he would also snoop around the Doctor's office when he could.

"The sooner we get to the bottom of this, the better." John told him.

"If there is even a bottom." Moe said.

"Well Moe, can you think of any more questions?" John asked.

Moe said, "At the moment, no. But you guys are a special case it seems."

"How so?" asked Mary.

"It seems every time someone asks a question, all you get is more questions. It's kind of like shoveling sand against the tide." At that Moe looked at his watch and said, "Damn. My how time does fly when you are having fun. Are you guys hungry?"

"Getting that way." John said.

"Good, I know a place we can eat on your way to drop me off." Moe told him.

"Sounds good." Mary said. "Give us a minute to change cloths and we will be on our way."

John and Mary went into the bedroom and armored up. Mary grinned and said, "Don't leave home without it." As she patted her under armor.

"You got that right." John said. In a matter of minutes, they were out the door. They walked to the parking facility where they kept their vehicle and were soon on the freeway heading south.

Moe said, "Good thing it's still a little early, we will beat the noon rush. I hate standing around waiting for a table."

"Me too." Mary replied.

John asked, "Is the place that small?"

"No." Moe told him, "It is not that small, it's because the food is that good."

"Really?" asked Mary.

"You can judge for yourself when we get there. Take the Broadway exit and turn left at the circle and go under the freeway."

"Sure thing." John said as he was working his way into the exit lane.

Moe told him with a grin on his face, "You will like it, no worries." John turned left at Broadway and started around the circle under the freeway overpass coming out the other side, Moe pointed to a building on the corner to the right.

"Right there." Moe said. "They have parking on the side and in the back."

Mary looked up at the sign. Taqueria Del Sol. "Oh good. I have not had any good Mexican food in a while." John admitted the same as he turned onto an alley styled parking strip alongside of the building.

Although it was only eleven o'clock, more than a few of the tables were occupied. Some were workers and some were family groups. The walls were painted up with some Aztec looking Indians, some step pyramids and such. Moe explained that the owners were from the deep south of Mexico and this authentic food is a result of that. As they were seated at a table looking over a menu, Moe brought their attention to a young man bussing a table. Moe said, "That is the owner's son."

"Really?" Mary said, "Learning the family business from the ground up."

"Huh?" Moe replied, "No." John and Mary quizzically looked at Moe as he explained, "That young man is working his way through medical school. He wants to be a doctor."

"No shit." John said, "That's quit the honorable profession, especially for an immigrant." About that time the young man approached the table and asked if they were ready to order yet. They placed their order.

After a good lunch of torta's, cheesy enchiladas, and roasted garlic, they left a larger than normal tip to the future doctor who was bussing the tables. Up front they gave their ticket to the cashier and paid up. John said, "Wow, that was cheaper than I expected." As they were headed toward the exit, they were steered through the door on the left instead.

"Wow!" Mary exclaimed as her eyes were scanning all the glass cases with donuts, twists, Panera sweet bread until she stopped at the chiller next to the door. "Cream puffs! My favorite." With a greedy little smile on her face, she helped herself to some cream puffs and various other delights.

John looked over at Moe saying, "You better get me out of here. I could put on ten pounds just looking at all this." They all laughed and cashed out. On the way back to the car John thanked Moe for the excellent choice of eatery and looked at Mary and said, "What did Arnold say in that movie?" In a deep tone he said, "We will be back." They all cracked up as they were getting into the car.

After dropping Moe off and heading back, John's device vibrated and he picked it up. "Hello." It was Boston.

"That little critter we found on your ceiling was Russian." "How can you be sure of that?" John asked.

"After looking at it under my magnifier, it was easy. The components of that critter were all labeled in Russian script."

"Well now, that opens up yet another door to go through now doesn't it." John replied.

"Sorry to say." Boston told him. "That is what appears to be the case."

"Did you tell J-Lee?" John asked.

"I'm on my way over now to fill him in on this morning's progress."

"Thanks." John said as he disconnected the call. He turned to look at Mary and said "Russian."

"What the heck" Mary exclaimed. "A Russian listening device in our house somehow connected to our fine doctor, and speaking of him, what the hell was with that unexpected, unannounced visit this morning? That was plain crazy if you ask me."

"Yeah." John said, "Another missing piece of the puzzle."

Mary replied, "How can it be a missing part of the puzzle? We don't even have a picture of the puzzle yet to figure out where to start placing the pieces. We just have a bunch of random pieces that's like looking for a complete sentence in a bowl of alphabet soup."

John looked at Mary laughing. "Girl, where do you come up with this stuff?"

"It just spills out." She said, grinning.

"Well, now that we are out and about, I guess it wouldn't be a bad thing to swing by the commission lab and restock our stash of goodies." John said.

Mary agreed. Being as busy as they have been as of late, she was getting low on the yellow jacket serum and John wanted to return that empty packet of evergreen. Once they arrived at the lab, they both felt like kids going into the proverbial candy store. As they were walking around checking out the supply room, John was humming and then started singing. "You got to slip out the back Jack, make a little plan Stan, fifty ways to kill a scum bug."

Mary punched him in his side with her elbow laughing. "What!" He said laughing as they stopped at the service counter.

The attendant behind the counter was grinning. "I heard that." John blanched as he handed over the packet that had held that deadly concoction. "Oh, we have more ways of death than that, I assure you."

John replied, "Yeah, but if you changed the number, the tune just wouldn't sound right, would it?" They all agreed and laughed. John and Mary took a quick inventory of their tools of the trade and John doubled up on the evergreen as he was pleased with that old folk robbing Lezzy outcome. It was the first time John had considered this use of this product and he could just imagine the future prospects. "You never know now, do you?" He stated to Mary as she was stocking up on more of that injectable yellow jacket serum. They didn't see any other particular tool they needed at the moment, so they signed out for their stock and headed for the door.

On the way across the parking lot, Mary sang out. "God only knows how we find you; God only knows how we demise you. God only knows the real you. There is a second death for you that God only know."

"Hey, that was good." John said. "Where did that come from?" "From a tune I had heard on the radio recently."

"I need to hear the real version." John told her. "Yes, you do." Mary replied.

Mary's device buzzed and she answered. Lacy was on the other end. "Hey you. Rochelle and Kathy and I have been worried about you guys. Is all well?"

"Yeah, all is well at the moment but you wouldn't believe a couple of things that happened since we came back to the city."

Lacy said, "Well, I'm all ears. Fill me in."

"I can't over the phone. We were thinking about calling a meeting over at the park on the west side. You know the one that has a jogging loop around a golf course, tennis court, and a soccer field?"

"I know that park. It's just off the south of the freeway by the loop, right?" Lacy asked.

"That's the one. Maybe in the next couple of days things will work out and we can meet there." Mary told her.

"Sounds good. I'll tell Rochelle and Kathy to be on standby mode." They said their good byes and Lacy clicked off. Mary reached into a bag and pulled out an item and held it up to John.

"Cream puff mister?"

John chuckled and reached out and grabbed the cream puff and took a bite and some white cream squirted out on his cheek. Mary started laughing and unclipped her seat belt and leaned over and licked the cream off of his cheek. He swerved at that action. Mary sat back in her place. "No need being a reckless driver you know."

"I wasn't expecting that!"

"Good." Mary told him. "I have to keep you on your toes." "That you do." John said as he looked at her grinning. He drove on over to the parking facility. They grabbed their bags and headed back to the cubby hole. Upon entering their home, John disarmed the alarm and turned to Mary with a high tenor pitch in his voice and said, "Lucy, I'm home."

Mary kicked off her shoes and plopped into an easy chair. "All this excitement going on wears me out."

"Too wore out for a movie?" John asked.

"Nah, let me go change into something a little more comfortable." She replied.

"Great." John said, "I'll put a tub of popcorn on."

Mary came back in wearing sweats and a T-shirt. While John was gazing at her admiring her curves and bumps, Mary asked, "What's on?"

That broke John's trance and he replied, "I haven't had time to look at the list yet. Any suggestions?"

"How about 'Double Jeopardy'? It's an old one, I don't think I have gotten around to seeing it yet."

"Good choice." Mary jumped and landed on her favorite spot on the sofa. John grabbed the big stainless mixing bowl full of hot buttered parmesan popcorn and sat beside her.

"Yummy." Mary said as she grabbed a handful. John clicked down the playlist until he found the title and then clicked play. He then sat back, kicked his boots off and put an arm around Mary's shoulder. I must be in Heaven he thought to himself as the movie started.

A couple of hours later, with an empty popcorn bowl in his lap, John said, "Well, I like the way that turned out. You think that old graveyard really exists with all those above ground tombs and such?"

"Yes, it does. It's there in New Orleans where that part of the movie was filmed." She told him.

Hmm, John thought. If I ever go there, I think I would like to check it out. Some pretty old tombs with probably a lot of history to boot. Mary got up and took the empty bowl to the kitchen to wash up. Mary called first dibs on the shower. John still sitting raised an eyebrow in her direction. She just smiled at him and said, "Exit stage left." She was out of the kitchen before John could even reply. He gathered himself up and followed her into the bedroom, planning to get lucky so to speak. Lucky, he did get. Afterwards, it was the most restful night of sleep each of them has had in a while. No more concerns of someone listening in on them. That thought alone relieved them of a tense weight off their shoulder. Ending the night with blissful passion and then blissful sleep.

The sun was up in the sky by the time John opened his eyes. He turned his head to Mary's side of the bed and she was not there. He groaned as he rolled over and sat up rubbing his eyes. He felt more rested than he had in a long time. He slid into his boxers and strolled into the living room. "Well good morning sleepy head." Mary said to him.

John still rubbing his eyes, sat down at the table as Mary poured him a cup of coffee. "Where did the night go so fast?" He asked her.

"You used it up." She replied grinning at him looking very pleased.

John smiled at the thought of it. As he took a sip of coffee. Just what the doctor ordered he thought as he sat his cup back on the table. Mary handed him a plate with about a half dozen slices of fried bacon and a couple of slices of sour dough bread. John's eyes lit up. "Yum." He said as he dropped three slices of bacon on to a slice of bread and folded it over taking a big bite off of the end.

Mary watched him silently eating his breakfast and wondering what kind of target would be sent in their direction next. For some reason it seems they have been in a slow time so to speak since the unexpected visit from the commissions doctor. At least compared to the previous week's work. Again, she was puzzled as to how the doctor is tied into some of these aborts they have been sent on. John noticed the puzzled look on her face and asked her, "What?"

Mary blinked, coming out of her thoughts and looked back at John. "Just trying to figure out what is really going on."

John had just finished his second folded bacon sandwich and took a swallow of coffee and said, "I second that." With a serious look on his face. "Why don't you go ahead and call the gang together for that meeting in the park."

"Sounds good, I'm on it." She retrieved her device and started making calls as John strolled back into the bedroom to get dressed. When he came back out, Mary said, "Today is out of the picture."

"What's up?" John asked.

"It seems Randy and Rochelle got sent out of town for an abortion."

"Well, that is not unheard of." John replied. "Remember when we went across the Bay that one time?"

Mary interjected, "Yeah, but not half way across the state."

"What do you mean, half way across the state? Where are they?"

"They are all the way up in Worth town." Mary said.

"Damn, that's at least a four-hour drive. Are we the only environmentalist around?"

"I never considered the thought." Mary said. "Could be the local environmentalist up there had been exposed to the bad guys."

"That would not be so good." John replied. "That would mean those that we are working for are working against us."

"Scary thought." Mary said, "But if you look at it, it kind of makes sense. Look what happened to us as of late."

John said, "Call the gang back and tell them that the water is getting muddy in the cement pond. They will know what I mean."

"Gotcha." Mary said as she speeds dial on her device. After she completed her calls she said, "You know, it seems like the world is changing around us."

"It always does." John said. "It's just that most people don't notice or even pay attention. We on the other hand have to pay attention all the time because if we don't, our own world could come to a surprise ending at any time."

Mary thought on this for a while. "Do you ever think of changing jobs?" She asked.

"Nah" said John. "There is always a need to take out the trash. I'm not in for the thrill of the kill, although I have done my share in the war. It's more of a duty to try to keep the world upright and not flipping into chaos. Do you know what I mean?"

She thought for a minute and said, "I agree and I am in it to win it." At that, John got up to check their body armor and supplies. It was a force of habit. They had to be always ready at a moment's notice as they were basically on call twenty-four hours a day. The good thing is those who sent their assignments worked a nine to five job so they had never received a target in the middle of the night.

"Works for me." John said out loud. "What works for you?" Mary asked.

"Nothing," he told her. "I was just talking to myself."

"Fine, but if I hear you starting to answer yourself then I will begin to get worried." They both laughed.

"How about we cruise over and give J-Lee a visit?" John asked her.

"I'm game." They changed into their armor, dressed casually over it and headed for the door. Setting the alarm on the way out.

On the walk to the parking facility she said, "I wonder what is really going on up in Worth town."

"I was just wondering the same thing. Something is just a little out of kelter here."

"Kelter?" Mary asked quizzically.

"Yes. It's kind of like a half a bubble off of plumb." He told her.

"Oh, I get it." Mary said. "I agree, something is not right about this. Something has not been right about a lot of things ever since that morning that person shot you in the leg. You think someone was asking you to change jobs or something?"

"I never considered that." John replied.

On the way over to J-Lee's bookstore, Mary said "We might as well give Boston a visit while we are in the same neighborhood."

"Sounds good." John said.

Upon arriving at J-Lee's bookstore, they were surprised to see the fire department's fire trucks, ambulances, and all the flashing lights going on. "Holy crap!" Mary exclaimed. "What the heck happened?"

John parked out clear from the emergency vehicles. "Let's go find out." He said as they approached the store front packed with google eyed onlookers. J-Lee and Boston stepped out to greet them. "Thank God!" John exclaimed. "What the heck is going on?"

"We are still putting the pieces together." J-Lee told him. They stood out away from the crowd and J-Lee laid out his theory of what had taken place. A narrow strip of the building had been vacated for some months now so J-Lee had blacked out the buildings windows and covered it with a huge bookstore interior photo for advertising.

Mary said, "You mean the strip mall owners let you do that? A loss of lease space like that?"

"Nah, the owner doesn't mind. Remember when you first found me and asked what's all. this?" J-Lee said.

John replied, "Yeah, you just said mine."

"Well, the whole strip mall is mine." J-Lee told him.

"Son of a gun. I would have never thought." John said. "How did you manage that?"

"A poker Game." J-Lee said.

John's mouth fell open. "You're shitting me."

J-Lee grinned. "That I am. But really, It's a long story."

"So, what is with all the excitement going on here?" John asked pointing to the array of flashing lights.

"Some jerk came racing into the parking lot, found a vacant spot next to the curb, drove right through it and crashed into the store front. I don't think he was planning on that piece of metal stud slapping back into his side window skewering him through the neck. Lucky the lot was full in front of my store, it could have been much worse. That empty spot with the window covering did look like part of my store." J-Lee said.

"Lucky you." Mary said. They all nodded in agreement.

About that time a fire marshal walked over to the group. "Someone back there said I could find the owner over here."

J-Lee stepped forward. "That would be me." Sticking his hand out in greeting.

"Lacourse, Richard Lacourse." The fire marshal said. "Do you have any enemies or someone who may have a reason to do you harm?"

"Why do you ask?" J-Lee responded.

"Well, it seems, before that metal stud freakishly cut that fellow's spinal cord in the car, he intended to push a button he had taped to his hand."

"A button for what?" J-Lee asked him.

Lacourse said, "To light a bonfire. He had about forty gallons of gas and diesel in the back seat." "Jesus." J-Lee exclaimed.

Lacourse said with a dry sense of humor, "Maybe he didn't like books."

J-Lee asked, "Do you know who he was?"

"Waiting on homicide and the coroner to finish doing their thing. Maybe they will come up with some sort of ID. After they are done, we will get that mess out of there." Lacourse explained.

"Thanks." J-Lee told him and Lacourse turned and headed back to the scene of activity.

"Wow." Mary said as all eyes followed the fire marshal back to the scene of the crime.

A few hours later a crew was sweeping up the broken glass, replacing the metal studs and screwing plywood over the hole in the wall. J-Lee, John, Mary and Boston were now in J-Lee's office pondering the current events. J-Lee asked, "Anyone hungry?" Heads nodded. "Any objections to a redo?"

"Sounds good to me." John said.

"I knew it would sound good to you John, but what about the others?"

Mary said, "I'm game."

Boston said, "I'll second that."

J-Lee wrote down his note, pushed a button on his desk and a cashier came in. "How's it going next door?"

"Almost sealed up." The cashier told him.

J-Lee handed him the note and he turned and was out the door in no time. "Well at least the situation is not totally fubar." John agreed. Boston and Mary just looked at each other questioningly.

Boston was telling them what little he could about the bug he had at his disposal and how the parts came from different parts of Russia. He informed them it was not the standard KGB type of electronics, but was just as good or even better. The question kept coming up about who would plant this and why. The obvious choice kept circling back to the butcher and the doctor. Was the doctor on the take from the butcher or was the doctor being blackmailed for some services he provided for the butcher's mistreated product.

Mary said, "I never thought of that angle. Pull another piece of the puzzle off of the table John."

"What?" Boston asked a little confused as J-Lee grinned.

John told J-Lee about the freakish timing of the unannounced doctors house call just before Boston and Moe showed up.

Mary said, "Yeah, three minutes later and we would have had an awkward room full. I barely had time to get Boston in holding pattern around the block until the doctor left."

J-Lee said, "Yea, that is quite coincidental if you think of it." They all agreed.

A light lit up on J-Lee's desk. He pushed the button and in came the cashier with two large pizza boxes. John smiled saying, "Bibba's." J-Lee and Mary laughed.

Boston asked, "Is this the same pizza we had the other day?" The other three all nodded their heads, and Boston smiled. "I think I could get addicted to this stuff." He said as he pulled a slice out of the box and took a huge bite while the cheese dripped down his chin. He wiped his chin and with a mouth still full he said, "Yum mm." The feeling was unanimous.

John was the first to speak after eating. He told J-Lee about the message he got from Pat and how he was going to go meet with Pearl when he went to collect his Nilgai meat.

J-Lee said, "Nil-who? What the heck is that?"

John explained it to him. He then added, "Oh yeah, Moe is going to tag along. Any objections?"

J-Lee replied, "None that I can think of."

Mary spoke up. "Speaking of Nilgai, Boston, do you handle appliances?"

"No, but I know someone who does. Tell me what you want and I will get you a good deal."

Mary said, "We need one of those half size freezers, not full length."

"How about an upright?" Boston asked.

"Will it hold a few hundred pounds of meat?" She asked.

"Well, I figure it would hold more than that half size you bury stuff in. At least with the upright you have access to everything." Boston told her.

"Sounds good." John said. "Find a larger one. After all, we won't be losing any more floor space like a regular deep freeze takes up."

Boston agreed and made a mental note to contact his friend. "Ok then." John said. "Another item scratched off of the to do list." Mary grinned big.

J-Lee said, "A type of antelope you say?"

John nodded. He told J-Lee that Pearl had so many kinds of animals out at the ranch, he couldn't even remember their names, much less how to pronounce them all. Mary laughed at that statement of truth.

"How the heck do you find a place like that?" Boston asked.

John grinned and just said, "Well, let's just say a friend of a friend."

"A friend of a friend." Boston repeated.

John said, "It's a long story."

"I'll take your word for it then." Boston replied and J-Lee laughed.

"So, you are going to take Moe out to a sort of hunter's paradise then?"

John said, "That's the plan when it happens." "Lucky him." Boston replied.

John and Mary wrapped up the meeting by explaining another oddity. How another team had gotten sent up to Worth town. Again, that only raised more questions. J-Lee and Boston were not knowledgeable about the commission and how it operated, they only knew John and Mary and as it played out to them, somethings were just not right. John and Mary rose and said their farewells and headed for the door.

As they were walking through the bookstore and were passing an isle labeled murder/mystery, John wondered to himself if the accident next door had any connection to him and Mary and associates. He would put that thought on file in his mind for a future reference. As they walked out into the parking lot it was a beautiful day.

John said to Mary in a jokingly tone, "What a day. I wish I was at the beach."

"Be careful what you wish for." Mary said laughingly, "You just might get it." As they were pulling out of the parking lot, Mary's device pinged. She looked at it and said, "Looks like we have an abortion to perform."

"Fill me in while I'm driving." John told her.

"Well, it looks like a Hollywood type lady, mid-thirties." John raised an eyebrow as she continued, "Evidently she is the head of some drug smuggling group from Columbia."

"Ok." John said. "Last know location?"

"Down on the south side." Mary said as John exited onto the loop. It was faster than getting caught up in that mid-town traffic. As they approached their location, they found themselves looking at Hobby International Airport. "What the heck?" John asked. The location turned into a short-term parking garage.

John said, "Well this doesn't look good."

Mary replied, "Well, let's wait for the next update in a few minutes." John was contemplating the situation when Mary's device pinged. "What the heck? She is a hundred miles out to sea. She must be on a plane."

"Where to?" John asked.

"We will know when the next location ping comes through after the plane lands somewhere." Mary replied.

"Great." John exclaimed, "I guess we have to wait for her to come back to the states."

Mary just shrugged her shoulders holding her hands up in the universal 'I don't know' sign without speaking.

"Can't do anything sitting here." John said. "Just a waste of time. Let's head back to the cubby hole." To which Mary agreed. As they left the airport parking facility and headed back up the freeway, Mary watched a street sign go by on the corner. Her eyes lit up. "This is Broadway!'

John said, "And?"

"That means somewhere in front of us is that Taqueria Del Sol place."

Now John's eyes lit up. "Your right. I didn't even think of that on the way down. I only had thoughts on the task at hand. Well, Let's not let it just be a wasted drive down here." John started licking his lips causing Mary to bust out laughing.

Mary's device buzzed and it was Boston. He said, "I got a really good deal on that upright and my friend does deliver. Will tomorrow morning be good?"

"Heck yeah! That would be excellent." Mary replied. "Okay. I will give him directions." Boston said. "Great." Mary said. "Thank you, Boston."

"No problem." He said as they disconnected.

Once at Taqueria Del Sol, John and Mary found out what Moe meant about busy times. They had to stand around in the bakery before getting a small table for two. "Well, that only took twenty minutes. I've seen worse." Mary said.

"Not while standing in a torture chamber." John replied tilting his head towards the bakery room they just left. "I could have sworn every sweet in that place was calling me saying eat me, eat me. The one next to it was saying no, no, don't listen to that one, eat me."

Mary cracked up and said, "John, you are crazy." She reached over and patted his hand and said, "It's ok. You're safe now." John laughed.

They changed up their order this time. They ordered fajita's and ice tea. When the fajitas came, they were still sizzling on the platter. On the side was a dish of rice and refried beans and two round canisters of both flour and corn tortillas. They cut up their fajita meat, then chose flour tortillas to spread on some refried beans before adding the meat and rice and rolling it up. They started to chow down. Shucking some roasted garlic to add in it was delicious and just what it needed to hit the spot.

After the meal, as John was cashing out, Mary slipped into the bakery and restocked her new found supply of cream puffs. She joined John and they headed out to the car. A little while later and they left their vehicle in their parking facility and were back in the cubby hole. Mary said, "I'll send a report to the commission and let them know our target left the country."

John commented, "At this late hour, they probably won't see it until the morning."

Mary typed up the report and pushed send and laid her device down. She reached into a bag and pulled out two fresh cream puffs and sat down at the table waving one of them in front of John's face. Without hesitation, he reached out and grabbed it. Mary smirked and said, "Is that the one that was saying no, no, not that one, me, me?"

John looked at it and said, "Well, I do believe it was." They both cracked up.

Mary's device buzzed and she picked it up. "Holy crap. It's the commission."

John sat bolt upright. "At this hour? I thought they would have been long gone to the house by now."

Mary put the device on speaker as she answered. "Hello." She said with a tingle of excitement in her voice. They had never spoken in person to anyone in the commission before.

The voice that came out of the speaker sounded very familiar, like a person highest up the political ladder. "Mary, Is John there with you?"

"He is. I have you on speaker." Mary replied.

"Good, good." The commissioner said. "My name is Don T." John's eyes about fell out of his head and Mary had to cover her mouth to suppress the gasp. "I have been watching you and your little group and am pleased with what I see. I just received your report about the one who got away. Let me assure you there is no one who gets away. You will shortly be receiving a package with credentials. You are now official government environmental specialist. Passports come with the job and travel vouchers, the whole nine yards." John and Mary were both speechless just staring at the speaker. "Hello? Is anybody there?"

Mary replied, "Yes, yes. Just catching our breath."

"Take your time." Don T. said with a chuckle. "The target you are after is now in Belize. In a small town called San Pedro. You will be leaving first thing in the morning. All your papers will be in order. You will have the same clearance to carry weapons as the Feds and the Sky Marshals."

"You can do that?" Mary asked.

"You would be surprised what I can do. I am opening up operations so no matter where your targets go, they will soon find out that they can't hide." Don T said.

The possibilities were running through John's mind. He smiled and said, "Thank you, Mr. T. for the honor of the job."

"No, I thank you." He told them as he disconnected.

CHAPTER FIVE

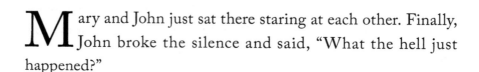

Mary and John just sat there staring at each other. Finally, John broke the silence and said, "What the hell just happened?"

Mary replied, "I think we just got a promotion, with benefits." About that time there was a knock on the door. John looked out and there stood a speedy delivery guy in his striped shirt holding a package about the size of a shoe box. John opened the door. The delivery guy asked to see some ID. John showed him and he said, "Sign here." John did. He peeled a copy and handed the package to John and was out of there.

John closed the door, sat the package on the table and opened it. Inside were the environmentalist credentials, passports, and any other documentation they needed for international travel. "Doesn't it take a couple of months to get a passport?" Mary asked.

"I wonder if the ink is still wet?" John replied.

Mary said, "Talk about a speeding bullet."

John sat there scratching his head before saying, "I guess we better go pack something."

"Crap." Mary said. "What?"

"I have to call Boston and cancel that freezer delivery in the morning." Mary told him.

"I hadn't even thought of that." John said.

Mary made the phone call and simply explained that something came up and they would be out of town for a couple of days. Boston understood and said, "Just call me when you are ready."

"Sure thing, Boston. Thanks again." Mary said before disconnecting.

Mary turned back to the task at hand and that was figuring out what to pack and take to Belize in the morning. She thought again, In the morning. My how fast their world has just changed.

John already had a couple of pairs of pocket shorts, a swimsuit, and two sets of casual wear and body under armor on the bed. The last item was not going into the bag. Mary said, "Darn. You act like you are in a hurry."

John replied, "Just want to be ready."

They were traveling light. One carry on each. That way easy in and easy out of the airports. When they were both satisfied and showered, they hit the sack. It was a near sleepless night as they were both contemplating this recent turn of events laid on them by Mr. T.

"Holy cow." John said. "He is the top dog and I meant the top, top dog. Who would have figured?"

Mary smiled and said, "He must like the way we work."

John said, "I hope so." Before rolling over to a restless night of sleep.

When morning finally rolled around, John and Mary finished a couple of fried eggs over easy with toast and coffee. As Mary was putting away the dishes there was a knock on the door. "Oh." Mary said, "Maybe Boston didn't get the message to the delivery man and he came early." Grinning she checked the door. "Strange." She told John as he approached the door behind her.

John peeked and then opened the door and said, "Yes?" The fellow standing there was in starched black slacks and a white shirt with creases to match.

The fellow asked, "Is this the residence of a John Myer?"

"Yes, it is, that would be me. What's going on?" John asked.

The fellow pointed to the street, "Your limo is waiting."

"Limo!" Mary exclaimed. "Wonders never cease." After the shock of it wore off, John and Mary grabbed their bags, set the alarm and closed the door behind them. Once up the street the limo driver opened the back door and Mary then John slid in and the driver closed the door. "Man, I didn't know these things had so much room in them." Mary said.

"Why do you think some people call them party wagons?" John asked her.

"Well, I know now." Mary exclaimed.

They joked around all the way to the airport when John noticed they were passing the arrival and departure concourse of the Hobby airport. The driver drove east on Airline Drive, turned right following the perimeter of airport. He pulled into a drive with access to the maintenance hangers. Turned left at a gate and rolled down his window and punched in a key code. Mary and John traded glances at each other as the gate rolled to the side. The driver drove through and pulled into a small garage door into the hanger. The driver then got out and opened their door.

John and Mary stood by the limo looking like two lost deer staring into the headlights. A young brunette approached them and said, "Welcome to Star Flight Services."

"What? What is this?" John asked.

The young lady pointed at a business class Learjet and simply stated, "Your ride."

Mary about wet herself. John shook like he just had an orgasm. "Holy, um." They both had to excuse themselves to the restroom before boarding the plane.

The pilots greeted them as the brunette guided them to their seats and said, "Welcome aboard. I hope you enjoy your flight. I will be your stewardess."

Still in a stupor of shock, reality finally set in when the wheels left the ground about three quarter of the way down the runway. Belize City, just over two hours away. At that moment both John and Mary's heads were literally in the clouds. Mary said, "I would have never imagined this yesterday or even in a million years."

"Same here." John replied. It seemed that even before they began to relax, they heard the turbines slow and they had started their glide path down over the jungles of the Yucatan Peninsula into Belize Only International Airport. It was located about twenty miles north of Belize City.

Once on the ground they taxied past a commercial gate and pulled up beside some small hangers and stopped. John and Mary got out and was met by an official who checked their papers. He didn't even check their bags and waved them through a side gate in the fence to a waiting taxi. "Wow." Mary said. "Talk about service."

They put their bags in the trunk and rode on in to Belize City. "Next stop," said the driver with a Jamaican accent, "Swinging Bridge."

"What's a swinging bridge?" Mary asked. "Is it a suspension bridge?"

"No." The driver laughed. "Some bloke put a pile in the middle of the channel and put a bridge on it that swings around to let boats in and out. It's just a motor and a big gear to swing it. No worries about a draw bridge with cables breaking and such."

"Makes sense to me." John said. "Where is this swinging bride?"

"Right there." The cabbie pulled to a stop. "There is a water taxi right down there." Pointing at the water front. They paid the land cabbie and went in search of the water taxi for whatever reason. They quickly found the water taxi office and went inside.

"May I help you?" The attendant asked.

"We are not sure." John replied. "We are looking for San Pedro."

"Well, you came to the right place. The next cab out is in forty-five minutes."

"Forty-five minutes?" Mary exclaimed.

"Yep, we only run two, maybe three times a day. The schedule adjusts to traffic. We aren't going to run all the way out there for just a couple of people." She said pointing towards the bay. "That won't buy the fuel much less pay the labor."

"That makes sense." John said.

John and Mary walked back up to the swinging bridge to check out a few shops and they got to witness railroad type arms come down on the street, bells ringing and the bridge turned perpendicular to the road. A couple of small fishing boats puttered by and the bridge and all returned back into position. "That's pretty slick." John said as they headed back to the water taxi office. Activity had picked up since they left a little while ago.

Finally, someone said, "All Aboard" as they collected tickets from everyone as they stepped onto the boat. The boat filled quickly. They shoved off and slow cruised until they were out of the 'no wake zone', then the pilot rolled back on the throttle and lit those two huge mercury's up. It took them about forty-five minutes to make the little pier to dock and every one off loaded. John and Mary spotted a little hotel to the left of the pier about a block or so up the beach. They strolled up the beach and turned in at the hotel check in. Second floor facing the beach. Crystal clear water and you could see the waves breaking about a quarter of a mile out on the famous barrier reef. "Awesome." Mary said.

They found a restaurant next door. They ate and returned to their room and settled in. "Now what?" Mary asked. "Here we are, all dressed up with no place to go."

"Well, there is a white sand beach right outside. Are you game?" John asked.

"Heck yeah." Mary said. As they were laid out on some beach loungers, she told John, "Remember what I told you the other day about being careful what you wish for?"

John said, "Yeah."

"Well, here we are. I bet you didn't see that coming now, did you?"

John laughed, "Nope, I sure didn't."

After an hour or so of afternoon sun, they decided to go back to the room before getting lobstered. Once showered and changed, they sat out on the balcony overlooking Main Street in front of the hotel. They watched the hustle and bustle of people traffic, golf cart traffic, and bicycle traffic. It was noisy and jam packed. Looking across the town, they could see the Blackwater Bay behind the town. Mary said, "This town is about as wide as the Rock."

John laughed. "A lot longer on this sliver of land and a thousand times more crowded."

Mary agreed. It was about that time Mary's device pinged. "Looks like we are in business."

"Alrighty then." John said. "Time to suit up." And so, they did.

As they walked north up to the end of the street where there was a band playing at a huge tiki party. They mingled into the crowd and found themselves a couple of virgin marys and commenced to mingle with all the tourists. Soon enough Mary befriended little Ms. Hollywood. John kind of stood off on the side. It didn't take him long to spot little Ms. Hollywood's associate or body guard or whatever he was. Where ever she went, he was there like a shadow. Mary eventually came over to where John stood and he said, "Well, it's not happening here."

"Why not?" Mary asked.

"She has a shadow." John told her.

"Really?" I did not notice that." After they got a refill Mary said, "I think I will go see if she will divulge any plans to me."

"Great." John said. "Good Luck."

About forty-five minutes later, Mary came back. "Good thing we didn't completely unpack. We are taking a small plane up to Pine Ridge. Seems there is a resort of sorts owned by Francis Ford Copella."

"Really? First, there is an airport here?" John asked.

"Yeah, it's a small airstrip too short for jets and at this Pine Ridge, there is a little dirt strip on top of a ridge line of hills. Who would have thought?"

Little Ms. Hollywood was slightly hung over when they left in the morning. They flew over Belize City in a matter of minutes and headed west into the hills and the heart of Belize. A bouncy landing on the dirt strip got everyone's attention. They taxied to the end of the runway and stopped. The pilot shut her down. Everyone clambered out, pulled their bags out of the cargo hold and walked down the hill. They crossed the road and into the lodge. John and Mary checked into a room and came back to meet the others standing in the lobby. Ms. Hollywood said, "That's the one." Pointing at an old wooden blade ceiling fan.

Mary said, "And fishing for some enlightenment. That's the famous fan from that scene in the movie Apocalypse Now." "No way!" John said. "I remember that show."

The desk clerk said, "Yep, that's the one and it still runs."

"Wow." John said. Him and Mary still haven't figured out the timing to abort the target.

"Ok everyone, into your swimsuits, it's time to go."

"Swimsuits?" John asked. "The beach is a long way off." They all made a quick change. A car pulled around and they loaded up. After riding through the Hills for a while, they came to a dead end at a small river. The car parked and everyone got out. They walked down to the river that seemed to be just flowing out of a rock wall.

"Now that is different." Mary said.

A guide came out carrying an arm load of inner tubes. "This is getting more interesting by the minute." John said. All said and done, everyone had a tube and a headlight.

"Weird." Mary said.

The guide said, "Follow me." He waded across the river onto a trail everyone else followed like ducks in a row. The guide was pointing out all the medicinal plants along the way and he said, "Here we are."

Everyone gathered to witness all this water flowing out the side of one hill and back into the side of another. Somebody asked, "Are we going in there?"

The guide said, "Unless you want to walk all the way back, yes."

There were no takers on the walk back. Nobody chickened out. Everyone clambered down the bank, flopped their tubes in the water and themselves into the tubes, and into the darkness they went. The light at the entrance of the cave grew smaller and smaller as they drifted with the current. John and Mary still trying to pick the right time to abort Ms. Hollywood the drug smuggler. They started around a bend and were in total darkness for a few minutes until a little light appeared in front of them. "Oh good." Someone said as the mouth of the cave grew larger and larger.

When they popped out the other side, they found themselves in a huge bowl. In the hills, the guide pointed everyone to pull over to the gravel beach. "Wow." Mary said.

Everyone had time to stretch their legs, swim, walk into the bushes to relieve themselves and out of nowhere a helper of the guide showed up with lunch for all. Cold cut sandwiches and bottled water. Mary found a few pretty flowers on her walk through the bushes and set them beside her and John. She looked at John and smiled. He then knew that Mary had a plan.

After lunch Mary had kept about a half of a bottle of water. John pulled another pack of evergreen and quickly sealed the bottle and set it aside. It was soon time to get back in the river for the last leg. They soon floated back into another cave as the light was dimming Mary paddled up to Ms. Hollywood. "Can you hold these flowers for a second before it gets dark?"

"Sure." She replied.

Mary held the bottle away from herself and opened it. She told Ms. Hollywood to stick the flowers quickly into the bottle and she did. She handed the bottle/vase to Ms. Hollywood and asked, "Do you like them?"

"Yes, I do." She instinctively lifted up the bottle to smell the flowers and a minute later she dropped the bottle and Mary retrieved it as they floated into the darkness.

Mary sunk the bottle in the river and rinsed it. John said, "Smells like someone has been eating bad eggs." Everybody but one laughed in the darkness. Soon after the light appeared before them. When they arrived at the mouth, they realized they were back where they started. All but one started to clamber out of their tubes.

Someone said, "Hey" as they caught Ms. Hollywood from floating on down the river. "She must have passed out."

John and Mary knew better and high fived each other. An ambulance came and collected Ms. Hollywood. Authorities concluded it must have been a drug overdose. John and Mary headed back with the rest of the group to the lodge. The next day they got the pilot to drop them at Belize City airport, tipped him well and he was on his way back to San Pedro.

The Learjet was sitting there waiting for them. The stewardess met them and asked how it went. They gave her a thumbs up and she said, "Now let me go round up those fly boys." Soon they were lifting off of the ground and heading back north. John and Mary still could not get used to this type of travel but they intended to. When they landed at Hobby International, they taxied back and into the little hanger they had left from three days ago. No surprises this time. There sat the limo and driver waiting for them.

"Am I still dreaming?" John asked. Mary laughed as they slid into the back of the limo and they were out of there. A short while later they walked back in to their cubby hole. John and Mary both plopped on the couch. "I don't know if it's jet lag or what, but I am beat." John said.

"I'll second that." Mary told him. "We have got to go back sometime."

"Why?" John asked her.

"We didn't get to see any of the many pyramids, or the two blue holes, or dive in the reef or any of that stuff."

John smiled and said, "I guess it's time for you to start drawing up your bucket list then." Mary laughed.

Mary called up Boston to let him know that they were back. Boston laughed and said, "So what you are telling me is that you are on for a tomorrow delivery."

"That I am." Mary replied. Boston said, "I'll take care of it." Mary

Then filled out her report to the commission that the abortion of their target was completed successfully. She then turned to look at John only to find that he had dozed off on the sofa. "Hey you!" He blinked his eyes open rubbing his face. "Are you hungry?" She asked him.

"Nope." He replied getting up. "I am heading for the sack."

As he disappeared into the bedroom, Mary said "I'll be right behind you." Mary looked around the room saying, "Home sweet home." She flipped the light switch and followed John's footsteps.

The next morning after coffee, they got around to unpacking their travel bags. John's device buzzed and he answered. "J-Lee. What's up?"

J-Lee said, "I heard you were back in town about the same time I heard you had left town."

"Yeah well, it was kind of a sudden thing." John replied. "Where did you go if you don't mind me asking?" "Belize." John told him. "It's a long story."

"How can it be a long story? I see three things here, palm trees, white sand, and clear water." J-Lee said.

"All of that and then some." John told him. "As I said, long story."

"I can't wait to hear about it." J-Lee replied.

John jokingly said, "It might cost you a pizza or two."

"Sounds like a deal to me." They both laughed. J-Lee continued, "Moe caught a trail so to speak on the one called the butcher. He is sniffing around on that."

"Great." John said. "Can't wait to see him in the next few days."

"What?" J-Lee asked.

John told him, "Don't you remember he wanted to tag along out to the ranch when we went out to pick up our Nilgai meat?"

"Oh yeah, I forgot all about that." J-Lee said.\

"As a matter of fact, we are sitting here right now waiting for that friend of Boston's to deliver that upright freezer so we can fill it up with meat."

"When are you going out to get it?" J-Lee asked.

"Just waiting for the call." John replied.

"Good deal. Gotta go." J-Lee said and disconnected.

"What was that all about?" Mary asked.

"Seems J-Lee just found out we left town. He must have bumped into Boston this morning. It seems Moe is cold trailing some leads on our butcher fellow."

"Good." Mary replied. "I hope he finds him. Then I will take it from there.

John told her, "Don't get excited now. I know you hate that sick business he is in, but if he is not a target, he is off limits."

"Oh, he's a target alright." Mary said. John decided not to push it. It would only make Mary more angry and more determined to make it personal. Mary said, "John, back in high school one of my best friends got sucked into the sex business. First it was by choice, then it was by force after she realized what kind of monsters men can turn into once that bedroom door is closed. She said the money wasn't worth it anymore. Some bad guys had evidently taken control over her and the next thing she knew she was basically a prisoner serving whoever they sent to her. She said you would not believe some of the nasty gross things that somehow excited those sickos. When she found an opportunity, she absconded."

"Where did she go?" John asked curious.

"She actually ran into me on the street. She was kind of in a stupor from the drugs they were pumping into her. She pilfered some guy's keys and took his car and lit out. She recognized me driving by and pulled out and clipped my back bumper."

"Wow. She actually ran into you with the car she was driving?" John asked.

"Yes. She had no phone and no way to contact anyone. She had no idea what to do. Her parents had moved away and then she saw me like a light in the night."

"What happened next?"

"She didn't make it. The addiction pulled her back into the gutter. They found her dead in an alley." Mary told him.

"I am so sorry." John said.

"I am too." Mary said. Now John understood.

There was a knock at the door that pulled them back out of their thoughts. John checked first before opening the door. "You expecting a freezer?" A big guy holding a dolly asked.

"Yea, yea." John said as he swung the door open wide for him as Mary started rearranging things to make a spot for the upright. "Damn tight squeeze."

"Nah. Sometimes we have to take the door off just to get them into a place. Some morons don't even think to measure the opening." The big guy told John as John winced thinking, lucky me it fit. The big fellow placed the upright at Mary's direction, pulled a pad out of his coveralls and handed it to John. "Just put your X right on that line." John laughed and signed. The big fellow grinned as John slipped him a twenty for having to dolly that freezer down the alley. "Thanks man." He said, and he was out of there.

John looked at Mary and said, "I was a quarter of an inch from being a moron just then." Pointing at the door. They both busted out laughing.

After sitting back down for another cup of coffee, Mary said in a comical tone, "Where's the meat?"

John looked at her and grinned. "Should be any day soon now. Just waiting to get that call from Pat."

They both sat in silence rewinding the tape in their minds and reviewing the past few days events. "I still can't believe it." Mary said.

"Can't believe what?" John asked.

"That we were down there in a place infested with all those old pyramids and we didn't even see one of them." Mary told him.

John nodded and said, "What about our ride down there and back?"

"Oh, that too." Mary said smirking at John. Mary knew John was still in a kind of wonderment of what had happened after that late evening chat with the one know as Mr. T, and not the one with the Mohawk and the ton of gold chains hanging around his neck. She looked at John and told him, "It will be alright."

"What?" He said looking up. She laughed again as she went to the fridge and pulled out a cream puff.

Later John was doing his daily chore of checking their gear and keeping weapons cleaned and lubricated. Mary was in the kitchen chopping some veggies to make a tossed salad when her device buzzed. She looked at it and then answered chuckling, "Mary, Mary quite contrary."

Rochelle said, "Oh really?"

Mary said, "I saw it was you before I answered. How was your trip half way into Yankee land?"

"You got it all wrong. We were halfway up to Indian territory." Rochelle responded.

"Oh yeah, I forgot about them." Mary said laughing out loud. "So, what's up?"

Rochelle said, "Well, it was an interesting trip. Another up-and-coming gangster climbed to the top so he thought he could rule the roost."

"How come they can't figure out that the top step is basically a death warrant?" Mary asked.

"I don't know." Rochelle said. "Maybe blinded by greed or power or both."

"That's how it seems." Mary said. "Well now that you are back in town, maybe we can get the rest of the gang together for a stroll around the park."

"Sounds good." Rochelle said. "I'll check in with the others and try to figure out when we can all do this."

"Great." Mary said. "Later." She disconnected. John said, "What's up?"

"Rochelle and Randy are back in town. She is going to try to find out when we can all get together and stroll around the park."

"Good." John said, "I want to talk to the guys."

Mary laughed. "No John, you want to brag to the guys about our recent travels."

John blanched and looked at her and said, "So?"

Mary laughed. "I don't blame you. I plan on doing the same with the girls."

John said, "What will they think when we tell them it took us less time to fly across the Gulf, about half the time as it took Randy and Rochelle to drive all the way up to Worth town."

"I hadn't even thought of that." Mary said grinning. Yeah, they had bragging rights.

A little later it was John's device buzzing. He picked it up and it was Pat on the other end. "Hey John, your meat is ready. I'm going to pick it up tomorrow and bring it back and put it in the meat locker down at the barn."

"Great." John told him. "Tomorrow is Friday already again, if nothing comes up, we will head out in the morning to go meet Bobby for a little practice."

Pat laughed. "You like that don't you?"

"Yes, My idea of a fun hobby. Just like what they say, go out into a pasture with a club and hit a ball as hard as you can, chase it. When you catch it, you hit the darn thing as hard as you can again, chase it. Repeat." Pat laughed. "Now riding horses on the move and shooting targets, that's the way to do it."

"I see your point." Pat said. "You know how to reach me." They disconnected.

He looked at his phone and hit a speed dial. It buzzed a couple of times before Moe answered. "Que paso John. What's up?" "How's your schedule?" John asked him.

"Why? What do you need?"

John replied, "Well, the good Lord willing and the creeks don't rise, we are headed out to the country around lunch time tomorrow to beat the rush. Then come back either Saturday or Monday. Just have to see how it plays out."

Moe said, "I can rearrange my schedule, no problem. I will be good to go then."

"Great." John said. "I think you are going to enjoy yourself. See you in the morning then?"

"Sounds good." Moe said and he disconnected.

John hit the speed dial on another number and Randy answered. "Hey John, What's up?"

John explained how he had to go pick up his meat and he figured he would get a little shooting in while he was at it and asked Randy if he could set up camp at his place again. Randy said, "I told you guys that you were welcome to use the place anytime."

"I understand." John said. "I just wanted to give you a heads up, you know? You might have something else going on."

Randy said, "Thanks for the courtesy. Might just see you out there." He then disconnected.

Then next day mid-morning Moe showed up. He walked into the living room with his big bag and a little white box. Mary asked Moe, "Are you hungry?"

Moe said, "I already had breakfast."

John was eyeballing the little white box. He looked at Moe and nodded towards it, "What's this?"

Moe stiffened looking all serious and said, "If I tell you I might have to kill you."

John raised an eyebrow about that time Mary put a cup of coffee down for Moe. He smiled and handed Mary the box. She took it and in a childish way peeked under the flap. Her eyes got big and she burst out, "Cream puffs!" John busted out laughing. Mary exclaimed, "Moe, you are my hero." The all laughed.

"As I said, I already had breakfast and now you know where." Moe said.

John and Mary both said "Taqueria Del Sol" in unison and another round of laughter filled the room.

Moe said, "Something looks different in here. I can't pinpoint it but something looks different. Did you all move your furniture around or what?"

"Or what." John said pointing to the upright freezer.

"I knew it." Moe laughed. "I couldn't put my finger on it."

John said, "and soon to be put to work as soon as we get back."

Mary said, "Yea, it's going to be filled with meat."

"What?" Moe said. "You going to rob a meat market or something?"

"No." John said. "You don't remember our conversation about the ranch?"

"Oh yeah. Kind of like a killing zoo." Moe replied. Mary said, "I guess that's one way to look at it." Moe said, "I can't wait."

John said, "Good. Let us clean up and grab our stuff and be on our way." They just barely drove out of the parking facility and ping. John said, "You have got to be kidding me."

"Really." Mary was looking at her device and said, "The target is right up the road by the freeway. What about Moe?"

John looked over to her and said in a tone she knew all too well, "What about Moe?"

Moe was sitting in the back wondering what the hell. John pulled into the bank parking lot. The ID says it's a known robber of banks with a long string of them as a matter of fact. John parked and stepped out of the vehicle just as a man came running out of the bank with a Samsonite briefcase. "That's him." Mary said. Before anybody even blinked, John drew and placed two nine-millimeter slugs in center mass. The guy dropped like a rock just as the security came running out of the bank.

"Holy crap!" Moe exclaimed. It was over before it started. The bank president came out shaken up. "Oh, thank God.

There is a small painting of a gold finch in that briefcase worth millions. We don't need this to get out."

"In that case, do you mind if we vacate the area?" John asked him. The banker asked why and John said, "As much as you don't want your gold finch in the news, we don't want our faces in the news either." John gave the banker his official business card. John Myers-Environmentalist.

The banker said, "I think we can come up with a plausible story, right Jake?"

Jake the security guard jumped and said, "Right boss."

The banker winked at John and said, "That was some damn good shooting, Jake."

John and Mary smiled and got back into the vehicle and went up the ramp onto the freeway.

"I hope that banker takes care of the video camera recording." Mary said.

"I'm sure he will. He has too much at stake for the truth get out." John said.

"I can see the headlines tomorrow." Moe said. "Heroic security guard shows up just in time to take out a robber and saves a bag of money."

"That's right." Mary said. "Nothing taken, no disclosure." About that time the radio started playing 'Carry on my wayward son, there will be peace when you are done.' "Good timing." Mary said.

"You sure got that right." Moe replied as John just grinned and slid on over into the HOV lane.

"It's time for a change in the scenery." John said and all heads nodded in agreement. After cruising down the road in silence for a while John spoke up again. "Moe, what do you know about horses?"

"Horses? Well, they are big and have four legs and I see them on TV on all those cowboy and Indian shows, why?" Moe asked.

Mary looked at John with a mischievous look and said, "Oh this is going to be fun."

John cracked up. "It sure is."

Moe said, "What?" Silence. Just grins. Moe repeated, "What?" John said, "You will see."

After a bit Moe said, "I'm not sure if I want to know or not." John and Mary both cracked up again.

After stopping in C-town for supplies, they cruised on over to the Rock. When they pulled in, John said. "Well look who is here." There was Randy and Rochelle. After they got out and greeted, they introduced Moe.

Randy said, "Look here John." As he pointed at a new little structure.

"What is it, a tool shed?" John asked.

Randy said, "Take a look for yourself." It was built upon a little raised slab about five feet by ten. John opened the door and as he looked in, he let out a whistle. Then he started singing 'Moving on up, moving on up to the east side of town.' Randy and Rochelle busted out laughing.

Mary was curious. "What?" John held the door open and told her to go on in and see for herself. She did and exclaimed, "Oh my." There was a working toilet, a shower and a deep sink. "Wow."

Rochelle said, "Sorry. Cold water shower, but it is a work in progress."

"Beats the heck out of a bird bath." Mary said as they all agreed.

Moe asked, "What?"

John said, "Oh, just a minor improvement. The last time we were here, it was like we were out in the wilderness."

Moe turned around with his arms extended and said, "Well, what do you call this?"

Randy smiled and repeated, "A work in progress." There was laughter all around.

John gave Moe a quick tour. The new outhouse and social area where the wood was ready for a fire. He walked him into the shrubs and showed him Randy's Scooby doo van and Moe's eyes lit up. "No way!" He had a sudden flash of memories. Smiling he said, "Well, don't that beat all." As they walked back to the social area, two more vehicles showed up.

Mary said, "Well, well, the gangs all here."

Rochelle said, "Since we never could make it to the park, I kind of let it slip you guys were headed out this way."

John said grinning, "Yeah, I'm sure it was just a slip."

Kathy spoke up saying, "you two can't have all the fun now, can you?"

Mary said, "Oh you would not believe."

Lacy said, "like what?"

Mary pointed towards the outhouse. John and Mary cracked up and Lloyd said, "I need a beer." At that everyone busted out laughing. "What?" Lloyd asked.

Moe was introduced to the rest of the gang, and John asked in general "how's work?"

"Well now, I think that question requires a fire and some chairs." Randy said. Everyone sat about setting up camp. Lloyd offered Jay a cold one as they all went about setting up their tents in their previous chosen locations. Moe aimlessly wondered around trying to give any assistance he could. Randy approached him and said, "Here. Try this."

"What's this?" Moe asked.

Randy pointed, "you see those two hackberry trees over there about a dozen feet apart?"

"Yes." Moe said.

Randy told him, "Go stand between those trees and unwrap that bundle in your hand. I'm sure you will figure it out."

About that time, Jay came over and said, "Come on Moe, I'll help you out."

Moe said "thanks" and they were off on a mission. After Jay and Moe finished their task, Moe stood back in admiration. "That's the neatest thing I have ever seen."

Jay laughed and said "It's only a hammock."

"Wrong." Moe said. "This is a house hammock with a roof and bug screen walls. I would have never thought." Again, Jay laughed and headed back over to the group in the social area.

After everyone was settled around the newly lit fire, Jay said "anybody hear about that foiled bank robbery today?"

"Nope." Randy replied. Moe's eyes just got big. Randy asked, "what happened?"

"Well, it seems a habitual heister ran out into the parking lot and right into a couple of bullets from a security guard that was just returning from running an errand that his boss had sent him on."

Moe was looking back and forth between John and Mary about to fall off the stump he was sitting on. Finally, John laughed and said, "Good story."

Mary grinned at John. "That's what you said would happen."
"Hold on, hold on." Lloyd said, "What do you mean that that

is what you said."

"Long story short" Mary said, "We left on our way out here and we got a ping." Now everyone was staring at Mary. "It was on our way. We pulled in and the bad guy came out, John shot him. We squared with the banker and we were out of there in under ten minutes before any officials or cameras showed up."

"No way." Jay said.

"Oh yeah." John told him. "The banker didn't want to let on that he almost lost a painting worth millions. So, it worked out mutually for both of us. He kept his little birdie and we in turn aborted our target. Happiness all around."

"You said a picture of a little birdie, what kind of little birdie is worth that much?"

Mary said "Evidently a little birdie called a gold finch."

"I've heard of that." Rochelle said.

John spoke up, "Say, Randy and Rochelle. How was your trip up into Indian territory?"

"The drive sucked." Randy said. "The job wasn't that bad. We actually had two abortions to take care of."

"Really?" Jay asked. "Why did they pull a couple of out of towners to do their work for them?"

"Maybe they have some of the same issues such as those with our fine doctor and associates." Randy said. That raised a few eyebrows.

Jay said, "We had a slow week. We only aborted an unlicensed illegal abortion doctor who has killed six of his patients in the past year."

Lloyd laughed. "So, you aborted the abortionist?"

Jay said "yep."

Lloyd said, "Well, I'll drink to that."

"What did you do this week Lloyd?"

"We had to abort a pharmacist. It seems he wasn't happy with the money he was making filling prescriptions so he started substituting high dollar meds with placebos and sold the real pills on the street. I guess he thought he needed or deserved a thousand percent profit to pay for that fine education." Lloyd told them.

"That's sad." Mary said. "Another full-blown case of greed. It's like one of those evil things that spilled out of Pandora's box," They all agreed.

"So, what about you two?" Jay asked if John and Mary.

"Well, you already know about the bank situation." John said.

"Don't hold out on us." Randy told him.

"Our house was bugged as we suspected it to be. The morning the debugger was coming our fine doctor made a house call."

"No way." Randy said as Mary just bobbed her head.

"Then we got a late call from the commission."

"Those people don't call us. We just get targets and information from them and they work nine to five." Jay told them.

John said, "Listen." All ears were on him. "Mary got a call from Mr. Don T."

"Holy Moly!" Lloyd exclaimed. "Do you know who his is?"

John said, "Yes. I know who he is and then some."

"What do you mean, and then some?" Jay asked.

"He is the top dog in the commission, also known as commander and chief."

"Hold on. You are talking about the P word right now, aren't' you? You say he called you? Ok, this is funny." Jay said. "What was in that Kool-Aid you have been drinking?"

Mary looked Jay dead serious, "do you want me to hit this call back number?" Holding up her device.

"Hold on, hold on and listen." John continued. "We had a target and we went for it. By the time we made the last location the target was a hundred miles out to sea."

"How is that?" Lloyd asked him.

John said, "They have these things called airplanes." Everyone busted out laughing.

"So, you had one that got away." Randy commented. "That must be a first."

"Listen you guys. Mr. T. said there won't be any that get away. As soon as Mr. T. disconnected the call with us there was a package delivered with passports. All I know is it does sound crazy. The next morning a limo picked up and off to the airport we went. It was not to a commercial plane either. The limo wheeled us into a little hanger and the next thing we knew we were climbing out of a Learjet in Belize."

"This is crazy." Jay said.

"I know." John replied.

"Did you find your target?" Jay asked.

"Mary completed the abortion tubing through a cave." "A cave?" Lacy asked.

Mary replied, "It's a long story, but as John said the job is done and here we are."

Rochelle said, "So you jetted off and spent a couple of days in paradise. Just like that? Then you jetted back."

"Right." Mary said. "Don't forget the limo ride back home too."

"Again," Jay said. "I think this is still crazy"

John said, "Look." He pulled out his new ID that said John Myer-Environmentalist United States government.

Randy and Jay both said, "I want one of those."

John said, "I think it is in the works for all of you. Oh, not you Moe, but I think it is in the works.

Lloyd started singing 'you know we're bad, we're nationwide.' Everyone busted out.

"Almost." John said. "Don't cut yourself short."

"What do you mean short?" Lloyd asked. "It's a little bigger than that, It's globally."

"Wow." Jay responded. "It's a little hard to wrap your head around."

Lacy said, "This is going to be fun."

"What?" Rochelle said, "This is only the second time Lloyd has been out of the city in years and now he is going to have the whole world in his hands?"

Lloyd spoke up, "That is a scary thought." Laughter all around again.

Randy pulled out the grill and put it over the fire. Rochelle pulled out that jumbo cast iron skillet and soon cheese burgers were grilling. About that time, just like clockwork, Bobby slid into camp holding out his token six pack. "Hell yeah." Lloyd said as he helped himself. Jay took one as well.

Moe asked, "do you mind?"

Bobby told him, "Go for it, I got more." Tops were popping and Bobby was introduced to Moe.

John looked at Bobby and said, "Moe here is a green hand."

"Is that so? Well, we will see if we can fix that." Bobby replied. Everyone laughed knowing what was in store for him, but no one let the cat out of the bag. Bobby pointed to the little shed and asked, "What are you building?"

Randy said, "We now have an official outhouse."

Bobby laughed, "I should have known. That's where the bathroom was back in the day when this was a drugstore."

Burgers were served so the chit-chat stopped. You could only hear the lips smacking and an occasional umm to go with it. After a bit, the conversation picked back up. The girls put the food away and the guys cleaned up around the social area. Everybody but Moe knew what was coming next. Eventually Randy got up to gather sticks. Rochelle broke out the bag of marshmallows and it was on. After a while, Bobby left and everyone started migrating to their respective tents. Moe went to climb in to his hammock and he darn near rolled himself up. Finally settled in, he thought to himself, why has he never done anything like this camping thing before? He thought this might just turn in to a new hobby and soon found a peaceful sleep.

Somewhere in the distance a rooster crowed bringing Moe and the rest of the gang awake. Randy was already kicking the embers left over from the nights fire feeding dried leaves and twigs and soon had a blaze going in which he added larger pieces of wood. He adjusted the grate and put on the pot of water and sat in a chair and watched the blaze grow.

Moe rolled out of the hammock and fell on the ground laughing at himself while looking around to see if anyone had seen him fall. Quickly finding his feet, he strolled over and sat by the fire. "Water is hot; you need a shot of coffee?"

"Sure." Moe said. Randy told him it was instant to which Moe replied, "I'm not picky." He watched Randy poured hot water into a cup and stirred before handing the cup to Moe who wrapped both hands around it. After taking a sip he spoke up. "Man, I never knew the city was so loud."

"What do you mean?" Randy asked him.

"I got a neighbor a couple of houses down from me that raises chickens. I don't recall ever hearing a rooster crow, but out here I heard that rooster and he must be blocks away." Moe explained.

"Actually, it's a little farther." Randy said. "More like a quarter of a mile away."

"No way!" Moe gasped.

"Yes sir!" Randy said about the same time the rooster crowed again in the distance.

"There he goes again." Moe said as he started sipping more of his coffee. "Man, this is nice. You know?"

Randy smiled. "If I didn't know, would I be here?" "I guess not." said Moe.

The rest of the gang was stirring and that new out house was getting well broken in. Moe was amazed at how everyone came together and in no time had breakfast ready. It was a scramble for the tortillas. Moe soon found that he had to fend for himself if he was to get a toasted flour tortilla. "This is crazy." Moe said to no one in particular. "But it's a good crazy." After everyone finished, Moe said "That was better than home made." Everyone just looked at him.

Bobby showed up and asked Moe if he was ready. "Ready for what?" Moe asked.

Bobby just said, "I'll be back later for you guys."

Everyone said, "Have fun Moe." Moe did not know what he was in for.

After Bobby and Moe left, Jay turned and said "So What's the story on Moe?"

John told him, "He does some work for my friend J-Lee and he sometimes helps Boston do sweeps."

"Sweeps?" Jay asked.

"Yes, and I highly recommend him. He has a magical upright vacuum that kills the crap out of bugs and finds them too." John explained.

"What are you talking about?" Jay was more confused.

"Ok." John sighed, "We suspected a listening device in our house. We found one and fried it. We were able to do that with the magical vacuum."

"I give up." Jay said. Randy started laughing as he was listening to the whole conversation. "What are you laughing at?" Jay asked him.

"You guys." Randy explained. "It almost sounded like some kind of Laural and Hardy skit you guys just did."

"And the bug, what kind was it?" Jay asked.

"Russian. Not the KGB type." John said.

"How do you know all of this?" Jay asked.

John replied, "Boston."

"Who the hell is Boston?" Jay asked.

John told him, "A fellow that is pretty spiffy with electronics."

Lloyd chimed in, "Electronics for what?"

John shook his head. "I recommend Boston to go to your homes and check for bugs."

"Bugs? We got tree roaches." Lloyd said.

Randy just busted a gut. "We are talking about listening devices and cameras Lloyd."

"Oh." Lloyd said. "Is it too early for a beer?"

John had to walk away. He went to the new outhouse and washed his face with cold water before he walked back over. "Let me try this again. Do you remember last week on the news where that suspected terrorist crashed his car into that bookstore?" They all did. "Well, my friend J-Lee owns that bookstore and Mary and I just happened to show up right after that non-fireball."

"Wait." Jay interrupted. "What do you mean non-fireball?"

"Here we go." Randy said grinning.

John put his hands up. "Ok, just listen. Ok? Ok? Fine." John continued, "That fellow had forty gallons of fuel in his back seat rigged to blow but it didn't." John held up his hands to stop the questions that were about to pour forth. "God, karma, whatever you want to call it. Fortunately, the car hit a void between businesses so damage was minimal."

"Lucky for your friend J-Lee." Randy stated.

"Yes and no. You see, that empty space belongs to J-Lee. As a matter of fact, that whole strip mall belongs to J-Lee." John explained.

"Wow." Jay said. "And this is the fellow you said you used to work with?"

John replied, "The one and the same and Moe is his number one man for snooping around on the low side of town if you know what I mean, jelly bean. Now Boston, he operates first-class electronics store next door to J-Lee's bookstore. If you need any type of quality electronics, I suggest you pay Boston a visit. He is on top of his game. He proved that with that old upright vacuum." John held up his hands again, "Trust me, it's a long story and I would rather let Boston explain or demonstrate his bug zapper."

"Now I'm confused." Lloyd stated. "I thought you were talking about a vacuum. Where did the bug zapper come in?"

John could barely hold a straight face at this point. "They are one and the same. Just take my word for it. Speaking of Moe, Mary and I need to go fetch him to ride over for a meeting with Pearl."

"You mean that guy who brought you that meat last time we were here?" Randy asked.

"The one and the same." John said. "Maybe you guys can take the girls over there after I pick up Moe and you all can play shoot'em-up."

"Sounds good." Randy said as he turned and said, "No, you can't have a beer, Lloyd. We don't want you to shoot yourself in the foot." Lloyd grinned and headed for the coffee pot.

John and Mary headed over to pick up Moe. When they drove in, there was Moe sitting astride that big paint with a bigger grin on his face. John said, "Hey cowboy. Are you ready to go to the ranch?" Moe's eyes lit up and he came sliding down off of that horse like he knew what he was doing.

Mary said, "I'm impressed."

Bobby strolled over and said, "He's a natural." Moe said, "I never messed with the guns much."

John replied, "Good, that means that you didn't pick up any bad habits."

"That's right." Bobby said adding "With a little practice, he should become very proficient."

Moe still grinning said, "Man, you guys have all the fun. I never even knew this existed."

John laughed and turned to Bobby. "The rest of the gang will probably be easing this way shortly."

"I'll be waiting." Bobby said. "Meanwhile, I'll go see if Jude got a sandwich handy."

"Jude?" Mary asked.

"Yeah, that's my wife." Bobby told her.

"Oh, I didn't know." Mary said. "We will have to meet sometime."

"That you will." John told her as he headed for the vehicle.

On the way over, Moe still grinning ear to ear said, "Man, I want to thank you guys."

"For what?" John asked.

"So far, this has been one of the best weekends I can remember in my life and its only Saturday." Moe said.

John and Mary laughed. "Who knows." John said. "Still got a day or so to go." Moe just kept grinning. Before long, John pulled up to the huge gate and he keyed in some numbers causing the two huge swinging gate doors to swing inward.

"Wow." Moe said.

"My exact word the first time I came through them." Mary replied.

Moe turned to look back and watch those massive iron gates close up behind them. He turned back forward just in time to see some Axis deer cross in front of them. "Wow." He said again.

They drove past the little lakes and as they rounded the curve, the huge lake and huge house came into view. "My favorite view." Mary said.

"Holy moly." Moe said.

John laughed as he crossed a cattle guard and drove up into the circle drive and parked in front of the house. The three of them got out and stretched their legs for a minute and went up the steps to the massive oak door. Just as they reached it, the door swung open. Peg greeted them and invited them in.

Pearl guided them to the sofa and he took a place across from them. Moe was introduced and John acknowledged to Pearl that he could speak freely. Pearl nodded and said, "Your doctor friend is still trying to schedule a hunt, but is having conflicting schedules with his two associates. Between their schedules and the hunts, I already have booked for others, they are having a hard time fitting into my slots."

"I see." John said.

"I think it will be soon." Pearl continued, "Maybe they are waiting for a short-term notice."

"How short?" John asked.

Pearl said, "I have had slots filled at the last minute."

"I see." John said. "No time to plan anything so to speak."

"My thoughts exactly." Pearl replied.

Moe interjected, "May I make a comment?"

John and Pearl said, "Sure."

"Is there any way I can act like a hired hand or something? I can be good at sweeping the barn or something. That way I might hear something. I have good ears." Moe told them.

Pearl said, "That might work. I could put you as Pat's assistant. He can show you around. Teach you how to fill the feeders and all that. Those Fellows stay in a suite built into the barn and that's where we will set you up a nook over in the maintenance area."

"That might work." John said.

Pearl buzzed Pat, and about five minutes later he came in.

Pearl told him, "You need to give Moe here a full tour." Pat looked at Moe and said, "Let's go."

While Pat and Moe were gone, John revealed the identity of the doctor's associates. "What on earth is that man doing with the likes of such?" Pearl asked.

John told him, "We are working on that. Mary has a friend in an agency digging and Moe is a good snooper. He's like a blood hound. Give him a scent and he's locked on the trail. The only thing is he's already ran into a couple of brick walls."

Pearl said, "Well, he didn't appear to have a broken nose." With that, John and Mary both cracked up. Peg said, "Hey

Mary, why don't you come over here." Mary got up and joined her in her huge open kitchen dining area. Just as she slid out a tray of baked cookies and slid in a tray of dough balls into the oven.

"Smells so good." Mary said.

So that is how the afternoon went. Mary and peg making cookies and Pearl and John trying to figure when the doctor's group would make their move. John said "Let's see what Moe has going and you can tell the doctor you have a last-minute cancelation."

"Sounds good." Pearl replied.

Finally, Pat brought Moe back all big-eyed exclaiming "Man, you sure have quite the operation here."

"Glad you like it." Pearl said.

John asked Moe, "How's your schedule?"

"It's open at the moment, what do you got?" Moe replied.

"Do you want to come back out here Monday when Mary and I come back to pick up our Nilgai on our way back to the city?"

Moe replied, "Man, those things are huge. Pat showed me a group of them on our ride through."

John said, "Moe, do you want to come out here for a while and get used to the neighborhood so to speak?"

"That would be great." Moe replied. "It's like living in a zoo."

Pearl gave him a look. "It's not a zoo Moe, It's an exotic game ranch."

"Oh, sorry." Moe said. "I won't say that anymore. Pearl just chuckled under his breath.

"Ok then." John said. "We better head on back to the Rock." "Here." Peg said handing a plastic dish of cookies to Mary. "I know there are cookie monsters that are hungry."

"You sure have that right." Laughed John as they were heading out the door.

The three of them stopped on the steps to watch a group of blue Wildebeests wander down to the lake for an evening drink. "Look, look." Mary said. Out of the woods close to the Wildebeest, came a half dozen Zebra's. "That is so awesome." Mary said. "I didn't have to go to Africa to see them."

"Finally." John said. "We need to head out."

They got in the vehicle and drove out of the circle drive, retracing their route back to that massive gate and they were out of there.

When they got back to the Rock and stepped out of the vehicle, John asked Randy if he had a rope. "I can find one, why?" Randy asked.

"Well, Moe's head is so far up in the clouds, we may have to tie a rope around his ankle and that tree over there to keep him from floating away." Everyone busted out laughing, even Moe.

"That good?" Lacy asked.

Moe said, "Yes. It was, and still is. Thanks to you all."

Mary then held up the plastic dish. "What's that?" Rochelle asked.

"Hot off the press, chocolate chip cookies." Yum, they all said and the cookie monsters came alive.

After the cookies were devoured and everyone sat around staring into the blaze, John spoke up. "We have a plan to try to find out what is up with that fine doctor of ours and those sickos he seems to be hanging out with."

"Well," Jay said. "Fill us in."

"We are going to try to manipulate them to come out to the ranch, and when they do, Moe's going to be there working as a hired hand. He will be sleeping in the same barn that they that has the hunting suite." John told them.

Moe grinned and said, "Yep, who is going to suspect a short tattooed up Mexican?"

"That's great." Randy said. "Do you know when it will happen?"

"Moe is going back on Monday when we go back to get our meat."

"So soon?" Jay asked.

"I don't have any other plans at the moment." Moe told them. "It's all about being in the right place at the right time." Then Moe had a thought. "Hey Randy, can I borrow your portable house bed?" He was pointing at the tent hammock combo. "I can rig that up in the barn and dress like I just came across the river."

"That is a good idea." John said.

Randy smiled and said, "Sure, why not? If you break it, you buy it."

"Randy!" Rochelle exclaimed as everyone cracked up. "Just kidding." Randy said. "No problem."

The rest of the evening the group had John and Mary retelling the trip to Belize. Quizzing them as to assure no detail was left out.

It was a natural campfire story hour and all present were enthralled, listening and staring into the blaze of the campfire. One of the group members spoke up saying "I never thought of using that H25/evergreen in such a way."

John said, "It's going to be Mary and I's choice in future situations. We have used it twice with perfect success. Take in the ramifications on the area of use, wind drift, the environment around you because if you make a mistake, it could be not only your target's life, but yours also. There is no room for miscalculation and absolutely no carelessness. That is why it is double packaged with that color bar to detect any leaks. If that color bar is the wrong color, take that crap back to the lab and let them either destroy it, or repackage it." Nods of agreement from all around the campfire.

It was getting late and John spoke up before everyone started dispersing to their designated areas. "Who's up for church again in the morning?"

The gang all said yes except Moe who asked, "Church? What the heck, it's been a while, I'm in."

The sun came up clear and bright on Sunday morning and everyone got up to the morning activities. Randy as usual already had the fire stoked and hot coffee was served all around. The breakfast taco routine came together better than last. At the swiftness of the teamwork dealing with the meal, Randy grinned. "Practice makes perfect."

Lloyd said, "Man, if they had breakfast taco competitions like they do those chili cook-offs, I think we would kick some butts." Everyone laughed at the thought.

Then came the squeals. Each a different tone as one by one they sucked air stepping into that cold water shower in preparation for church. Kathy afterwards said, "I would almost have preferred a warm bird bath." The other girls chimed in agreement. Randy pointed to the fine toilet, shower accommodations and said, "I told you it was a work in progress. Not enough roof area for a solar powered water heater or we could put a tub of water on and fill a garden water bucket and have a hot hand shower." "Or." John interjected pointing to the corner of the property where the power pole was standing and said, "maybe you could try that." Everyone laughed.

"Then it wouldn't be like camping." Randy said. "First hot water, then lights, then fans, then heaters."

Rochelle spoke up, "Randy, I think we might be able to adjust." She looked around at the group to see all heads were bobbing.

"And a mini fridge to put some beer in." Lloyd said. At that everyone cracked up.

Lacy asked him, "Lloyd, is that all you can think of ?"

Lloyd said to her "No, I like food too." Lacy just shook her head.

The church service was about blessings and forgiveness and when you learn forgiveness, blessings follow. After services everyone visited with each other. The group then headed back to Randy's place. What seemed to be turning into a home away from home. Moe said, "I like that little church."

"We all do." Rochelle told him.

"I'll second that." Kathy added grinning.

For the line of work that they were in, one sometimes wondered on the blessings of forgiveness and God's grace. It was not a choice in their duty to take a life. Just like it was not a choice for a soldier to take a life in battle. After all, the bible tells of killing whole towns of men, women and suckling's leaving no survivors. God created the governments, but it was the officials in said governments that became corrupt. Same today as two thousand years ago when Jesus wrecked the temple yard. The job of this little group of environmentalists was to expedite evil to put them in line for their second and final death. No eternal promises for them. Choices have consequences. Praised be to those that see the light. Pity be to those headed for eternal darkness.

After lunch, Bobby came by in his pickup and asked if any-one wanted to go to Burkes water hole and swim awhile. The vote was all ayes and they soon found themselves in a cool water irrigation reservoir pumping a six-inch flow of water into it. Actually, the water was cold coming from around six-hundred feet below the surface. It was all sun and smiles. Moe said, "Man, you guys have opened up a whole new world to my eyes I never knew existed and I like it. I never in all my days knew there was more to life than the city life."

"Well." John said, "Old dogs can learn new tricks, you know."

CHAPTER SIX

B ack at the camp, everyone got into some dry cloths. That rope that John had asked about the night before was strung up from a couple of trees and everyone's wet stuff was hung out to dry. Randy said, "Hey John, do you have a minute?"

"Sure, what's up?" John asked as he followed Randy to his vehicle.

"Let's take a little ride." Randy said.

John raised an eyebrow as he pulled the door closed and said nothing. They headed south out of town. The road had a couple of slow curves, then it straightened out. Randy turned right into a long horseshoe drive. In the middle of the loop back was a gazebo. Randy stopped. They got out and John looked around at all the tombstones. Randy walked to the south side of the gazebo to a plot of headstones. John followed. Randy said, "I have family here."

"Oh really?" John replied.

Randy said, "Multigenerational." He pointed and said, "There is my mother and father. Over there is my sister, and back there is my brother."

"Wow." John said. "I didn't know."

"Well, it's not something people hold conversations about now, is it?" Randy said.

"No, it's really not." John said. "The work we do, keeps places like this in business.

"Do you ever think about where you are going to be planted John?" Randy asked.

"Come to think of it, I don't think I have ever considered that thought." John replied.

"Most people don't. They just roar through life full speed ahead and then something happens and it turns out that either families or strangers have to figure out where to plant you because your life was just so busy with other things to do." Randy explained.

John looked at Randy staring at his mother's headstone. "Are you alright Randy? I never took a minute to think of final details like that."

Randy looked up at John. "Yeah, it's kind of like you can't get off the crapper until the paperwork is done." John looked at Randy in silent thought. Randy pointed to an empty spot and said, "That's mine. Paid in full for future use of course. At least I know where I will end up."

"Wow." John thought after Randy visited a couple of headstones. He walked back to the vehicle and they got in and headed out the drive back to camp. "Thanks for sharing that with me Randy." John said. Randy nodded as they pulled back in at his place.

The grill was hot and Rochelle was doing her magic. The evening meal was soon served and the sky was getting dark. The first evening star was out. There was a debate on whether it was Venus or Mars or Mercury. No conclusions were made and Lloyd said, "I need a beer." Now everyone shook their head. Lloyd looking at them grinning. "What?" He started laughing.

Kathy told Rochelle some kind of sense of humor and Rochelle replied, "You think?" They both started laughing between themselves.

Lacy said, "Anyone up to singing around the campfire?"

John stood up, "Not me." They all looked at him questionably. He was still thinking about the previous excursion and talk he had with Randy. Thinking how right he was. No one here was immortal.

Mary came over to him and asked him what was up so he explained what was bothering him and how he never even considered getting planted somewhere. Mary said, "Well John, who does?"

John said, "I think I am going to buy a plot out there. You get burned in the city. Someone comes in with lots of money and wants to build a high rise and they might come in and dig you up and put you who knows where."

Mary pondered this and said, "Let's go turn in." "Sounds good." John said. So, they did.

The sun was well up before everyone was awake. John and Randy had already had their fill of coffee. Lloyd stumbled out of his tent and said, "Dang, that sun sure came up early today, didn't it?" Everyone just looked at him. He was rubbing his eyes and exclaimed, "Did I miss something?"

Jay replied, "No Lloyd, you didn't miss anything."

After breakfast everyone started folding tents and packing up. Moe took special care to roll his house bed into a tight roll and tied it and put it in the back of John's vehicle by the huge cooler they brought to haul John's meat in. After sitting around the dying fire, everyone started leaving by the twos. Lacy and Lloyd headed out first, then Jay and Kathy. Finally, John, Mary and Moe headed back over to the Ranch. Randy and Rochelle still had a few things to do so they stayed behind.

Upon arrival at the ranch, Pearl had them follow him down a winding dirt road following a creek through the woods. After about a mile or so, they arrived at the barn. Pat was waiting on them and waved John around to the back where the meat locker was and parked. They all got out and walked through the overhead door into the barn. The first thing to hit you was the smell of alfalfa hay. Almost half of the huge barn was stacked three quarters of the way up to the ceiling with the stuff. Pearl had to have it to supplement winter forage and a backup for those random dry spells in the summer when everything sometimes dried out in drought conditions.

As they continued into the barn, Pat pointed to an area with a fridge and freezer and hand tools, compressor and various other tools. A wall of shelves with oils and pesticides and fertilizers and other various items such as game cameras and sodas. Moe said, "This looks like a good place for me to hang out. Literally."

Pat said "What?"

Moe grinned. "I can tie off my hammock to one of those gaps in those metal wall panels and the other end to that pipe column."

Pearl looked at it for a minute and said, "That should work." He then turned to Pat. "Why don't you help Moe get set up."

Moe and Pat headed back out to retrieve Moe's gear. Pearl, John, and Mary continued towards the front of the barn and turned in to the hunter's suite. It contained a kitchen area, a living room with a huge flat screen, two multi-bed bedrooms and a full bath. Mary said jokingly, "I like this. Do you mind if we move in?"

John laughed and said, "Yea, sure and we will have the doctor and his friends set up tents outside, right?"

Mary said, "Darn, I forgot about them."

Sitting down to a table, Pearl said "We might have a go on them coming out this week. I contacted the doctor and told him I had a cancellation, if they were interested in a quick slot. The doctor said he would have to get back with me. I am still waiting on that to happen. You never know."

John said "It still bugs me. Why would our fine doctor associate with the likes of those other two?"

Pearl said, "Well, maybe they are gay for each other."

John's eyes got big on that one. "Gross." Mary said, and John agreed.

Pearl said, "You never can tell. I see a lot of so-called Hunters who use hunting as an excuse for one to get away from their partner, or to meet another partner and not the one at home. I have seen some real Jeckel and Hydes. What you may see out here is a one-hundred-and-eighty-degree different person than when you bump into them on the street."

"I can imagine." John said. About that time Pat and Moe came in and told Pearl that Moe is all set up and ready to act the part of a wetback when the time comes. Pearl informed them it may be soon.

Pat asked Pearl, "Do you want me to show Moe some of the equipment?" Pearl agreed. Pat said, "We will start with those four wheelers out there."

Moe smiled. "Sounds like fun."

John decided it was time to load up and head back to the city, so they got up and went back out to start transferring packages of meat with John's name on it from the locker to the cooler. It didn't take long for John to figure out that he didn't have enough cooler. Oops. Pearl had John go over in the corner and grab a cooler out of a stack he had there. Relieved, John said "Thanks." Pearl helped him find a suitable one and took it to the water hose and gave it a good rinsing. They placed it in the back seat and started filling that one also. "Man, that's a lot of meat." John said. "Maybe I should leave a few steaks and some links for Moe." Pearl pointed to the fridge right over by where Moe set up camp, and John took an armload to the fridge. On his walk back, Pat and Moe came pulling in on their four wheeled ATV's. Again, Moe was grinning like a kid in the candy store.

After showing Moe his new stash of meat, they all said their goodbye's. John and Mary followed Pearl back up that winding road leaving Pat and Moe standing, looking out those big overhead doors of the barn. At the fork in the road, Pearl headed to his house and John and Mary headed for the gate. Mary said, "I can almost still see Moe's smile from here."

John laughed. "Yea well, he seems to be having fun now."

"I hope this all works out. Why would the doctor bug our house?" Mary asked.

"Why do you consider it to have been the doctor?" John asked.

"Because." Mary said. "Every time you mentioned going to see him, we were side tracked on an abort mission. I mean every single time."

John thought on this as they went through those big automatic gates and said, "I don't really know what is going on, but it is more than meets the eyes." Mary agreed.

The drive back to the city was uneventful. Except for the part where they had to squeeze the vehicle down their ally to pull the coolers into their front door. Mary stayed and started transferring into that glorious new upright freezer as John took the vehicle back to the parking facility. When John returned, Mary was finishing up. A shelf of roast, a shelf of ribs, a shelf of steaks, a shelf of links, and a shelf of slim link packages. One of which was open and a stick hanging out of Mary's mouth. She grabbed it as she stood. "You want one?" He did. He later said that those little suckers were kind of addicting. Mary agreed.

After unpacking the rest of their belongings, John began to inventory and check out their tools of the trade while Mary put things away and started laundry. Once they both caught up and sat down, John and Mary got ready for a movie night. John made the popcorn as Mary went and changed into her favorite sweats. "What is on tonight?" Mary asked.

"Oh, I don't know. How about Enemy of the State? You know, with Will and Gene?"

"Sounds good." Mary said as John strolled back into the room with a big bowl of popcorn. After the movie ended, they got up to head for the shower when John's phone buzzed.

It was Moe. He told John that the doctor and his crew were tentatively going out in a few days to meet at the ranch. John pumped his fist in the air in excitement. Moe explained that Pat had it set up where Moe will be working around and with the group whenever they show up. "Good." John told him. "In the meantime, what are you doing to pass the time?"

"Oh man, you aren't going to believe this. I'm sitting in a big air-conditioned tractor riding around shredding the weeds and grass along these little roads. Tomorrow, I start on a one-hundred-acre pasture. It's like a giant lawn mower on steroids." Moe told him.

John laughed. "It's good to hear that you are not bored to death out there." Moe said he had to go and disconnected the call. John turned to Mary who was standing in front of the shower and told her, "No worries about Moe. He is having way too much fun." He peeled his shirt off and headed in Mary's direction. He gave her a quick kiss and invited her to join him in the shower. When his pants hit the floor, he followed her into the shower. Sometime later after a lot of bouncing and banging on the shower walls, the sliding door opened and they both nearly fell out laughing and giggling. After they dried off, they finally found their way to the bed.

Mary looked John in the eyes and said, "In all the excitement, I forget. Is this round two or round three?"

John giggled and said, "Who's counting?" Just as they were finding themselves in a semi-tangled position, Mary's device buzzed on the bedside table. John asked her, "Are you expecting a call?"

Mary replied, "No." Reluctantly she reached over and picked it up. She turned to look at it. "Oh." She screamed as she pushed John to the side. Her eyes were big as she answered. "Hello." She had only seen that number once before.

"Hello Mary. Is John around?" Don T. asked.

"He is sir; I'm putting you on speaker as we speak sir." Mary said.

"Good, good." Don T. said. "Now to the point. I like the work you did down in Belize. You chopped one of the snakes heads off of a Medusa. With that said, I am here to tell you that I am going to authorize your fellow teams. Hold on, let me see here. That would be a Jay and Kathy, a Randy and Rochelle, and also a Lacy and Lloyd if my information is correct."

"Yes sir, it is." They replie

"Good, good. My delivery man is on his way as we speak to bring to you all of their credentials. The same as yours. Your little group is going to spear head, so to speak."

John spoke up, "Sir, does that mean we are going somewhere in the morning?"

"No, no." Don T said. "Besides the credentials, my messenger is also bringing you information on the next job. You have tomorrow to sort it out with the others."

"Great!" John replied.

"Keep up the good work." Don T. told him and disconnected the call.

John and Mary just sat there in a daze. Mary came to and looked over at John and told him, "You better put some pants on." He looked at her quizzically and about that time there was a knock on the door.

"Crap." He said jumping up and grabbing a big thick robe and heading for the door, all the while Mary was laughing at him.

John peeked out the window and confirmed it was the same guy. The same striped shirt holding a package about the size of a hatbox. John opened the door. The guy recognized him and didn't ask for an ID. He just handed the paper over and John signed it and got his copy. Mr. Stripes turned around and left. John brought the box to the table as Mary said, "Leave it until morning. Don't we have some unfinished business in here?"

"That we do." John said turning out the lights as he headed back into the bedroom. The next morning as they were having their morning coffee John said, "You know, at the rate we are going it is going to take forever to break this coffee pot in."

Mary laughed and said, "Yeah. We have been gone more than we have been home lately. Speaking of gone, you better round up the gang for a walk around the park. I hope Randy and Rochelle came back in yesterday."

John said, "Call them first. If they are the farthest, we need to set some time to meet. I am not going to just drive across town and hang out for the fun of it all day."

"Aww, come on." Mary said kiddingly.

John looked at her then down at the package. He said, "Well, doggies. Let's just see what is hiding in here."

After opening the box and looking at the contents, John pulled out two photos. Mary said, "I wonder why they sent two photos of the same guy."

John looked at her and said, "It's not the same guy. Look closer, It's twins.

"Wow." Mary said. "You think they try to look alike."

"That would be my guess." John said. He read the Modus operandi of the twins and said, "The names Ricky and Dicky. How easily confusing that could be growing up in school. We can review all of this at the park later with the gang."

Mary started making her calls. Soon she said, "We are in luck. Everyone is in town."

John said, "Good. Let's meet around two-ish at the tennis courts. Go after the lunch rush. Then we can be out of there before evening rush."

"Sounds good." Mary replied. "I will let them know."

John walked over to the new upright freezer and opened the door and stood staring. "What are you doing John?" Mary asked. "Are you trying to cool your toes off?"

"What?" He asked.

She said, "You're letting all the cold air out."

He smiled and said, "But I was admiring your fine work, Mary." He swung the door back into the closed position.

A few minutes later Mary said, "It's all set up. Tennis courts at two."

"Good." John said. "We have time to go look for something under the covers of the bed."

Mary said, "Did you lose something?"

"Maybe." John replied.

"Do we need a flashlight?" Mary asked.

"I don't think so." John told her. "I had more in mind of us getting under the covers and feeling around and see what we could come up with."

"I see what you mean." Mary said grinning. "What are you waiting for mister?" They went and they went until they were spent. As they lay there, Mary looked and John and asked, "Did you ever figure out that cigarette thing after sex?"

"Heck no." John replied.

"You are the one who brought the subject up a while back." Mary told him.

"Mary, you are crazy." Laughing together, they just held each other for a few more minutes.

A quick lunch, then John and Mary geared up. Anticipating how the gang was going to react on the news and the new mission. John laughed when he remembered the conversation out in the country. A couple of the group said, "I want one of those." Well, here and now, John was bringing them one of those and boy were they going to be happy. This makes it official. His gang are all going to be official environmentalists under the guise of the department of agriculture. So their comings and goings won't raise any eyebrows.

After everyone arrived and high fived, John looked at them and said, "You guys are not going to believe this." He opened the box and gave each one of them a brown envelope with all their official papers, new passports, and the works. Holy this and wows and Jesus's and all sorts of exclamations as everyone opened up their envelopes. John looked around a couple of people were playing tennis. One or two were just batting balls off the walls. John said, "Now, we walk." They walked around the club house past the practice range and on down the gravel three-mile-long path that circled the park.

As they walked, John passed around the pictures of the twins. He said, "It seems our little Ricky and Dicky here seem to be running a slick operation making millions off of poor and dead people.

"How's that?" Jay asked.

"Near as I can make out, weapons and drugs." John said.

"Why have they not been caught?" Jay asked.

"Money talks, and bullshit walks." John said.

"Ok." Randy said. "What is the game and how does it work?"

"These two are running a never-ending circle that we have to break. The thing is it is a multi-state thing and each one of these fellows are either in one place or the other." John explained.

"How so?" Jay asked.

"It seems that one makes a run from the city out to New Mexico with an assortment of weapons and returns with a load of assorted drugs." John continued.

"How do they get away with it?" Lloyd asked.

"They won't." John said.

"What do you have in mind?" Randy asked.

They got about half way around the park and found a picnic table to sit at. John said, "This is like a snake with a head at each end. Tomorrow someone is going out to New Mexico and someone is going to work this end."

Randy said, "We will go." Looking at Rochelle.

John said, "So will Mary and I. That leaves you four on this end. It seems when one leaves the city the other leaves New Mexico. They don't meet in the middle. Maybe for a minute at a fuel stop, but I don't think they would be so foolish to both get caught in the same place."

"Yeah." Jay said. "The way I figure, they pretty well sound alike. So, to everyone they are dealing with on each end, they think they are dealing with just one person who never leaves town. I can see how that works for them. They are each other's alibi."

"How's that?" Lloyd asked.

"Well." John said. "Suppose someone in the city accused Ricky or Dicky of something while one was in town and one was in New Mexico with a boat load of witnesses saying we were all with this fellow at the time you made accusations or whatever."

"A near perfect alibi." Randy said.

"That's what I am thinking." John said. "This isn't going to be our regular wham bam thank you ma'am and go home. The four of us are going to follow the red dot out there and you four are going to wait for the red dot that's coming this way and intercept it. No strikes before they make delivery. Let's see what is up that food chain. After delivery, then it's abortion time at your discretion." At this John rose and everyone followed and they continued on around the park working their way back to the tennis courts where they started from.

Jay said, "Wow, that was a quick three-mile hike." The girls stopped by the big swing sets across from the tennis courts and chatted excitedly about the recent turn of events.

John gave Jay and Lloyd one of the photos. "Which one is this?" Lloyd asked.

"Who knows." Jay said. "We will just call him Ricky Dicky."

"Works for me." Lloyd said. John and Randy just chuckled on the side.

"Okay Mary, it's time to roll before we get stuck in traffic." John said.

"I'm there." She said walking across the street to their vehicle. John and Mary as well as Randy and Rochelle took off. Jay and Kathy, along with Lacy and Lloyd stayed back to brew a plan for their end of the game. John swung by Boston's electronics to visit with him and to seek his technical expertise in the upcoming work that was before them. Their mission was still to find and abort their designated targets but with the recent turn of events and the fact that they were no longer just taking walks in the city so to speak. Their game has been stepped up to travel and who knows what kind of global travel lay in their future. After his and Mary's sudden and unexpected trip to Belize and the doors opening up for the rest of the group. John planned on getting his hands on every tool he could or would need in future missions. He also wanted to ensure the safety of his team from let's say unwanted ears. So John asked Boston to go to each member's home at their nearest convenience and perform the same cleaning process he had done on John and Mary's house. John gave Boston contact information for the three other teams and he also told Boston how Moe was having the time of his life out at the ranch playing with all the big boy toys. Boston grinned and asked if Moe would be back to help him with his house cleaning. John told him, "Probably so." John also asked Boston if he had any tracking type of devises and listening devices, he could put in his travel bags.

Boston said, "Walk this way." They went into Boston's office. By the time John and Mary left Boston's, they had trackers, little ears, a modified high-end purse with video and audio recorder and a briefcase to match. John and Mary were happy with the new toys. He asked Boston, "Do you think you can scrounge up three more packages like this?"

Boston said, "Give me a few days. What I can't get, I will build."

John said, "Thanks. It's good doing business with you. Mary and I have to run."

John and Mary stopped in next door to check in on J-Lee noting how that damaged store front was as good as new. Upon greeting J-Lee, John asked him if there was any information on why a suicide bomber would attempt to burn his store down. J-Lee didn't have a clue. "Maybe he didn't like the way a book ended." He said with a chuckle.

"No, seriously. You have no idea?" John asked.

"None." J-Lee said. "I'm still waiting to hear back from the investigators."

John said, "You ought to call Moe and razz him about playing too much."

"What?" J-Lee asked. That's when John told him about the ranch work. J-Lee said, "You know, I can just picture that little fellow driving a big assed tractor around listening to the stereo and enjoying the air conditioning all the while mowing acres and acres of pasture land.

Mary came over to where they were talking with a paper back in her hand. John asked, "What's that?"

She said, "It is for the road trip."

"Oh." John said. "I didn't even think of that. What is it?"

"One second after." Mary said.

"One second after what?" John asked.

Mary said, "I guess you will just have to read it."

J-Lee laughed. "She got you there."

Mary went and paid for the book and upon her return, it was time to leave. As they turned to walk out, John said, "Don't forget to razz Moe now."

J-Lee said, "I'm heading to my office to do just that."

Back home, John and Mary finished eating supper and John said, "Well, I might as well check the gear and add our new toys to the goody bags."

Mary told him, "I will go pack our travel bags."

John said, "While you are at it, put our papers and passports in that new briefcase."

She did so plus changing contents from her well-worn purse to the new one. Smiling to herself thinking that it's no time to start breaking it in like the present. When Mary came back into the living room, John asked, "What do you think? One car or two?"

"I don't see why we can't take just one." Mary said. "After all, it's going to be around an eight hundred or so mile trip one way. If needed, we could relay drive. No stopping for motels right."

"That's right." John said. "Why don't you give Randy and Rochelle a buzz and have them meet up at the first ping. Then we will shadow this Ricky Dicky which ever one he is. His whole route out to his delivery and pick up point."

"Sounds good." Mary said. "And John, don't let me forget to take a pack of the little Smokey's with us for road snacks.

"That's a great idea." John said. "I think I could get used to this hide and seek game. Get paid to travel and do things like we did down in Belize."

Mary said, "Yea, but the down side is that while we were busy, we did not even see not one pyramid and that place is full of old ruins."

John smiled and said, "I thought you were going to put that on your bucket list."

"I already did." Mary said as she picked up her device to call Randy and Rochelle. After the call, Mary looked into the refrigerator and turned to John and said, "cream puff."

John smiled and said, "cream puff? You are my cream puff."

Mary blushed and said, "Aww, that was sweet of you to say. We have to finish them off. I would hate to throw them away.

Who knows when we will get back."

John said, "Fine." Then he took a cream puff from her. He looked around the room making a mental note that all was ready and turned to Mary. "Time for some shut eye. It's going to be a long day tomorrow and then some." So, they polished off the cream puffs and licked their lips. They got up and hit the light switch and headed for the bedroom.

CHAPTER SEVEN

In the morning John was drinking his first cup of coffee waiting on Randy and Rochelle to show up. He gave a chuckle. Mary said, "What was that about?"

John said, "Remember the other day at camp and Lloyd got up and said how the sun must have come up early?"

Mary laughed and said, "Yes."

John said, "Well, I guess I can feel his meaning."

Mary said slyly, "Oh, you thank something was lost in the translation?"

John said, "I guess you could say that." About that time there was a knock on their door.

John got up and let Randy and Rochelle in and they all gathered at the table. Mary said, "Ok, now eggs. Sunny side up, scrambled, an omelet or what?" Sunny side up was unanimous so Rochelle went into the kitchen with Mary and helped by making a stack of Texas Toast to go with the eggs. Pace picante and a honey bear bottle on the side. Meanwhile, John was showing off the new freezer and his new collection of toys he had gotten from Boston. John asked if Boston had contacted them to which Randy replied, "Not yet."

John told him what the plan was. They agreed it wouldn't hurt to have the houses swept. After all, they still didn't know who planted the bug in John and Mary's cubby hole. John still suspected that maybe the doctor and friends, but hasn't been able to figure the connection between the doctor visit and coincidental job assignments. The pieces just wouldn't fit.

Shortly after breakfast they got their first ping. One of many in the day to come at thirty-minute intervals. John had figured the commission had been satellite tracking and the commission had worked out Ricky Dicky's schedules close enough which was all fine and dandy. A satellite could not do the close-up work of boots on the ground. So now, John and the crew went to the parking facility and transferred Randy and Rochelle's bags into the back and they loaded up and hit the road. Ricky and Dicky had about a fifth-mile head start. "Good enough." John said. If Ricky and Dicky had a tail looking to spot a tail, they were well out of that range and they would keep a distance. No worries as long as the satellites stayed up in the sky.

Once on the freeway heading west, Randy spoke up told them that him and Rochelle had made several trips out to New Mexico over the past few years. "Really?" Mary asked.

Rochelle said, "I have a thing for the hot springs."

Mary's eyes lit up. "Really?" She said again. "Then I hope we stumble across one somewhere along the way".

Rochelle said, "Well, that's very likely. They have them all over southwest New Mexico."

John looked at Randy who in turn smiled, nodded his head and gave a thumb up. John thought to himself that this was another item to add and check off on his bucket list. Randy said to the girls who were chatting, "Might as well get all comfy now. Next stop is Kerrville, hours down the road". And so it was. Randy said, "First exit, take a left under the freeway. Go about a half a mile. Stripes will be on the left." It was a pit stop for the girls. They headed straight for the lady's room. John filled up with fuel and then made his pit stop. The four then walked out with soft drinks and dogs off of the rotisserie and Randy said, "My turn at the wheel." John handed him the keys. So far, every thirty-minutes the ping would let them know Ricky Dicky was anywhere from forty miles to sixty miles ahead of them.

Mary said, "It's been a while since I've sat in a vehicle for so long."

Rochelle said, "yeah, may as well get used to it. Make you a comfy nest. We are just getting started"

"Oh, Oh." Mary exclaimed as she reached into her purse and pulled out a brand-new paper back novel."

"Well, there you go." Rochelle said.

Randy said, "Ok, now the next stop is Ft Stockton." It was the same as the last stop. First exit to the left under the freeway and into full truck stop. Back on the road, John got behind the wheel again. Randy said, "Next stop will be El Paso." As they came to a ridge of Rocky Mountains, they passed an enormous border check point. It was mainly used for east bound traffic. It had lights, electronic x-ray, dogs, the whole nine yards. Once past that, the road turned North following the Rio Grande up to El Paso.

John asked Randy, "How do you suppose Dicky Ricky brings a load of drugs past that check point?"

"Good question. How long do you think the commission has been tracking those yo yo's" Randy asked.

John thought about it a minute. "This is probably the first time to actually track them via satellite. The time is on the tax dollars. They can't spend days and days just following someone around."

"Yeah, I think you're right." Randy said as they were rolling into the southern limits of El Paso.

Rochelle spoke up loud surprising everyone, "Chicos Tacos." John asked, "What's that?"

Randy said, "Don't ask. Pull off at the next exit." They did and found themselves enjoying a bowl of taquito soup covered with shredded cheese.

"Yum," Rochelle said, and they all agreed.

Walking back out to the vehicle, Mary said "Man, I'm glad you came Rochelle. We would have missed that." Laughter rang all around.

"Ok." John said, "Now we are fueled up. I need to find a station to fill the vehicle."

After they got back on the freeway, they got their latest ping. Mary said, "Interesting." "What?" John asked.

Mary told him, "Take the right turn northbound out of Las Cruces."

"What the heck is up that way?" John asked.

Rochelle said, "Hatch. Truth or Consequences and on up to Albuquerque and on to Colorado."

So, when John got to the interchange, he also turned north after a bit. "Ping." Mary said. "Left turn, Clide."

"What?" John said again. "Our Ricky Dicky fellow is heading west out of Hatch."

"Darn!" Rochelle exclaimed.

Mary said, "I agree with what Rochelle said. They have some nice hot spring bath houses in Truth or Consequences."

"I think I know what he is doing." Randy said. "What's that?" John asked.

"Well, if he would have gone straight west to Deming, there is another check point there. They check you coming and going." Randy explained.

"That makes sense. I guess it's time to close the gap between us up a bit." John said as he exited the freeway and drove through Hatch out on the two lanes. He put a little more weight on the gas pedal and cruised along across the arid hilly terrain. Patches of green where irrigated fields were adding a contrast of color to the otherwise rugged looking landscape around them.

After the second Ping Mary said, "Hey, Ricky Dicky stopped moving. I'm going to pull it up on the map. What is a City of Rocks?"

Just as they were coming around a rise in the road, Rochelle pointed and said, "That."

"Holy cow." John said. "Look at the size of those rocks"

"Don't stop." Randy told him. "Cruise on by. See that rise a little further up with the trees?"

"Yea." John replied.

"Pull in there." Randy told him.

Rochelle looked at Randy and was grinning from ear to ear. "What is in there?" John asked.

"Faywood. Hot springs. If Ricky Dicky is going to sleep in the City of Rocks for a bit, no sense we can't soak up some hot water straight out of a Tufa Dome now is there?" Randy said. Smiles all around.

Not knowing Ricky Dicky's plan, the group decided to go ahead and rent a cabin for the night. All the convenience of home. The next ping indicated Ricky Dicky was not in a hurry to move so the gang went to the public side of hot pools. The other side was clothing optional. Mary laid back and said, "I have always wanted to do this, but I was never around this kind of place."

John said, "Well now that's another one to check off your bucket list." He turned to Randy and asked, "Since you are familiar with this area, what do you suppose our little Ricky and Dicky is up to?"

"Well, he could be resting up and refreshing himself before meeting someone." Randy replied.

"That would make sense." John said.

Randy said as he pointed to the west, "About a mile or so from here, you have no choice but to turn right and go north to Silver City. Turn south and you go to Deming. Silver City is a nice college town right on the edge of the mountains. That is where Billy the Kid lived and also where he broke out of jail. Between here and there is a huge copper mine. So big that they have to literally consume a small town and the mountain the town was on."

Mary asked, "They can do that?"

Randy replied, "They can and they did. But still, Silver City would be a good place for a business. Now you go south to Deming and it's a nice sized freeway town with Pecan orchards and other irrigated crops. Now eighty miles south of Deming is Columbus. Which is next to the Mexican border. Columbus has the bragging rights of being invaded and shot up by a gang lead by Poncho Villa. Our Ricky Dicky could be working his way around to any one of these locations."

"I have an idea." John said. "Mary the next ping I want you to pull up the exact location and then zoom in so we can see exactly where and what Ricky Dicky is driving." Which she did. John asked Randy, "Are you up for a late-night hike if Ricky Dicky doesn't move?"

"Sure, what's up?" Randy asked.

"Maybe we should test out this new tracker I got from Boston. That way, where ever he moves around locally in town we will know and can just kind of hang out in the vicinity and try to see how this is going to go down." John explained.

"Heck yeah." Randy said.

"I guess Mary and I get the job of hanging out in these hot pools." Rochelle said.

Mary laughed and said, "That works for me."

So later that night, John and Randy hiked over to City of Rocks about a mile or so away. It was a clear and moonless night with a ka-jillion stars shining above the high desert. The night optics worked like a charm. When they located Ricky Dicky's camp so to speak, John eased silently over and magnetically put the little tracker under the inside of the back bumper and they slipped back into the darkness. About half-way back to Hot Springs, John finally spoke. "Can you freaking believe it? This son of a gun is hauling weapons and drugs back and forth in a big black shiny hurst."

Randy said, "What?"

John said, "A big black hurst with a casket in it."

Randy said, "How is he doing it? Like hauling a load in the casket or is there some kind of storage area under the casket?"

"I don't know, but I'd like to find out." John said.

"Wait until we tell the girls." Randy said.

John said, "I bet they will find this as freakish as I do."

After telling the girls back at the cabin, Mary as quick as usual said, "Do you think they are using some mortuary as a front?"

"That's very possible." John said. He added, "You girls need to get on the link and find all the area funeral homes."

Randy said, "I will relay the same message to Kathy and Lacy. At least that narrows down the vicinity for them to look for when Dicky Ricky rolls into the city. That is if these twin brothers have twin rides."

"Who the heck would have thought." Rochelle said.

"Better catch some shut-eye." John said. "Don't know what is going to happen in a few hours when the sun comes up."

In the morning, John and Randy were up before the girls drinking their coffee. Randy was looking around the cabin.

"What are you looking for?" John asked.

"Nothing." Randy said. "I was just looking at how they built this cabin. It's a pretty simple design. I might be able to put one of these together back at the rock."

John looked around the room and said, "That would be awesome for you and Rochelle. A regular cozy little home away from home. Dibbs on that old Scooby Doo van." They both busted out laughing and woke the girls.

"What is so funny?" Mary asked rubbing her eyes.

"Nothing, nothing at all." John replied.

The girls made a pot of cinnamon oatmeal for breakfast. John said, "I'm thinking Ricky Dicky won't head into town until normal business hours as not to turn heads. We have time for another quick soak." And so, they did.

They got their ping at first movement of Dicky and Ricky and Randy walked up on top of Tufa Dome and watched the black hurst go by. He waited and watched and then at the T in the road, it turned right. He went back to the cabin and said, "Silver City." So, they loaded up and headed out the gate.

They made a pass-through town to familiarize themselves and suddenly Rochelle said, "Pull over right here."

John did so without question. Mary asked, "What?"

Rochelle pointed at a little cabin across the street. "That was where Billy the Kid used to live."

"Really?" John asked.

"Come on, let's take pictures." Mary said. "Another check to a new item done on my bucket list." They all laughed.

John said, "Ok. Back to work." And they all loaded up. John handed Randy the little GPS type of screen and said, "Let's see where Tricky Ricky Dicky is about now."

"Go about a half mile up and turn right by the big ditch." As they pulled up to and parked by a hippie type of farmers coop. "That big ditch right behind this place was at one-time main street full of horses and buggies back in the old Billy's days. Then the rains came and the well-worn street just eroded away leaving this big ditch across the street from the co-op."

A fellow had a coffee shop there so the group migrated over and ordered a coffee. Randy said, "Check this out." John turned and Randy was pointing to a government building with various agencies as its occupants. Border Patrol, FBI field office, Immigrations.

John said, "Why would Tricky Dicky have any business with any of those services?"

John sent Randy and Rochelle to ease up one side of the street and him and Mary the other. As John and Mary approached the building their target and a fellow in a suit came out. The suit looked in the back of the hurst and gave Dicky and Ricky a package. They shook hands and Ricky and Dicky climbed into the big black beast and drove off. Randy and Rochelle crossed the street. "What the hell just happened?"

John said, "I don't know."

Mary said, "I got it on film." Holding up her purse.

"Great." John said. "I forgot all about that. Let's roll. It's cat and mouse time." They made their way back to their vehicle and started tracking slicky Ricky across town. He soon hit the highway heading south. "Here we go again." John said.

They kept going south past the hot springs exit across ten through Deming and on south. "Hell." Randy said. "Looks like he is running for the border."

"That's okay." John said. "We can go there." Finally pulling into Columbus, their target turned left and on the outskirts of town was a little border patrol outpost building. A single-story box with a garage door on the side. Just up the street was a tire shop. John pulled in and Randy and Rochelle went in to talk to the owner like they were lost while John and Mary watched the hurst. John had his digital recorder on the window ledge and zoomed all the way in as he recorded Tricky Dicky and another suit slide the casket out on to a roller dolly and slid another one back into the hurst. Dicky handed the suit the package and the suit handed Dicky a large envelope and Dicky got back into the black hurst and drove east bound.

"Now where the hell is he going?" Mary said as she pulled up a map. "Oh crap. This is like a back road that skirts the border all the way back to El Paso."

"Imagine that." Randy said.

"Better call the others and let them know it's time." John said. Randy said, "I got it." He called Jay and Kathy and Lloyd and Lacy.

John said, "Hold up. Tell them to be on stand by and if the other little tricky Dicky pulls out of town to follow him."

"Right." Randy said and he finished the call.

John pulled in to the border patrol outpost. Everyone looked at him quizzically. He said, "Get out your credentials and let's see what's up in there."

They did and the group walked up to the door and was met with a suit. "Can I help you?" The suit asked.

John said, "That's why we are here." He then introduced them all and showed their environmentalist badges that said they were with the department of agriculture.

The suit said, "What brings you here?"

"Here." John said pointing at the map on the back wall and said, "We are looking for the Sanchez place."

The suit said, "I've never heard of it."

Randy asked, "Do you mind if we look at your map? This place has a huge pecan orchard but we were told they were using some kind of poison to kill the varmints, but it's also killing the crows that fly in for a snack."

"Really?" The suit said.

"We have to make sure that stuff don't get in the water supply as in the run off after a heavy rain." Mary explained.

"That makes sense." The suit said and he pointed them to go across the little room to inspect the county map.

As John and Randy studied the map the girls asked if there was a restroom handy. The suit told them to hold on a second and he left the office. A minute later he was back holding a roll of toilet tissue and handed it to the girls. He pointed back at the door and said, "Through there and to the left."

When they left the room, John got the suits attention and pointed at the map and asked, "Is this a huge pecan tree operation?" Pointing at the map.

"It sure is." The suit said. "But I don't think it's called Sanchez."

Randy spoke up and said, "Maybe we are mistaken. Maybe it could be a Vasquez or Cortez and not Sanchez. Could be something got lost in the translation."

John laughed out loud at Randy's quick thinking and said, "It wouldn't be the first time." The girls came back into the office much to the suits relief and John said, "Let's go check this place out." Satisfied they thanked the suit for his help and left. Once back in the vehicle John asked the girls, "Well? What did you find?"

"Not much besides that casket covered over with an old tarp." Mary said.

Rochelle asked, "Don't you find it odd to have a suit manning a border patrol out post and no border agents at all?"

"That struck me as odd as well." Mary said. "The only vehicle there looked like a borrowed undercover clunker."

"It probably was." Randy said.

Mary replied, "Have purse, will travel. I have a picture or recording of the whole garage area and the vehicle license plate and all."

"Good." John said. "Could you send that make and model to your friend to run a check on the plates?"

Mary said, "As soon as I transfer information off of the sim card."

John said, "Good." They then headed east on a two lane road in the direction of El Paso a couple of hours down the road.

Randy said, "So, are we going to abort our target in El Paso?"

John said, "I don't think so. I want to see how you have a boat load of drugs around a major check point like that one at that mountain pass on the other side of El Paso"

"I haven't thought about that." Randy said.

Rochelle said, "Good bye hot springs." To which Mary laughed.

Mary said, "I have a few of those slim links left." Before she could aske who all wanted some, all hands were in the air.

Randy said, "You know that fellow back at that outpost sure dressed like one of those Washington D.C. Men in Black types."

"That he did." John said. "I have heard rumors of some DEA or FBI or somebody thinking of selling weapons to the cartels, so they could "wink, wink, wiggle finger, wiggle finger" track the weapons back to drug leaders."

"That's about as stupid as giving a six-year-old the keys to the car so they can drive to kindergarten." Rochelle said. They all agreed.

"Who thinks this kind of stupid stuff up?" Mary asked.

"That would be the genius of some of those left leaning fools in Washington." John said.

Randy said, "I don't think they are left leaning. I think they completely fell over the left cliff into left LaLa land." They all got a laugh from that group.

Mary said, "Well, at last 'ping' Ricky and Dicky were back in Texas rolling into El Paso."

"We need to do a little catching up." John said as he put the pedal down as the long back road had minimal traffic. He then said, "I want to get into that five-mile range so we can track him with our little tracker in real time. I don't want him to stop between pings and we blow right past him somewhere." Shortly they were in the flow of freeway traffic and pulling out of town. John did a pit stop. He said, "Mary, grab us a fountain drink while I fill up." She did so.

Finally on the open freeway heading south, Randy said, "I got him looking at the little hand-held GPS Device."

"Alright." John said. "Time to kick back and just put it in cruise control."

After a bit, Randy said, "It looks like old Tricky stopped up ahead." Everyone sat up and looked at the road. Up ahead was an exit and Randy pointing at the device said, "He is right there." They drove past going over the underpass and John looked down and there was the black hurst sitting in the shadows of the north bound overpass.

"Now what?" Mary asked.

John said, "We find a scenic spot to pull over and then we wait." And so they did. After the long curve in the road to the east, there was a ridge of mountains and sloping off to the west was the Rio Grande Valley. "I wonder what he is waiting for." Mary said.

"Who knows." John replied.

"Well." Rochelle said, "It's been too long now for a pee break."

"Yes, it has." John said.

It was coming up on three o'clock. The hottest part of the day and Randy said, "I've got movement." Looking at the device in his hand. "He's heading this way." So, they all scrambled out of the vehicle. Randy and Rochelle stood back to the fence in a tourist pose as John snapped a couple of photos as a big black hurst blew by them.

"Let's roll." John said.

As they neared the check point, Randy said, "Must have just had a shift change." Pointing to a line of border patrol cars heading north towards El Paso. Tricky Dicky had not changed course. When approaching the guard shack, Tricky Dicky pulled right over to the inside lane. John slid in behind him. At the check, Tricky Dicky said something to the guard who in turn went into the building.

John asked Randy, "Are you getting this?"

Randy said, "Every second."

About that time the commander of the guard walked out and waved the guard with the dog on down the line. Randy filmed Tricky Ricky handing the commander of the guard an envelope who in turn waved the big black hurst merrily on his way. The man with the dog circled their car and asked where they were headed and waved them on. After driving away John said, "Son of a gun. So, Dicky had to wait for shift change for his get out of jail free card to work."

"From the size of that envelope, I don't think it was a get out of jail free card. I think it was a pure and simple pay off." Randy said.

"So, how the heck did the little twit and twerp get so well connected is what I want to know." Mary said.

"Story of my life." John said. "Ask a question and the only answer you get is a whole bunch of more questions. Okay, I have a plan. We stick with him and see where his next stop is." They did so and it turned out Tricky Dicky pulled off the freeway in Vanhorn. Dicky was gassing up when John pulled around to the side and said, "Wait here. Randy let the other end know that it is abort time." He nodded and picked up his device.

John went into the convenience store with his silent stinger. He was hoping Dicky would have a need for the men's room and he did. It was a single occupant only so as Dicky was just stepping in, John hit him with the yellow jacket and pushed him on into the restroom and pushing the button on the inside, John pulled the door closed and checked it. It was locked. John walked outside around the back of the big black hurst sitting at the gas pumps and retrieved his little magnetic tracker before turning and walking around to the side of the building where the others were waiting. He climbed into the vehicle and said, "Next stop, Fort Stockton." He then called the local tip line and said, "Some fellow at the gas station was acting really spaced out and to top it off, he was driving a hurst. You just might have a body snatcher on your hands. There are some really sick people out in the world, now aren't there." He then hung up.

Randy said, "That should rattle the local sheriff's cage when they peek inside that coffin don't you think?" John laughed.

As they were cruising on down the freeway, John finally spoke up, "More puzzle pieces. How was Mr. Dicky and Mr. Ricky so well connected to whatever agency in Silver City? Whoever that suit was in that border patrol outpost and then the connection at the checkpoint. Was this just a tricky Dicky or Ricky operation or is it something more?" They all sat in silence contemplating as the Texas desert blew by them at about ninety miles an hour.

After a bit, they made Ft. Stockton and pulled into the same truck stop on the east end of town. Everyone got out for the usual relief and to stretch their legs. It had already been a long day and they still had about eight hours to go to get back to the city. Randy had been napping since leaving Van Horn so when John asked the group if they wanted to find a room because he was getting tired, Randy said "Onward through the fog. I can drive in to Kerrville the next gas stop." They all agreed. They grabbed some snacks and hot cappuccino and headed east.

Mary said, "You know, I kind of miss just getting up and getting an abort mission out on the city streets and being back home in a few hours." Rochelle nodded in agreement.

Randy said, "Yea, I can adjust to getting out of the noise and pollution and breathing some fresh air now and then."

John said, "Besides this travelling around, you get to check boxes off of your bucket list that you haven't even added to your bucket list yet." They all laughed in agreement. John was making himself comfortable and he asked Mary what the story in the book she picked up at J-Lee's was about.

Mary said, "The story is when I am done, you are going to have to read it."

John said again, "What's it about?"

Mary looked at him and said, "Life without lights."

"Curious." John said as he melted into the seat and closed his eyes.

The car stopping at the light at Kerrville exit brought John's eyes wide open. John said, "What's the matter?"

"Gas stop." Randy said.

"No way, I just closed my eyes a minute ago." John replied.

Mary said, "John you have been snoring for the past three hours."

John looked at her perplexed and said, "I don't snore."

They all laughed at him and Mary said, "You would if you could." As Randy pulled up to the pumps at stripes. John took the wheel for the last leg of the trip. If they kept up the pace, they would blow through San Antonio before the bars closed putting the drunks on the road and then roll into the city before early morning rush hour traffic jam. He thought to himself the timing could not have been better.

Mary got a message for Lacy. Abortion completed. Everyone in the car did a High Five. That's one bad circle that has been totally broken in two. Randy said, "You know, I never looked at it like that but your right. The world we live in is nothing but circles. Good, bad or indifferent."

John said, "Yea, I can see more bad circles in our future. Some will be harder to break than this one was."

Mary said, "You have to wonder when we break a bad link or circle, what floats up from the depths of evil to fill the void."

They rode in silent thought. About that time the song Live and Let Die came on the radio and everyone looked at each other and Rochelle said, "How weird is that?"

They rolled into the city to ghost townish like traffic. They were well ahead of the morning rush and it didn't take long to reach John and Mary's parking facility. There Randy and Rochelle transferred their bags to their vehicle and John invited them down to the cubby hole and they went. Opening the door, John and Mary checked the house and all seemed to be as they left it. Mary put on a pot of coffee and her and Rochelle went into the kitchen. John said, "Now, for the hard work." Mary knew how John thought so as she and Rochelle filed the report to the commission, they kept it to a minimum. Basically, they stated that the double abortion was completed, no frills. That way they would not draw any unnecessary attention if there was a leak in the commission offices.

John pulled the memory card out of the camera and put it into the laptop. He played the exchange with the border patrol commander and Ricky or Dicky which ever he was. He backed it up a little and freeze framed a straight up face shot of the commander. He then screen shot the image and opened a new file for it. He also printed a copy. He moved the mouse around and focused on the envelope exchanging hands and he stopped the picture just before commander grabbed it. He zoomed in and said, "Look on the upper left-hand corner."

"Wow." Randy said. "What do you make of that? Looks like some shady government business going on here."

John said, "That is why none of this is going into the report." The girls had stepped back into the room and John said, "Let's have the memory card out of your purse." Mary retrieved it and handed it to him.

John started playing the recording and when he got a good face shot of mystery agent in Silver City, he did the same print and file. He then went to the suit and did the same again for the border patrol outpost. He also printed a picture of the undercover clunker and tarped over casket beside it. A close up of the clunker with the license plate as well.

"Weird." Randy said. "You would think that high dollar suit that fellow was wearing that he would at least have an agency car, don't you think? It would seem that way. Unless of course you were either trying not to draw unwanted attention from so close to the border or you were just flat out hiding the chance that some good soul might ask what's up with so many different government cars all the while dealing in weapons and drugs."

John said, "Mary, do you think your pal in the agency can get us an identification on these three musketeers?"

"Ha, ha." Randy laughed. "That's a good one. Three musketeers."

Mary said, "I can only ask and hope she can keep it on the down low."

"What about running the plates?" John asked.

Mary said, "Oh, that's the easy part. No questions asked there." So, John sent her a copy of a file now called the three musketeers and she started working on her request to an old school friend. About that time, John's device buzzed and he answered. It was Moe. "Did I wake you?"

"Nope." John said. "I haven't been to bed yet. Long story."

"Well to add to your never-ending story, they took the bait."

Moe told him. John sat forward and put his devise on speaker phone for all to hear. Moe continued, "When I brought the tractor in from shredding, they were already set up in that hunter suite in the barn. They were supposed to go out for a hunt this morning but plans changed last night."

"How so?" John asked.

"Well as near as I could hear, the undertaker fellow got a call. It must have been some kind of bad news because he started yelling at his phone I guess." Moe explained.

"What do you mean?" John asked.

Moe said, "Well, he was not talking to the other two men with him, but he was yelling loud enough to wake the roosters."

"And?" John prompted.

"He was yelling and cussing something about two lost shipments." Moe said adding, "I don't know what was lost. It could have been girls, drugs, or anything. That's all I got."

"That's it?" John asked.

"Well, that mad fellow loaded up right then and there and left in the middle of the night like a mad hornet. Your doctor and friend are leaving shortly. The good news if Pearl is paid up for the week and in all the excitement, no one has asked for a refund." Moe said.

John smiled and said, "Well, there probably is no refunds on hunts. You pay whether you get an animal or not."

Moe said, "I didn't think of that."

John said, "Well, that's done. When do you need a ride back?"

"Oh." Moe said. "I haven't even thought of that."

Randy spoke up, "Hey Moe, Rochelle and I are going out to the Rock in a couple of days. We can bring you back then unless you are in a hurry."

Moe contemplating then said, "No hurry. I am having too much fun out here."

John spoke up and said, "Fine. When you get back Boston needs your assistance for some more house cleanings."

"Sure thing." Moe said. "Gotta go." Then he disconnected.

John sat back thinking. Mary spoke up. "I know that look! I can see those gears turning behind your eyes. What's up?"

John said, "Thank about it. It was late when the other crew took out Ricky or Dicky. Shortly after that the undertaker wigs out and bales out on a multi-thousand-dollar hunt."

"Do you think they could have been connected?" Rochelle asked.

"Damn." Randy said. "Simple is as simple does. In the left hand, you have a fellow known as the undertaker and in the right hand you have Tricky Dicky and Ricky driving a real undertaker's tool of the trade to make a very prosperous living."

"Now." John said, "It we can connect the dots. We have got to figure out how the three musketeers fit in with the undertaker now, if that's the case."

Mary said, "Moe is right you know."

"Right about what?" Randy asked.

"This turning in to a never-ending story." Mary said.

Rochelle said, "This is all starting to give me a headache. What happened to the good old days? When you get a job, go out in the streets and abort a target, then home by supper. Even home by lunch sometimes. Life was simple and now it's getting really complicated. Too many mystery players in the field."

"So, what do we do with all these mystery players?" Randy asked. "We can't just go walking around picking our own abort targets, now can we."

John said, "No, we can't. We can't give out what we know to the commission either. We don't know what the doctor's connection is or who the leak is if it's not the doctor. Somewhere in the crate there is a bad apple or two."

Mary said, "Who knows. We rattle the right cages and shake the right limbs maybe. Just maybe some of our mystery players will come up on our abort list. You never know."

John said, "If we all work this right, we may be able to make just that happen."

Mary said, "Man, I am feeling rather frazzled all of a sudden."

Rochelle said, "Yea, I feel it coming on like jet lag."

"That's my cue." Randy said. "Time to head home." Randy and Rochelle said their good byes and left.

Mary said, "I have got to hit the shower before I fall out."

John said, "I will be along shortly." He went back to his laptop opened up the three musketeers file and watched all three videos over again. In the sweep of the garage at the border patrol outpost he stopped the video in an area over in the corner. It appeared to be like an open-ended closet. Normally he would not have noticed, but it was the gold print that caught his attention. He zoomed in and then set back scratching his head wondering what the hell was a Mexican Federal uniform doing hanging in and American Border Patrol outpost. If that is even what that building was. John thought back on the chain of events. How this whole damn trip of follow the bouncing ball went. How and if the undertaker was actually involved in any of this. At this moment, John knew two things. Only time will tell, and boy was he too suddenly tired.

After John showered, he climbed into bed and just lay there. Mary asked him, "Are you okay?"

Tired, John admitted, "I am more confused now than I was fifteen minutes ago."

"How so?" Mary asked as she placed her hand on his chest.

"It's kind of like a three-dimensional puzzle with moving pieces and it's really hard to find the place to fit the pieces in. Before this job, our abort missions were pretty simple. Go out on the streets, find our target, then figure out the least disruptive means to abort. Then do it without drawing attention to ourselves. Pretty cut and dry. Basically compared to a walk in the park. This Tricky Ricky Dicky job just threw a whole lot of bumps in the road and I am afraid someone is going to have to level those bumps out."

Mary said, "Are you suggesting?"

John put up his hands. "No Mary, I am not suggesting anything. I am just thinking out loud. Who was that person or agent or whatever in Silver City? Who was that suit in that border outpost and why was a Federales uniform hanging in the outpost garage?"

"What?" Mary exclaimed. "I didn't notice any such thing."

John said, "I barely caught it on your video. You were probably more concerned about the tarped over coffin and if Mister Suit was going to step out there to check on you and Rochelle."

"Yes, I will admit I was a little nervous." Mary said.

"You did good Mary." John said. "I only chanced to see some gold writing on the uniform so I had to really zoom in to make it out. Then there was the top dog at the Texas check point on the evening shift accepting envelopes and waving boat loads of drugs right on through without a second glance. All of this is so wrong, but it is happening here and if it's happening here, then you can bet your sweet bottom dollar the very same thing is going on in other places. It is just too well organized."

Mary asked, "You think the undertaker is involved with this also?"

John said, "It is sure starting to look that way. Dots."

"What?" Mary asked.

"Dots." John repeated. "More damn dots to try to figure out how they are connected. They lay there in silent thought and were both soon asleep.

It was after noon before John opened his eyes and rubbed them. He gave a good yawn and a stretch before rolling out of bed and he wandered into the living room in his boxers and sat at the table. Mary asked, "How are you feeling?"

As she got up to get him a cup of coffee, John said, "Much better." He looked at the clock and said, "Darn, the day is over half gone."

Mary said, "John, the day was well started before you went to bed. You haven't missed anything."

He smiled. "I guess you are right."

Mary said, "I got a report on that car out in New Mexico."

John raised an eyebrow as he took a sip of coffee. "It's getting better." He said.

"Yes, it is." Mary continued. "About the car."

"No, the coffee. The coffee is getting better." John said and Mary laughed. "Now, about the car?" John said with a grin.

"The car belonged to a drug cartel member who was killed in a shootout with the Federales five years ago. Somehow this dead guy has managed to keep his registration and insurance up to date."

John looked at Mary blankly. "Who the heck would keep a dead guy's registration for license plates and insurance on an old car like that?"

"Duh, big red truck." Mary said.

John busted out laughing knowing the story leading up to that punch line. John said, "Well now. The plot thickens on that little outpost. That truly is an undercover clunker junker but the question is which cover is it under? Cartels? The Federales? The Department of Homeland Security or Drug Enforcement to many other possibilities to make some kind of conclusion. Another dot with no solid point to pin it to."

Mary asked, "Soup or sandwich?" John just shrugged so Mary said, "Fine." and turned to the kitchen area. John was still sitting there in thought when Mary sat a bowl of Chicken noodle soup and a plate of grilled cheese sandwich in front of him. He looked up at Mary as she said, "You didn't answer me, so you got both. Now deal with it." John smiled and did just that.

Afterward, John asked Mary, "So, what did the others find out on this end when Dicky Ricky made his pass through?"

Mary said, "Pretty cut and dry they said. They slid in traffic along side of the hurst for a positive identification of the driver then changed lanes a few times and got back behind him Jay and Kathy in one car and Lloyd and Lacy in the other tag teaming him. If he made a turn the nearest tail would go straight until the next block while number two would fall in behind at a visual distance. They said a big black beast like that is like following a candle in the darkness. Anyhow, it ended up at a tilt wall warehouse." Mary then looked at John and asked, "What's a tilt wall warehouse? Is that like that burger chain where the building looks like an upside-down V?"

"No." John laughed, "That's an A frame. A tilt wall is basically every mall. Every big box store and every big warehouse complex."

"Oh." Mary said. "Why do they call them tilt walls?"

John explained, "They lay out the walls on the ground and leave out the window and door openings and add designs or borders to fill form with rebar steel and fill with concrete. Once cured, they bring in a really big crane and hook on to the top of the wall and they tilt it up to its upright position. They brace it off with tooth picks until iron workers come in and weld everything together."

Mary said, "What's tooth picks got to do with anything?"

John laughed and said, "It's really like four-inch tubing pipes with adjusters on each end and once the wall is stood by crane, they then angle the pipes and bolt to the wall and floor. These hold the wall up until iron workers come and do their thing. When you are looking at a massive forty-foot-tall wall just standing there and nothing but these pipes holding them it makes the pipes just look like tooth picks."

"Oh." Mary said.

"Anyhow." John said. "What do we know about this warehouse?"

Mary said, "You are not going to believe this, it's a coffin manufacturing business."

"Imagine that." John said. "A warehouse full of coffins. What better place to hide a coffin full of drugs."

Mary said, "It gets better."

"How so?" John asked.

"Well, it seems Lloyd and Lacy rode around the block and guess what they discovered?" Mary asked.

"No idea." John said.

"Well, on the back side of the coffin warehouse, there is none other than a guns and ammo outlet." Mary told him.

"You have got to be kidding me." John said.

"They both share the same loading dock." Mary said.

"How convenient." John said, "More dots."

CHAPTER EIGHT

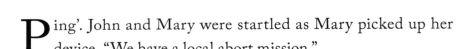

Ping'. John and Mary were startled as Mary picked up her device. "We have a local abort mission."

John said, "Good. I need to get my mind on something else for a bit. This last job is giving me a headache." John rapidly checked out their gear and him and Mary armored up. They unplugged the coffee pot and set the alarm on the way out the door. "More questions." John said. "Who owns the coffin business and who owns the weapons business and if and how are they tied together? When is all this mess going to just stop unfolding or did we accidentally fall head first into Alice's rabbit hole? Ok, what do we got?" John asked concerning the local mission as they headed up the street.

Mary looked at her device and looked up at John and then looked back at her device. "What?" John asked.

"Our target is a Catholic Priest." Mary said.

"What the hell?" John said.

"Yep." Mary said. "That's where he is going."

"What again?" John said.

"It says he has been relocated multiple times and now he is here." Mary said as she pointed to the big church up ahead. "It seems that where ever this fine priest goes he tends to convert choir boys into boy toys."

"That is disgusting." John said. "How many young minds has this monster screwed up?"

Mary said, "Just one is too many."

"I got this." John said as they entered into the massive church. John looked once more at the man looking back at him on Mary's device. They went through the motions and then went to light a candle and went back about midway to sit on a pew.

After a bit, a priest came in from somewhere behind the pulpit. He eventually wandered over to greet them. It was their target. John told him that he had done some bad things and would like to make a confession. The priest said, "That is what I am here for son." So, John got up and Mary stayed seated as John followed the priest over to the confessional booth. The priest went into his side, and John went in the other and sat down. The priest said, "You may begin."

John sat there for a minute in silence slowly pulling out his silenced nine-millimeter. He could see the outline of the priest's head. He finally spoke. "Forgive me father for you have sinned." About that time the priest understood what John had said as he heard a pfft. That was the last thing that sick bastard ever will hear. John stood up, holstered his weapon and walked out of confessional and Mary joined him. As they walked out of the church John said, "Abortion complete."

Mary put her arm in his and they returned the way they came. As they walked Mary said, "Now that's what I am talking about."

"What?" John asked.

"Wham bam thank you ma'am and the job is done." Mary said. John laughed. They soon arrived back at their cubby hole. Mary sat down to make out their report that the abortion was a success and send it to the commission. Then she said, "Hey John."

"Yes?" He asked.

"Randy and Rochelle are headed out to the Rock."

"Good. When are they planning on returning?" John asked. "Probably tomorrow after they retrieve Moe from his new found playground."

John laughed at that and said, "Good. That means Boston will be able to make sure none of the gang have bug infested homes. Did you hear back on your friend's facial recognition thing yet?"

Mary replied, "No. Not yet. Hopefully sometime today if she isn't tied up with a big load of her regular work."

John just said, "I just want to get this three musketeers file in some sort of order and maybe we can get it to Mr. Don T. without the rest of the commission's prying eyes."

"I didn't think of that." Mary told him. "Good idea."

John said, "I still think that the undertaker is in this up to his ears. Why else would he flip out when he was at the ranch either just after Dicky number two was aborted or he got word from someone out west about a hurst full of drugs had been impounded and someone tried to contact the registered owner of the hurst who may have then contacted another up the ladder until the undertaker got the news. This is all speculation. You know?"

Mary said, "Yes, I know. It all does really make sense now that you lay it out like that, but where is our proof?"

"That's just it." John said. "Without proof, it won't fly."

Mary said, "Speaking of flying, did you know that mathematically speaking that a bumble bee and a helicopter cannot get off the ground. In theory, it is impossible."

"But they do." John said.

"That's just it." Mary said. "Think outside the box."

"Okay." John said. "Let's just say someone way up in the government is pulling strings and let's say has ties to our man the undertaker. Who is supplying weapons to some drug cartels for whatever reason an in return the payoff is loads of drugs that the cartels don't have to try to smuggle in to the country. Hell, the doors are open and deliveries are done for them."

Mary said, "Can you imagine the payoff for something like that?"

"Yea, billions in the long run." John said. "We got to get this report together for Mr. T. He can set the big boys on it." Mary agreed.

Mary said, "It makes you wonder."

John asked, "What?"

"Our trip to Belize. Little Ms. Hollywood. Do you think she was running from something here or was she down there to make some kind of a deal?"

John said, "I never considered it. Our focus was on our target and just doing our job that we did."

Mary said, "Kind of like that medusa theory. Cut one snake's head off and two grow back."

John considered this and just shook his head. At least he hoped little Ms. Hollywood was not in any way connected to this other mess he was trying to deal with. Mary said, "I wouldn't mind going back to Belize if we had to, but if we did, I would darn sure make time to visit some old Aztec ruins and Pyramids."

John said, "You just want to check another box."

Mary said, "What box?"

John said, "On your bucket list." They both laughed. "I am curious about something." John continued. "Let's take a ride over to check out the coffin factory."

"Are you serious?" Mary asked.

John told her, "Dead serious. 'snicker, snicker'" Mary laughed.

So, they armored up and headed out the door. Once in the vehicle Mary got the warehouse location from Lacy and they headed across town to check it out. Upon arrival they slow cruised around the complex, a coffin factory on the end and next to it was a furniture warehouse and so on. After rounding over to the next block on the backside was the same large tilt warehouse. Basically, a city block under one roof. John noted the gun and ammo outlet next door to an Indian import warehouse. Making the last turn of the block. He noted the convenient high loading dock for loading and unloading eighteen wheeled freight trucks. He told Mary, "Look at those overhead doors on each side of that dock."

Mary said, "You have a point there. No one would notice at all."

John drove around to the coffin factory and parked and told Mary, "Go see if they have some kind of brochure. You know, showing all their makes and models." He pointed to the sales door. "It's that one."

Mary looked up and said, "I can read John." Giving him that smirky look and he laughed. A couple minutes later she came back with a booklet.

John said, "I didn't know there were so many kinds of coffins."

Mary kiddingly said, "That's not all."

John asked, "What do you mean? That's not all. They make round one's?"

Mary said, "No, John. The thing is they deliver nationwide."

"Holy cow." John said. "Now we have the distribution point." Mary smiled.

On the way back to the cubby hole, John said, "Man, this is huge. We need to send and SOS to Mr. Don T. How can we do that without drawing unwanted attention from any of the others in the commission?"

Mary said, "I can try to reverse call the number I got on my phone when he called."

John said, "Wait a minute. Don't you think a man in his position would have caller I.D blocked?"

"You would think." Mary said.

"When we get back to the cubby hole, you need to try that number just to see what happens" John told her and she agreed. John said, "I think I could pig out on a great big double meat double cheese jalapeno burger from Miller's. How about you?"

"A single meat is fine with me." Mary said.

He dialed in the order and exited the loop and turned north on Shepard. He dipped under the tracks and tuned right into the parking lot. Perfect timing. Just as they approached the cashier the burgers were coming off of the grill. John and Mary sat down to feast. "That hit the spot." John said and Mary agreed wiping a little dripping off of John's chin and he grinned.

"Ok." John said. "When we get back to the cubby hole, I need to update my file on what we found out about a probable drug distribution point and how all of this ties back to the three musketeers by association with Ricky and Dicky, but we still don't know who is behind the curtain pulling the strings."

Mary said, "Well, at some point this gig should start to unravel without Ricky and Dicky unless these people have a backup set of identical twins hanging out in the background somewhere.

John said, "I don't even want to consider that possibility but you never can tell, money talks."

Finally, back at the cubby hole, John started updating his file on the three musketeers' distribution point and a very slight chance that the undertaker was maybe involved. Mary reverse called that number that Mr. Don T. had used, it rang twice before some lady answered and said, "Let freedom ring services, may I help you?" Mary said, "Oh, I am sorry. I must have dialed the wrong number and hung up."

John asked, "Do you ever wonder why we still say we dialed the wrong number when the rotary dial phone went the way of the dinosaurs?"

"What?" Mary said, "Am I supposed to say oops, I punched the wrong number? That sounds a little violent does it not?" John laughed.

A few minutes later, Mary's device buzzed. She answered without looking at it. "Mr. Don T." She jumped up startling John all big eyed. "Yes sir."

"Is John with you?" Don T. asked.

"Yes sir. I am switching to speaker now. What can we do for you sir?"

Mr. T said, "You called me or am I mistaken?"

"Oh, no sir." Mary said. "I thought it was a wrong number."

"Well, you did right. If you need me, call that number as you did and hang up. I will be notified. Now that we have that straight, I want to tell you congratulations on the twin operation. Good work."

John spoke up, "Mr. T, there is a matter that we feel is out of our jurisdiction but needs to be brought to your attention."

"Is that so?" Mr. T said.

"Yes sir." John continued, "I have made a file that would be of interest to you to review it. I may be wrong but this is something big."

Mr. T said, "You make it sound interesting John, I will relay Mary a code and she can transfer the file there. It's very secure and encrypted."

"Good." John said. "Thank you, sir."

"No, I thank you and Mary." Mr. T said before he disconnected.

"Wow." Mary said. "I can't believe that we actually have a hot line to the big cheese himself."

John laughed and said, "Imagine that."

It wasn't long and Mary received an anonymous message with a coded address. She turned to John and said, "you better get the file ready."

"Just finishing up." John said. He typed three musketeers on the correspondence and attached the file, entered the code and pushed send. "Good one, that's a big headache gone. Let them figure it out." He finally relaxed with a job done, or so he thought.

After their shower, John was staring at Mary in her birthday suit. "What?" Mary asked.

"Oh, just admiring all those perfect curves of yours from your calves to your hips and around to your butt to your waist and up to those magnificent breasts and on up." John told her.

"Stop, stop John." Mary said blushing. "I love you too." She said looking down below his waist. "You are perfectly fit."

John smiled and said, "I can't wait to test that theory out."

Mary said, "Then why are you still standing there like a stump?" It was on. It ended up in the first blissful night's sleep either of them had in a little while. Both smiling in their sleep.

The following morning, John was up early. He even had the coffee made before Mary came strolling in. "So, how did you sleep?"

"Like a baby." Mary replied as she poured herself a cup of coffee.

"So did I." John said. "Now that all that stuff is off of my mind."

"Good." Mary said. She then asked, "Eggs, oatmeal, or waffles?"

John said, "Eggs the usual way."

"I know." Mary said, "Sunny side up. Fine." She went to the fridge.

John said, "Do you think later we should start eating some of that Nilgai? We only have a few hundred pounds of it."

"Heck." Mary said, "I forgot about that." She went and got a package of breakfast sausage out and did a quick defrost and fried some to serve on the side with the eggs.

"Give my compliments to the chef." John said as he finished his off. Mary grinned. "How about we cruise over and give J-Lee a visit this morning?"

Mary said, "That sounds good." They cleaned up the breakfast mess and John did a quick once over on their gear and they armored up and headed out the door. Mary habitually taking one last look as John set the alarm and then pulled the door closed behind them. Soon they were moving right along with the flow of mid-morning traffic. It had already thinned from the morning rush.

John said, "Wasn't there an oil changing place down on the end of J-Lee's strip?"

Mary said, "I do believe I remember seeing one or a tire joint, not sure."

John said, "We put a lot of miles under us this past week, It's time to service old Betsy here." Patting on the steering wheel.

Mary looked at him, "Old Betsy?"

"Well, what do you want to call it? George? Or Fred?" John asked.

Mary thought for a moment and said, "Betsy will do."

John said as he was laughing, "I am glad you see it my way."

They pulled up into J-Lee's parking lot and drove all the way to the end and sure enough there was a 'Lubes A lot' and he pulled in. One car ahead of him in line. He told the attendant he wanted full service. The whole nine-yards. He handed him the keys and said, "I will be back for it."

The attendant was quick witted and said, "The customers usually do."

John asked, "What?"

The attendant smiled and said, "Come back for their vehicles."

Mary busted out laughing and John just shook his head and walked out with a smirk on his face. They strolled on down the mall window shopping all the way to the book store. When they met up with J-Lee, he said "I was going to call later."

"Oh yeah?" John said, "What you got?"

J-Lee said, "Let's go into my office." Once everybody got settled in, J-Lee said "Since you guys have had Moe out playing farmer in the dell on green acres, I have been doing a little research. It seems those two characters you told me about, that undertaker and that butcher seem to have some strange connections."

"How so?" John asked.

"Well, as near as I can tell without some serious digging, they seem to both have ties to a California politician." John raised an eyebrow. "It seems the undertaker is tied into a really big drug outfit from down in South America and that other fellow seems to have some sort of ties to China."

"Really now." John says.

J-Lee continued, "I am just scratching the surface you know. I don't want any attention, but this is what it is looking like so far."

Mary said, "I wonder if that Federales uniform fits into any of this?"

J-Lee asked, "What Federales uniform?"

John said, "Long story, but all is not as it appears in the land of enchantment."

"What?" J-Lee said.

"Just as I said, a long story." John told him.

Mary said, "And a long ride to figure it out."

J-Lee was scratching his head. John said, "We had to abort a twiddle dee and a twiddle dum and it was quite the road trip."

"Oh," J-Lee said, "Your two persons of interest seem to have their connections."

John said, "Let us know if anything else floats to the surface. You said a political California connection?" "Yes." J-Lee said.

John stood up and said, "Don't you just love the land of fruits and nuts?"

Mary said, "Maybe it will slide off into the ocean. Then that Arizona desert would be prime beach front property."

J-Lee said, "I'm not going to bet on that investment." They all laughed.

John said, "Well, Moe should be back soon."

J-Lee said, "He already is. Him and Boston went over to do a house cleaning job for some of your friends."

"Good." John said. "I hope they come up all blanks."

Mary said, "Excuse me. I need to go pick up another book." She left the room. Mary was waiting for John by the main desk when he finally came out.

J-Lee said, "We will be in touch."

John said, "We have to go fetch our vehicle." J-Lee gave him a look. "Oil change." John explained pointing in the direction towards the end of the mall.

"Oh." J-Lee said as they waved each other off.

On the walk back, John said "South America and China. Man, the trail is getting bigger and bigger now, isn't it?"

Mary said, "Not our problem, is it? We handed our information off. It's not in our jurisdiction, is it now?"

John said, "You know what, your right. Can't let it bother me." John paid up and collected his keys and started the vehicle and he said, "Listen to Old Betsy purr."

Mary laughed and said, "I guess you're stuck on that." John winked at her and smiled. He put Old Betsy in drive and off they went. It didn't take long and they were back at their cubby hole.

South America and China were rolling around in John's head. He kept asking himself how was the commission doctor tied up in all of this? He just could not figure out an angle. John was absently fighting with that book of caskets and it fell open to a familiar face. This was the owner/CEO of the casket company and John looked down at the name. "Shit." He said so loud that it scared Mary.

"What on earth John?" He pointed at the picture. "Micky. Oh my God. Not identical twins, but identical triplets. Now how rare could that be?"

John said, "Parents had some kind of sense of humor didn't they. Ricky, Dicky, and Micky. Who knows who is who. Okay then. Doesn't this throw a cog in the wheel?"

"How did the commission miss this one?" Mary asked.

John just shrugged his shoulders. "Get Lacy and Lloyd over there to schedule an appointment with Micky to maybe try to solicit some charitable donations."

"I'm on it." Mary said as she was hitting speed dial. She told Lacy what was up and they could not believe it themselves. The warehouse was closest to them, so it was their gig to go fish for the owner and or his where abouts.

After disconnecting, Mary said "How could they miss a little detail about five-foot-nine? It's not like he was a good guy and his brothers just rolling loads of dope and guns in and out of his business and him not knowing."

"I agree." John said. "I get the feeling we are about to fall back down that rabbit hole."

Mary said, "I guess it's a good thing they didn't have sisters named Pixy and Trixie."

That got a laugh out of John and he said, "You sure got that right."

After a bit, Lacy called back. "We went in there with a good plan but hit a brick wall."

"How's that?" Mary asked.

Lacy said, "I guess ole Micky didn't take to well to giving up some of his ill-gotten gains. Every clerk and secretary we tried to speak with pointed to the big sign on the wall. It was a huge circle with a half an X mark over the big letters saying solicitors."

Mary said, "Well, that don't help us now does it?"

Lacy added, "So, we went around to the loading docks and waited. Sure enough a dock worker came out to smoke a cigarette, so you know Lloyd. He grabbed a couple of beers out of his cooler and walked up to the fellow and struck up a conversation. It seemed that the dock worker has a weak spot for ice cold beer on a sunny day like this. Anyhow, all said and done, it seems our Micky abruptly absconded the building. The dock worker didn't know if it was an emergency vacation and or a business trip. His personal secretary doesn't even know where he is off to or when he will be back according to the scuddle butt in the lunch room."

"Thanks." Mary said as she turned to John and said, "Micky is missing in action."

Lacy said, "Boston and Moe were now in the process of cleaning our house. That's the damndest contraption I have ever seen." They both laughed and Mary said, "Trust me. It may look odd for what it does but it works and that's all that matters." They finished their chat and disconnected.

Mary said, "Well, what do you think John?"

John said, "I think that after the demise of his brothers, he bolted like a grey hound out of the chute. No telling where he went. He may not even be in the country for all we know."

Mary agreed. As Mary turned to walk back into the kitchen area 'Ping". She stood by the counter next to the refrigerator just staring at her device.

"Hello, earth to Mary." John said. "What's up?"

Mary looked at John then back at her device and said, "Enemy of the state, drugs and weapons smuggling, bribery of foreign officials, threat to national security."

John said, "Holy Moly." He got up to check out their gear. "What part of the city?"

Mary said, "The Silver part."

John blinked. "And that would be?"

Mary looked back at him and said, "That would be Silver City."

"What?" John exclaimed as he stood up and walked over to her and looked at the photo of a face looking back at him. A photo they took while out there. A photo straight out of his three musketeer's file.

Mary continued, "A traitor to his country and a subordinate to a certain California Democratic Politician.

John sat back down and said, "The rabbit hole just swallowed us."

After a minute Mary said, "Good thing you changed the oil in Betsy, huh?"

At that John smiled and said, "When do we leave?"

Mary said, "That was at our own discretion. Who is going to go with us?"

John said, "I think Randy wants to do some work out at the Rock. Let's see if Jay and Kathy are up for a road trip."

"Sounds good." Mary said as she picked up her device and hit a speed dial button. Kathy answered after the second ring. Mary said, "You guys up for a road trip?"

Kathy said, "Hold on." As she spoke to Jay in the background. When she came back on the line she said, "Yea, sure. We could use a little change of scenery. Where are we off to?"

Mary told her, "New Mexico."

Kathy said, "Didn't you just get back from there?"

"That is correct." Mary said. "Get your gear in order while we work out some sort of schedule."

"Will do." Kathy responded.

Mary then asked, "Has Boston been by your place yet?"

"We were waiting on him to come over from Lacy and Lloyd's." Kathy explained.

"Good." Mary said. "We'll be in touch." Then she disconnected the call.

John was back at his laptop looking at his file of the three musketeers. He was focusing on their new abortion target and trying to remember what was that government building. He drew a blank and said, "Well now, when we get back, we just might have to get to know that fellow that runs the coffee café right up the street. At least that's a start."

Mary asked, "When do we leave so I can let Jay and Kathy know when to meet us."

John replied, "Might as well get this done the sooner the better. Let's try to hit the road at first light. Traffic will be coming in so it should be no problem heading out."

Mary said, "I will let Jay and Kathy know to be here at first light."

"Sounds good." John said as he turned back to review his file again.

Mary put her hand on John's shoulder and said, "Why don't we just kick back and relax and have a quiet dinner and a movie?"

John said, "Sounds good to me. What do you suggest?'

"How about 'All the President's men'?" Mary asked.

John replied, "That sounds good. That sort of fits into the scheme of things." He got up to make the popcorn and said skip the dinner."

After the movie, Mary asked, "Why is it you never hear of a bad or crooked politician go to jail? It's like once they ever get elected, they act as if they are above the law. Bribery, corruption, murder and all sorts of shenanigans and they are lucky to just get a slap on the wrist. It's just not right."

John agreed and the thought of it made him angry. He then told Mary, "Power corrupts and absolute power corrupts absolutely." Mary nodded in agreement. John asked, "How do politicians go to Washington on a two hundred thousand a year payroll and leave four years later with a multi-million-dollar bank account? It sure is not from some book sales now, is it? Just do the math. Look at our next target. Crooked as a dog's hind leg."

"Yes, but now it's our job to eliminate this rotten corrupt link in this chain of evil." Mary said.

John agreed and said, "Time to pack up and hit the sack." And they did.

Jay and Kathy arrived about the same time the coffee finished brewing. They greeted and Jay said, "What have we got?'

John said sarcastically, "A long ride."

Jay said, "I hope you don't mind, but I brought some plastic."

John raised an eyebrow and thought a minute and said, "you never know. It might come in handy."

Mary served up some hot buttered biscuits and a side dish of jam. They all dove in afterwards. Mary and Kathy cleaned while John and Jay carried their bags over to their vehicle and when they came back. The girls were done with the chores and were ready to go. They all strolled back to the parking facility and Jay said, "No bugs."

"So, Boston and Moe did finally make it over?" John asked.

"Yea." Jay said. "That is some kind of contraption Boston has there."

"It works." John said.

Once on the road, John was thinking to himself that the other three houses did come up clean which was a good thing. Then he thought back to when he got shot in the leg and the doctor and the bug and he still could not fit the pieces together. About that time an old tune came on the radio. 'It was early morning yesterday; I was up before the dawn.' "Oh, Oh." Mary said, "That is an old group called Super Tramp. I like their music, even if it is old."

That broke John's line of thinking so he just listened and drove on. He pulled off the freeway at Pyka Road into a little truck stop. He pulled up to the pumps and topped old Betsy off. "Last piss stop." John said. Everyone took the hint. The morning coffee flushing their system. Next stop Kerrville. And so it went. Then on to Fort Stockton. Then on to El Paso with a minor stop at Chico's Tacos of course. Remembering the check point, he right turned at Las Cruces and rolled on past Hatch and pulled off at Truth and Consequences. He said, "Randy told me about some cabins on a bluff overlooking Elephant Butte on Elephant Butte Lake."

Mary was looking at her device and said, "Turn right here" she said pointing. "Now just drive straight through town" As they crossed over the Rio Grande she said, "Next left." John did. The road wound around and up past the Dam which was holding back twenty-two miles of Lake in the middle of the desert. There it was.

A huge formation sticking up out of the water that sure as heck had the shape and look of an elephant, looking west.

"Wow." Jay said. "That's kind of neat." Just then they found the old cabins overlooking the huge Dam site marina full of luxury house boats down to homemade cabins on pontoons.

John looked around and said, "I guess we have to go down to the marina to rent a room." "Well, a bed, a bath, a stove, and a refrigerator. What more could you ask for with a giant elephant out the front door?"

Mary laughed and said, "This is kind of neat and quiet. I'm going next door to get Kathy and see if we can toss up a salad between us."

"Sounds good." John said as he strolled across the street and sat on a boulder that was placed there so no one would drive off the cliff into a seventy-foot drop off. Jay came out and joined him.

After a bit, Jay said, "You got a plan?"

John replied, "Not at the moment." He pointed westward and said, "Over in Silver City there is this little coffee café where we may learn about or the whereabouts of our target."

Jay then asked, "How do you feel about this? You know, um" searching for the right word, "government."

John interjected, "scumbag."

Jay said, "Well, yea. This is sort of something you might expect from a third world country."

John said, "At the rate we are being invaded by immigrants, we are turning into a third world country. When you were young, I bet you and the other kids played games in the streets in the evenings."

Jay said, "Yea, those were the good old days."

John said, "You are right. Were, being the key word. Now you have kids selling drugs to kids. You have those drive by shootings. You have these sicko's taking kids for all kinds of ungodly reasons and some of those we are assigned to abort are a big part of why our world is the way it is today. It's greed. Pure greed. Greed corrupts the best of them. Again, look at how some of those politicians get rich quick. How else can you explain it? It's not book sales. It's insider trading. Pure and simple bribery for no telling what kind of business or trade and we have to deal with it."

Jay thought on this while staring out at some quarter-million-dollar double decker house boats out in the marina and he asked himself, how does one even be able to afford one of those just to have sitting around for a random weekend visit or a private love nest and he just shook his head. John was right.

Mary called out, "Come and get it." They did. It was a huge tossed salad with diced sandwich ham and turkey breast blended in. It was good.

The next morning produced some hot coffee, scrambled eggs, pace picante sauce and flour tortillas. Afterward, John said, "I'll take the keys down to the marina."

Jay said, "I'll walk with you."

The girls got stuck out with cleaning up which wasn't much. Clean the skillet and throw the paper plates in the trash. Done deal. Then they freshened themselves and packed the bags so all was ready when the guys got back. John and Jay came walking back up the hill from the marina. John told Mary, "We just might have to come back for a longer visit."

Mary said, "Really?"

John said, "Yes, the marina operator said he would give us a good deal on the use of a pontoon boat or up towards the other end of the lake they rent out jet skis and there is a place about midway that even rents out paddle boards."

"Yea," Mary said, "Sounds like fun."

John said, "Let's see how this play's out."

Jay said, "I'm good for a couple of days' delay before heading back."

Kathy said, "I'll second that."

So, John and Jay started loading up Betsy. They took one last walk through to ensure nothing was left behind and then loaded up and backtracked their way out of there. Once back across town, John made a left at the freeway underpass, turned south and headed back toward Hatch.

Exiting the freeway at Hatch for the backroad, Mary had to explain all those red and green clusters hanging out in front of various shop stands were all chili peppers. Hatch is supposed to be the chili pepper capitol of the world. "Wow. I'm impressed." Kathy said. "Another place I can say I've been there and done that." Everyone laughed.

Soon they were out in the foothills and desert. "Look." John said as a couple of road runners ran across the road in front of them.

Mary said jokingly, "They are real." Everyone busted out laughing.

Mary finished up her first book from the first trip and asked Kathy, "You want?" holding it up.

Kathy said, "What is it?"

Mary said, "One second after." "One second after what?" Jay asked.

Mary laughed and said, "May be one second after the lights went out in Georgia. You want to know you have to read it."

"Fine." Kathy said taking the book from her.

During this conversation no one noticed that they blew right on by the City of Rocks and Faywood hot springs so John didn't even bother with that conversation. He had other things to think about.

Right turn at the T and they were less than twenty-miles from Silver City. John did point out the strip mine on the right as they passed it for a couple of miles. John explained how they had moved a mountain from one end and leveled it out on the other. Jay said, "No wonder copper prices are so high."

John pulled into the Silver City Walmart. John said, "A couple of days." And Mary and Kathy went in for supplies. John got fresh ice for their cooler. The girls came out with a couple of bags. Everyone loaded up and were soon enjoying a fresh brew of coffee at the coffee café. John pointed out the building down the street and said, "That is where Dicky or Ricky met that agent fellow who was now their target.

Mary and Kathy went down to explore the little co-op store and then eased across the street to the little bakery. Nothing like the smell of fresh baked breads. They bought a small twisted loaf of sour dough bread and headed back to the guys. When they reached the street, Mary looked down towards the dead end and froze in her tracks. Kathy about bumped into her and said, "You look like you seen," as she turned her head to look in the direction Mary was looking and barely finish, "ghost." There at the dead end of the street was all five-foot-nine of a Ricky, Dicky, Micky whoever he was crossing over and heading down the alley in the direction of the big ditch.

Mary grabbed Kathy's arm and said, "come." When they made it to the coffee café, John was just finishing the story of how the big ditch came to be. Mary said, "Big ditch." Pointing down the alley across from them.

John said, "I know Mary."

Mary said earnestly, "No, John you don't. Watch the big ditch."

Puzzled by Mary's action, John turned and looked down the alley and suddenly out from behind the Co-op across the alley and disappearing behind the next business was none other than Ricky, Dicky, Micky or whoever he was. "Damn." John said, "What's he doing here? Jay, stay. Mary, come." They trotted up the street in the vicinity of the last place they saw Dicky, Ricky meet with their target. They stopped across from the government building and waited and sure as heck, out came Ricky, Dicky, Micky heading into that same building. A few minutes later, John said, "Hold up Mary." He then walked across the street up the steps to the door before he saw the sign, closed for remodeling. John cut a turn and motioned for Mary to meet him as they headed back to the coffee café.

Jay said, "So, what was that all about?"

John said, "To tell you the truth, I don't know."

John asked the coffee shop man how long that government building has been closed and the coffee shop man said, "It's been about six months now. It sure has put a dent in my business. All those workers are in a temporary building across town."

"So, what's the story?" John asked.

"They have to do an asbestos abatement to that old building. Gut it out, the contaminated old stuff and replace it all." The coffee man said.

"I see." John said.

"It's been six months and I haven't had not one construction crew worker show up for a cup of coffee."

John said, "I would be willing to bet the government accounting office has already written a couple of checks by now."

Jay said, "What do we do now? Micky is not on our list to abort."

"For now, anyway." John said as he turned to Mary. "I think you need to write a special report to add to that file you sent the other day."

"I'm already working on that." Mary said.

John went to the car and retrieved his camcorder and handed it to Jay. "If you see anyone come out of that door, I want them on film."

Jay was rolling the camcorder around in his hand inspecting it and said, "Nice."

John said, "I like the double zoom feature."

"How's that work?" Jay asked.

John explained, "You zoom all the way in, say at the front door. It brings it halfway to you, then when you look at the picture, you can zoom in on it and the door would appear close enough to reach out and grab the handle."

"I like it already." Jay said as he changed seats to face the building.

The coffee man came back out to check for refills and said, "If you folks are interested, I could probably roust up some grilled ham and cheese sandwiches and a garden salad."

"That's sounds good." Mary said looking at her watch. "I didn't realize it was so late."

John said, "Count me in." Jay and Kathy nodded in agreement as well. Mr. Coffee man smiled and turned back inside his little shop and went to work.

After the sandwiches and salad were brought out, John asked the coffee man, "In the past six months have you noticed any thing out of the ordinary over there?"

"Not really. Hard for me to watch up that way, but on occasion I have noticed a big black hurst sitting out front a few times. I kind of thought that was odd."

"Seems that way." John said.

John looked at Mary, "Let's walk." He said as he dug something out of his bag. "Jay, you and Kathy watch that door." John led Mary up to the old building, then they started around the block before John found what he was looking for. The employee parking area. Empty except for two vehicles. One had a flat and was covered in dust. The other a big shiny four by four. John sarcastically asked, "Which one would you think we should put our little tracker on?"

Mary looked at both vehicles and then slapped him in the arm. "I am not even going to answer that." John stepped over the perimeter cable and stuck the magnet under the back bumper as he had done to the hurst.

"Now let's see where that leads us." John said.

On the walk back as they rounded the corner, just in time to see Micky crossing over towards the big ditch. They got arm and arm and followed him. Kathy and Jay read the plan and headed down toward the dead-end street they found the path and stairs leading up to the next block. They quickly went up the steps and down the street in front of some other small shops. It was not long and Micky popped out onto the street. He walked across and went into a mini warehouse. "B-17" Jay said and they headed back down the stairs to meet John and Mary.

Jay repeated, "B-17."

John asked, "What?"

Jay pointed over his shoulder. "That is where he went. Mini-warehouse numbered B-17 on the door."

"Nice work." John said. They all exchanged high fives.

As they headed back up the street, Jay said "You reckon the coffee man is excited?"

"About what?" John asked.

Jay said, "In all the rush, I don't think we settled up with him."

"Oh, heck." John said.

When they made it back, Mr. Coffee man was just pouring them another round grinning. He said, "I knew you would be back because you left something behind." Pointing at Old Betsy. They all laughed. John paid up and threw in a twenty-dollar tip. "Gee thanks Mr. That's the best tip I've had all week."

As they headed to the vehicle, John said "We will be back." Mr. Coffee man smiled big and waved goodbye.

John headed out of town, going back the way they came. Jay said, "I got a good shot of three men standing out front of that old building while you and Mary was around the other side."

"Oh, really?" John said. "Nothing like perfect timing. I will look at them when we get to the cabin."

Jay said, "We're going way the heck back over to the lake?"

Mary replied, "Not hardly. No lake where we are going, but there is water." John smiled and winked at her. She knew his plan.

As they pulled in the gate at Faywood hot springs, Kathy asked, "Is this what I think it is?" Mary reached back and high fived her.

Soon they were settled in and unpacked. Jay was looking around at the cabin and said, "Nice."

John said, "That was Randy's thoughts exactly. I bet that is what he is doing right now. Building him and Rochelle a little cabin in the Rock."

"Cool." Jay said.

"Don't even think about it. I already have dibs on his red Scooby doo van." John said as they all started laughing.

Mary said, "Why not go have a little soak before we start working on some sort of strategy to abort our target."

"Sounds good to me." John said coming out of the rest room in his bathing shorts.

The rest changed and Kathy said, "Lead the way." They did.

While they were soaking, John told Jay how him and Randy had hiked to the City of Rocks to put the tracker on the hurst. Jay asked, "City of Rocks?"

John said, "You have to see to understand. Maybe we will do a drive through on the way back in to Silver City."

"Sounds good." Jay said.

"I think I am going to go back to the cabin and do some homework." John said stepping up out of the pool grabbing his towel before he left.

He enjoyed a few minutes of peace and quiet in solitude. He had time to reflect on the recent changes in his line of work. It just was not so simple of a task anymore. He plugged the camera into his laptop and down loaded the photos Jay took. "Yes indeed." He said to himself. The first of the three musketeers was standing there as well as the left-over Micky from the Ricky Dicky trio. The other was a fiery red-head of obvious good health and matching form standing there in a black silk Pinafore. Flame on, John thought to himself. Who the hell are you and what is your business with these two vermin? John stood up and got dressed. He walked back to the group hanging out in the hot pool and said, "I have to go back into town to retrieve information from the tracker."

It was set on auto-track so it stores a map of every change of location so I need to dump its information for review. Jay said, "Hold up a second. I'll ride with you." He climbed out of the pool and hurried toward the cabin.

Mary looked at Kathy and said, "Well, looks like we have the tough job of holding down the fort now don't we." They high fived.

Jay was ready when John got back to Betsy and they climbed in and drove out the gate. On the way in John said, "What do you think the lady's business is in all of this?"

Jay said, "The red-head?"

John said, "So, you did notice when you snapped that photo."

Jay grinned and just said, "Curious?"

John handed Jay the little GPS looking device. He told Jay to just turn it on and it would locate the tracker when they were in range. It did just that. Jay said, "I think we already missed our turn off."

"What?" John asked as he slowed and pulled over to the shoulder of the road to bust a U-turn.

Jay said, "That Road back there by the old fort site. It runs up into the forest." John headed back and turned left at the fort. A couple of miles in was the four-by-four sitting in front of a huge log home. Jay said, "Wow. This is nice."

"Okay now." John said, "When I turn around, on the way back you need to hold that little button in on the side and keep holding it from approach until we are past. That should do it." That's what they did.

Back at the cabin, John downloaded the GPS information into his laptop. "Well." John said, "Not much here. Let's take a look. The first mark is the parking lot where we placed the tracker. Let's follow the yellow brick road now to a bank. Okay." John said to no one in particular. "Next stop, a warehouse. Last stop must be home."

Jay said, "I wonder why he would go to a warehouse?"

John said, "Let's google earth this. Better yet, let's use street view of the warehouse coordinated." Suddenly a street view was on the screen with a blinking dot on the side. John put camera in forward motion until the dot appeared on the edge of screen. He then rotated camera to the right and a door came into view. "Will you look at that?"

On the warehouse door was an identifying address and it was B-17. "So, did our target pick up Micky or did he pay off Micky? That's the question." Jay said.

John said, "Either we take him out as he leaves his house or as he shows up for work. Any suggestions? Anyone?"

"This is a little different than targeting someone on a crowded city street." Jay said. "How about plain and simple ambush at that old fort site?"

"Why didn't I think of that?" John asked.

Jay said, "I would use that handy little tracker and when he approached, I would pull out in front of him and distract him while someone steps out from behind a tree and does what needs to be done. Not so neat, but short and sweet."

"Sounds like a plan." John said.

Mary said, "Supper is on." They sat down to eat. A little later after cleaning up, the girls were reading their books and John and Jay sat out on the porch enjoying the cool desert breeze. Way off in the distance, they watched the flashes of lightening that rolled out of an evening thunder head many miles away. Mary was just turning the page to start a new chapter and 'ping, ping, ping'. Like a ricochet rabbit. Mary sat up saying, "What the? I have never heard that before." She yelled for John. "You better get in here!"

"What's up?" John asked.

Mary said, "I just got a three-ping thing."

"Wow." John said. "That is new. Let's have a look."

First on the list is a drug dealing Federale in Columbus, New Mexico. Second on the list is the commander of evening shift at the check point. Third on the list is none other than our boy Micky. "Wow." John said. "This is all new. The outpost in Columbus is not a problem but the top guard of the check point could be another story."

Now John's headspace was just packed full of thoughts that need to be sorted and filed. "Okay." He said out loud. "No more dicking around. Target number one, first thing. Then let's hope Micky is still in town. That means someone has to be at Mr. Coffee's to watch out for Micky while someone has to take out number one. Jay, I need you and Kathy at the coffee shop."

"That is fine." Jay said as he thought about that little bakery nearby. They all said their good nights and hit the sack.

CHAPTER NINE

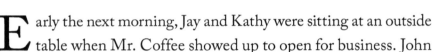

Early the next morning, Jay and Kathy were sitting at an outside table when Mr. Coffee showed up to open for business. John found a little turn off just north of the old fort site and backed in. He sat with Mary until his little tracker activated. Now Mary slid over into the driver's seat. He pointed to a big fir tree beside them and said, "I am right there. When I wave, you shoot out into the street. Basically, blocking it. I will do the rest."

"Got it." Mary said. As the vehicle approached, John waved to Mary who shot out into the street almost going on into the ditch on the other side. She stopped in a dust cloud. In turn, the big four-by-four skidded to a stop. John swung around the fir tree, but didn't pull the trigger. He stepped back behind the tree. Mary saw his response and looked at the driver of the four-by-four. Holding both her hands up and mouthing the words 'I'm sorry' as she put Betsy in reverse and backed out of the way. The four-by-four continued on its way. John came around to the driver's side and Mary said, "Where the hell did that red head come from?"

John said, "I am still trying to figure that one out."

When they made it back to the coffee shop, Jay and Kathy had some fresh donuts waiting. Jay asked, "How did it go?"

John replied, "It didn't"

"What happened?" Jay asked.

"Murphy's law. What can go wrong, will go wrong." John said.
Mary said, "Red head."

Then Jay understood and said, "Isn't that a kick in the pants."

"So what." Kathy said, "Maybe our target never left the building. It is a big old building."

"I never considered that. Well, now. Here we sit." John said.

About that time, Jay said, "Look. There is that four-by-four. It sure looks like it. Must have taken the long road for it to just now be getting here."

"You think?" Mary said. "Maybe she picked up a hitch hiker or something."

John said, "I need to walk around that building." As he got up, he retrieved his GPS device.

Jay said, "Let Kathy and I go for a walk. We have already been here a while."

John handed the device to him. "Hold the button and walk by." Jay said. "I got this." They strolled up the street leaving John and Mary to deal with the left-over donuts. After a bit, Jay and Kathy came strolling back and handed off the device. John retrieved his lap top from the vehicle and downloaded the tracker location map.

John said, "Okay, here we go. First stop at old fort." Mary smiled. "Second stop was at Walmart. Third stop, please mister please, don't play. B-17"

"You're kidding, right?" Jay said pointing just on the other side of that building.

"X marks the spot." John said. "I need to take a look in X."

Kathy elbowed Jay and nodded down the street. Jay said, "Well look yonder. Micky must have another appointment."

"Perfect timing." John said. "You girls stay put. Jay, let's walk."

Standing in front of B-17, Jay pulled out his special tools and in seconds they were inside the door. The roof had sky lights. No need to turn on the overhead. John let out a low whistle. "Looks like I put our tracker on the wrong vehicle." Sitting in the mini warehouse was a shiny Maserati and a new hummer. Overhead door in back. "Well, that explains two things." John said. Pointing at the doors. "That's why no one was seen leaving for one. The other, we tagged the wrong vehicle." Jay nodded in silence. "Let's get back to the coffee shop. I have a couple more of those trackers in my bag of goodies from Boston. If the coast is clear, we tag these and retrieve the one from Red later." In less than ten minutes, they were back, trackers attached and they were out of there. Just as they made it back to the coffee shop, they spotted Micky coming out of the building taking his usual route.

John said to Mary, "Stinger, now." She jumped up and her and John went around the end of the building at the end of the street. When Micky came around from the big ditch with an envelope in hand, he just saw a couple making out against the wall. He never saw Mary reach out and pop him in the leg with the yellow jacket. He looked around before he fell and the last thing he saw was John bending over him and relieving him of the envelope.

Arriving back at the coffee shop, Mary said in a hushed voice, "Abortion complete." Silent high fives.

John said, "Now we wait. Nah, just kidding. Let's go for a ride."

They paid up and did some site seeing. John drove by and showed Jay and Kathy where Billy The Kid lived. Then they made the drive all the way out and checked out the Gila Cliff dwellings and were back in Silver City by mid-afternoon. Back at the coffee shop the coffee man made them the same meal he had made the day before. John told Jay, "When that tracker alerts, we have got to go in a hurry. I want to be in that warehouse when Mr. Bigshot shows up to retrieve his mode of transportation."

Ironically, their target did faithfully keep to a schedule of holding regular business hours. As a so-called public official while abusing his power and privilege to maintain his real task as nothing more than a gun-runner and drug smuggling kingpin of sorts. At just after five-o'clock, the tracker on the big four-by-four alerted Jay. He stood and John looked up at him and he nodded in the direction of the mini warehouse and John jumped up and him and Jay took off at a fast pace to get to the warehouse before.

Red and her big four-by-four could circle around the eight-block stretch to reach the upper road. John and Jay were inside the storage building for a few minutes before they heard the four-by-four go by to the cul-de-sac and turn around before pulling up at the door to B-17. After a minute, the four-by-four drove away and the sound of keys were rattling. The knob turned and in walked the man of no-good means. John and Jay had stationed themselves on each side of the door. Jay grabbed the fellow before he could react. John stuck him with the tranquilizer dart. They walked him over and set him in the driver's seat of the Maserati as the man lost consciousness. John went back and picked up the ring of keys. He then walked over to the hummer and retrieved his tracker from that vehicle. He looked in the driver's window and smiled. The keys were in the ignition. John reached over the column and started the Hummer. He told Jay to start the Maserati as he walked around behind it and collected the other tracking device. He held them up for Jay to see and said, "Seems we didn't need those after all." Jay hit the ignition on the car which put out a low rumble of power. They then exited the building.

On the walk back down the stairs, John said, "That sleeper shot should hold him for about twelve hours. It won't take that long for those two vehicles to run out of gas causing a permanent sleep by carbon monoxide poisoning. Now all we have to do is wait for our Lady in Red to show up in the morning for work as usual to confirm a truly successful abortion and to retrieve that last tracker during all the morning excitement and confusion."

"Sounds like a plan." Jay said as they were approaching the coffee cafe.

The girls greeted them and asked how it went. John said, "Well, let me put it this way. Abortion is in progress."

Jay smiled and said, "I think our man is sure to wake up dead."

John said, "I think we need to go check out the construction project over there." He pointed at the government building. John held up a ring of keys smiling. The group strolled up the street and then up the steps to the front door. John tried a few keys until he hit on the right one. John led the group in cautiously searching. John said, "Yes, this old building does need an upgrade. I don't see any electronic alarm for one. I don't see any sprinkler system for fire suppression. There may be a little asbestos abatement needed. So truly this old building needs to be brought up to code for general occupancy. This must be Red's reception desk." After looking in several doors, they found one with a desk and another with office amenities. They went upstairs and found all rooms empty. Back on the ground floor, they found a basement door inside of a closet.

Going down the stairs, they found a light switch and turned it on. Mary said, "Oh my."

Jay said, "Wow."

On one wall, stacked like bricks were trash compactor bags of marijuana. Thirty-two of them. On another wall was kilo bags of cocaine. Under the stairs was an ammo can with around fifteen-hundred dollars. "Not much." John said, "Enough to make change for cash sales."

They didn't take any but before they left, John found a metal trash can and put some marijuana in the bottom and then added some newspaper in and lit it. No way to set the concrete floor on fire, but a sure way to set off the smoke alarms. The only updated thing in the old building. Back at the coffee café, they watched and sure enough, here came the fire department.

Jay said, "Good thing you left that front door unlocked."

It didn't take long for the Silver City police to arrive after the Fire Department found the source of the fire. Eventually and investigator came to the coffee shop and asked if anybody had seen any suspicious activity. The group agreed that they saw nothing suspicious. The rest of the evening dragged by. They had stopped in for groceries and made it back to the cabin. "Better soak while you can." John said, "We checkout in the morning."

The following morning, John drove in early. No need for the rest of the crew. He stopped by the mini-warehouse as he still had the keys and he opened the door to verify the job was complete. It was. Both vehicles were no longer running. Mister suit had a gray tint. John closed the door and left. He then went and parked on a side street by the building parking lot for Red to show. The front of the building had yellow tape across it. (Do not enter).Then he had thought, maybe he should have waited a day to light that trash can. It turned out to be so. Red never showed up, so he pulled out his tracker GPS and turned it on. Nothing. "Well, crap." He said to himself. Now he had to take a detour up that road past that old fort site. Nothing there as he made a big loop around Silver City. He was unable to pick up a signal. "Well, that's a goner." He said to himself. Time to head south after all, they had aborted the two local targets.

He had arrived back at Faywood, he was just in time for a late breakfast. Afterwards, the group packed up and continued south to Deming. In Deming he refueled and they continued south for almost another eighty-miles. John was still complaining about losing his tracker when they rolled in to Columbus, New Mexico.

He turned left and headed for that little border patrol outpost. John pulled right up to it and said, "Wait here." He went inside and met the on-duty person who was the same person that was there the last time. John pulled out the envelope he had taken from Micky and said "I was told to bring this here."

The agent looked at John and then at the envelope and back up at John. He told John, "I was expecting that yesterday."

John laughed and said, "Micky got delayed." John tossed the envelope on the desk and the agent grabbed it. When he looked back up, he suddenly grew a third eye right above his nose.

John again pocketed the envelope and walked back out to Betsy and said, "Jay, time to play with your toys."

Jay smiled really big and retrieved his special bag of goodies. It seems Jay likes things that go boom. They went through the office to the garage area. Under the tarp was a casket. John opened it and found it was full of white powder and not weapons. "Help me out here Jay." They pushed the cart over dumping the caskets contents across the floor. Now John looked at Jay and said, "Do your thing." That's what Jay did.

He placed a charge under the gas tank of a car and a few more at load bearing beams in the walls and then asked John, "How long do you want to delay?"

John said, "A minute ought to get us down the road a piece."

Jay said, "Yea, that should do."

Jay set the timer as they were headed out for Betsy. After hurriedly getting in the car John faked turning the key and said, "Oh, crap. It won't start." Jay's eyes bugged and John said, "Gotcha." He turned the key and Betsy came alive. John burned rubber getting out of there. About a half mile down the road there was a flash and about two seconds later a kaboom. John looked in his mirror and he was pleased.

A few minutes later, Kathy spoke up and said, "Well, now. We are moving right along aren't we. Three down, one to go."

Mary said, "The last one may be more dicey."

Jay was still looking back at a pillar of smoke rising in the ever-increasing distance. "That was good." Jay said.

"It sure was." John replied. Now he was no longer concerned with having the plastic explosives at the Texas checkpoint. Weapons were not a problem.

As they drew near El Paso, John asked Mary for an update on Mr. Commander of the border patrol check point. Evening or second shift? John already figured that they would have to lay over in El Paso Del Norte because it was too late in the day by the time they rolled into town. About that time, they were crossing the Texas state line. Mr. Commander was crossing the El Paso city limit line to the south east heading for the check station. There was no way they could cross through the city and catch up with him.

They settled on a room at the Inn. As they had time to kill, John said, "Anyone interested in a little sight-seeing?"

"Like what?" Jay asked.

John said, "I want to go indulge in some chrome.

"Do what?" Kathy asked.

John laughed and said, "I want to go over and stroll through the world's largest Harley dealership and it's right up the road.

Mary said, "Sure."

Jay and Kathy followed suit. That's where they went.

They walked through the huge showroom with all models of motorcycle. Factory and custom designs. John was impressed. Mary looked at the amazement in John's eyes. A certain model just kept drawing him back. She said, "I guess this is the one you can scratch off of your bucket list, huh?"

John smiled. Jay and Kathy laughed. John said, "I had a little motorcycle when I was in Junior High. My older brother gave it to me when he joined the marines." John was reminiscing and continued, "Four or five of us boys were tearing up the streets before going to school every morning. I later followed in my brother's footsteps and went into the marines. I did a four-year hitch and made Sargent. I came home with a Harley Sportster in the back of my pick up. Life happens. I later fell in love with that." He pointed to a motorcycle. "On first sight at a dealership, I passed through a few years back in Montana."

Mary pointed and said, "That?"

Amused John said, "Yea, It's a real beauty. It's an FXSTS." He then broke out of his trance and said, "Just may be, one of these days. Now, let's get out of here." They did so after acquiring various shirts and John a leather vest. Next stop is Chico's Tacos.

Back at the room, they were trying to get a strategy together on a way to abort Mr. Checkpoint. Mary asked no one in particular, "What would make a good person turn to accepting bribes?"

John said, "That brings us back to greed. For whatever the excuse is. I am sure some of those agents took those jobs not to serve the country but instead to get placed at certain border crossings or checkpoints where they are guaranteed to receive envelopes and brown paper bags full of money. Tax free of course. All you have to do is just wave them on past. I am sure it happens every day just as we filmed Mr. Commander do to that coffin full of drugs. He got what he wanted but he could care less about all the overdoses. All the deaths and all the associated crimes created to and for a bag of white powder. All the lives affected after he waves his hand is of no concern to him. It's all about me, me, me, in his eyes."

John got a call from Randy who was checking on their progress on the mission at hand. John updated him and told him they should be back in a day or two. Randy said, "Sounds good. I have been kind of busy myself these past few days."

John asked, "On a job?

Randy said, "Not that kind."

John laughed and said, "A cabin?"

Randy said, "Yep. I am working on just that."

John said, "Maybe when I get back, I can help."

"Sure thing." Randy said.

"See ya then." John said and he disconnected.

Mary turned to John and said, "I have been reviewing the satellite tracking history of our target since he was put on the abort list."

John said, "And?"

"Well, it seems out target has been stopping at an afterhours lounge on the way home every night. He's been there long enough to register one or two pings each night." Mary told him.

"Creatures of habit. That will be our target's downfall." John said.

"It appears our targets shift is ending at eleven. It then takes him an hour or so to get back to the outskirts of town. He then pulls into a night club with a two-o'clock license. He then washes down a few of his daily crimes then he goes home." Mary explained.

"Okay." John said, "Nap time. It's going to be a late night. First, we need a means and a method plan."

Mary said, "Maybe Kathy and I can get close enough to spike his drink and if that doesn't work, one of us can abort him out in the parking lot." After discussion all around, Mary's plan was agreed on. Now it was nap time.

The alarm went off at eleven. That gave the crew enough time to get ready and go to this club well before the time of arrival of their target. They paid their cover charge and found them a booth along the wall with a full view of the front entry. The juke box was blaring some honky-tonk heartbreaking song. Most of those in attendance were already near or over the legal limit state of mind. John and Jay found an empty pool table and began to play. Jay ordered up two beers and set them at the table. The girls ordered Virgin Mary's. It took a few games of pool before their target showed up. He entered and scanned the room. Then he noticed a fellow in the far corner booth and went directly over and joined him.

Mary put her purse up on the table and acted like she was digging for something as she engaged the hidden camera in the direction of the corner booth. Assured that she got a good face shot, she put her purse back down on the seat beside her next to the wall. Kathy said, "I hope that turns out to be just a fishing buddy or a golf pal. I am ready to go back to the city already."

Mary laughed and said, "You? This is our second trip out here." She watched John sink the six ball and then line up on the two.

Kathy said, "Ok, now do we go with injection or do we go with ingestion?"

Mary said, "You pick one and I will pick the other and we will see how it play's out."

The hard-core late-night bunch were all that was left and they still found no reason to approach the two men in the corner. They were well placed so no passerby could listen to their conversation. No nearby bathroom door, nothing. Jay and John continued knocking balls around and finally John said, "This does not seem to be going as planned. Let's regroup." He motioned for the girls and they headed for the exit.

Once outside, John said, "Plan B. Anybody have one?"

Jay said, "Boom."

John laughed and said, "Nah, we don't want it to look too obvious. No real attention getter, you know. Maybe a physical malfunction or an auto accident or even a drive by."

Jay said, "A drive by probably would not draw any attention. After all, just across the river is Juarez. They have more killings going on over there in a year than they had in the whole of the Iraq take over."

"Ok then." John said, "I guess we tail him and wait for a moment of opportunity."

Just then, Mary took off at a fast walk digging in her bag a car door slam shut and Mary knocked on the driver's side window. The driver rolled down his window and said, "Can I help you?" Mary said, "Yes, you can. You can take a message to the Big S for me."

The driver said, "I don't understand. Who is the Big S?"

"Oh, you will know him when you meet him." Mary said as she stuck the yellow jacket stinger in his neck. His eyes got big at the sudden paralysis and Mary said, "That would be Satan." She turned and walked away.

"What was that?" John asked.

Mary grinned and said, "I asked someone to say hello to Satan for me."

Kathy said, "No way!"

Mary said, "Yellow jacket in the neck."

Jay said, "Ouch. I bet that hurt."

Mary said, "Not for long." After a positive identification, everyone did the high five's and they headed back to their room.

After the late-night activities, it was mid-morning before the group pulled themselves together and loaded up. They fueled up and then headed out of town. An hour or so later they passed through the Texas checkpoint with minimal delay. With the checkpoint in their rear-view mirror, Kathy said, "I wonder how that's going to work out for the bad guys since the commander of wave troughs just won't be on duty this evening?"

Mary said, "I for one hope the replacement will be one of the good guys and in turn, the bad guys get what they deserve."

Van Horn came and went in pretty much silence. Kathy was reading that book Mary had given her and Mary asked her, "Well, what do you think?"

Kathy said, "You know I had never even considered the possibilities of some electromagnetic pulses could actually knock us back to like living in the eighteen hundreds. Yet, it is a possibility and a scary thing to consider. No wonder the leaders of the free world frown on the possibilities of North Korea and Iran and the likes to be able to create nuclear weapons."

This was more food for thought. Ft Stockton fuel stop came and went and after a bit, they were looking at all the giant wind turbines scattered for miles and miles along scattered plateaus of land. John said, "Funny how man can grow things out of seemingly nothing." They soon passed all the wind farms and rolled on into Kerrville for a leg stretch and fuel stop. They should make it back to the city about dark or just after.

Jay and Kathy left straight from the parking facility and John and Mary were soon settled back into their cubby hole. John unpacked their gear and stored it in the usual location. Mary started laundry and then made a snack. As they sat there Mary did the so-called paperwork on the successful aborts of all four targets that were assigned to them. She then entered a code and pressed send. She turned to John and said, "Done, done, and done."

John smiled and said, "And done. You missed one."

Mary said, "Boy, am I glad that trip is over."

"I know what you mean." John said, "It's not the destination, it's the journey to and from that tends to get old."

The next morning over coffee, John got a message from Moe. Pearl had Pat call him back out to the ranch as a new unscheduled hunt had been purchased at a premium for the doctor and his two associates. John turned to Mary asking, "Well now, I wonder what this meeting is about"

Mary said, "At least with Moe there, we may find out."

John said, "Speaking of finding out. I would be curious to know how someone could acquire casket loads of weapons without a suspicion by Alcohol, Tobacco, and Firearms agents or the Department of Homeland Security catching wind of this. With the required background checks, I don't see it possible for and individual to make mass purchases as those time and time again."

Mary said, "Unless you are well connected to the powers that be."

John said, "That's what I am afraid of."

Mary said, "Maybe you should send Lacy and Lloyd out to do some dock fishing."

"Dock fishing?" John asked.

Mary said, "Yes. Send Lloyd back to that service dock between the casket place and the sporting guns and ammo place. He can go with his six pack and fish for information on weapons shipments in and out."

"Well Mary." John said, "That is a great idea." He immediately got on to his device and called Lloyd. After he filled Lloyd in on all the adventures they had been through out in New Mexico and back he then asked Lloyd to go fishing."

"That's all?" Lloyd asked. "Just a fishing expedition?"

"You might also inquire to the chain of command next door at the casket factory. Might be good to know who is stepping up to fill the void so to speak." John told him.

Lloyd said, "I will have Lacy work that side and I will snoop around at the gun warehouse" He then disconnected.

J-Lee called John and asked if he could stop by the store for a chat and John agreed and let him know they would be on their way. After disconnecting, John told Mary to suit up and so they could go see J-Lee. On the way across town, John had many things going through his mind and as usual, not enough answers. They soon arrived at J-Lee's and were ushered into his office. Once the greetings were done, J-Lee said, "So, Moe is back out playing farmer in the dell again?"

John said, "I just heard this morning."

J-Lee said, "Well, in my searching around that California connection of the one called the butcher dealing in young live meat I found he has a preferred shipping company that uses containers and regular freighters and it seems that the containers go to California and the regular freighters run back and forth from L.A. to Houston via the Panama Canal."

John said, "What would a freighter bring from California?" J-Lee told him, "On the surface it looks like pipes." "Pipes?" John asked.

J-Lee said, "Yes. Your regular pipe line pipe and huge pipes for massive water lines."

John said, "Curious."

J-Lee added, "The pipes just move back and forth. They send them from California down here to the Gulf Coast and bring them in to Texas City. They put a thick protective coating on them and load them up and send them back."

"Why?" Mary asked.

"I guess things get done a lot cheaper in Texas, but I also think it's another way to smuggle humans in." J-Lee said.

John thought back on the van load of young girls that the driver had that became an abort target and he wondered if it may be connected. "Okay, where does this freighter dock up?" John asked.

J-Lee said, "That's just it. It doesn't' dock up. It pulls just inside of Galveston Bay and then off loads the pipes on to barges. The barges are then taken up into the shallows to the coating facility over at Baytown."

"That makes sense." John said. "Baytown is an industrial area."

J-Lee said, "But, I don't think those pipes are the only thing coming in on those barges."

"I see." John said, "Now if we can just connect the dots to the butcher."

J-Lee said, "Maybe that is why he is here and not in California."

Mary added, "Who is to say that if girls are being sent like from China, maybe they are picking more up along the way like in the Panama for prompt delivery to the states?"

J-Lee said, "I had not even thought of that."

John rubbing his head said, "Always more questions. I think that the undertaker is tied to that mess we created for someone in New Mexico and his side kick the butcher are evidently working with or for the same people which so far seem to be California politicians. If we can verify any connections, just maybe those faces will appear on our abort list. That would make my day."

J-Lee said, "Maybe if Moe can get off that tractor, he might be able to help." All three of them laughed at that remark.

John said, "Remember a short while back we had to abort what we thought were twins?"

J-Lee replied, "Yea."

John said, "As soon as someone realized something was astray with them the undertaker wigged out at the ranch and bailed out on the hunt/meeting. For the life of me, I cannot figure how in any way possible that our commission doctor is involved with these two."

Mary said, "Well, maybe they were old school chums or something."

J-Lee said, "I will see if I can backtrack his life and see if there is a connection in the past."

"That's a good idea." John said.

John saw that Mary was looking at her watch and told J-Lee that they needed to roll. They said their goodbyes and walked out of the bookstore.

John told Mary, "Let's pop in and see if Boston is in." So, they walked down the way.

Boston was a little surprised to see them. He said, "I thought you guys were out of town."

"We were." Mary said.

John added, "I heard there were no bug infestations with the rest of the crew."

Boston said, "That's right and I think it is odd that you were the only ones to have such an infestation."

"So far, I am the only one who has been shot at also." John said.

"Good for the others, bad for you." Boston said.

John told him, "J-Lee is going to try and find any past connections with the doctor and his friends. Oh yea, I had one of your trackers run away."

"How so?" Boston asked.

"Here tonight, gone tomorrow." John replied.

"Oh, I see." Boston said. "Oh well. If it is found, it can't be traced so no worries."

John said, "It's not the worries that bother me. It's the fact that a new person of interest is missing with it."

Boston said, "You never know. When you least expect it, it might show up."

John said, "I don't think I am going to drive another nine hundred miles one way just to see if it went home."

"I understand." Boston said.

Mary spoke up and said, "I want to commend you also on creating that lady's handbag camera. It has already proven its worth a couple of times."

Boston grinned and said, "Thank you Mary."

John turned to Mary and said, "I guess we are ready then."

They said their farewells and headed for the door. As they were leaving the parking lot Mary got a 'ping'. She looked at her device and said, "Good. It's a local target to abort."

John said, "What's the information?"

Mary said, "Well now." She turned her device for John to see. Looking back at him was a familiar face that had been in the news as of late.

"Oh." John said. "That's the fellow who sweet talked all the company employee's into buying into the company stocks and such. Those poor souls invested their life savings on a shell game with the promise of a bright future of life on a beach somewhere and this fellow took their sand away."

Mary said, "It all came crashing down over night. One afternoon the employees go home in a happy world with a bright future and the next morning they are locked out of the building. Not even allowed to enter to collect their personal affects."

John said, "And this target of ours is responsible for it all. His fiscal duty was to rob from the poor to make himself and others on the top very rich. Greed has won out. Greed, greed, greed. That is what drives most of the evil that we have to contend with. I would say about ninety percent greed and ten percent are just plain and simple sickos."

John and Mary tracked their target to the southwest of the city and on the last locator blip found him sitting in his vehicle in and empty industrial parking lot. As they pulled up to him and got out of the vehicle the distraught looking fellow turned his head and looked up and John and Mary approaching. Before John could react to the sight of a pistol in their targets hand, the fellow quickly raised the muzzle up under his chin and pulled the trigger.

John and Mary just froze dumb founded as to what just unfolded before their eyes. The impact rolled the targets head back and then came to a rest in forward down facing position with bodily fluids oozing out of the newly formed eighth hole in his head. "Wow, I didn't see that coming." Mary said.

"Neither did I." John said as he grabbed Mary by the arm and turned her back to their vehicle. They were out of there, leaving a lone vehicle in an abandoned parking lot.

"Well, I bet that will be on the evening news." Mary said.

John replied, "I am sure it will."

As they were driving back to their cubby hole, John glanced down into the side door pocket. He reached in and pulled out the white envelope that he had taken from Micky in Silver City. He held it up for Mary to see and said, "I forgot about this." He grinned and said, "It looks like we got some homework to do when we get back."

Mary said, "Yea, and I have to make a report about our target's self-abortion."

John said, "Well now, do you reckon that will be a first?"

Mary said with her palms raised, "Who knows. Do you think he had a sudden attack of guilt or did he just take the easy way out instead of facing life in prison where you could also be short lived as of late?" John had no comment.

Back at the cubby hole like clockwork, John checked and inventoried their gear to make sure none was inadvertently left behind somewhere. It still bothered him that Boston's little tracking device had gotten away from him. He had not even considered Red when he set those smoke detectors off. She must have been on a notify call list if there was a problem pertaining to the building. Now John thought of the coffee man. Maybe now, his business would pick up if crews showed up to restore the old building back to use as intended. At least he hoped so anyway. John then opened his photo file looking through, he stopped at a picture of Randy and Rochelle haplessly posing while waiting for the hurst to drive by and ahead of them. He printed a copy and sent a copy to Rochelle. Laughingly, he thought to himself that this just might be the first picture on the wall of that cabin Randy is working on. He then flipped through a few more until he found the one with the fiery red-head with those other two now dead targets. He zoomed in and got a good face shot of Red and printed one of those and sent a digital copy to Mary so she could maybe find out from her connections just who and what this was. He then leaned back in thought.

After a bit, his eyes fell on that envelope he had taken from Micky. About that time Mary said, "Here."

She handed John a photo of a man. A mystery man just like old Red. He was the fellow sitting in the dark corner booth at the afterhours bar where Mr. Commander of the check point got checked. Now in thought again, John asked himself, "Now who are you? How do you fit into this mess?" More questions. If Mary's person could get an identification on them, then J-Lee and Moe could sniff them out. About that time, John's device buzzed and he looked and answered it.

"I was just thinking about you, Moe." John said.

"Good things, I hope." Moe replied.

John said, "Are you having too much fun on that tractor?"

"I never get tire of that. About your trio. They are out here now. I took a load of firewood in for the fireplace and over heard one of them complaining about some distribution line had been broken and cash flow stopped." Moe said.

"Good." John said.

Moe added, "That it was. They stated that it could be a while before being able to re-establish a trade route. I didn't hear much more. I can only piddle with stacking wood for just so long, you know?"

John said, "You did good, Moe. That pretty well verifies that the undertaker is more or less overseeing the trafficking of drugs and weapons and we think his partner Mr. Butcher is using the shipping way to do business. No land road blocks or check points to worry with."

"No kidding?" Moe said. "I heard that other fellow say something about ships last night."

John asked, "What did he say?"

Moe said, "Something is arriving in port today. I just thought they were talking about a cruise ship or something. I didn't pay any mind to it."

John said, "That helps. Keep your ears open. You are doing mighty fine for a farm hand." Moe laughed and they disconnected.

John turned back to his computer and located the local Port Authority website. He then went to a page marked tracking. Opening his page, John found the active list of ships coming and going. It listed those on the docks, those that were departing and those anchored off shore in the gulf waiting their turn in line to get up into the shipping channel. He soon found what he was looking for. It was a midsized freighter unlike those super tankers or those monster container ships. This mid-sized ship could pull out of the shipping lanes and anchor on the industrial side of Galveston Island on the edge of the intercostal waterway. John looked at the ships name 'Kasyade' and thought that to be an odd name. Out of curiosity, he opened another search window and typed in Kasyade. Looking at the results he said, "Well, I'll be." Fitting. Kaysade is one of the watchers of ancient times. A fallen angel who taught every wicked stroke of spirit and devils. John then thought well this is the pipe hauler that is now suspected to be deep in human trafficking.

John turned to Mary and asked if she had any luck on those I.D.'s. "Not yet." Mary told him.

John then asked, "Are you up for a trip down to Galveston?"
"Sure." Mary said. "It has been a while since I have smelled some salty air."

John said, "Let's pack an overnight bag just in case we end up stuck down there."

"I am on it." Mary said as she walked into the bedroom. In less than five-minutes, she was back with a shoulder bag and said "Ready."

They geared up and headed to the parking facility where Betsy was waiting. In a matter of minutes, they were in the flow and heading south. Mary said, "You know what this means?'

"What?" John asked.

Mary smiled and said, "Fresh cream puffs. Coming and going."

John laughed out loud and said, "Fine."

After driving up and letting Mary run in for her fresh cream puffs and a couple of other pastries, she came back out and they were on their way. After a while, topping out over the intercostal water way bridge, John looked to his left and sure enough. There was a freighter sitting just off the shore with a barge tied to its side. The ships crane was swinging over and lowering some pipes down onto the barge. "There she blows." John said. "It looks like it will be a while so let's cruise the seawall."

They turned right at sixty-first once past the lagoon, they turned right again and cruised past the glass pyramids and on until the airport turned left, then again at the seawall. They then slow cruised the sea wall past the condos and townhouses, past the big elegant hotel built on top of old military bunkers, and pulled into the sandwich store across from the statue on the seawall. They grabbed a couple of sandwiches to go with the dessert Mary had previously acquired then cruised on eastward past the poop deck where Lady Liberty was watching over traffic on down past the Ferris wheel. They then looped back around the back side of the island past the shrimp boats and others. They passed the shops and cruise ship terminal and back to the industrial sector of the island. John pulled off by a business that was actually building a huge steel barge. Mary said, "With those welders working in the open end of the barge, it makes you see actually how big those things are."

John, looking out at the 'Kasyade' said, "This is not their first rodeo. They parked and put the barge on the opposite side away from the shore. We cannot see a damn thing going on. Just the crane lowering pipes onto the other side."

Mary pointing toward Texas City said, "What about over there?"

John said, "That is too far. Besides, you would need a telescope. It's even too far from the old remnants of the flat bridge. I don't happen to have a boat handy in my back pocket, and since we are just scoping things out, I am not ready to rent a fishing boat."

John then turned Betsy around and went to the four-way crossover and turned left and cruised all the way down to Sea Wolf Park. Home of the captured World War Two German Submarine. Still no clear view of the goings on at the 'Kasyade' besides the crane swinging pipes to the side and putting them out of sight onto a barge to be taken to get coated. John said, "I am sure another barge is probably on its way over here from Baytown with a load of coated pipes for the return trip."

Mary said, "We still don't know if any human trafficking is involved in this for sure."

John said, "I have a feeling for sure that they are. We came, we saw, but we did not conquer. We need to go over to Baytown and see what we can see as we cross that ship channel bridge."

Mary said, "John, are we going to eat these sandwiches before they go plum soggy?" John pulled off of the shoulder where other fishermen had been parking and they ate their sandwiches. Mary asked, "Do you think they stuff a bunch of people in a stack of pipes?"

John said, "No. I think they put them down inside the barges. The tug boat operators would never see them. The tug will just show up and tie up to the end of the barge and just shove it to wherever it needs to go."

"Oh." Mary said.

"Now if you would Mary, get on the link and search for pipe coating facilities in Baytown area." John said. She did so as John drove back over and stopped by the barge building facility. He just watched the crane in action back and forth.

Mary said, "There are two metal coating facilities in Baytown."

John said, "How about a map view?" So, she pulled it up for him. The first one was nowhere near the water or a set of railroad tracks. John said, "Next."

Mary pulled up the next on and said, "Now look at that. Let me put it on bird's eye view."

Once she did, John looked and said, "Mary, I think you hit the bull's eye. Zoom in on it. I am sure that has to be it. From first look it has a barge slip and those tracks on either side indicate a huge trolley crane that can traverse over the barge and back into that long massive warehouse. Zoom back out some. There you go. Just north of that suspension bridge. That makes it easy to find. Can't see nothing here and it will take a little over an hour to get over there. Time for Betsy to fly." Mary busted out laughing. John took one last look over his right shoulder at the 'Kasyade' as he topped over the tall bridge that connects the island to the mainland. He soon exited on the beltway to the east and followed it around to the north. "Darn." Mary said, "There goes my cream puff stop."

John laughed and said, "The day is not over dear."

"I like that." Mary said.

As they came over the suspension bridge, John tried to look over to the left but the view was obstructed by oncoming traffic lanes. John took the first exit and doubled back to turn under the bridge and soon found himself looking straight at a huge barge loaded to the gills with freshly coated green pipes. A tug was just finishing tightening up the lines to the barge getting ready to pull it out of the slip and head across the bay. "I see how this works." John told Mary. "This barge is going to go to the 'Kasyad' and tie up on the island side of the ship. Then the tug will swing around to the other side then tie on to the fresh load and bring it back here. By the time he gets back here it will be late night and this doesn't look like a twenty-four-hour facility."

"Meaning what?" Mary asked.

John said, "After hours delivery of barge with a load of live bodies in it is perfect. Load them up and ship them out in a van or a truck maybe. Even a bus. Drive off in the night and no one is the wiser."

Mary said, "But John, all of this is still out of our jurisdiction."

John said, "I know, but it's all part of the puzzle and it's tied to the butcher and to California and who knows where. I'm guessing six to eight hours for the road trip and I want to be here when it comes back."

As the tug boat pulled back out of the slip. John made a reverse U-turn and drove away. John told Mary, "Later you are going to drop me off and if I have to walk the streets all night with a bottle of water in a brown paper bag looking like a lost wino, then that's what I will do. I want to watch that barge from delivery until daylight if that is what it takes."

Heading back to the cubby hole so John could dress the part, he then kicked back in his easy chair and said, "I am going to try to get a nap in. It could be a long night. It might not hurt to send a report on our activity to Mr. T, but send regular report on self-abort to the commission."

Mary said, "I was already working on that."

"Fine." John said sarcastically. "Give me four hours and I will be good to go."

Mary said, "Will do just that and besides you owe me." "Say what?" John said.

Mary said, "Taquaria Del Sol." John smiled and closed his eyes.

It was almost ten o'clock when Mary woke John and said, "You want a burger before we go? You better eat something."

John said, "It could turn into a long night."

Forty-five minutes later, Mary dropped John under the bridge with his water bottle wrapped in a brown paper bag. He grabbed his trusty camera and put it in to the hand pocket in front of his sweatshirt. It was kind of warm at the moment he thought. It didn't take long before the gulf breeze was blowing off of the water. John spotted the running lights of the tug boat heading his way pushing the pipe loaded barge right along. John walked a distance away from the slip that the barge was going to get parked in. He would wait until the tug left if it was. Before he eased his way back up that direction. About a half hour later, the barge secured in its slip the tug cut it loose and headed up the channel. Day's work done.

John wandered aimlessly up the street taking little sips of water now and again. Out of an office on the corner of the warehouse, John observed six men walk out. One of them crossed over to a bobtail truck and started it. While the other five men went to the end of the barge and slid a ramp out on it. The truck driver backed the truck right over adjacent to the ramp. He parked and got out and slid the back door open. One of the men gave an order. John could not quite hear. Then one by one, chained together with a lite chain, twenty-four young females of various races were loaded into the back of the bobtail truck. John paged Mary. The door closed and a pad lock was place on it.

John was photographing the driver and the rest of the group as best he could. As he headed up the street a way and waited. All but the driver returned to the corner office. John kept on walking away. The bobtail pulled out of the coating facility and headed John's way. He was already about two blocks up the street by now. As the bobtail was passing by, John quickly put a round in the front tire. John crossed over to the other side of the street and the bobtail traveled almost another block before pulling over. After it stopped and the driver was looking at his flat tire, John crossed back over behind the truck and left a tracker up under its frame. He stepped out on the flat tire side looking at the driver thinking to himself, "Yep, it's a flat alright." The driver looked up at John and his little brown bag and John said slurry, "Ya winna some help?"

The driver said, "Beat it on down the road wino." That's what John did.

About six blocks up, Mary drove up locating John with the special sunglasses they had. John got in and said, "We were right, Mary. I just watched them load up two dozen young women into the back of a truck out of that barge." He was digging in his pack and said, "Let's wait here." He turned on the GPS device and tuned it to the tracker. The truck was still where it stopped. John sarcastically said, "I wonder if they have triple A road service? Not."

It took the driver about twenty minutes to change the tire before John detected movement. He let the truck cruise on by and out of sight before starting Betsy back up. "Now let's see where this bouncing ball leads us." John said as he started following from a distance. They followed the truck west on Ten, then North around the loop as it continued northwest on Two-ninety. John said, "I hope he is not going all the way to Austin. If he does, I will have to fuel up quickly."

"Speaking of fuel, where do ships fuel up? I never heard of a gas station for ships." Mary said.

John replied, "That depends. If they are dockside, some places have hook ups or they call in a tanker truck or two at ten thousand gallons a shot. They can fuel on the run out on the high seas as well."

"Really?" Mary said. "How so?"

John told her, "Easy. A fuel tanker ship pulls up along the side of other ships cruising along side by side. Let's say that the 'Kasyade' uses like a shot gun with a sort of plug with a nylon line attached. It shoots the plug over the refueler. The deck hands catch the line and hook a cable that is then pulled back across to 'Kasyade' then a fuel hose is trolleyed across and attached. Then the tanker kicks in the pumps and delivers about a thousand gallons a minute. At that rate, it doesn't take long. They disconnect and pull the fuel hose back to the refueler. Then they disconnect the trolley line cable and they pull it back and go their separate ways."

Mary said, "That's pretty slick and it keeps the snoopers from hanging around the gas pumps, so to speak."

On the northwest side, the truck exited and made a left under the freeway. It went a few blocks and then crossed the railroad tracks. It made another left into another huge industrial complex with blocks and blocks of Tilt wall warehouses. They caught up with the bobtail just as it was backing into an indoor dock and a big overhead door came down. Out of sight, out of mind. The indoor loading dock was on the corner of the building.

John then drove around to the end of the building and there was a store front. Topsail Industries. Before John could say anything, Mary said, "I am already searching. Topsail Industries. Replacement nylon sail of any shape or any size from your small boats to your masted ships. Also, custom tents, para-sails and canopies and any other type of specialty items you may require."

John said, "Now, that's puzzling. Why would they bring a bunch of young females under the cover of darkness in the back of a truck to a place of business like this?"

He then circled around the block and got back just in time to see the truck pull out of the dock and the dock door closed behind him. The driver stopped and got out of the truck and closed his back door. "Empty now." John said. "More questions."

Just as John was beginning to wonder how far and how he was going to retrieve his tracker, the bobtail pulled into a fast-food joint. "Bingo." John said startling Mary. They pulled in on the drive through lane. "Slide over here." John told Mary. "I will take two of those sausage biscuits and I will meet you at the street."

Mary continued through the drive through and John walked over and around the bobtail. Looking through the window at the driver who was busy placing his order. John reached up under the frame and retrieved his tracker. He then walked out to the sidewalk, crossed over to the drive through side and waited for Mary at the exit. He hopped into the car and reached into the bag and pulled out a breakfast biscuit and said, "All that walking around over in Baytown made me hungry." He then looked at Mary and said in a pompous voice, "Home Mary," and started laughing.

She looked over at him and said, "I will home Mary you mister if you don't watch out." Then they both laughed.

CHAPTER TEN

Back at the cubby hole, John was loading the photos of the driver and his associates at the pipe coating plant. Mary was searching history and ownership of Topsail Industries trying to find some string that connected the pipe coating plant with the sailmaker but that began to look like a dead-end road. John was rubbing his eyes yawning and said, "Time for a break. Day light soon." Mary agreed.

John was awakened by the buzzing of his device. He looked at it and it was Lloyd. John grinning answered by saying, "Wow, the sun must have come up early today."

Lloyd replied, "You know, that sometimes happens to me. It looks like business as usual at the casket factory but talking to the dock workers, it seems that there has been a slump in sales at the weapons store. His boss has not been happy the last few days."

"That's good." John said. "Can you make it a habit to visit a time or two each week and if there is a sudden uptick in sales, we will be the first that they don't want to know, to actually know."

Lloyd said, "No problem. That fellow turns out lives over in our neighborhood."

"Good." John said. "Stay on it and thanks for the update." They disconnected.

John rolled out of bed and headed for the shower. Afterwards he strolled into the kitchen. Mary said, "The coffee is on. My turn." She in turn headed to the shower.

Shortly, they were both sitting at the table sipping their brews and John asked, "Are you up for a visit to the sail makers? Aren't we looking for our own special 'Love Tent'?" Wink. Wink.

Mary busted out laughing and said, "That might work. All we can do is ask. Either they show us around, or they show us the door."

After coffee and a snack, they geared up and went out setting the alarm behind them as usual. They were soon in Betsy cruising across town to the northwest side. Pulling into the parking lot out front of Topsail Industries. Mary looked at John and said, "A love tent."

John said, "Can you think of anything better?"

Mary laughed and just said, "Not off the top of my head, no."

"Then its settled." John said grinning. "We are looking for a love tent."

John and Mary went into the place of business and were greeted by a young blonde clerk. "May I help you?" She asked.

John said, "We saw on the link that you make custom tents."

The blonde said, "And more. Would you like to look around?"

"Sure." Mary said. The blonde explained how they make ships sails, tents, canopies and even parachutes and parasails. As they circled around to the back where there was all the tents and designs. In the back wall was a sound proof window looking out over the massive sewing tables with all sorts of colored nylon sheeting being cut and sewn.

John said, "Wow." The blonde brought their attention back into the showroom and Mary was looking at two-room tents and three-room tents. John stood back as Mary kept on debating and John was glancing back into that huge fabrication room in silent motion.

Finally, Mary said, "I can't make up my mind right now."

John said, "Are you sure?"

Mary took the information on three different styles and said, "I need to think on these." Holding up the pamphlets.

"Fine." John said, acting impatient.

The blonde said, "That is okay. You can come back anytime."

As they made their way back to the front of the showroom, John turned to the blonde and said, "Parachutes. Now why would anyone want to jump out of a perfectly good airplane?" The blonde had no answer. John and Mary turned and walked out the door.

Once back out in the car, John asked Mary, "Do you see anything missing?"

Mary said, "No, why?"

John said, "All the employees in the back of this place. Where do they park?"

It was then that Mary noticed only a few cars parked around in the business parking area. "You are right. Do you think they bus them in?"

John said, "More like lock them in. Some sort of slave shop maybe."

"Who knows." Mary said.

John said, "I want to know. I saw twenty-four persons climb up out of a barge into the back of a truck and brought to this location. Is this some sort of holding pen for the girls to be distributed at a later day?"

"Now, that's a possibility." Mary said. "I am starting to change my views on warehouse businesses. You have the one across town delivering drugs and weapons in coffins and now you have this kite maker here doing who knows what in the human trafficking. Don't you think there would be at least a few men in the group. There were none. So that only leaves one conclusion and it's not a good one."

John looked at Mary and said, "Kite store. That was a good one." The joke helped quell the anger Mary was starting to feel. "Let's roll Betsy." John said as he hit the ignition and said, "Vroom, vroom, vroom."

Mary started laughing and said, "Thanks, I needed that." John smiled and put Betsy in drive and they left that place.

On the way back to the cubby hole John said, "Now what?"

"Now what, what?" Mary asked.

John said, "Well, we know their ways and means. So how do we stop it?"

"We are going to have to find a way." Mary said.

John said, "We can't just sink the ship now can we. They would just find another one to put an evil name on."

Mary agreed and said, "I am not putting sinking ships on my bucket list."

John laughed and said, "Okay. At least we can track the 'Kasyade' and it's not on a weekly cycle like Dicky and Ricky were. The ship with its cargo is just a piggy back ride arranged by a mystery person but I suspect it sure ties to the butcher."

Once back at the cubby hole, Mary put together a report on their extracurricular activities and forwarded it by code to Mr. T. Meanwhile, John was printing the best face shots he could pull out of his night photoshoot in the dim dock yard lights. About that time, Mary's device goes 'ping'. John's eyebrows raised and Mary said, "Looks like we got some work to do."

"No rest for the weary." John said. "What do we have?"

"Oh wow. He's a doctor." Mary said. "It's not our doctor either."

John said, "I don't know if maybe it should have been."

Mary went on and explained, "Looks like it is an abortion doctor. His clutch must be slipping in his old age. He has sent an excessive number of patients to the hospital with internal injuries and has earned the state's highest death rates on patients in the state."

"Okay then." John said. "Let's go look this mad abortionist up and just abort him." On the way over to the abortion doctor's office, John asked Mary, "What do we have on background for this guy. Where does he live, who lives with him, kids, wife, grandkids?"

Mary searched and said, "It appears this old goat was so busy killing babies, he never married nor had any kids of his own. He lives over in the Oaks area."

John said, "How about we just meet him at home alone then."

Mary mapped out the address and John made a detour from the office directions. Mary suddenly spoke up, "Oh look. House of Pies."

John smiled and said, "Tag that on your map for later." Mary grinned and said, "I already did, you are too slow."

John said, "Mm boy. What I could do to a slice of strawberry cheesecake."

Mary laughed and said, "John, would that be your creampuff?"

"Yes." John said.

A few blocks and a few turns later, they were in front of a stone-faced house of midsize for the neighborhood. It had a two-car garage that appeared that only one side ever gets used. No tire wear marks, no oil drop stains or battery stains. "I guess he doesn't have a roommate either." John said.

John eased on by and made his way around the block. It was on his way back around the block that he noticed the for-sale sign on a house which was a few houses down from the abortion doctor's house. "There is our parking spot." John said.

"How convenient." Mary replied.

John said, "I think we have plenty of time to go enjoy a slice of pie before our good doctor gets back into the neighborhood." After enjoying their pie, John and Mary arrived at the house for sale and parked in the driveway like they lived there. They looked around for a few minutes in case the neighbors had prying eyes. Then they wandered up the street. They walked up the doctor's drive way like they knew what they were doing. Mary pulled her lock pick set and went to work as John shielded her from view and looked around for prying eyes. The door popped open and John looked quickly in. He found no visible keypad for and alarm. He quickly went to the back garage entry way and did not find one there either. Relieved, John said, "Well now, shall we make ourselves at home?" He then looked into the garage and found nothing in there.

"John." Mary called out. "John, you had better get in here now."

John fast walked across the living room then down a short hallway towards the bedroom areas. Mary was holding the door open and what John saw almost brought him to his knees. The room had floor to ceiling shelving. Wall to wall with what appeared to be large pickle jars. Hundreds of them. Each one contained a fully formed fetus. John asked, "What kind of really sick person actually collects all his murder victims as trophy's?"

Mary said, "He has collected all he is going to collect and he can't take them with him where he is going."

"How do you suggest we do this Mary?" John asked her.

"A bullet is too fast and too good for this bastard. Just give me a pillow. That will be slow enough, and he can listen to me tell him how much of a piece of crap he is on his way to hell." Mary replied.

"Sounds good to me." John said. "Let's put a few of his prizes up on the bar here. That should jack up his mind a little when he comes in to the house."

After a bit, they heard the vehicle arrive and John peeked out and made sure the doctor was alone. John stood behind the door and Mary just sat in the middle of the floor and waited. The doctor rattled his keys and then unlocked the door. He stepped into the house with another trophy in a jar under his arm and pushed the door closed behind him. The jars of dead babies on the counter first caught his attention. He was all confused now. Then he saw Mary sitting on the floor. He quickly asked, "Who are you and what do you want?"

Mary stood up and asked, "Me? I am Mary and I want an abortion." She could barely hold her anger in check.

He sat the jar down and said, "I don't do abortions here, you have to go to my office."

Mary said, "I think you are a little confused doctor; I am not here for an abortion on me. I am here to abort you."

It took a few seconds for that to register and just as the panic took a grip on him so did John. The panicked doctor spoke up, "What are you doing?"

Mary just started singing an old tune. "Round and round, what goes around, comes around". As she pushed a plastic pillow over his face as John forced him down on the floor. The doctor could not speak, but Mary gave him plenty to think about in hell. It did not take long and the struggle and spasms ceased and Mary was still giving him a piece of her mind when John finally reached down and touched her hand and said, "Mary, it's over."

At that moment Mary just burst into tears sobbing. She then said, "All those beautiful babies lives ended by his hands and then he collected them like some sort of merit badges."

John said as he was finishing wiping down all that they had touched, "You did the world a favor Mary. It's time for us to move on."

Mary leaned heavily against John's shoulder on the short walk back down the street to the for-sale sign and Betsy. Driving out of the neighborhood John said, "Another house soon to be on the market."

"I pity the coroner." Mary said. "How is he going to deal with that insanity? All this hoopla of woman's rights. It is a woman's body is bull crap. The sure-fire God given right to not make a baby is for the woman to be responsible. Either take your pill as a prevention or simply don't spread your legs. Once a woman freely spreads her legs and accepts the donation of sperm, half of what grows inside of her is the mans. She can't get pregnant by herself, can she? Just because she has the burden of carrying the child, does that mean it is her sole choice to do what she may? Choices of five minutes of feel good have lifelong consequences. How simple is that to understand?" John shook his head in agreement. Then Mary added, "Sixty-five million babies assassinated in what started as a racist way of population control. Now it is just an inconvenient ritual for plain and simple irresponsibility. My body, my body, my ass."

John drove silently back to the cubby hole. It was not often that Mary had to vent, but when she did, he gave her all the time she needed to get it out of her system. Finally, she looked over and John and said, "I am done."

He smiled and asked her, "Do you feel better now?"

She said, "Not really. It's been bottled up for a while and mister abortion doctor just popped my cork like a champagne bottle and it just kept flowing and flowing."

John said, "Well now, at least you got it out of your system for now."

They were back at the cubby hole and John was checking over the gear. Mary went straight over and sat down and made her report to the commission. The abortion doctor has been aborted, period. "Wow." John said, "Nothing like short and sweet."

John sat back for a rare occasion of watching the local news. He told Mary, "It looks like someone found that suicide over on the southwest side."

"Oh yeah?" Mary said.

John said, "Yea, and the talking heads are getting their two bits in."

Mary said, "You just wait until they find out about a house full of dead babies. That ought to get their teeth to chattering." John chuckled at that. Mary then sat down by him and said, "Are we ever going to get to the top of the food chain?"

John said, The way I see it, if we keep cutting off the legs eventually the top will be down here at the same level with us."

Mary said, "I never thought of it that way."

John looked at her and said, "Just keep your axe sharpened."

After a few minutes of relaxation, John's device buzzed and he looked at it to see that it was Moe. Answering the buzz he said, "What's up Moe?"

"That undertaker fellow said something about catching a plane and the three of them packed up and left just a bit ago." Moe said.

John asked, "You didn't catch a destination, did you?"

"No." Moe said, "They don't say much if they notice me in the area."

"Well." John said, "If you can manage to break away from green acres, we have a couple of locations you can sniff around in."

Moe said, "I will head back in the morning. I don't want to just disappear on Pearl and Pat. I want to keep the welcome mat out so I can come back and play at another time."

"Sounds good." John said. "We will meet up tomorrow then." They disconnected.

John looked at Mary and said, "Moe is heading into the city in the morning. The meeting is done out there."

Mary said, "And?"

John said, "We don't know any more now than we did. All we know is the undertaker has to catch a flight to somewhere."

Mary said, "Well now, that's kind of open ended, isn't it? He could be going to New Mexico or Los Angeles or Washington D.C. or maybe even South America for all we know."

John added, "I want to know who is keeping them from being our take-out targets. It is still open for too much speculation. Where is the puppet master? Who is pulling the strings? This is above gang activity. Yea, they may participate on the lower end of the supply and demand chain, but who is really driving the train?

It's like the shell shuffle game but the shells keep on shuffling so no way to know what shell to look under. Texas, New Mexico, California and Washington D.C. At the moment and how do we possibly sift through that. Plus, the fact that a player or two may also be in the commission keeping or trying to keep tabs on us."

Mary said, "My brain is getting tired. Let's go to bed."

John said, "I am with you on that thought."

As they rose to go to the bedroom, there was a knock on the door. John asked Mary, "Are you expecting anyone?"

Mary said, "No."

John glanced out the window and was surprised to see a familiar face in the now familiar striped shirt. "What the?" As he opened the door, the messenger handed him the receipt book to sign and John did. Then he received the brown envelope. Mr. Stripes then turned and walked away. John closed and locked the door in reflex as he stared at the envelope in his hand curiously. He walked over to the table where Mary had already occupied her usual place.

"Now what? Another trip to Belize or something?" Mary asked.

John shrugged his shoulders as he picked up a letter opener and cut the end of the envelope open and looked in. He then pulled out the contents. "Pictures."

The first one was a picture of Red with the governor of New Mexico. The next was Red and the governor of California. The next a California state senator. The last one, Red was with the assistant director of the department of Alcohol, Tobacco, and Firearms. "Wow." John said, "Looks like we had a kingfish in our sites and didn't even know it."

Mary said, "So, what is all this?" Waving her hand over the spread of pictures.

John then pulled out the last one and showed it to Mary. There stood a trio at some function and it was none other than the Butcher and Red and the Undertaker.

"Well," Mary said, "That explains a lot. No wonder she absconded at the first sign of trouble. She didn't want to get caught with her hand in the cookie jar."

John said, "She never came up as a target either now, did she?"

Mary said, "Not so far, but I have a suspicion that may change, why else would we be looking at this collection of photos from all over the country."

Again, they went to bed that night with more questions than answers. Both had a restless night of sleep and as usual when John opened his eyes, he could smell the fresh brew in the other room. He got up and trailed the aroma of coffee. Scratching his head, he said, "I didn't sleep well. How about you?" Mary just shook her head from side to side. John's device buzzed and it was Randy. "Hey, how's it going?" John asked.

Randy said, "It is coming along just great. If you were referring to my little cabin project."

"Oh." John said, "That is good."

Randy said, "Four walls and a roof now. Next, I have to build in a kitchen area. You know a sink, stove, refrigerator and a place to hang that picture you sent to Rochelle. She said to tell you thanks. Besides all that, we are in high cotton."

Laughing, John said, "That's great." His mood was improving. "Mary and I need to come and check it out. We already could use some fresh air."

Randy said, "How so?"

John told him of their adventure concerning the 'Kaysade' and confirming the human trafficking. He added how Lloyd is trying to keep tabs on the coffin warehouse and he is thinking of getting Jay and Kathy to watch and snoop the Topsail Industries, that is if they are not on another target project at the moment.

Randy said, "Wow. Sounds like you have been as busy as a three-legged dog."

John said, "You sure got that right."

Randy asked, "Why did you not call us to help out?"

John said, "You have a pretty important project going on yourself. If we need you, we will call. Moe is heading back also. It seems the hunting party has dispersed with nothing really to add to that adventure. Oh yeah, do you remember that little outpost we stopped by where the coffin swap took place?"

Randy said, "Yea, sure."

John grinned and said, "Well, Jay likes things that go boom. He is good at it. First chance we get, Mary and I are going to come out there and lay claim to that old Scooby doo van." Both John and Randy laughed at that one. John then said, "Well, we will be in touch. I don't want to hold up your project any longer."

"Fine." Randy said and they disconnected.

John turned to Mary and said, "Good news."

Mary said, "You mean some of that stuff is still laying around?"

John laughed and said, "The Scooby doo van is ready for new tenants."

That got a laugh out of Mary. Now Mary's device buzzed and it was Lacy. "Yes?" Mary said.

"Hey." Lacy replied. "Lloyd wanted me to relay that something may be going on over at the coffin factory warehouse. He said that his dock working neighbor says that some new bigshot is moving into Micky's old office and she is making quite the stir."

"Well." Mary said, "That usually happens when there is a change of command. The one taking over usually brings trusted number two also, so I would guess that is normal restructuring."

"You think?" Lacy asked.

Mary said, "Why don't you try to get us some photos and we will see if we can check them out."

"Will do." Lacy said and disconnected.

John sat down and was buttering a slice of toast and asked, "Well, what was that?"

Mary said, "New management moving in to the coffin warehouse."

John said, "I was wondering how long that would take after they found Old Micky on that less beaten path. I kind of wish I had a Silver City newspaper to see what all happened after we left."

Mary asked, "Do you think anyone has looked in B-17 yet?"

John said, "I am pretty sure of it. That was Reds drop off and pick up point. You can bet she peeked on her way out of town or she had someone look for her."

Mary said, "Makes you wonder who was the boss and who was the clerk in that building."

John said, "A pretty high dollar car for a clerk but maybe that's why he kept it in B-17 and not out on the lot. It would look kind of strange to see a reception clerk walk out from behind a counter desk and then climb into a car such as his, don't you think?" Mary nodded.

John started buttering his second piece of toast when he noticed that envelope, he took from Micky had slid behind his laptop. He stared at it a minute then considered his toast and coffee a priority at the moment. After finishing up, he refilled his cup and said, "It's getting there." He sat down in front of his laptop.

Mary said, "Do what? What's getting there?"

John looked at her and smiled and said, "The coffee pot. It seems to be getting broken in."

Mary said, "John, you are nuts."

John said, "I know." He reached behind his laptop and produced that white envelope. He flipped it back and forth. Bureau of Alcohol, Tobacco, and Firearms.

John picked up his letter opener and sliced the letter across the end. He tilted the envelope and shook out the contents. The first page turned out to be a universal pass and get out of jail free card signed by the assistant director of the ATF. John then said, "So, someone in the government is actually running guns to the bad guys. I guess for a tradeoff for all the white stuff they can carry back or something like that. This sounds like some failed logic that got that ambassador killed smuggling weapons to a bunch of rebels. The second page held a login code to a bitcoin account and a pass code for access to the digital funds in that account. You just have to enter a bank account number to transfer the funds. Once transferred the digital currency turns into cold hard cash. Digital value fluctuates so you get whatever the going rate is at the time of sell. No telling how much money is socked away in bitcoins. Just might have to look into this account at a later time."

Then John shuffled through the pictures that arrived the night before and pulled out the one with the assistant director of Alcohol, Tobacco, and Firearms with that fiery red head. "Well, our Miss Red is sure well connected. I can't wait for the order to start disconnecting this mess."

Mary said, "Be careful what you wish for, you just might get it."

John said, "What worries me is at some point, we meet up with the men in black types and they take us as the threat."

Mary said, "Let's just hope that event never comes to be."

John was studying the picture of the man and he started up his laptop. He went to his photo files and opened the photo of Mr. Checkpoint commander and his drinking buddy in the back of that club in El Paso. He cropped Mr. Unknown's face and magnified it. Still, it was a dark and fuzzy picture. He asked Mary, "Do you see what I think I see?"

Mary compared the photos and squinting, she said, "It could be the same man."

"Now," John said, "I would be willing to bet, he sent the pass to Silver City and Red and associates added page two with the bitcoin information. The bitcoin currencies were to be delivered back to the director by Mr. Commander of the guard."

Mary says, "Why would you think that?"

John laid down both pages of paper side by side and said, "Look at the difference in the texture of the paper. This one is almost photo quality and the other is the cheap run of the mill office supply type."

Mary said, "You are right John. I would have never noticed that two types of paper as two different points of origin."

John said, "You think Mister Director is upset about losing these codes?" Mary just smiled and John said, "Greed."

John just sat there thinking and then said, "You know, we just might end up back in El Paso or New Mexico again in the coming future."

Mary said, "I just had a light bulb moment."

"What?" John asked.

Mary said, "You tracked Red to her home at Silver City, right?"

"Yes." John answered.

Mary said, "Can you still pull up that track map to her house?"

John said, "Sure."

"Well." Mary continued, "Who owns the house? Was it some sort of rental?"

"That should be easy to find out." John said as he started by getting his GPS tracker and reviewing it until he came to the location where the tracker spent the night. Once the location was retrieved, John entered it on street view to make sure it was the house he remembered and it was. Then he copied the address off of the mail box out front. He then searched and logged on to the Silver City tax assessor and collector site. He typed in the address and found a Rose Smith listed as owner and tax payer. Now he had to google search for a Rose Smith. "Jesus." John said, "So many Smiths." He found about a dozen Rose Smiths but only one had such fiery red hair. "Bingo. Well, at least now we have a name to go by. Who knows if it is a real name or not."

"It's more than we had five minutes ago." Mary said.

Looking back at the pictures, John said, "Okay now, how is Mr. Director and Miss Rose connected?"

"Time will tell." Mary said.

John added, "That's something J-Lee can check out for us."

John called up J-Lee and asked if he could find any connections between a Rose Smith and the Assistant Director of ATF. J-Lee said he could do more snooping around for them and he told John to keep it coming. It keeps him occupied. He also told John that Moe had stopped by and was on his way over to meet John as they spoke. John told him thanks and they disconnected.

"Man." John said, "Is it just me or have we been busy since we woke up?"

Mary said, "Since before we tried to go to sleep."

John laughed and said, "You sure got that right."

Next there was a knock on the door. "That should be Moe." John said walking to the door taking a peek before unlocking it. John greeted Moe and invited him in. As they walked over to the table John said, "Oh my. What a farmer's tan you have going on." They both laughed.

Moe said, "I have been outside a lot. I have a red neck thing going on."

John didn't let up and said, "You mean you left home without your sombrero?"

Moe cracked up and replied, "I never in my life owned one of those big floppy hats. Not my style."

John turned the conversation down to business. He asked Moe, "How do you feel about night duty?"

Moe said, "It makes no difference to me. What do you have?"

John filled him in on Topsail Industries and the truck load of girls that were hauled there. John asked if he could somehow watch the place at night and record the afterhours coming and goings on the place. Moe held up his sunburned arms and laughed and said, "Keep me from getting any more sun, sure."

At that John gave him the location and a quick review of 'Kasyade', the barge transfers and the truck he managed to tag with his tracker. "Dang." Moe said, "When do you get time to rest?"

John said, "Sometimes I wonder that myself. All of this stuff just keeps on unfolding."

Moe said, "Well, I guess I should go back and give Boston a visit. I need to see what kind of night time toys he may have on the shelf."

"Good idea." John said.

Moe said, "Night goggles, infrared cameras, things like that can see through the dark."

John said, "I can only imagine what kind of toys that Boston can dream up." Moe agreed.

Moe had nothing new to add about the meeting out at the ranch. He then cut the meeting short and said he would see what Boston had and then he would try to sleep the evening away to get his body to switch over to a night time schedule. They said their fair wells and John locked the door after Moe stepped out. John sat there thinking of all the recent past events and decided he had to do something about Topsail Industries. He called up J-Lee and asked J-Lee how well he knew that fire marshal that came to investigate the crash but no burn of his store front a while back. J-Lee told him, "We had a few meetings. He seems like an honest person just doing his job."

John said, "Do you think we could get him to do some kind of code check on a place of business that also does business in the human flesh?"

J-Lee said, "Something like that might pique his interest. Let me give him a call and see if he bites. It may not even be in his area."

"I don't know." John said, "You would think that a fire marshal for the city would be city wide."

J-Lee said, "Let me give him a call and have a talk and see what happens."

"Thanks." John said. "Something is better than nothing." They disconnected.

John looked at Mary and said, "Well, we can't just sit back like nothing is going on over there now, can we?"

Mary said, "No we cannot. Why don't you go ahead and see if you can get Jay and Kathy on over there for some day light snooping. Then Moe will have the night watch."

John called Jay and updated him to the activities at the Topsail facility. Jay said, "Sure." They would look it over inside and out and get back with him as soon as they could. John told him that Moe was going to be on night watch for afterhours traffic. Then they disconnected.

John said, "I don't know what else we can do without just going in there and hurting someone."

Mary said, "John, you've got the ball rolling. Now we wait on J-Lee and Jay and Kathy and Moe. Something is bound to come out in the wash."

John said, "Man, I would like to just get a green light on the Undertaker, the Butcher, and even Red or Rose Smith an on up the ladder to vacate that director's chair. You know just rip the spider's web of evil connections to shreds."

John's device buzzed and it was J-Lee. He answered, "What goes?"

J-Lee said, "You aren't going to believe this, but Lacourse is on his way over to Topsail Industries to perform an unscheduled code enforcement check. You know, sprinkler systems, no interior exit doors locked during business hours and up to date permits. All that kind of stuff."

"That's good." John said.

"I told him there may be some kind of child labor going on over there and he said it would not be the first place to do that in the city. So, he agreed to do a walk through." J-Lee said.

"That's great." John said, and they disconnected.

"See there." Mary said after John told her what was in progress.

John was back sitting at the table looking at the pictures and said, "I find it hard to believe that Red was in our sights. Plain and simple."

Mary said, "Well, if you would have had an itchy finger, she would have been out of the picture back when I stopped her in the road."

John said, "Yes, that is true. She was not on out target list, just as that Assistant Director as he sat smugly in that dark corner of that bar. That's two big birds we didn't know we had in our grips and they both are still doing whatever it is that they do. I do know it isn't any good whatever it is."

Jay and Kathy arrived at Topsail Industries about the same time that bright red car arrived. Kathy said, "I got the inside, and you got the outside." They split up. Kathy went in before the fellow in the bright red car. The blonde greeted Kathy and was about to give her a tour when she spotted the fire marshal exiting his car. She told Kathy to wait right there a moment and she bee lined straight to an office and said something which in turn created a stir of activity as several persons skittled off in different directions. The blonde came back to where Kathy was waiting and told Kathy to go ahead and browse around. The blonde then intercepted the fire marshal.

Kathy watched as the blonde stalled the fire marshal for a few minutes by checking his identification card and he finally held up his code book and pointed around and the blonde had no choice but to relent. Finally, she started to escort him around the show room. He then pointed to the offices and door into the fabrication room. He was checking tags on fire extinguisher and overhead sprinkler systems. Finally, after a bit of hesitation they made their way into the warehouse section. Kathy found that window back by the tents and observed the marshal checking the exits. There were only three people working on all those sewing tables. Kathy though that was odd. Kathy headed back to the front of the showroom and waited.

Jay was walking around the building and happened to be walking by when the fire marshal opened a door and closed it. Jay looked up at the height of the tilt walls and he noticed that the rectangle scupper holes to let out the excess water off the roof in case the drain clogged. He said to himself, "That's a lot of wasted space." Those drain holes in the wall were somewhere around ten feet lower than the top of the wall. He continued his walk around the block and back to the store front. Kathy then came out and they left.

Jay and Kathy stopped by John and Mary's and told them about the fire marshal showing up and the way the blonde stalled him. Jay said that he didn't notice anything but the excessive height of the walls according to the placement of the roof drain holes blocked out of the concrete walls. Nothing else to speak of. Mary asked Kathy, "Did you make it back by the tents?"

Kathy nodded. Then John asked, "Did you see that window?"

Kathy said, "Yes, I watched that fire marshal check that the exits were not locked."

Jay added, "I was just going by that door when he opened it."

John said, "So you saw all those people back there sewing up all kinds of stuff?"

Kathy said, "I only observed three people back there working on a big table. That is all."

"What?" John and Mary said at the same time. John added, "There should have been at least almost thirty people back there. That is what Mary and I saw the other day. All those sewing tables were busy."

Kathy said, "I thought that was an awful big operation only to have three workers on the floor."

John's device buzzed and he answered it. J-Lee said, "Well, the fire marshal said that was quite the strange visit. Such a big business with a handful of employees. He only cited them for a couple of expired fire extinguishers and one for blocking access to an exit. He almost let that one slide but he didn't. It was the exit to the roof. Now if you have a fire, who is going to run up on the roof? He also commented that they sure looked understaffed."

John said, "Thanks." and they disconnected.

"What the hell is going on over there?" John said out loud. "I know I followed a truck with twenty-four warm bodies in it and they got dumped at that place."

"Unless they have already been moved." Mary said.

John said, "That could be, but now we wait and see if Moe observes anything out of the ordinary."

Mary asked Jay and Kathy if they were hungry and they said they would take a rain check on that. They needed to roll so not to get stuck in the evening traffic jam. John thanked them and they left.

Mary looked at John who was still showing signs of frustrations and said, "You going to make the popcorn or what?" That snapped him out of his thoughts and he got up and headed for the kitchen area. While the corn was popping Mary said, "What about Men in Black?"

John absently said, "What about the men in black? We don't want to deal with them."

Mary said, "John." He looked at her and she said, "The movie."

"Oh, That Men in Black." John said, "Yea, that sounds good." He finished popping the corn and came in and sat by Mary as she just pushed play.

All through the movie, John was searching his mind for clues. Where could all those people have gone? Did they get split up and moved? That could have been done with just a couple of unmarked delivery vans. He was missing something and he just could not put his finger on it. After the move was done, John went back to the table and laptop. He told Mary, "We have pictures. We have people. We have the place, but our hands are tied and we can do nothing. I was sure hoping that the fire marshal thing would fix something, that even came up a blank."

Mary finally said, "John, let's go to bed. I think I can take your mind off of all of this."

They shut off the lights and went to bed and she distracted him as promised. John woke up well rested and headed to the shower. He then strolled in to the living area and Mary was pouring him a coffee. Mary smiled at him and said, "What happened? Did I wear you out last night?"

John grinned and said, "Whatever you did, that was the best night's sleep I have had in a while.

Mary asked, "Eggs?"

John replied, "Over easy." And so the morning began. John had finished off his eggs and toast. The dishes were finally put away when the knock came on the door.

John got up and checked. It was Moe. John unlocked the door and in came Moe all excited. He said, "I came straight over, except for a breakfast taco stop. But you have got to see this." He held up a sim card.

John said, "What is that?"

Moe said, "Well, when I went by to see Boston for some night eyes, he let me use one of his toys. So, between two and three this morning, nothing was going on. So, I started playing with a drone he sent. I was flying around the parking lot. Then I figured out the infrared camera thing on it and as I was flying it around, I was watching it on my laptop. Like that bird's eye view thing. So, I was flying this thing around an I flew it over the top of the building and man was I surprised. Plug this card in. You have got to see this for yourself."

So, John slipped the card into his reader and downloaded the video. Once John started playing it, Moe said, "Fast forward. This is all my learning junk. Go in to about the twelve-minute mark and go from there."

John did and in a minute, he was looking down on the parking lot and soon went over the wall above the building. John said, "What the heck?"

Moe said, "Every one of those glow in the dark logs, is a person. It's like a tent city on the roof of that warehouse John."

John's brain started clanging. No wonder the fire marshal didn't see them. They took a fine for blocking the access to the roof just so the fire marshal wouldn't go up the stairs.

Mary said, "Didn't Jay say something looked weird about the drains?"

John said, "He did. He said 'an extra ten-foot of wall. What a wasted of space.' A perfect place to hide people. The wall is too high to jump from, too high to see in, even from the building across the street. A perfect prison so to speak." John counted about thirty visible hot spots and said, "That should be about right." John looked up at Moe and said, "Now that we got them, what do we do with them?" John then got up and hugged Moe. "Thanks for saving my sanity."

Moe said, "Well, if I wouldn't have been just goofing around playing with Boston's toys. I would have never figured that I would find a tent city on the roof."

John rubbing his head, "Okay, now we have to figure out how to do this."

Mary said, "Give it to Immigrations."

John said, "No. We have to think this one out. Who can we trust who is least likely to be bribed and not just sweep it under the rug?" John thanked Moe again and said, "Man, you hit the goldmine."

Moe grinned and then asked John, "Does that mean I am done?"

John said, "Can you hang in there for a few more days? I need to see when that pipe hauler is coming back."

Moe said, "Yea, I can hang around and do the night watch."

"Good." John said. Moe got up and John followed him to the door and he left.

"Wow." Mary said, "Hiding all those workers up on the roof. Who would have guessed."

John said, "I knew it, but now to the hard part. Mary you just might sink that ship yet. Not literally."

Mary smiled at that and said, "What's the plan?"

John said, "I can see one starting to fall into place. We need to figure out who in the government can pull this off without Mr. Director or Ms. Senator or any uppity-ups ever seeing this coming. I have got to call J-Lee."

Mary pointed at his coffee cup and he nodded as he dialed up J-Lee. He then looked at his watch and thought to himself that it's a bit early for store hours but he let it go through and ring. On the second ring, suddenly J-Lee said, "Early bird gets the worm in the morning." So, John had to fill him in on Moe's major discovery and how those people hoodwinked that fire marshal. J-Lee said, "You want me to suggest he go back over there?"

John said, "No." He then explained that he wanted to drop the hammer on the whole thing, but did not quite trust the various agencies that would normally do this kind of work. "I want to drop the hammer on those human traffickers so hard and fast that they never see it coming."

J-Lee asked, "Well, what do you want me to do?"

John said, "I am not sure, but we need to find some capable person in some kind of law enforcement with enough scruples to take care of this."

J-Lee said, "I might know someone who can help you."

John said, "Really?"

J-Lee said, "You will have to talk to him to see if he can help you. You want me to see if I can set up a meeting or something."

John said, "If you say he is good, then I'm good. Go ahead and let me know something when you can. Thanks J-Lee."

"No problem." J-Lee replied and they disconnected.

John's brain was in high gear at this point as he sat down with his laptop and searched the port authority for Los Angeles and sure enough the 'Kasiyade' was already scheduled for departure later in the day. "Man, that was fast." John thought, but he had been so busy, he lost track of the time. "Okay then." John said, "However long it takes, the 'Kasyade' to get back to Galveston, we have got to be ready."

Mary was drinking her coffee and watching John and she finally spoke up. "John." He turned and looked at her and she said, "It's filth and it will all come out in the wash."

John smiled and said, "I sure hope so."

Mary said, "How is it that all these running the show seem to be untouchables. The Butcher, the Undertaker, the Director of ATF and not to forget our little Ms. Rose Smith who is chums with all the above and that's not even beginning to climb up the ladder to see who is on top.

John's device buzzed and he answered, "Hello?"

The voice on the other end said, "Is this Mr. John Myers?"

John said, "It is."

The voice said, "I understand you have an interesting story to tell."

John said, "Who is this?"

The voice said, "My name is Bill. J-Lee contacted me."

John said, "Oh, good. Where would you like to meet?"

Bill said, "I have your address and I will be there in two shakes of a stick."

"Well, alright then." John said, and they were disconnected. John turned to Mary, "Two shakes of a stick. We got company."

Mary looked at him and said, "What?" Then there was a knock at the door and Mary's mouth dropped open. "Oh."

John got up and looked out before opening the door. There stood a six-foot-four, creased pants, creased shirt with a Stetson in his hand man. "John Myers?" He asked.

John said, "Yes, and you?"

"Bill Esterling, Texas Rangers."

'Oh wow', John thought.' I didn't see this coming.' John said, "Come in, come in." John led him over to the table. Mary offered coffee to which he accepted.

After he sat, he looked at John and said, "Tell me a story."

John did. The ship, the barge, the roof top tent city, the expected return of the ship. How the whole port to shore delivery took place and how Topsail Industries managed to fool the Fire Marshal. Bill looked at John and said, "I am impressed and most cases fail to impress me." Bill then gave both John and Mary a card and said for John to keep doing what he was doing and if anything new came up to contact him on any changes. In the meantime, he would look into a few things for himself. He then rose to leave and with a handshake headed for the door.

John closed the door and turned to Mary and said, "Holy crap. The Texas Rangers. I would have never thought, but you can bet your butt that nobody in Washington is going to be jerking on his chain." John smiled really big and added, "Now that's what I am talking about." He even gave Mary a high-five and did a little jig. At that, Mary laughed. For once John felt good as it seemed that maybe things might just go their way.

CHAPTER ELEVEN

―――――⊰∘⟨⟩∘⊱―――――

A couple of hours later, Mary's phone buzzed and she just reflex answered it. "Mary." Came the voice and she straightened up. "Yes sir?" Mary said.

"Is John with you?" Came the voice.

"Yes sir. I am switching to speaker. Okay sir, go ahead." Mary said.

"First, that was a job well done out in New Mexico, but it seems some wounds heal faster than others. Our man from Washington is already setting up a meeting with the replacement commander of the guard. We don't want that meeting to be a success. We want that meeting to be an example."

John said, "Sir, other players were not designated targets and we didn't know their parts until after the fact."

Mr. T. said, "We understand and I believe your next target will be meeting in the same place he is comfortable with. You know the place. You did your job there."

"El Paso it is." John said.

Mr. T. replied, "Be on standby to hop a flight out at a moment's notice and take another team with you for back up. On confirmation of target, you go." And with that he disconnected before John could ask about the other evil doers.

Mary said, "Well, at least we don't have to deal with a twelve-hour drive, now do we."

John smiled and then said, "I think I am going to call Lloyd and Lacy. This could be interesting. I don't think Lloyd has ever had his feet off the ground."

Mary laughed as John picked up his device and called Lloyd. Upon answering, Lloyd said, "Hey John, what's up?"

John smiled and said to Lloyd, "You will be." Lloyd laughed and said, "No, really."

John said, "You and Lacy are now on standby. Pack a carry on. We go on short notice."

Lloyd said, "A carry on what?"

John said, "Lacy will know."

Lloyd asked again, "What's up?"

John laughed and said, "After I get you on that airplane you will be up to around thirty-five thousand feet. You aren't scared of heights, are you?"

"Hold on now John. Back up a minute. You said airplane. I ain't never been on no airplane in my life." Lloyd said.

John said, "I know. That's why you're going so you can check it off your bucket list. Now listen Lloyd. What if you got sent to Europe or Japan, are you going to row a little boat over there?"

"I haven't thought of that." Lloyd said.

John said, "Will, if your good to go when we get up a couple of miles, I will buy you a beer."

Lloyd asked, "They have beer up there?"

John laughed and said, "Just for you, but pack a one or two-night bag."

"I guess I can do that." Lloyd said.

"Thanks." John said and disconnected.

Mary said, "That sounded like you were having fun with him."

"I was." John said.

Mary said, "So, we wait until our dear Assistant Director flies back out to El Paso. We abort him before his meeting with new recruit."

"Something like that." John said adding, "You might call Lacy so she is up to date on this short notice. Lloyd may lose something in the translation."

Mary laughed and said, "I could see that happening."

With the gear ready and the bags packed, the rest of the afternoon was spent piddling around the house. John checked on the 'Kasyade' and it had left port heading south. "Come on." He was talking to the screen. "We will be ready for you this time." He looked at the stack of pictures and pulled the one with the Assistant Director and Rose Smith and said, "I guess their back ground doesn't matter anymore. Well, his anyway, and where the hell had Miss Rose Smith absconded to?"

It was about four a.m. when the device 'pinged'. John got up and called Lloyd to meet them at the front of Hobby in forty-five minutes. Time to roll. John and Mary quickly dressed and grabbed their gear and were out the door. At the Broadway exit, Mary said, "Aww. It's too early for cream puffs."

John laughed. A crescent moon was coming up in the East and that old Credence Clearwater song came on the radio. 'I see a bad moon a rising, I see trouble on the way'. John cruised right on into the short-term parking and walked across and then up to the departures. It took Lloyd and Lacy another ten-minutes to show up and find them. They looked on the flight schedule board and got the first flight out to El Paso.

Way down at the end of the terminal, waiting to board the flight, Lloyd was starting to get antsy. John eased around behind him to prevent a last-minute escape and Lloyd did turn and John laughed and said, "Oh no you don't. The door is that way." Lloyd reluctantly went. "Get you a window seat Lloyd, so you can watch the world go by."

Lloyd said, "I don't know if I want to."

John told him, "Sit."

He did and Lacy pulled in beside him and showed him how to buckle in. Then Lloyd sat back and watched all the people filing on, stuffing the overheads as they went and he said, "Where are all these people going?"

Lacy said, "El Paso for starters.

Once the wheels left the ground and the city sank away from them and after popping up through the clouds into the clear blackish blue sky, all the twinkling stars and dawn cracking behind them, Lloyd finally relaxed. "Wow. You can see the curve of the earth. That's crazy." It didn't take long before they started their slow glide down into El Paso International. Lloyd said, "Man, that was fast. I couldn't drive to San Antonio that fast."

John said, "Well, what do you think now?"

Lloyd said, "I could get used to it." John smiled.

At the terminal with bags in hand, Mary found the car rental place. They got a mid-sized, so not to feel scrunched. They pulled out of the rental and headed to the south side of town back to the same place John and company stayed before. Once they were settled in, Mary said, "Well, it looks like our target is a late sleeper. He is just now leaving the D.C. area."

John said, "That ought to take him around six-hours to get here. He won't get here until afternoon so he must be going to meet the replacement afterhours."

Mary said, "He must be comfortable in his zone. Probably thinks that last fellow just keeled over on his own."

John said, "I hope so. Bad for him, good for us."

After a little while, Mary said, "What's the matter John? You mean you're not going to take Lloyd over to the Harley shop so he can watch you have eye sex with that FXSTS you were google eyeing?"

Lacy busted out laughing and said, "John, you're not cheating on Mary now, are you?"

John started blushing a bit and said, "No. I don't think so. I can't do like a puppy and say Mary, it followed me home. Can I keep it. It won't fit into my suitcase. So, I guess I better not indulge." They all laughed a little, then John said, "That's a long ride on two wheels."

Lacy said, "What, make your butt sore like a few hours on Bobby's horse did to mine?"

Lloyd said, "So, what's Randy and Rochelle doing?"

John said, "The next time you go out to the Rock, he will have his cabin in good shape."

"Cabin?" Lloyd asked.

Mary said, "He studied the one we stayed in over in New Mexico and decided to build him one."

Lloyd said, "What about the Scooby doo van?"

John replied, "Don't even think about it. We claimed first dubs on it."

"Shoot." Lloyd said, "Put Lacy and me next in line then."

"Fine." John said.

They ordered pizza delivery and watched TV for the afternoon. Lloyd found a six pack somewhere so he had him one. The pizza showed up so they all pigged out. The girls hung out by the pool as the evening sun went down. They decided to take a little nap as the day was growing long and Mr. Target was at his hotel out by the airport. John had trouble dozing off. He kept thinking of the ship and the kite store and the roof top city and he felt sorry for those persons that were being held captive. He even wondered if that guy they had to take out in that broke down van and all the girls that were being transported in it. Was there a connection? The thoughts rolled around and around until his eyes finally slide shut.

Mary woke John and said, "We have movement. It seems to be at one of those nice steak houses. The kind with a floor to ceiling glass wine lockers, complete with a librarian sliding ladder to be able to reach all the wine bottles."

John said, "We need to be able to track our targets in real time in situations like this. The thirty-minute updates are good for sure, but a lot can happen in thirty-minutes." The rest agreed. John then told Lloyd and Lacy they were going to a late-night bar where they believed the target was going to go and wait for the new commander to get off duty. At least that is what John hoped for, if not, they would just have to follow the bouncing ball irregardless.

The next blip was moving their way. John said, "Time to get to the club before he does." They loaded up and went. They were already settled in with a little closer booth to the corner. Not too close and were playing pool when Mr. Assistant crooked Director came in and took his corner booth. John looked at his watch and said, "If he drives like the last fellow, he will walk in here in about fifteen to twenty-minutes."

"So, how do you want this to go down?" Lloyd asked.

John said, "Mary just stung the last guy out in the lot, but we need to send a real message to the commander that this is not a game he wants to play in."

Lloyd said, "Easy then. Get Mary over to that jukebox and drop a few quarters. Lacy and I will just dance our hearts out between the target and the bar and you just give him a quick third eye. Lacy and I will be making enough noise and dance show that no one will even notice a dead stiff in the dark corner."

"Sounds like a plan." John reached into his pocket and pulled out a half dozen quarters and told Mary to go play some loud stuff. She dropped the quarters and on the first song, Lloyd and Lacy lit it up. The waitress went and served the man in the corner and John thought it was perfect timing. She won't be back for a while. John went up and cut in on Lloyd and danced with Lacy kind of over in the corner. Lloyd then came back after a drink of beer grinning and laughing and when he cut in on John, John turned and silently planted one between Mr. Assistant's eyes. Just like the suicide fellow, Mister Assistants head went back and then leaned forward and down like he was sending a message. And soon would be. John went back to his booth and watched Lacy and Lloyd cut it up out there on the floor.

Mary came back from the jukebox and said, "Okay. What now?"

John said, "Wait and watch."

"Watch what?" Mary asked.

John said, "The reaction of that fellow when he meets a dead man."

Mary said, "Dead?" "Very." John replied.

"I missed it?" Mary asked.

John said, "I hope everyone else did too."

The new commander came in and tried to get the directors attention. It must have been that extra hole he saw when he bent down to speak. He suddenly went rigid. He stood and looked around with a look of I don't need to be anywhere near this place and he rushed out the door. Lloyd and Lacy were still cutting the rug. Finally, the bar maid went to see if Mr. Director was thirsty. He wasn't. She screamed so loud that it stopped the dance and everyone was looking from the corner to the door that someone had just hurried out of.

Again, John thought, perfect timing and a clear message sent. He bought Lloyd a beer and they sat there and listened to the music John paid for. It just didn't seem right to try to shoot a game of pool with all the excitement going on. No one could figure out who that was that left in such a hurry.

The body got hauled out and plenty of witnesses stated that someone rushed out of there but no one could identify him. Soon they were all free to leave. When they made it back to the motel, Mary filed the report and they soon called it a night.

On the news the next morning, the police were looking for a person of interest in the murder of a government employee. Specifically, the Assistant Director of the Department of Alcohol, Tobacco, and Firearms. John smiled and said, "That ought to rattle a few cages up there in Washington D.C. and a few other places." After their continental breakfast, they loaded up and checked out and headed to the rental return place at the airport. Once the car was returned, they went and found the first flight back to Hobby Houston. John asked Lloyd, "Are you ready for this?"

Lloyd replied, "Piece of cake."

They touched down just after two p.m. and were soon on their way back home. Mary said, "That's what I am talking about. Jobs that are short and sweet. At least we didn't have to drive all the way out there and back."

John said teasingly, "Yea, I could have let you drive that motorcycle back."

Mary laughed and said, "In your dreams, Mister. In your dreams."

All in all, it was a good day's work. Mission accomplished. John pulled over at the corner of Broadway and Forty-five and Mary jumped out and ran in for a couple of minutes. She was returned back with a big white bag. "Not only did I get my cream puffs, I also got some fresh baked bread, some sweet rolls and you have a half dozen cinnamon twists." Mary said.

John was already chewing on a cinnamon twist before he hit the entrance ramp to the freeway. It didn't take long and John and Mary were back in their cubby hole. Mary put the pastries away and then sat down to do her report to Mr. T. One dirty crooked Assistant drug and weapons smuggling director has been aborted. John was thinking he hoped this cleaned up that line of work or should I say put them out of business. It will take a very long time for something like that to be replaced. Now the only loose end on that whole situation would be the missing Miss Rose Smith. He spoke out loud, "Most trash floats, she will pop up somewhere."

Mary asked, "Who?"

"Oh." John said, "Our missing Rose." He then took the photos of the now aborted Director out from the others and said, "Another one bites the dust."

Mary said, "Yea, if we could just make this pile go away." John sighed in agreement.

As the evening passed, John's device buzzed. He answered. "Hello Moe."

Moe said, "Evening. I just wanted you to know that last night or should I say early this morning, there was a couple who visited Topsail Industries for about fifteen-minutes."

"When was this?" John asked.

Moe replied, "Between three and four in the morning."

John said, "That is strange business hours."

Moe said, "That's what I thought also. I could not get a good look at all. I know it was a man and a woman. They pulled up to the front door. The door opened and they were gone. There are no lights on so to speak in the showroom except at the window displays. Curious as to who stays in the building at night besides those on the roof and their watchers. How do you find this crazy stuff? First those weird hunters and now these human traffickers and slave laborers."

John said, "I think it is all tied together." He then told Moe, "Thanks and keep on watching the watchers, whoever they are. This whole mess over there is not going to last long."

"Good." Moe said and they disconnected.

Mary was in the kitchen browning some hamburger meat to add to the pot of spaghetti that was on the boil. She would just blend it in with spaghetti instead of dealing with meatballs. John liked it that way. It was then that Mary's device 'ping' and she just looked over at it and thought to herself, 'I will wait', in which she did until after they ate. Mary picked up her device and looked at it. She said, "Well, what have we here? Mid-eastern decent wanted for murder by bombing roadsides and with associates of the poppy plantations. He is a chemist who creates opium from poppy and a master at cooking crystal meth.

John said, "Sounds like he has been a busy fellow, only putting all his good talents to the wrong use."

Mary said, "He is personally responsible for an outbreak of more than forty high school age kids' deaths who got served up an extremely potent concoction of his. Look at this. He is going somewhere now. He's on the move."

John said, "Let's follow the bouncing ball until it stops somewhere." The next ping was on the east loop northbound. The next was on the north loop west bound. The next was the south loop eastbound, and on and on. "What the hell is this guy doing?" John asked. "He is just riding around in circles. This doesn't make any sense."

Mary said, "Well, this sucks. He's driving around in the traffic and we don't even have a clue to what he is driving."

John said, "I have an idea." He pulled up a map of the city and he told Mary, "Back up to the first ping location." She did. Then John put a time and flag on that location of the loop. "Next." He said to which Mary pulled up the next time and location on the loop. "Next." He told her and so it went until they had multiple flags and time stamps of this target going around and around the loop. As it was getting late, John said, "We can calculate future pings at the thirty-minute intervals. Traffic is thinning and being he is going round and around we can either go back and forth on ten or up and down on forty-five and try to be near him on a ping to possibly identify.

In Betsy, heading east, they figured the next ping would be somewhere close to the ship channel bridge. They exited south off of ten and went down to turning basin to turn around. They found and empty stretch and waited. The 'ping' happened on the bridge this time. John calculated the time and speed and pointed for Mary to take a picture of that group. She did. He fired Betsy up and got back on ten wests and cut across town. He took forty-five norths and then sixteen west and exited at Shepherd and waited. The 'ping' went off at North Main. John did another quick calculation. Another cluster of vehicles came by and Mary took another picture. John started Betsy and got on the six-ten west.

Mary was looking back and forth between the photos like a what's missing picture puzzle. Finally, she said, "The only thing I see is back in this group." She held the photo up. "That container hauler. Then almost in front of this group is a container hauler. Most of the other vehicles in both pictures are not the same that I can see."

John said, "Okay. Now let's tag along with that container then." That was about a quarter of a mile ahead of them.

Mary said, "I wonder how many times this guy has run around the block. We have been pinging him for about five laps now and there is no telling how long he has been driving before we got our first ping." Finally coming around the west side again the container truck exited and pulled off into a huge mall parking area. John pulled in a different entry way watching the truck. The driver got out and went into a fast-food joint. John said, "It must be a piss break."

Mary said, "That's not our man."

John said, "What?" Mary showed John the picture of the mid-eastern chemist/bomber and John said, "That driver is a black man. Hold on." Digging in his bag, he pulled out one of Boston's trackers. While the driver was still inside, John eased Betsy up alongside the container hauler and stuck the tracker up in the pin point used when they stack them. "Now, let's compare notes at the next ping." It came too soon. The driver was still in the food joint and the 'ping' coordinates and John's tracker coordinates matched. "Weird." John said as they sat a distance away from the container.

Mary asked, "Do you think he is locked in that container?"

John replied, "I don't know about being locked in, but he must be in there."

About that time, the driver came out with a carry out order and was talking on the phone. He walked to the back of the container and opened one of the doors. A man climbed down and took the bag and started eating. Mary said, "Now that is our man. What's he doing riding around in really big circles in a container for?"

John sat up quickly, "Holy smokes. I bet that is a lab on wheels. I read somewhere that a lot of times these chemists get busted is because of the odor that is created in the process. A lab on wheels, you will have no oder to pin-point to any specific spot."

Mary said, "How do they come up with all this? If they had their right minds, they could help solve the world's problems instead of creating some of the world's problems."

John just shook his head. Then he said, "The cooking party must be over. Let's follow this container home."

Their target finished up his either late supper or early breakfast then waved off the driver and started walking across the parking lot towards a lone vehicle that was parked under a shade tree. The container truck rolled out of the parking lot and turned right at the tracks. John said, "It looks like it's a drive by." Then he rolled Betsy around the parking lot and intercepted his target just as he was closing his door. John pulled up beside him and motioned for him to roll down his window, which he did while starting his ride. John smiled at him. Then Mary cut loose two quick rounds and John watched the man's head change shape as the man fell over in his seat.

John turned to Mary and said, "Any closer and I am afraid I would have a pierced ear. I heard both those rounds zing by."

Mary started laughing and told John, "What? I had two inches to spare."

John turned Betsy and rolled out of the lot. "Mary, get my GPS tracker out of my bag please. Now, let's see where this portable lab is going."

Mary switched on the device and for a minute it had two blips on opposite ends of the map. Then the one behind them disappeared. "Wow. That was weird. Must have been some kind of glitch that it mirrored itself."

John said, "I never had that happen. Might have to talk to Boston about that."

They continued to follow the blip on the GPS. It continued moving northwest past the beltway and then turned left. After about a mile or so, it turned into an empty lot. The driver backed his trailer between two other containers and then unchained the container and tilted his hydraulic controlled trailer to let the back of the container rest on the ground. He slowly pulled ahead and the container was soon on the ground. The driver reset his trailer to the road position and drove away.

John drove on down the road a couple of miles before turning Betsy around. Upon returning to the container lot, John pulled in and retrieved his tracker. He also took down the numerical code that was painted on the container. John got back into Betsy and they were out of there. John said, "You might send Mr. Bill the location and numerical code of that container and tell him probable meth lab." Mary sent the message. Another long night and day light was coming as they pulled into the parking facility. John laughed at a thought and told Mary, "We might have had to stop that truck to buy some product if we were going to keep chasing it around the loop."

Now Mary laughed saying, "John you are still crazy."

Back in the cubby hole, John sank back in his chair and said, "That was crazy. Chasing a rolling lab on wheels. If it was not for the satellite tracking, we would have never figured out what was going on." Mary was typing her report to the commission. One mad chemist successfully aborted. John told her, "You are getting good at writing those short and to the point reports."

Mary laughed and said, "Why waste the space in a file somewhere with a bunch of words that don't really matter. Abortion complete. The end.

John got a call from Bill asking what was this story out of left field about a lab in a container. John could only tell him it was something he stumbled across but it was not in his scope of work to cut a lock and take a look inside and added, "I don't think you will be disappointed if you just take a look."

Bill said, "I will go check it out now before it grows legs."

John said, "That would be good because I don't know if the driver had some sort of schedule or not." Then John added, "The 'Kasyade' was already well on its way back. I have been busy, but it may be back in the Caribbean or the Gulf by now."

Bill said, "Now, on that matter, I plan to be ready with the cavalry when that ship gets back and proves to be doing what you claim."

"Good." John said, "Maybe we can put this human smuggling ring out of business."

Bill said, "That is my sole intention."

John said, "Again, you will be the first to know of 'Kasyades' arrival." At that, they disconnected. "That's a good thing." John said to Mary.

"What's that?" Mary asked.

"That Bill has some sort of a plan to execute upon 'Kaysade's' arrival and I just can't wait." John said. "I need some sleep." He and Mary went into the bedroom to do just that for a couple of hours.

About lunch time, John's device buzzed and pulled him out of a deep sleep. It was Bill. "Hello?" John answered.

Bill said, "That was a damn good tip you gave me." John said, "So it was some kind of lab."

Bill replied, "That and then some. There was enough crystal methamphetamine to wire up half the city. Whoever is running that operation just took a major hit in the pocket book. We had to have a hazmat crew come out to clean out that container and whatever they left behind is going to the scrap yard to be chopped up and recycled into rebar or something."

John said, "No paper trail in the container? Like receipts for chemicals or anything like that?"

"No." Bill said. "Clean as a whistle."

John asked, "Do you know where the container came from?" Bill said, "We are back tracking that now. If we can find the point of sale, we might have something, but with the wide spread sale of those things, who knows if it wasn't just stolen from some other lot somewhere."

"Good luck with that." John said and disconnected.

By the time John finished his conversation with Bill, Mary was already in the kitchen rounding them up a meal. "Well, that was some journey last night, wasn't it?" Mary asked.

"Yes." John replied. "And how lucky they were to figure it out when they did. Otherwise, the lab on wheels would still be in business. After the meal, what do you say we ride over to Bay town to check if they are loading up that barge with pipe yet or not?"

Mary said, "Sure, why not."

"Besides, all that riding around last night, Betsy is getting thirsty." John said. So, they headed out.

Once Betsy was filled, they found their way onto Ten east and headed for Baytown. Once across the river, they headed south to the water front. When they arrived back by the pipe coating facility, they found that the barge was being loaded with freshly coated pipes. John said, "They must be loading them as they coat them."

"Why do you say that?" Mary asked.

John said, "The building and the barge and the trolley crane I can see, but what I don't see is a bunch of pipe racks taking up space." Mary looked around at the absence of any storage room for a large lay out of pipe. John said, "They must haul them all inside and stack them, treat them, and coat them before bringing them back out and stack on the barge for the shipment. From the looks of it, they about have a full load. I'm getting excited. Let's get back to the cubby hole and I will check if the 'Kaysade' has scheduled an arrival time."

On their way back, John's device buzzed and he answered. It was Lloyd. "Hey John. I just wanted to let you know that my neighbor told me that his boss is getting in a better mood. It seems there has been a slight uptick in weapon sales and he seems to think it has something to do with the new boss next door."

"Oh yeah?" John replied, "Well that didn't take long. I wonder if we are going to have to start following coffins around again?" Lloyd said, "That may be the case. My neighbor has not witnessed weapons going across the dock between the two businesses, but that don't mean it doesn't happen after hours."

John agreed and told Lloyd, "Thanks and stay on top of it." He then disconnected.

John looked at Mary and said, "It seems the dead don't stay dead long."

Mary asked, "What?"

John said, "We might have to get Moe on night watch as soon as Mr. Bill takes care of the kite store and company. It seems there is a chance that the coffin factory is starting to stick it's fingers into the gun business. Going to have to get Moe to watch for any afterhours transfers across the docks. It's the only way we will know. I am not chasing a bunch of hursts to a bunch of funeral homes just to deliver a special-order casket, but suspected gun deliveries, I will chase."

It was almost dark already by the time they made it back to the cubby hole. John commented on what a short day it was. Mary laughed and said, "That's what happens when you're out chasing around all night."

John laughed and said, "Wrong context. That sounds kind of juvenile."

Mary laughed and said, "Got ya!"

John's device buzzed and it was Randy. "Hey." John said, "What's up?"

Randy said that him and Rochelle were back in the city for a bit and he was just checking in. John grinned and said, "Oh, I see. You came in just in time for the fireworks."

Randy laughed and said, "Well, John. I can't let you have all the fun now, can I?"

Then John told him, "You're not going to believe this, but we got the Texas Rangers on our side."

Randy said, "A baseball team."

John said, "No. The Texas Rangers as in Texas lawmen that Washington can't rattle."

"Oh wow. Those guys. They have a long history of history. I sure wouldn't want to be on the wrong side of the fence with them."

John then told him about the late-night rodeo of chasing the dot around and around the loop and subsequent actions. Randy said, "Wow, I have been missing out on all the fun."

John said, "Yeah, and we put the Texas Rangers on the drug lab that is now out of business. A lot has been going on, on multiple fronts. We might start chasing caskets again."

Randy said, "No way."

John said, "There is a stirring in the works. Maybe the demise of that Assistant Director of the ATF might change things."

Randy said, "I heard something about that on the news. They were looking for a mystery person."

John laughed and said, "Lloyd and Lacy can sure shake up a dance floor."

Randy said, "No way." John said, "Yes way!"

Randy said, "We have been missing out on all the fun."

John said, "tell the truth now. You have been having fun building your little mini mansion out at the Rock."

Randy said, "I suppose you got me there."

"I thought so." John said. "I will let you know when the party starts."

Randy said, "Good deal." They disconnected.

Mary sat a plate with a couple of grilled ham and cheese sandwiches on it and John dove in. Between bites he said, "Thank you Mary."

She nodded in acknowledgement while she chewed on hers. Then she said, "Movie?"

John asked, "What do you have in mind?" Mary replied, "How about Deja Vue?" John said, "That sounds good. Popcorn?"

Mary replied, "Of course." And so it was. After the movie they hit the shower and then to bed and a restful sleep for a change.

It started early. John's device buzzed. It was Moe. He said that the couple who were there the other night came back for a visit last night and stayed for almost an hour. John told him that he suspected another load of warm bodies was soon to be on the way. John then asked if he had seen any of the captives get taken out of there.

Moe said, "Not yet. I do a nightly fly over and the number of glowing warm bodies has remained the same."

"Good thinking." John said, "This job is soon to be a done deal. Are you up to another all-night job at another location?"

Moe said, "Sure, what do you have for me?"

John told him, "Just need a set of eyes on a loading dock to watch for afterhours transaction between the coffin company and the weapons store."

Moe asked, "The same one that you guys have been dealing with?"

John said, "The one and the same."

Moe said, "I thought that was a done deal."

John replied, "So did I."

Moe said, "Well, sure. I don't have anything else to do at this particular point in time."

John said, "Good. First, we try to wrap up this mess." Moe agreed and they disconnected.

A cup of coffee appeared in front of John and he looked up at Mary and said, "I didn't even hear you."

Mary asked, "Eggs?"

John nodded as he fired up his laptop. He went to the Port Authority site he had flagged. He typed in the 'Kasyade' and there it was. Early afternoon arrival. "Crap." John said, "That little bugger got here sooner than I guessed, but I forgot they chug along twenty-four hours with no rest stops." Then John thought, where is the second barge? The one loaded goes out after to trade out. There is only one barge slip at the pipe coating facility. "How did we miss that?" He said out loud.

Mary asked, "Miss what?"

"The second barge." John replied. "An empty barge goes out to 'Kasyade' to get unloaded and the full one goes to Baytown. I watched the tug boat cut loose the loaded barge upon delivery and then he went through the channel, not back out to retrieve the empty. So where is the empty one? Still out in Galveston?"

Mary said, "Maybe at that barge building yard. That's right close by."

"That would make sense." John said, "Just tie it off to a pile or two until needed. Man, I wish I knew where it was. It would be slicker than greased owl poop to have someone in that barge when they decided to put those other warm bodies in there."

"Oh." Mary said, "Better yet, wouldn't it be a surprise to have a bunch of badges crawl out of the barge as they are putting those girls in the back of the truck?"

John smiled at the thought. He had to talk to Mr. Bill now. If they could find the empty barge, they could get set up fast. John called Mr. Bill and explained the situation about the missing empty barge. Mr. Bill told John that it was a good catch and he may know someone who prowls around those waters down there who may be able to help him out. He told John to keep on top of it. Ranger Bill then called his old pal Game Warden Leo K. and talked to him about the goings and comings of the 'Kasyade' and the subject of the whereabouts would the pipe coating facility leave a spare barge in Galveston for use to unload pipes on. Game Warden Leo said, "I know exactly where. I have observed that very ship come and go while checking on the fishermen for proper licenses. I happened to be in the area a time or two when that ship departed and you were right to guess a little tug from the barge facility comes out and moves the empty back to a set of concrete piles and ties it off."

"Where would that be?" Bill asked.

"Not at the barge building yard, but across the intercostal in the shallows. Fishermen fish around it all the time. I guess the fish like hanging out under such structures."

Bill told Leo, "I will meet you down at your boat shortly." Leo said, "I will be here." They disconnected.

Bill called John and said he had the Galveston end under control but John needed to be ready at the Baytown end when the pipe barge arrived. John said, "I can't wait."

Bill said, "We are going to tip one domino at a time. First the barge, then the men at the pipe coating facility, then send an unexpected load to the Topsail location. Take them all out in one fell swoop. I will let you know when we are headed that way."

"That's great." John said, "Talk to you then." They disconnected.

CHAPTER TWELVE

———❦———

A while later, as the 'Kasyade' was approaching and called in for the barge, the little tug boat packed like sardines with borrowed Galveston SWAT officers. Their instructions were to hide in the darkness of the barge for the load up and delivery of pipe to the pipe coating facility. Mr. Bill rode in the pilot house to make sure the tug pilot and crew didn't alert anyone.

Once the 'Kasyade' dropped anchor and was set in position, the little tug pushed the barge up to it on the Bayside of the ship just as before. No eyes to see. Right away, the pipe dance began. Clank, bang, clank is what the SWAT officers had to listen to for the next few hours. Finally, the clanging and banging stopped as the last of the pipe was set and chained and boomed down. The SWAT team heard the other tug arrive with its barge load of coated pipes.

Then the hatch opened and one by one, as if on a leash, the women were made to crawl down the ladder into darkness. All thirty of them. When the last one was in, the hatch was closed. The women were in total darkness, but the SWAT team had their night eyes on and could see every one of them. They felt the bump as the tug butted up against the barge to tie on. This caused a couple of the woman to give a little shriek. The SWAT officers could see the pure fear and panic on every one of their faces and none of them had a clue that they were in good company.

The tug tooted its horn and the barge started to vibrate as the tug began to push the barge away from the 'Kasyade'. Bill, watching from the game warden's boat in the distance said, "One domino falling over, fixing to hit the next." He then called John and said, "Package is on its way."

John called Randy and Rochelle to hurry over if they wanted to come out and play. And they did. It would take the barge some time to get back up to the Baytown facility. John and company would be waiting in the neighborhood.

Bill and Leo followed at a distance stopping every now and again to check out a few night fisherman. To some, it was their lucky night. Leo just gave them verbal warnings as him and Bill had a lot bigger fish to catch. Finally, the barge was pulling into its slip with a bump and a stop. Once secured, the barge did as before. It cut loose from the barge and headed up the channel. Bill and Leo eased up behind the barge out of sight. John called Bill and told him to watch the corner office since that is where he observed the group of men emerging from the last time.

Sure enough, after a while, that office door opened and just as before, the five went and put the ramp out and the other went and got the bobtail and backed it over near the ramp. The men then opened the hatch and said something and one by one, the women followed their chains up and out of the darkness. As the men were laughing and making wise cracks escorting the girls and started loading them in the bobtail, they did not see the dozen black suited men silently climb up out of the barge and then fan around them. One of the men saw a red dot on another man's back and looked around saying, "Oh shit." The others all looked around and froze in silence and confusion.

Bill called Baytown Police who had a paddy wagon and a bus on standby in the neighborhood. Then he called John to come on in and enjoy the show.

John and company arrived just as Bill was telling the Coast Guard station of the human smuggling ship. Within minutes, the Coast Guard boarded the 'Kasyade' and placed every person on board in custody. The officer in charge asked the captain if this was his ship. The captain told him it belonged to a company out in California. The Coast Guard officer told him, "Not anymore. This ship has now been seized for conducting human trafficking." The captain tried to claim that he was just hauling pipe. The Coast Guard officer then said, "We have half a hundred witnesses to say otherwise." That is when the captain knew the gig was up.

Back at the Baytown pipe coating facility, the six men were cuffed and stuffed into a paddy wagon and hauled out. Ranger Bill then told John, "Let's finish this. I want you to make delivery to that Topsail place."

John said, "I can do that. All I have to do is to back into a dock."

Bill said, "That's all you have to do. When they open the back door they will be surprised."

Mary said, "We will go and meet Moe in the neighborhood."

John said, "Good. I will see you there."

Mary, Randy, and Rochelle left. John grinning from ear to ear turned and told Bill, "You don't know what a relief this is for me."

Bill looked at John and said, "Well, let's go make the fat lady sing then." John laughed. Bill said, "Now, don't go hitting every pot hole in the road now. I am going to be back there with the men."

John said, "Gotcha." The men in black uniforms started climbing into the back of the truck. Once loaded, John pulled the door shut and latched it. Then he climbed into the cab and headed out.

On the way over, John called Moe to let him know he was driving a surprise package over to the kite store. Moe laughed and said, "I can't wait to watch this. I will meet the others a couple of buildings down and then walk over."

John said, "I just had a thought Moe. We might need someone at the back door fire exit just in case."

Moe said, "I will see if Randy and Rochelle want that task after they get here."

"Good." John said, "I should be there in about fifteen minutes."

Moe said, "See you soon." He disconnected.

Moe moved up the street to intercept Mary, Randy and Rochelle. He could spot Betsy as she came around the corner. Randy and Rochelle agreed to the back door duty although they might miss the excitement that was soon to take place at the front of the store. Mary got positioned to where she would watch John back in and Moe stayed up at the store front. All bases were loaded. Moe said to himself, "Batter up." Just then the bobtail truck rounded the corner being followed by a bright red car driven by none other than Richard L. the fire marshal. John had given Mary a quick call and told her he invited his red caboose to be a witness to all this and had instructed him to drive past. As John turned into the parking lot, the red car drove by and Mary intercepted it by flagging him into the next lot.

Richard recognized Mary from that attempted failed bomb plot over at J-Lee's. He said, "I'm not exactly sure what is going on, but a fellow named John said that there could be a lot of fireworks going off shortly and I should be here, so here I am. Fireworks are prohibited inside the city limits."

Mary grinned and told Richard, "There won't be literal fireworks but follow me and see for yourself." She walked towards Topsail Industries pointing at the place. The overhead door opened and John backed in like he knew what he was doing. After he was in, the overhead door closed. Mary said to Richard, "The trap has just been sprung." The fire marshal was still confused. About that time a paddy wagon pulls up in the parking lot and Mary told Richard, "Looks like Bill is on top of it."

Richard asked, "Who's Bill?"

Mary looked at Richard and explained, "Bill is a Texas Ranger and he is now in there." She pointed at the overhead door. Then it dawned on Richard, he must have seriously overlooked something on his fire code inspection. He didn't have to ask; Mary could see the look on his face. She said, "It's okay. They were on the roof; how could you have known."

Richard said, "So, that is why that stairwell was blocked."

Soon the overhead door rolled back up and John pulled the bobtail out into the lot and parked it. Upon seeing Mary, he busted out. "You should have seen the look on their faces when that door opened up and they were staring down the barrels of a dozen or so weapons." He waved to the fire marshal and said, "come on, let's go have a look."

So, John and Mary and Richard joined Bill and they went and found the stairs. A few SWAT members not guarding the newly arrested traffickers were doing a search of the showroom and the warehouse sewing room. As the group stepped out on the roof, Bill said, "I would say that you were quite right in your investigation John. We might have to hire you to do some work for us sometime."

John blushed at being flattered by a Texas Ranger. The fire marshal said, "How could I have missed this?"

Bill responded, "It might be a good thing that you didn't insist on coming up here, you probably would have never made it back down again. All those men down there had weapons on them. We just caught them with their pants down is all. They sure was not expecting SWAT in the back of their truck."

The fire marshal said, "That blonde was pretty adamant that she was not going to have anyone move those supplies right away. That's why I gave her a citation."

Ranger Bill asked, "So, she more or less forced the citation?"

Richard replied, "Yes."

Ranger Bill said, "Well now. That is aiding and abetting in my books."

The walls were too high to see over and the roof was covered with tents. Finally, Mary spoke out loud, "Wake up girls, we need to talk."

One by one, the sleepy faces began to show up. Once they realized it was not their captors, word spread rapidly through the little tent city in multiple languages and soon there were around thirty girls standing in front of them. Some kept glancing their eyes at one in particular to see what her reaction was, then one by one they pointed at her and said, "She is not with us."

John stepped in front of the door to block any chance of fleeing. Bill walked over to her and put cuffs on her and said, "You must be the house keeper." He then turned towards the group and asked, "Are there any others?" He continued to hold the housekeeper by the cuffs. The rest of the girls either said no or shook their heads in confirmation.

John called down to Moe, "Do you see a bus down there yet?" Moe replied, "One just drove into the lot."

John told Bill the bus was there and Mary told the girls to take what they want as they would not be coming back here, and so they did. Once the girls were on the bus, the little tent city was searched to make sure no one was hiding or left behind. Back out in front of Topsail Industries, John was explaining to the fire marshal how Moe had accidently stumbled across the tent city on the roof. Then John looked around and said, "Well now, what have we got here?"

All eyes looked in the direction that John was looking and here came Randy and Rochelle and a reluctant blonde in between them. When they got near, Randy said, "Yea, we had one try to slip out the back Jack. We waited until we figured no one else was coming out."

Bill asked Richard, "Is this the one showing you around the place the other day?"

Richard said, "Yes sir, it is."

Bill motioned for a SWAT officer to come over and he pointed at the blonde and said, "Throw her in the garbage truck with the rest of them." They cuffed her and lead her away.

Moe said, "Too bad those other two were not here when it happened."

Bill asked, "What other two?" Moe told him of the two late night visits. The short one days ago and the hour long one just last night. Bill said, "There goes my idea of a clean sweep. I hate loose ends. It may take a while, but we have over fifty females that we have to interview and then see if they have a life somewhere so we can figure out what to do with them."

Moe then asked, "Am I done here?" John looked at Bill and said, "Well?"

Bill thought about it for a minute then said, "If you can hang around for a few more nights, I would like to know who is going to pick up the pieces."

"Okay." Moe said. "Maybe if that couple comes back, I can get a photo. It's hard to get a good photo in the dark."

Mary said, "I am so glad the girls are safe."

Bill said, "I am glad that not one shot was fired. We completed this whole operation with each step being an utter surprise. Now there are going to be two businesses with employees wondering what the heck is going on when they show up for work shortly and no one to welcome them."

Mary put an arm in John's and said, "Maybe now we can get out there and remodel that Scooby Doo van." Randy and Rochelle busted out laughing.

John looked at Mary grinning and said, "Yea, yeah, I would like that."

Bill asked, "Scooby Doo van?"

John replied with a grin, "Yea, that's another story."

Moe said, "Daylight is coming, if you don't need me anymore, I am out of here." He shook hands with the fire marshal and the Texas Ranger and said, "Nice to meet you. John knows how to find me." He then turned and walked away.

Bill turned to John and said, "This is a nice crew you have here."

John replied, "I know, but this is just the half of it."

Bill raised an eyebrow at that but chose not to ask any other questions as a professional courtesy. The paddy wagon pulled out of the lot just after Moe left. The bus was still awaiting orders which Bill gave them to take the women to the same location as the others to keep them in one big group. Keep it simple with no confusion that arises when you have two or more groups trying to do the same thing but end up doing things differently. Bill said, "I think I will tell the coast guard to confiscate both of those barges. They were also used in the trafficking of humans. Might as well take all their toys away." John nodded in agreement.

John said, "In no way could they try to claim the barges innocence, after all, you had twelve officers on the ride to prove it."

"That is true." Bill said.

John said, "Well, if you don't need us, we will be on our way."

Bill said, "I guess I have to drive that bobtail all the way down to Galveston now. I have to get these fine men back to where they belong."

The senior SWAT officer came up to John and said, "I don't know who you are, but this mission has been the best my men have done and not a shot was fired. It has been an honor to work with you."

John replied, "Thanks. It was you guys that made it work. I just stumbled across this mess."

They all shook hands and parted ways. Yellow police tape was cross the door and when John looked in Betsy's rear view mirror, he saw some fine men climbing into the back of that bobtail. He smiled big and realized a great weight was now lifted off of his shoulders. Mary watching him said, "You did good John. You saved a lot of females from no telling what. You did good."

On the way back to the cubby hole, John asked Randy, "How's the mansion building coming along?"

Randy said, "Livable now. Roof, walls and screened windows. What else would you ask for?"

Rochelle said, "An indoor kitchen." They all laughed.

Randy said, "We are getting there. That's one reason we came back into the city. I need some electrical supplies and appliances. I need to wire up so I can hook up to the power grid. A meter on a pole will be a real biggie. For now, we have a gas stove. We don't need power for that. Just a big propane tank and maybe not even a big one. We just have to have some oversize bottles for cooking and who knows, maybe some hot water."

"That would be a big improvement." John said. "No need to go bum a tub of hot water from Bobby."

"That's right." Rochelle said, "It's also easier to wash dishes with hot water."

Randy and Rochelle left from Betsy's parking facility and John and Mary went to the cubby hole just as day was breaking. John said, "I am still excited. I can't believe we pulled that off and no one was hurt."

Mary agreed and said, "But some bigshot is going to wake up to very bad news and people may die yet."

John said, "That is a high possibility. If I were a fly on the wall,"

Mary said, "I would swat you." They both laughed and headed to the bedroom to catch up on another nights lost sleep. For not feeling as tired as they were, as soon as their heads hit the pillows, they were out.

Around noon, John's device buzzed pulling him back to the awake world. It was J-Lee. He said, "Are you watching the news?"

John replied, "Actually I was watching the backs of my eyelids for holes."

J-Lee said, "Oh, sorry."

John replied, "It's okay, what's up?"

J-Lee said, "It seems like the coast guard with the help from other agencies busted and international human smuggling ring."

"Really." John said scratching his head.

"Yea." J-Lee continued, "They seized a ship and some barges and no telling what else. It's on national news."

"On national news, huh." John thought to himself, 'good choice Bill, who is going to pick on the coast guard for doing what they are supposed to do." John said, "I guess I had better go see what this is all about. Why don't you give your fire marshal a buzz?"

J-Lee asked, "Why would I call him?"

John said, "You want some inside scoop?"

J-Lee said, "Hold on, don't tell me this is what Moe has been watching now is it?"

John said, "That is exactly what I am telling you. Later." They disconnected.

As John sat and watched the news, he was amazed at the speed in which the TV station had already did a fly-by of the 'Kasyade' and barge still beside it full of pipes. It then showed a bus unloading thirty young ladies at a facility. John said, "Bill must have tipped them. No mention of the pipe coating facility or Topsail Industries. But he got the message out there and some big cages were being rattled. Good job Bill, good job."

He went back to the table and opened his laptop. His mind was off of the human trafficking finally. He looked at the photos of the trio. The Undertaker, The Butcher, and Rose Smith. How in the hell are fine upstanding citizens like you staying out of my target? It damn near makes me just want to go on a killing spree but I won't. Mary came strolling in and said, "What, no coffee?" John had nothing to say. She loaded the coffee pot and sat down. John said, "The coast guard made national news busting an international human trafficking ring."

Mary said, "Oh really?'

John replied, "Yes really. I just got finished watching it on TV."

Mary looked over at the TV and there was the 'Kasyade'. She said, "Oh wow."

John replied, "Yea, blame it on the coast guard. Good for them and good for us, right?"

Mary thought a moment and said, "Yea, they got just what Bill fed them and no more. Smart man that one is." John agreed.

"So." John said, "Six men at the pipe coating and six at the kite store and probably close to a dozen on the pipe hauler. That's a lot of bad guys to talk to."

Mary said, "There might be some good guys in that lot and they just got caught in the net."

John said, "That is possible. All we need is as the aliens would say, 'Take me to your leader.' Someone hired them, someone paid them. It could be a fake company or a ghost check writer. Someone is pouring money in on this. Maybe a couple of them didn't see this possibility coming and will now want to cover their asses. We can only wait and see."

At that, Mary poured them a cup of coffee and stared at the images on the screen. John broke the silence by asking, "I wonder who those night visitors to the kite store are." John picked up his device and buzzed Moe.

"Yea." Moe answered.

John said, "You tried to get pictures of the night visitors, right?"

Moe said, "Yea, but nothing on facial to be able to identify."

John asked, "What about what they were driving?"

Moe replied, "Yea, I probably have that."

John said, "Look through your photos and see if there is a license plate we can track."

Moe replied, "Yea, I can do that. If I come up with something, I will send it over to you."

"Thanks." John said and they disconnected.

John went to his bag and pulled out his GPS tracker and sat back at the table. He plugged it in to his laptop and pulled up the map of when he started following that container and he freeze framed it when he got that double blip. It seemed to be on Ten going east inside the loop because John was going northwest at the time. Thirty seconds later and the device would have never picked it up, whatever it was. John was asking himself if it was just a fluke or some kind of interference. Whatever it was, that was another puzzle for a later day and he disconnected and put the GPS back in his bag. He turned to Mary and said, "I hope Moe comes up with a plate."

'Ping'. That got John and Mary both to flinch. Mary looked at her device and said, "Okay then."

John asked, "Well, what do we have now?"

Mary said, "Another scum sucker."

"Okay." John replied, "That is a broad category, what kind?"

Mary said, "A bail jumping serial rapist waiting on another trial. Seems his lawyer got him out of his last two on technicalities."

"Well." John said, "I guess it is time to end those kinds of excuses."

Mary said, "This bastard is not choosy. He raped a twelve-year-old as his youngest and a seventy-five-year-old and a few in between."

John said, "Where do these people come from? Worse yet. They walk amongst us."

"That is a scary thought." Mary said.

They geared up and went out the door. John backed in and armed the alarm. Then they were on their way. They were about ten blocks from the marker, so they walked. The streets were busy, so it took some time to get there. When they got to the location, they looked all around to no avail so they had to wait until the next ping and when it did, John said, "Oh crap."

He was like five blocks behind them. They must have passed on the street and didn't even know it. John and Mary turned back and back-tracked for about six blocks at a fast pace. Whoever they were looking for was a slow mover. If they could gear up and leave home and walk ten blocks and their target only moved five blocks total.

John and Mary split up on opposite sides of the street and moved ahead looking for a slow mover. Mary said to herself, "This guy might just be trolling looking for his next victim." They slowly worked the sidewalks a couple more blocks and John motioned to Mary to look ahead of him and there was the fellow they were looking for. She got a good identification from her side of the street. John was behind him so he had to have Mary verify. The buildings here were set apart by a few feet. Old-style so the brick layers could lay up the walls.

The target grabbed a single woman and backed into the narrow alley and Mary shot across the street like a bullet. John saw their target disappear so he cut down the narrow space between buildings at a run. Mary entered the other ally pistol in hand and yelled, "Hey!" The rapist did not let go of his soon to be victim, but held her as a shield as he backed down the alley towards the back of the building where the street alley was. Mary followed him step for step telling him to let her go. He just kept backing up almost into the car alley watching Mary and that pistol in her hand. He never saw the hands that reached around and grabbed his chin and gave his head a twist beyond its turning point. There was a snapping crunching sound in his neck and then he heard no more as he fell to the ground twitching. The woman looked at Mary and then looked at John and then looked at the dead man and fainted. John barely caught her. He held her up by one arm and Mary took her other and they walked her out of the alley and around the corner to a street café and sat her in a chair. As she started to come too, John and Mary disappeared into the crowd.

Mary said, "Almost missed that one." John agreed that they had luck with them today. That thirty-minute time between pings has almost caused several bad incidents. He wondered if Boston could hack the system and get them real time locations like the trackers do. Mary said, "Don't you think maybe we should ask Mr. T. first. Maybe not have to hack."

"Well hell Mary." John said, "That would be too much like doing the right thing. What about our trio? Why not target them? How can they be immune?"

Mary had no comment. She understood John's frustration with the situation. They were back at the cubby hole in to time. She sat down and filed her report. Abortion successful. No more court cost or other fees needed.

John said, "Sometimes things just work out like it is supposed to. I need to call Lloyd." He picked up his device and made the call.

"Hey there." Lloyd said. "You must be a mind reader; I was thinking of calling you."

"What's going on?" John asked.

Lloyd said, "I can't figure out what is going on over at that casket place. It is like the leadership is a now you see them, now you don't thing over there."

"What do you mean?" John asked.

"Just what I said." Lloyd told him. "New boss moves in, then nobody knows when the new boss is going to be there. One day in the office, two or three days gone."

"That is odd." John said.

"That is why I haven't been able to get you a photo yet." Lloyd replied.

John said, "That is okay Lloyd. Moe may be over to help out in a few days. He is finishing up a project. He will be our night watchman over there when he finally makes it."

Lloyd said, "That's good. So, you managed to do it didn't you."

John said, "What?"

Lloyd replied, "I'm not stupid. All that stuff on the news. I know you had your fingers in that cookie jar."

John laughed and said, "You can sure cut a rug out on the dance floor."

Lloyd laughed and said, "You got to do what you got to do."

John said, "Exactly. Later." They disconnected.

John put his device down and again looking at the pictures, he picked up one of the first. The Butcher, the Doctor, and the Undertaker. It was the picture he got from Pearl. He studied for a long time and finally spoke. "What are you doing Doctor? Just what is your game? I intend to find out." With that he put the picture on top of the stack and got up and took a shower.

After the shower he laid down. Eventually Mary did the same thing. She said to John, "We can only do what we are ordered to do. We can't turn into vigilantes."

John looked at her for a moment and said, "I know that. We were not ordered to interfere with those human traffickers but we did."

Mary said, "You have a point there. We saved people from who knows what, but we didn't kill anyone. Besides, the coast guard did that. Remember?"

John looked at her and laughed saying, "You are right."

Mary said, "They can't hide or be hid forever. One day their number will pop up."

With that, John looked at Mary and said, "You want to play?" And they did.

After breakfast; John asked Mary "Do you feel like going to the Rock for a day or two?"

Mary replied, "Let's go. I'll pack up right now."

John said, "We will leave before the noon lunch break. You should call the others."

Mary said, "I think Randy and Rochelle may already be out there. Rochelle told me we just caught them basically on a shopping spree, then they planned on going back out there. I will call Lacy and Kathy anyhow."

John checked their gear bags to make sure all was accounted for and then he went to the table and picked up his GPS tracker and put it in the bag. He wondered again about that mystery blip. Another puzzle and not even a piece that fit in his puzzle play board. Then he considered his puzzle and smiled. Only a few pieces missing on that one.

John said, "Don't forget to let the commission know that we will be out of pocket for a few days."

Mary said, "After I call the others, I will do just that, but it shouldn't matter anyway."

"Why is that?" John asked.

Mary replied, "It's Friday already. The weekend."

"Holy moly." John said. "This day and night then night and day work sure knocked my days out of whack."

Mary grinned and said, "Maybe that is why they put days and dates on one's watch."

John looked at her grinning, "Smart ass." He set their gear bags by the door.

Mary said, "Lloyd and Lacy are packing as we speak. Lloyd said he is not waiting to get hung in Friday Night exodus like before."

John laughed stating, "Old dogs can learn new tricks."

"Jay and Kathy are tracking a target at the moment. When they complete their abortion, they will be on their way." Mary said.

"Good." John replied. "Anything special you might want to add to the Scooby Doo van?"

"Oh." Mary said, "I forgot about the Scooby Doo van. I don't think much cause for remodeling." They both laughed.

John said, "Don't forget to take a couple of packages of that Nilgai sausage and pencil sticks."

Mary said, "Will do."

On one of the slow days, as John was piddling around the house, he put together a four-wheel rectangle shallow box with wheels and without a top and added a piece of rope for a handle. He retrieved it out of a little storage closet and put that heavy when empty cooler in it.

"Cute." Mary said, "Maybe you should paint it red and stencil radio flyer on the side.

John laughed and said, "I thought about a little red wagon, but I think they have shrunk since I was a kid. Not as sturdy either. Greed. Take your everyday candy bars. They shrink them and put them in a fancy new wrapper and then jack up the price on them. It is a win, win for the candy maker. Charging more for less."

Mary said, "I never looked at it that way but come to think about it, you are right."

John said, "Now I don't have to make two trips to Betsy's house." They finished packing. Gallon jugs of water out of the freezer. No need to buy bagged ice until another day. They set the alarm on the way out and the little not red wagon followed John to Betsy's house. At nine-thirty-three, they hit the road. Mary turned on the radio and Willie was singing 'On the Road again.' As they headed out of town, the remainder of the morning rush was still driving in.

As they crossed the Brazos River, Mary asked, "Where do they get the names of these rivers? Surely when man showed up there was no signs saying this is so and so river".

John laughed and said, "I think this one was a map maker's prank."

"Why do you say that?" Mary asked.

"Look at the water, what do you see?" John asked.

Mary said, "Mucky reddish looking water."

"Exactly." John said. "Somewhere in this world the word Brazos means bottle green."

Mary said, "Not in that water."

They travelled the next thirty or so miles and upon approaching the Colorado John said, "Now look at this water."

As they crossed the bridge, Mary said, "It is almost bottle green clear."

"Yes." John said. "Somewhere in the world, Colorado means something I guess having a clay red color."

"Weird." Mary said.

John said, "I think it was a map maker's prank, but it got published before the prankster could fix it and now, we are stuck with it. There are millions and millions of cars a year that cross over these two rivers and nearly all of them don't know they have been pranked."

They soon pulled in at Randy's and Mary said, "Oh wow." As she laid her eyes on the mini mansion.

John said, "Quite the upgrade from the Scooby Doo."

Mary said, "It sure is."

John and Mary got out of Betsy and were greeted by Rochelle grinning big. "So, do you like?" Rochelle asked.

Mary said, "It is great."

Rochelle told John that Randy was around back and she led Mary inside. John walked around back and Randy was closing the eve in. He looked at John and said, "Darn Starlings are already trying to make themselves at home." John laughed. Randy came down off the ladder and said, "Well, what do you think?"

"Nice." John said, "How did you settle on the size?"

Randy replied, "Easy. Twelve sheets of sub floor or four by eight. I could have gone thirty-two by twelve, but I chose the sixteen by twenty-four. I didn't want that trailer home feel."

John said, "It looks good."

Randy invited him inside so they went in and joined the girls. After checking out the bare interior except a bed a table and chairs, Randy told them "I still have to run wiring and then cover up the walls."

John said, "Keep it up."

Rochelle pointed to the far end and said, "That's the kitchen, eventually."

They all laughed and John said, "Well now, I suppose Mary and I should go move in to the Scooby Doo van."

Randy said, "It is ready and waiting."

John and Mary went out to Betsy just as Lloyd and Lacy drove up. High fives and hugs. Then Lloyd and Lacy went to investigate the ongoing construction project. John and Mary moved their belongings over into the Scooby doo van. Mary said, "No sleeping on the ground."

John laughed and said, "Yea, quite the upgrade." He placed the cooler wagon by the door and said kiddingly, "No bears in this neighborhood."

John took a pack of pencil sausage sticks and went and sat down in the social area. He closed his eyes and started listening to all the different bird songs playing around him. He could not remember the last time he just listened to the birds. He did remember the rooster though. Lost in the sounds, soaking in some high noon sun, a thought hit him like a ringing bell. He opened his eyes and looked around. The others were all inside the mini mansion. He got up and went to join them. They all looked at him when he walked in. Mary said, "What is it? You have that look."

John asked Lloyd, "When was the last time that new boss was at the coffin factory?"

Lloyd said, "Thinking back, it must have been around Tuesday."

John asked, "And the boss has not been back since?"

Lloyd replied, "Not to my knowledge she hasn't." "She?" John asked.

Lloyd said, "I suppose. I don't think many men wear dresses to work on occasion but the way the world is going, you never know."

John asked Mary, "What day was it that we followed that container home?"

Mary said, "I think it was Monday night, Tuesday morning."

John asked Lloyd, "Did you get a good look at that new boss?"

Lloyd said, "No, too far away."

John said, "Did you notice anything else about this new boss besides wearing a dress?"

Lloyd replied, "Yea, yea I did. Her hair was rose red."

John almost fell out of his chair. That got not only John but Mary, Randy and Rochelle. They all said, "What?" They were all aware of Rose Smith from New Mexico. Only Lloyd and Lacy didn't know because they weren't there.

John said, "I bet that chance ping on my GPS the other night was Ms. Rose coming into town for the day."

Mary said, "It could very well have been. The timing seems right." John was fidgeting and Mary said, "John. You already looked down your barrel once at Red, remember?"

He calmed and said, "Yes, and I will again."

Another vehicle arrived and it was Jay and Kathy. They were greeted with a bunch of high fives and then given the grand tour. After the dust settled, they all ended up standing around in the cabin. Jay and Kathy got caught up on John's mystery blip and the possibility that Red was in the city a few days ago. That caused a little stir. After all, Red was associated with Micky, Ricky, and Dicky. It made sense.

Jay and Lloyd re-established their tent sites and soon had their tents up and mats aired up. Back at the social area, John's pack of stick sausages was disappearing at a steady rate. Lloyd said, "Man, these things are good. I bet they are better with a beer." He then popped a top.

John told Randy and Jay how Lloyd tried to crawfish out of getting on that plane to El Paso. They all laughed. Then John said, "Lloyd and Lacy can sure cut a rug. They could be on that dancing show."

Jay looked at Lloyd and said, "You mean that you dance?"

John said, "I would be willing to bet he would dance you under the table."

"Well, thank you." Lloyd said grinning as Randy just shook his head.

After the evening meal of grilled over the fire Nilgai sausages and fried potato wedges, the porta grill was removed and the gang was sitting around the fire. A familiar figure stepped into the fire-light holding a six pack and a grin. "Hey Bobby." Randy said, "Come on in."

Lloyd and Jay reached for a cold one as he walked by them. Randy told the group that Bobby had been helping him out a little here in there. Somethings on the mini mansion a man just can't do by himself. He would need to have arms like an octopus which he didn't have. After a bit, they were all kind of silent and gazing into the flames.

John said, "What is that?"

Jay replied, "Sounds like a helicopter."

Bobby said, "Sometimes life flight lands on that foundation over by the highway if they have to give a life flight ride." The sound got nearer and it did sound as if it touched down over there and then it took off. Bobby said, "Maybe they are practicing a night time touch and go. You never know." They listened as it circled around the town and then began to fade into the distance. John just came out of the can and he thought he noticed movement on the street behind the cars. He stopped and looked at a man in a black suit that walked up to the edge of the property and stopped. Now all eyes were looking in that direction and John was thinking to himself, "Oh shit. The men in black."

The man said, "John Myers."

At this point, John's brain was still catching up. He replied, "Yes." He had already had his hand on his shoulder weapon.

The voice said, "May we approach?"

John replied, "Talk to him. This is his property." Nodding towards Randy who was also standing confused.

The black suit said again with his hands spread wide with a tone of urgency, "May we approach please?"

Randy said, "Well, come on then."

Him and three other black suits lead another person in with them. When the man approached the campfire the group about fell out of their chairs. Mary gasped, "Mr. T."

He said, "Hello Mary." and then, "John and Randy and Rochelle and Jay and Kathy and Lloyd and Lacy and you must be the shootist, Bobby." Bobby's mouth fell open when Mr. T called him by name. He continued, "I have three more sharpshooters with night eyes out in the darkness so I will be fine."

John said, "What brings you to our little camp? Don't you have armies to command?"

"That I do." Mr. T said. He continued by saying, "If I could give you all a medal for the recent work you have done, I would. But we don't advertise, now do we? That clean up out in New Mexico was great."

John said, "Yea, we still have a loose end there."

Mr. T said, "That would be a wild Rose." John nodded and Mr. T. continued, "In due time. Remember, I told you that there is no one who gets away. The way you got all those different agencies involved in squashing that human trafficking, that was pure genius. Some at the top see these operations being planned for months only to foul them before execution. You blindsided them so hard, a couple of them had to go back to California to try to figure out what the hell happened. Especially after their scheme in New Mexico got wiped out. I hear that even the next in line commander of the guard who had been groomed for years to take the last man's place had a crap in his pants come to Jesus meeting and no longer wants anything to do with those in the business with drugs or weapons."

"That's good." John said. "The message was received and understood. With all due respect sir, who is keeping those such as the Undertaker fellow and that Butcher smuggler and as you say, the wild rose from popping up on our screens to abort? While I'm at it, why can't we have real time tracking? We almost lost some innocent victims due to the thirty-minute timing."

Mr. T. answered, "As for the timing of the target locations, that has to do with invasion of privacy if someone tried to sue about twenty-four-hour tracking. Now the thirty-minute pings give a loop hole in the invasion scenario. We just say we are spot checking and that gets us around a lot of obstacles. I may be able to look on the target time and get the commission to change things since the targets have not complained yet."

John said, "That would help. We walked right by our target the other day and had to double back only to catch him in the act of committing another crime."

Mr. T. said, "About those other three you mentioned. They are bad apples. The problem is, they are well connected bad apples and I think a few more bad apples are in a seat on the commission so they are being watched out for. Our problem is we don't know who is who. That is why I am here." He looked down and saw those few remaining sausage sticks and said, "May I?"

John said, "Sure."

Mr. T. bit off a chunk before saying, "I'll say, these are good. What is it?"

John replied, "Nilgai and pork."

"Whatever it is, this is good. You don't find this in the D.C. area." Mr. T. said.

John motioned to Mary as he asked Mr. T. "What can we do about a bad commissioner?"

Mr. T. said, "We are working on that also."

Mary came back from the Scooby Doo van and presented Mr. T. a package of smoke-dried pencil sausage sticks and said, "Enjoy and share with those in the dark."

"I will." He said as he motioned to a suit behind him holding a briefcase. The suit opened the briefcase and Mr. T. said, "In my honor, I give these to John, Mary, Randy, Rochelle, Jay, Kathy, Lloyd, Lacy, Boston, J-Lee, Bobby, Moe and Ranger Bill E." He shook all their hands and when he came to Bobby he said, "I've seen you in video on horseback. Damn good shooting." Bobby was about to drool all over himself and Mr. T. added, "I trust his meeting won't be in the local paper now, will it?"

At that, Bobby straighten up and said, "No way."

The helicopter was coming back and Mr. T said, "Thanks for the hospitality." He turned and walked into the darkness.

John sat down looking at the medals in his hands wondering how does this man know so much. Boston, J-Lee, and Moe? It was then that he heard the helicopter lift off and fade into the darkness. He even knew where we were. Mary said, "At first sight, I thought, Oh crap. Men in Black. Then it was men in black."

Bobby said, "I can't believe I am sitting at a campfire in a little nowhere town and get presented a medal from the main man himself. I about wet my pants."

The group of them laughed and Lloyd said, "I need a beer."

After the merriment of pinning medals to shirts and dancing around high fiving each other, they all finally settled down. John said, "How is it that they know where we are and who we work with but we can't find out crap about the bad guys?"

Randy said, "It must have something to do with that crappy invasion of privacy thing."

John said, "I will know more when I talk to Ranger Bill and ask him what he put in his report. We reported nothing. Remember the coast guard did it."

Jay and Kathy said, "We didn't report anything." It was the same with Randy and Rochelle and Lloyd and Lacy didn't even know.

Mary said, "Well, I hope nobody else knows."

Bobby asked grinning, "Knows what?"

John laughed and said, "Lloyd, get this man a beer."

He did so and sat back down by the fire. Now, they have all settled back into the circle watching the fire. Kathy said, "I still can't believe what just happened here."

"I second that." Lacy said.

Randy said, "Maybe I should get a bronze plaque that said 'On this day of this year, Mr. T. stood right here.' pointing to the spot on the ground vacated by Mr. T.

The whole group busted out laughing and John said, "I dare you." More laughter.

The next morning, the rooster was crowing. That brought John awake. He fumbled around getting dressed and Mary said to him, "You're rocking the boat."

John replied, "Sorry. Randy and Rochelle must have worn out the shock absorbers."

That got an early morning laugh out of Mary as John stepped out into the world. He was over poking the coals restocking the fire to make some hot water when Randy came out. Randy sat down and asked, "Do you think New Mexico Red or Wild Rose is in the city now?"

John replied, "It kind of looks that way but I am not positive."

Randy said, "You think you got a momentary hit off of the tracker?"

John said, "That is my speculation only."

Randy said, "Well, John. Why don't you go fishing?" John just looked at him. Randy said, "Plug your tracker in to Betsy and have it on wherever you go. If Red is in town, you could be passing her anytime and not know it."

John said, "I never had a thought that she would come here." Randy said, "It would be good to do a slow pass. If you found her and downloaded that map." John's eyes lit up. I wonder how much map is saves? I would guess if it filled up it would do a write over. Randy said, "You would know where she goes and where she stays. Maybe lead you to the other fellows." John was thinking of the possible enormity of this idea. We have to find that tracker. Randy repeated, "Leave your GPS in Betsy and leave it on."

John grinned and said, "I might even have to take a couple of Sunday afternoon drives."

Randy asked, "So what did Boston tell you the range was?"

John replied, "Roughly five miles."

Randy suggested, "Do the loop and you pretty well cover the inner city. If nothing there, then try the beltway. You will miss a lot but you will cover a lot."

John said, "I will have Lloyd and Moe watching the casket factory. If she goes there, I can ease by and collect her driving routine." He then high fived Randy.

The water was hot so Randy poured them both a cup and added the instant coffee. John was still grinning when Jay came over. "What's with the happy face?" Jay asked as he was pouring a cup of hot water.

Randy said, "John's going fishing."

Jay replied, "I like to fish."

John laughed and said, "Wrong kind of fishing. I'm going fishing for a two-legged red fish."

Randy laughed and said, "I like that."

Lloyd finally straggled over and said, "I like that rooster but he wakes up early." Again, laughter all around as Randy poured him a cup.

John said, "I wonder how Moe is doing?"

"What is he doing?" Randy asked.

John said, "Babysitting a fresh out of business, business. We hope an associate will snoop by in the dark and Moe will be waiting. It was Moe who found the tent city on top of that building. I need to call him before he goes to sleep."

John dialed and Moe answered on first ring. "Hey, John. I was going to call in a bit, what's up?"

John told him, "The gang is all out at the Rock."

"Oh yeah?" Moe said, "In that case, I'm busting a U-turn. You guys can't have all the fun. I'll see you in an hour or so." Then he disconnected.

John was just staring at his device. "Well, I didn't get anything out of that, but he is on his way out here now. He said something about us hogging all the fun."

Jay said, "Sounds like Moe."

The girls were rustling around now and that out house door was getting its morning workout. Kathy said, "I sure am glad you built this."

Randy said, "Thanks."

With the girl's faces washed and awake, it was time for them to tag team breakfast. In no time, there was a platter of fried eggs, toast and hash browns and a bottle of pace picante. Jay actually stood up and asked for blessings. He asked blessings on breakfast, and the cabin and on the day. Then the girls were talking about going over to Bobby's later to play on the horses. Lacy said, "Did you see the look on Bobby's face last night when Mr. T turned and spoke to him by name?"

Rochelle said, "Yeah. That kind of knocked his sox off."

Randy said, "Hey, that's a good one. Bobby Sox."

John laughed and said, "Bobby Sox, that might stick."

Lloyd said, "It about Knocked my sox off. Who would have thought that the leader of the free world would just drop in for a fireside chat?" No comments were made.

They sat around enjoying the morning and John asked Jay and Kathy, "So, what was that job yesterday morning that you guys had if you don't mind me asking?"

"Oh that. That was an easy job. We just had to take out a black widow so to speak. This woman had already married a half dozen men only for them to mysteriously die shortly after the wedding leaving her to inherit all that they had. She was heading for wedding number seven when we intercepted her." Kathy said, "Woman can't resist smelling the flowers."

John said, "Evergreen." Jay nodded.

"You said it worked well." Jay said, "We tried it. We were pleased with the outcome."

Kathy said, "It worked better and faster than we would have guessed."

About that time Moe pulled up. "Hey." He said to all as he walked up to the group. He asked, "Do you have another one of those cups?" He then looked up and pointed at the mini mansion saying, "Man, that's great." He took his cup and found a log to sit on. He continued, "That didn't take you long."

Randy said, "Thanks."

John said, "Don't move. I got something for you." He went to the Scooby Doo van and back.

Everyone but Moe stood up grinning and Moe said, "What is going on?"

John said, "By the power vested in me. Oh, never mind. You seemed to have caught the big cheese's eye and he stopped by last night to give this." He handed Moe his medal of meritorious service.

Moe said, "What? Is Boston pranking me or what?" John said, "Or what."

Moe still didn't understand as he looked at the medal. He looked up at everyone grinning and said, "I don't get it."

Randy said, "Moe. Who is the big cheese or top dog of this country?"

Moe's eyes got big and he said, "No fricking way!"

The whole group said, "Yes way! And he stood right where you parked that log to sit on."

"Holy guacamole." Moe said.

John said, "We all got one. Even Boston and J-Lee."

Moe was having a hard time accepting the fact before John told him of the helicopter and the men in black. "If you don't believe us, go on over and ask Bobby Sox about it."

"Bobby Sox?" Moe asked.

John said, "That fellow with the horses." "Oh Bobby!" Moe said.

"Yea, the big man almost knocked his sox off last night as he got one also." John explained.

"Well, I'll be." Moe said. "This is the real McCoy. It's not a piece of fake jewelry."

"Yes." John said, "But you can't publicize it."

"Why would I want to do that?" Moe said. "I have to stay on the down low to do my work. I don't want anyone to know who I am or what I do. That could be bad for my health."

He started laughing and then they all started laughing with him and everyone settled back in to their seats. Moe was still flipping the medal on the ribbon over and over. He started chuckling. "Maybe I will hang it on my mirror. You know, like those big dice you see all the time."

Mary said, "Really?"

Moe replied, "No, not really. But I do have a special place for it."

After everyone was settled back in and coffee refilled, John said, "So, anything going on over at Topsail?"

Moe replied, "Oh, Yea. We had a visitor last night. A big four by four with New Mexico plates."

"Yes!" John said, "I knew it was all tied together. Did you see the driver?"

"Oh yes." Moe replied, "She made a couple of laps around the building like she wanted to go in but it's all taped up, so she left. The police got a security guy sitting out front also."

"That's good." John said, "I wonder what may be in there that she is after?"

Mary said, "Maybe you could get Mr. Bill to meet you over there Monday so we can have a look and see."

John said, "I will give Mr. Bill a call later and see if we can do that. I have a medal to present to him unceremoniously. Just to be sure, Moe. You said it was a she? Just how good of a look did you get?"

Moe replied, "I was down on the corner by all those lights when she first drove in and it was that bright red hair that caught my eye."

John said, "Yes, double yes! We are positive now. I am going red fishing when we get back. If I have to drive around that loop all day like that container truck did."

Randy asked, "What's with the container truck?"

John explained, "Our target was in a container truck cooking meth. A lab on wheels, so it went around and around she goes, where it stops nobody knows. We finally pin pointed it and at the end of the cook, our target came out and never left the parking lot."

The girls hiked it over to Bobby Sox's to play on the horses. The guys helped Randy build a lean-to porch on the front of the mini mansion. Randy said, "I didn't need a loft over porch. This is easier and cheaper. John, what do you think it is with this wild rose?"

John said, "I think she is the needle that sews our mess all together. I have pictures of her with the Undertaker, the Butcher, State Governors and Washington politicians. She is now supposed to be the new top dog at the casket factory and now she is snooping around Topsail Industries. Maybe there is a midget behind the curtain like on the Wizard of Oz. I wouldn't be surprised."

CHAPTER THIRTEEN

John got a surprise. A stranger's vehicle showed up out in front of Randy's place. A slim fellow in a striped shirt got out. Randy said, "I wonder what this is now?"

John said, "I know." John walked to meet Mr. Stripes. Same old routine. John signed and then received a large brown envelope. Lloyd and Jay and Moe were all wondering what the heck. John came over to the social area and Mr. Stripes vacated the area.

John sat down and opened the envelope and he began to read. The others started to gather around. He finally looked up smiling. "It seems some South American Ranking Official got fed up with his drug running leadership. He left his country and named names as to who is involved and it seems a certain West Coast politician's name was floating in the bowl. Now that the politician is being charged with money laundering and insider trading with a Chinese business. An impeachment investigation has begun and the rats are jumping ship. Including a sudden resignation of two members of the commission."

"This is good." Randy said, "Now maybe we will get the real jobs to take care of our little party. All we can do is wait and see if they come up on our abort list."

"In the meantime," John said, "I am going to find our wild rose and see if she leads us to the others. Oh, and by the way, there is a fifteen-million-dollar bounty now on that Country's crooked leader. Any takers?"

Randy said, "No way. If he has a fifteen-million-dollar bounty, imagine what he has to pay for protection just so his own people don't do him in. That is a viper's nest I would not advise stepping into."

John also said, "Jay, you guys up for a trip to Belize?"

Jay replied, "Belize, when?"

"Sunday evening." John told him.

Jay said, "Wait until the girls get back for sure but I am up for it."

Randy said, "Lucky you."

Moe and Lloyd had no comment. John said, "You and Rochelle are busy right now and Lloyd and Moe have to watch out for Red and any new weapons exchanges between those two neighboring businesses and I have to call Bill for a meeting tomorrow on our way in. I will just have to hunt for Red later. At least we know she is around."

The girls finally made it back to the camp and John told Mary about the trip back south. That made her happy. She said, "We are not leaving there until I see some of the old pyramids."

Kathy said, "I'm good to go." So, it's settled. The rest of the afternoon passed with talk and speculation about worldly politics and the upcoming assignment that John and Mary and Jay and Kathy were at task to take.

"This is weird." John said, "We have orders to go down there, but we have no target as of yet."

Jay said, "Maybe it's like that race. You get to one point and then you get directions to the next point and so on."

Mary said, "Some of my point is to see some sights this time and not just a cave." John chuckled at that. He thought she was right. All work and no play, does not a happy camper make.

Night came fast and so did the morning. The group did the Little Full Gospel Church Service then afterwards, John and Mary and Jay and Kathy headed back to the city. The others would go in on Monday. John had managed to get a hold of Ranger Bill and arranged to meet at two p.m. and they did.

The security officer started to challenge them until he saw the Ranger's badge and ID and he crawfished out of the way. Upon entering the building, they went to the offices. John said out loud, "What would Red be looking for or wanting to hide?" Ranger Bill started up the computer. John and Mary started going through the sales files and Jay and Kathy started going through the purchase orders.

It didn't take long and Kathy said, "How many girls were supposed to be brought here the other night?"

John replied, "Thirty."

Kathy said, "A couple of weeks before that, how many?" She was shuffling through the purchase orders.

John replied, "Twenty-four."

Kathy laid the first purchase order down and said, "Thirty bolts of fabric at three-thousand-dollars a bolt." She laid down another purchase order, "Twenty-four bolts of fabric at three-thousand-dollars a bolt."

John and Bill looked at each other and then Bill asked, "Who did they buy these bolts of fabric from?"

Kathy said, "According to this, it says Ling-Ling Imports, Los Angeles."

John said, "The Chinese connection."

Bill said, "Hand me those invoices. I'm not going to chance them disappearing."

John said, "I wonder if that is what Red was interested in?" Bill asked, "Who is Red?"

John replied, "A loose end, but we are working on that."

Kathy said, "You want me to keep back tracking here?"

Bill said, "No. I will have our people come and do a long-range back track now that we have something to look for."

John said, "You know if you go to the pipe coating facility and back tracked every shipment of pipe from the 'Kasyade' you will find a coinciding invoice there."

Bill looked at John and said, "I like how you think. I will get a team to both locations first thing in the morning. I sure would like to know who is running Ling-Ling."

John said, "I second that. Maybe the paper trail will lead somewhere." As they were locking up, John said, "Oh, hold up Bill." He trotted out to Betsy and grabbed something and came back. He looked at Bill and said, "I was directed to present this to you." He handed him the medal of meritorious service.

Bill looked at the medal and said, "I have seen one of these before and if I'm not mistaken, only one person hands these out. So, how did you get it?"

John smiled and said, "By sitting at a campfire."

Bill looked at him quizzically then said, "Just who are you people?"

John flipped his I.D. and said, "Department of Agriculture." He started laughing.

Bill looked up and smiled and said, "I am not even going to go there. Whoever you are, keep it up." John winked and they left. Bill was just standing there, eye balling the ribbon and medal in his hand and then watched that black sixty-three Impala roll out of the parking lot. He said in a low voice, "Some good guys do exist." He smiled, dropped the medal in his shirt pocket and patted it twice and started laughing and walked to his ride. As he sat in his car thinking, he said to himself, "Department of Agriculture my ass." He started laughing again as he drove out of there. John had his GPS tracker on all the way home with no luck.

Jay and Kathy detoured over to their place to repack some travel cloths before going back to John and Mary's. Once there, John showed them the pictures of Red and company. Kathy said, "She sure seems to get around."

John pulled the one with the Undertaker, Red, and the Butcher. John said, "This is the core of all that we have been working on lately.

There was a knock on the door. John looked out and started grinning. "The limo is here."

"Limo, what limo?" Jay and Kathy both asked. John said, "It only gets better."

He started grabbing bags. The limo driver took them back to the same private hanger. Jay and Kathy said nothing until they were in the air. "This is nice." Jay said.

John and Mary just grinned at them. John said, "Just sit back and enjoy the ride." As they were flying over the gulf, John said,

"The last time we did this, we were chasing a target. So, at the moment we are flying blind."

Jay said, "Are we really blind? Remember the other night and Mr. T. and Company just came in off the street."

John said, "That's right. So, how did they know we were where we were? There are no street cameras or any other identifier out in the country but they knew where to land and where to find us. Are we being tracked like our targets?"

Jay said, "That could be kind of a scary thought if the wrong people were doing it."

John agreed. They felt the plane throttle back and begin the decent down to Belize International. John said, "I presume we are going to a hotel. It's too late to send us out to San Pedro by water taxi. We don't even know yet where we are going and I am not too fond of blind traveling. No telling what you will run into."

The plane taxied back to the same spot it had parked last time they were here. They took a cab into Belize City to a hotel for the night. Once in their rooms, Jay and Kathy knocked on John and Mary's door. Mary let them in. John and Jay were still discussing the disadvantages of not knowing the where's and the what's. Mary was telling Kathy of the clear water and beach out on the barrier reef in San Pedro. Mary's device vibrated and she looked at the incoming message.

Mary said, "We are to go to a car rental place called Texas Jacks and pick up a vehicle. Then we are to go to San Ignacio over near the Guatemala border."

"Then what?" John asked.

"That's it." Mary said.

Jay said, "So, we are to just get up and go somewhere? Then what or for what?"

Kathy said, "I hope that someone is not just sending us on a wild goose chase."

They settled in for the night unsure of what tomorrow would bring. The next morning after breakfast, they took the courtesy car and arrived at Texas Jacks. Jack the owner of the car rental was a retired man who kind of fell in love with Belize so he moved down there. When he realized there were no car rentals to speak of with all the tourists who came south to see the sights, he found himself a niche. He shipped a few cars down in containers and he was in business. He could charge seventy-five to a hundred dollars a day and that covered well over any out-of-pocket expenses he may encounter. The group took a small SUV loaded their gear and plugged in the GPS for directions to San Ignacio and they drove out of Belize City in a westerly direction. They drove through the coastal flat land and eventually found some small rolling hills. The vegetation changed from mangrove and palm to a more forested scenery of hardwoods mixed with pine and still a few scattered palm trees.

As they entered San Ignacio, Mary's device went off again and she looked at it. She looked at John and said, "I'm going sightseeing. Finally."

John said, "Do what?"

Mary said, "Keep on driving. We cross into Guatemala shortly. Next stop is Tikal."

Kathy said, "Oh wow. Isn't that like an ancient city center full of pyramids?"

John replied, "Well, looks like another check mark on that bucket list of yours."

They drove on, arriving near noon and they checked into the Park Inn. "Now that we are here, what do we do?" Jay asked.

John replied, "When in Rome, do as the Roman's do. We go sightseeing, what else?"

The group left the Inn and walked the mile or so long path to the center cluster of pyramids that had been reclaimed from the jungles. The most magnificent were the Kings and Queens pyramids facing each other at what seemed to be a football fields length of grass between them. Some kind of Royal Plaza. Standing on the top of the Kings Pyramid, Mary hooked the heal of her tennis shoe and pulled her foot out and let the shoe fall. It fell to the next step, and then the next and on and on occasionally skipping steps until it came to a rest at the bottom. Wow, the group thought. Be very careful not to lose your footing. These pyramids could be deadly.

After Mary reclaimed her shoe, the group walked around and looked at other structures. Some were cleared while others were overgrown. Soon the girls said, "Okay. We have seen enough." They took the keys and went into town.

John and Jay were approaching a smaller flat top pyramid. All the tourists were out by now. The woods were alive. John stopped in his tracks looking into a group walking away from them and Jay asked him, "What's wrong?"

John said, "I saw a face and that face looked like our fine doctor's face."

Jay said, "No way. What would our doctor be doing down here?"

John said, "You are probably right." They went ahead and climbed the tree top high pyramid. This one was also different in step height. These steps were eighteen to twenty inches in height.

Jay said, "These builders must have been high steppers."

John laughed and said, "High steppers for sure."

Once on top, they could hear the howler monkey's cutting up in the jungle. John's device vibrated. A message from Mary. John urgent incoming message. Put on your locator sunglasses and you will see your target. He showed the message to Jay and they both reached for the case on their belts and pulled out their special GPS sunglasses they use to keep track of each other in crowded places. To the south was a not quite middle-aged man busy with his phone. John and Jay both milled around on top of that pyramid each taking turns watching that man. Finally, John asked Jay, "Is this that fella's office? He seems to be doing nothing but business and not site seeing." Jay agreed, not a normal tourist.

John told Jay, "We have orders from headquarters." When the man finally turned to walk back over to the steps down, John could not believe his eyes. He got a blood rush to the face. He was looking at the face of one who has been on his desk looking back at him for way too long. Taking his first step, John boosted his momentum. Just as Mary's shoe didn't stop until the bottom, so was the same results with the Butcher. By the time he hit the bottom, there was blood sprays on multiple steps. He was gone before an ambulance or a medical team arrived. One of the park rangers said that a tourist falls a couple of times a year. Some survive and some don't. This one did not.

John was still jittery with adrenaline as they walked the long walk back to the Inn. Jay said, "I can't say I have ever seen anything like that before."

John said, "I am going to have to check that box on my bucket list."

Jay asked, "What box?"

John said grinning, "Death by pyramid."

Jay laughed and said, "Man, you have got some sense of humor."

They were back at the room before the girls made it back from shopping in town. Jay said, "What now? Go home?"

John said, "We will leave tomorrow. I plan on hitting that swimming pool after a while."

The girls finally made it back and John told Mary and Kathy that Mary's shoe came out better than the Butcher did. Mary said, "The Butcher? And I missed it?"

Jay said, "You know how it is. What's that song? Oh yea, Girls just want to have fun."

John said, "On a more serious note, I want to know if that man was tagged somehow or did they somehow figure out a way to lock our locator glasses to a person's cell phone?"

Jay replied, "That may be it. The whole time we were on old flat top, that man was on his device."

"Doing business, I'm sure." John added.

Jay told Mary, "You know, before we climbed up on flat top, John thought he saw our commission doctor in a group of tourists that we walked past as they headed in the opposite direction."

Then John realized, "I bet that is the same way Mr. T. knew where all of us were at the other night. Technology is getting kind of scary."

Jay said, "I'll second that. I may start to think to leave my shades at home or in the vehicle."

John said, "Face it. The bad guys and the good guys can both run, but you can no longer hide."

Not only did the girls buy some colored hand-woven blankets, they also had fresh fruit and sourdough bread. A meal was made and topped off with a fresh fruit salad. A while later, John said, "I'm ready for a swim." The group suited up and hit the pool. Out in the middle, John told Jay, "Watch your step here, it's a gradual drop off from shallow to deep."

Jay said, "Let's get the girls." The guys chuckled.

First Kathy came and stepped over the edge but she caught herself. Then Mary came walking out across the pool towards the other three. She sank out of sight. Then she broke the surface and all were laughing. She said, "I see how it is." She started laughing with them.

Later they were sitting around the room recycling the day's events and all the lights went out. "Oh yea." Mary said, "They shut off the generators at nine, so if you want lights, that is what the candles are for."

John said, "I don't think I need any lights. The unexpected excitement today has me kind of off and feeling tired. I think I will go lay down."

Mary said, "I am with you." Jay and Kathy did the same.

No new orders came the next morning so the crew decided to head back to Belize. They stopped off at a few more pyramid sites in Belize before making it back to Belize City. They went back to Texas Jacks and returned the vehicle. He then offered them a ride to the airport as a courtesy in hopes that when and if they came back, they would prefer to use his services for transportation while there.

Texas Jack dropped the crew off at the hanger building where the jet was waiting for them. The stewardess rounded up the flight crew and as Ranger Bill once told John in two shakes of a stick, they were out of there. Once in the air, John and Company again pondered how a target could get identified with their GPS locator glasses that they use to keep track of each other. This is something John would have to see what Boston's thoughts were on the subject.

They watched the Texas coastline slide by under them on their descent down over Galveston Bay as they approached Hobby International. The 'Kasyade' and barge load of pipe is still anchored where it was when the coast guard seized it and carted the crew off to jail. John smiled to himself thinking that with no ship to smuggle with and now no smuggler to give the ship or ships direction. The Butcher was not only out of business, he was out of life. No more evil could come forth from him.

John's thoughts drifted back to the remnants. Wild Rose and the Undertaker. There was no means to prove that the Butcher was aborted. By all rights and reports, it appeared as a tragic tourist accident unless the doctor was there and recognized any of them. Time would tell on that matter. Now all John knew was another photo to take off of his stack and hope and pray that the Butcher didn't have a twin or more like Ricky, Dicky, and Micky. He soon cast that thought out of his mind. All he knew now was one down, two to go.

Mary touched John on the shoulder and asked him, "John, are you ready to go?"

John looked around and they were already in the hanger and John said, "Wow. I didn't even know we had touched down."

Mary laughed and said, "Yea, you kind of had that zombie look." That got a laugh out of Jay and Kathy. After loading up in the Limo, Mary said, "You think the driver would stop at Taqueria Del Sol?"

John laughed and said, "All you can do is ask him."

She asked him and he did stop. Back on the freeway, five cream puffs were disappearing at the same time. Smiles all around.

Back at the cubby hole, Mary was trying to figure out who to send the report to or not. This whole operation was carried out in a new parameter. Jay and Kathy high tailed it on back to their place of residence. John took the pictures of the Butcher off of the table and dropped them into a file 'Aborted' and smiled. Finally, John looked at Mary and asked, "How did you know to tell Jay and I to put on our glasses to locate the Butcher?"

Mary replied, "I received an unidentified message that came with the commissions logo but I don't have an identifier on it."

John said, "Just put 'abort successful' period. No names, no places, just mission complete. If they have a problem with that, then they will have to contact us for more details." That's what Mary did and the rest of the day was uneventful.

The following morning at the table, John told Mary that they are both broke in now. She looked at him and said, "What are you talking about John?"

John grinned pointing to the coffee pot and he said, "That, and the bed. I sure slept good last night."

Mary grinned and replied, "Me too."

John set about cleaning and inventorying the gear and Mary set about cleaning the house and catching up on the laundry from nearly a week of moving around. First out to the Rock and then back only to catch a ride south and out of the country. By mid-morning the chores were done. John asked Mary, "You ready to go surprise Boston and J-Lee with those medals?"

"Oh, heck yea. I forgot about those." Mary said.

John replied, "Well, let's armor up and get going." They dressed and grabbed their gear bag and headed out for Betsy. Once on the road, Mary reminded John to plug in this GPS tracker. That thought made John wonder how Lloyd and Moe were doing on post at the coffin factory. He was going to call and then decided if they had news, they would call him so he just drove on over to J-Lee's bookstore.

J-Lee was in the showroom when they walked in and he greeted them. They made their way back to his office. He asked if Moe was back at the ranch and John said, "As far as I know he was doing night watch over at the casket factory."

"Oh." J-Lee responded, "I can't keep up with him since you put him to work."

John laughed and said, "Well there may be a light at the end of the tunnel. If you do some research, I bet you will find our Mr. Butcher the body smuggler fell off of a pyramid while sightseeing in Central America."

J-Lee said, "You have got to be pulling my leg."

John said, "Look it up. Google tourist death in Tikal Guatemala recently and see what comes up."

J-Lee was typing in his computer and then sat back and said, "Well, look at that. Pure dee accident. Saves you the trouble of chasing him down."

John just smiled and said, "We just got back from Belize yesterday."

Before J-Lee could find his way out of his confusion, John said, "You think you could get Boston over here for a chat?"

J-Lee picked up his phone and speed dialed. J-Lee spoke to Boston and hung up. "He will be here in a few minutes."

"Good." John said.

The green light on J-Lee's desk came on and he pushed a button and Boston came walking in. He looked at John and said, "I thought that shiny black sixty-three Impala out front looked familiar", as they shook hands. He then said, "The only thing missing is the pizza you all had."

J-Lee said, "Well, we can take care of that easy enough." He wrote out a note, buzzed his clerk who came in and took the note and left. J-Lee then called Boston over to his desk to show him the report of an unfortunate accident.

Boston said, "Well now. That solves one of your problems now, doesn't it?"

John said, "Not really." J-Lee and Boston looked at him curiously. John began by asking Boston, "Is there a way that the powers that be can track a pair of locator sunglasses?"

"First." Boston asked, "Sunglasses?" John had to explain how him and Mary had proximity glasses so they could not loose each other in a crowd. Boston said, "That's sick. Can I see?" John handed him his pair and when he put them on, there was a dot to his right lens towards Mary as he turned in various directions the dot went high center in front, low center behind him, and right lens, left lens for whatever side she was on. He took them off and looked them over and said, "Why didn't I think of these things? I like."

John laughed and said, "Can these be hacked?"

Boston replied, "Hacked? What do you mean?"

"Just what I said." John replied. "Can someone tune in to our glasses to know where we are at any particular time, and can our glasses get tuned to a particular person's electronic device so we know where a target is without the use of the regular satellite tracking that gives us locations of our abort targets. I need some answers if my crew's safety is at risk or not."

Boston studied John's proximity glasses and was doing some serious thinking. He said, "Those are good questions. Say you're out in a remote area, how would it pinpoint a specific spot? A cell phone only pings off of a tower. That gets you in the neighborhood, but now say a person standing in a room or across the street. No, they don't do that. Unless there is a new and improved secret global positioning satellite not servicing the public sector. The kind of troop tracking on combat missions now, that may be possible if your glasses are tuned to a certain top-secret frequency."

John said, "That might make a little sense and it would be out of the full commission's control. Only top personal has military clearance. Politicians get left out of the workings of the military. Can't see a senator butting heads with a general on classified operations. That makes me feel a little better."

The green light on J-Lee's desk came on and he pushed the button and in came the clerk carrying two big pizza boxes labeled 'Bibba's'. John's face lit up. Once the lid was raised on the first pizza box, all conversation stopped. After finishing his second slice of pizza, J-Lee's curiosity got the better of him and he had to ask, "John, were you on that pyramid?" John just winked at him and smiled.

Boston stopped chewing long enough to look at J-Lee and then back at John and back to J-Lee as he just put two and two together. Mary saw him looking and said, "Yes Boston. Yes to what you are thinking."

John said, "Oh yea. I brought you guys a souvenir."

J-Lee asked, "From Belize?"

John replied, "No, not quite."

Boston asked, "Something from Guatemala?"

"Nope again." John said and Mary started laughing. John continued, "From a campfire chat last weekend." Boston and J-Lee were both lost at this point. John said, "Okay, long story short. You guy's work with us does not go unnoticed."

J-Lee said, "Uh Oh."

John said, "It's not like that. We are all but singing around a campfire when we heard a helicopter land up by the highway. We can't see it so we just took it as a life flight or something. Next thing I know a man in black is calling my name."

J-Lee said, "Aw hell."

John said, "Seriously. He was not alone. The next thing I know, Mr. Don T. is eating some of my little Smokey sticks I made from that Nilgai and he told me to deliver this." Mary handed him two medals. "One for you J-Lee, and one for you Boston."

They both eyeballed the medals and J-lee asked John, "Are you serious?"

John said, "As a heart attack."

J-Lee was typing on his computer and held his medal up to the screen and said, "Look at this Boston."

John said, "Yea, the big cheese shows up in the middle of the night and said that he cannot publicly give you guys a medal for your work, then before he walks away, he gets his man in black to open his briefcase and he hands out thirteen medals and then walks off into the darkness and was gone. He even gave Moe one for the work he helped in busting that human trafficking ring."

J-Lee was grinning as he looked around his office for a place to display his new souvenir. John said, "These are a private affair, not to make public on orders of Mr. Don T. himself." J-Lee and Boston both agreed.

J-Lee said, "My office is not open to the public so I can hang it anywhere I so desire."

Boston said, "I may do the same thing." They both stood and shook hands with John and Mary thanking them for the chance to help them.

John then said, "That's exactly still a good question I have about all of this. You guys have never been mentioned in any of our reports as far as Abort missions or any other reason. So, how did Mr. T. know your names and association with us?"

J-Lee said, "It really does not matter to me." Boston on the other hand had a few reasons to be concerned and was not thrilled at not knowing who knows what he does in his free time. "Well, it is what it is." Mary said, "Not a dang thing anyone could do about it." They all agreed and then emptied the last Bibba's box.

John said, "I don't think I could ever get tired of this stuff." The group laughed as John was rubbing his stomach.

Boston said, "I would sure like to meet that fellow or lady who came up with your guy's locator glasses. That was impressive."

John added, "And the one who figured out how to tweak them to locate our abort targets without full blown satellite tracking system."

Boston said, "Yea, that's like flying under the radar."

"Exactly." John said.

Finally, Mary said as she stood, "I need to walk a little. I think I will go and find that last book of that series that I was reading. I think it was called The Final Day."

J-Lee said, "Hold up, let me look it up for you." He typed into his computer. He looked back up and said, "Yes, we do have it. It is located."

Mary interrupted and said, "In the same location as the others." He grinned and nodded and Mary said, "I can find it. Thank you, J-Lee." She headed for the door.

"So." John said to J-Lee, "I guess you don't need to chase the Butcher's shadow anymore now that he is out of the picture."

"That." J-Lee said opening a file, "Remains to be seen. That import business out in California, Ling-Ling Imports. Turns out to be a subsidiary of a subsidiary of an industrial metals importer owned by the husband of a certain California Politician."

John replied, "You mean the one who's personal driver reports to the Chinese embassy once a week for the last twenty years? The same one that is soon to be impeached and kicked out of office?"

J-Lee said, "The one and the same."

John said, "I will pass that along to Ranger Bill when I catch up to him. Speaking of catching up, I better go catch up with my side kick." He bid farewell and headed for the door.

Mary was waiting at the main counter when he came out. She waved her new book at him and he grinned. He said, "Well, that is two medals down and none to go." After they got into Betsy he eased out of the lot and was heading back across town and his GPS tracker blipped. He said, "There you are Red. I knew you couldn't hide forever." She was at max range but it appeared she was heading towards the coffin factory area. John detoured and headed for the new found target. He grinned at Mary and said, "Before this is over, we just might get Boston's tracker back. First things first."

He called Lloyd to let him know the Wild Rose was heading in his direction. Lloyd said he was close by the coffin factory and he would go sit in a nearby parking lot to watch for her. Unlike Topsail, there were no indoor, out of the weather, loading docks. Just a recessed dock high pocket between two businesses. No place to hide a vehicle. John's blood was flowing in anticipation of the chance to pull the stored mapping from the tracker still on Red's big four by four.

An odd thought came to mind as John neared the coffin store. He asked Mary, "What do you think the odds are that Rose is there to pick out a casket for the recently deceased Butcher?"

Mary said, "Now would that not be ironic? They still think he died accidently. Not a clue we have them in our sights."

John grinned and repeated, "Not a clue."

John's device buzzed and he answered. It was Lloyd. "One big four by four present and accounted for."

John said, "Good." And he disconnected. Then he told Mary, "I don't want Rose to think she remembers you from driving out in front of her out in New Mexico. So, I will pull Betsy up to the four by four and I will run in for a brochure this time while you download all the tracking information that you can get out of that tracker, then clean it to start fresh from there. We can get more information at a later time."

Mary was already fidgeting with the GPS tracker before John came to a stop in front of the casket company and got out and ran inside. When John came back out, he hopped into Betsy and said, "This may not have been a smart move."

Mary asked, "Why is that?"

John said, "Good thing you were away from the building and could not be seen. Rose was staring at Betsy like maybe remembering what kind of vehicle pulled out in front of her in New Mexico."

Mary said, "Could be, and could be she has good taste in old cars."

John laughed and said, "Let's hope for the later." He drove around and found Lloyd and told him what happened and told him, "The next time we need to download that tracker, we will use your vehicle or we do a walk by." Then John filled Lloyde in on how the Butcher met his demise and the thing with identifying their target out in the country with monkeys howling and all.

Lloyd asked, "Do monkey's howl? I have never heard of that."

John said, "Well, those down in Central America sure do." Then he asked, "No new word on weapons sales?"

Lloyd told him, "My friend says that it is slower than molasses in the winter time."

John said, "Good. Let's hope it stays that way. Keep watch and I'll check in with Moe later." He then pointed Betsy toward the cubby hole and left.

He was halfway back to the house when 'ping' on Mary's device. "Really?" John stated.

Mary looked at her device and said, "It seems we have a wayward Afghan bomb maker drifted in from Mexico and is now recruiting Muslims for some kind of explosive event."

"Great." John said, "And his hangout?"

Mary said, "It's the downtown Islamic building of course." "Really." John said, "The heart of the city."

Mary said, "Yep, just off of main street."

John said, "That's right across the street from some attorney's I know. Their office is on the sixth floor looking down on that Islamic building."

Mary said, "Useful?"

John replied, "No, they are not useful. We won't even go there."

Mary said, "Well, maybe we can at least park in front of their building."

John relented and said, "That might work."

They parked Betsy and waited for their target to come out of the three-story building. The meter maid passed by twice but said nothing as the vehicle was not empty. Finally, they caught sight of the target walking out and going east. John fed a few quarters in the meter and him and Mary followed their target toward Main. They crossed the street and followed to Rail Stop. He boarded the Metro Rail going south and so did they. As it passed by Memorial Park Mary passed by the bomb maker with a yellow jacket in hand. She faked a stumble and stung him on his upper leg. He looked at her and then he looked at his leg beginning to realize something was seriously wrong and looked back up at her in total surprise. In his world women were nothing. He came to the wrong world. Mary smiled at him and walked away. The next stop, John and Mary got off just in time to catch the return Metro Rail back to downtown and Betsy before the meter expired.

Again, John complained about the old satellite system. If they had not a visual, their target could have been miles away before the next ping. Mary said, "I wonder how many times Mr. Boom is going to ride back and forth on the rails before someone tries to wake him up?"

John grinned and said, "That would make a good trivia question. How many round-trip rides can a dead man ride before getting kicked off of the train?"

Mary said, "That's a morbid question to ask."

John replied, "I can think of worse."

Back downtown, it only took John and Mary a couple of minutes to get back to Betsy. The meter maid was working her way back toward them. When they backed out of the slot, the expired flag popped up on the meter. "Perfect timing." John said to which Mary grinned. They headed back to the cubby hole which was not far. Once Betsy was put to bed, they walked home from the parking facility. John eager to retrieve what map information he could from the data grab from the tracker on the Wild Rose's four by four. John said, "I cannot believe the luck our tracker would actually follow us back to the city."

Mary said, "I thought that thing done high tailed it to California."

John wasted no time once back home. Mary filed the report for the successful abortion on Mr. Boom. John was finishing loading the map into the computer. "Kingwood." John said.

"What?" Mary asked.

"She must be staying in Kingwood. That would be why I could not pick her up around the city. That is well out of the tracker's range. We have a location in Kingwood and here's the coffin factory. It also shows a couple of trips to Topsail Industries. Oh, and look at this one. It's a funeral home. Maybe there is going to be a funeral, unless this is some other sort of smuggling operation." John said.

Mary replied, "That will be easy enough to find out."

John said, "If we have to attend a funeral, we will have to hitch a ride. Don't want Red to spot Betsy again."

Mary looked on the link for the funeral home site that the tracker had located. "Thank you, Red. Not only do we know your home in New Mexico, now we know your hang out right here in our own backyard. Just give us a 'ping' and we got your butt with no need of the big eye in the sky."

John just looked up and smiled at her. It was not often he ever just heard her thinking out loud. Finally, she said, "It appears to be a real funeral ceremony and the man is going to be planted in that little cemetery west of downtown by the Bayou. It's the same place where Howard Hughes is laid to rest."

John said, "I wonder if the Butcher was in a family business or is this something that he just put together himself?"

Mary said, "Now that we know his name was Farr, we can search the link and find if he has a twin."

John said, "You never know after our deal with those identical triplets."

"God." Mary said, "I would hate to even think that."

Again, John laughed and said, "You just never know."

Mary said, "I will soon enough." She was already typing in a search on her device.

John was still looking at the tracker trail backing up in time when he said, "Well, look at this. Our wild rose has also done a drive by of the pipe coating facility. It does not show that she entered, but just did a drive by like she was riding around the block at Topsail Industries."

Mary said, "How would she even know of those places if she had only worked with the Undertaker?"

John said, "It's what I have been saying all along. The three of them acted like one big happy family."

"But still." Mary said, "A big operation to be working here in Texas and only have the puppet master pulling the strings from out in California."

John said, "I intend to cut those strings and let the puppet fall like humpty dumpty and scatter the pieces so not to be put back together again."

Mary said, "Well, it appears Farr has no immediate family stateside. His mother was mid-eastern decent and his father was Russian. Both were killed in a bombing of a city in Syria. Looks like he had friends in high places that must have pulled the right strings to get him over here and then get him citizenship. No mention of siblings that I can find."

John said, "That makes it more the interesting." "Why?" Mary asked.

John said, "No family to be at the funeral. Let's see who's sandbox he was playing in. Who is going to show up for the services. We need to get Jay and Kathy to set up and take photos at the chapel services as attendee's leave and then have Lacy and Lloyde do the same at the graveside services. That way we don't miss anyone who may be trying to stay incognito. Then we can compare photos and see who is who at the zoo."

"Sounds like a plan." Mary said. "I will call them and let them know the schedule so they have time to site out a good place to photo from."

John said, "I have the Wild Rose's habitat at Kingwood, her favorite eating places and where she does her grocery shopping. Any place, any time, we are ready when we get the orders. Now we just sit back and watch like a cat watching a mouse. The funeral services are scheduled for tomorrow so all we can do now is make some popcorn and watch a movie to finish the evening before going to bed."

CHAPTER FOURTEEN

The following morning was a cinnamon oatmeal and coffee kind of morning as John pondered the upcoming event. Randy called to let him know they were in town. John said, "Perfect timing." He explained that he might need them to give them a ride to the funeral and back. Betsy would stand out like a sore thumb if Red laid eyes on her again.

Randy laughed and said, "Sure thing." He would be over in a few hours to pick them up.

John asked, "How's the mini mansion coming along?" Randy said, "Let there be light. Flip a switch."

John said, "That's great."

Randy said, "The indoor kitchen is up and running."

John started singing, "Moving on up, moving on up to the east side of town."

Randy cracked up and said, "You need to buy a new compass dude. I'm on the west side of the street." They both laughed.

"You can now bring your personal fan in warmer weather. We can run you out an extension cord to old Scooby Doo."

John said, "What no A/C hanging out the back window?"

Randy said, "I don't think so."

John said, "Okay then. I will see you in a little while." They disconnected.

John waited until just after services started before entering the chapel lobby. No one was present so he went over to the register and took a photo of which ever attendees took time to sign it. He then entered the chapel and sat on the back pew. There were between fifteen and twenty persons in there. As the ceremony came to an end, John eased back out the door before the wild rose had time to stand and turn to leave. She did not see him go. He went to the back of the line of cars where Randy and Rochelle and Mary were waiting for him. John said, "Closed casket. I guess those sharp ninety-degree stones really messed him up."

Randy asked, "Sharp stones?"

John said, "Yes. Death by pyramid." Randy said, "Oh, okay." And left it at that.

They followed the crowd over to the grave side services and watched from a distance around the corner. John got a good photo of the front row mourners. He said, "Why do all these faces look familiar? I hope the other two teams get close up headshots for a positive identification. Let's head back to the cubby hole." And they left.

Once back at the cubby hole, John put his pictures in the laptop and zoomed in and went down the line. Ms. Rose, Mr. Undertaker, California Chinese connection political chauffeur, and none other than the politician's rich husband. Crazy crew. Mary said, "I don't see the doctor in the crowd, do you?"

John said, "I will look at the register." He loaded that picture of signatures and scanned down through it. "Evidently there was no doctor in the house. I don't know what to think about that. We thought we saw him down in Guatemala but that could have been someone else." Looking back at the list of names John said, "Would this Mister Yekun be our Undertaker fellow?"

Mary said, "As soon as Jay and Lloyd send their pictures of going and leaving, we should be able to cross reference the photos to names by search of names on the link."

"That sounds easy enough." John said.

About that time, both Rochelle's and Mary's device went 'Ping.' Everyone just looked at each other for a second. Mary said, "Crap, John look at this." It was the same face as one of those on his computer screen. "Well, Mr. Moneybags otherwise known as a politician's husband, you are in for a surprise. You can't take that money with you."

Rochelle said, "That's weird. We got the driving Chinese importing spy."

John said, "We better get before they leave town." The group headed out. At the moment it seemed they were both going to the same place, but for insurance in case they split up, John and Mary took Betsy.

They headed west and John was trying to figure why then he remembered the little airport out at the Bear Creek. As they were getting close, the next 'ping' was farther out west. John pushed the pedal down some saying to Mary, "They are going to West Houston Airport way out at Brookshire." He passed through Katy then jumped over on ninety and Randy was struggling to keep up but he did. They pulled into the airport, got out at the big hanger and watched as a small jet took to the runway and vacated the area.

Randy said, "Now what?"

Mary said, "Well, hello there."

John and Randy looked around and there was the young stewardess from the previous trips. She said, "Come this way please. The engines are running."

They grabbed their bags and stepped through a door and there she be. The same jet that took them south. They trotted to the door and climbed in. The stewardess pulled the door closed and sealed it. She turned to the cockpit and said, "Roll." They went out in hot pursuit.

Once at altitude and the group all settled in, the captain came back to address them. He said, "We are on the edge of mach one. We will overtake the other jet. We will land before they arrive and you will be in their private hanger waiting for their arrival. We will be outside of that hanger refueled and waiting for your return. Their pilots won't interfere. We will be in communication with them on a sub channel on the radio."

John just smiled and leaned his chair back for the rest of the ride.

The girls were chatting and Randy was looking out the window watching the world go buy underneath them and John was thinking of how to cut these two strings from the puppet master. Then he considered the possibility of Mr. Moneybags as the puppet master himself, and Mr. Chauffeur as possibly the head of Ling-Ling imports. If that was the case, this was a major abort mission. In the timing of the 'Pings', every thirty-minutes of the four-and-a-half-hour flight, they had passed well ahead of the other craft they started following from Brookshire west Houston airport. Arriving at a small airport south of Los Angeles near the Marine Base.

John was considering the ways and means of an abortion technique as to not draw any attention. He told the girls to have their tranquilizer darts ready to knock out any personnel that may be waiting inside the hangar. John then told them, "We are going to walk right on in there like we own the place and if confronted by anyone, we will tell them we were summoned to meet the arriving jet from Texas."

The jet pulled up beside a single craft hanger whose door was wide open. They disembarked and their jet then taxied over to the fuel depot for refueling. The group strolled into the hanger and headed over to the Limo that was parked off to one side out of the crafts wingtip reach. There was a small office and restroom on the same side at the back of the hanger. John said, "I am going to go have a look." He had his silenced pistol in his hand when he opened the door. Inside the office sat two young men with full Mohawk haircuts.

The sight of the Mohawk set John in motion. As the two realized too late that it was not the expected person coming through the door and they were fumbling for their weapons when John placed two shots in each one's head. He then checked the closet and restroom. No more Mohawks. Randy stuck his head in the door and looked. He said, "Are you hogging all the fun or what?" "Or what." John said, "It was the team of Mohawk heads that made the mistake of a heart shot and not a headshot when they tried to take me down or I might not be here. I'm not giving them second chances."

Mary came over and said, "I believe they have arrived. A jet just touched down."

John said, "You girls go wait outside. Walk around the back of the hanger until the jet drops them off or pulls in whichever. Then come around from each side to make sure our targets don't get spooked and go running outside." So, they did and he asked Randy to make sure the keys were not in the Limo and to lock all the doors.

Randy ran and checked for the keys and pushed the lock button wiping the button and the door grip with his shirt tail. He went back into the office where John had moved the two Mohawk heads behind a desk and left the legs showing in a position of passionate pleasure at first glance. Toes up on bottom and toes down on top. John said, "That ought to throw them off for a second."

Randy said, "No keys in the Limo."

John pointed to the far wall by the restroom. "Check out that key cabinet."

Randy did so and sure enough, one set of car keys, a desk key, and a file cabinet key. Randy said, "Who locks the desk and file cabinets anymore?"

John checked the desk, it was locked. "People with things to hide I suppose and we need to have a look before we depart this fine facility."

At this point, the whine of the turbine engines approached. John cracked the office door to see the small Jet turn and coast right on into the hanger stopping the front wheels on a white square painted on the floor. John said, "It looks like this guy has done this a time or two." He turned to Randy and said, "Here. A paper towel wrapped pistol. He had another just like it." He smiled and said, "It seems like our Mohawk friends here killed the wrong people."

Randy laughed as he backed into the restroom with the door cracked open but he was in darkness. John saw the ramp come down and the two men emerge. They came straight away to the office. The China man first came in with money bags on his tail.

The China man said something and then stopped in his tracks and started laughing. He turned to Mr. Money bags pointing at the legs protruding from behind the desk. Before he could say anything, the office door closed behind him and Mr. China man's eyes got big. About that time, Mr. Politician's husband's eyes got big as Randy pushed the bathroom door open. Both men froze where they stood. Mr. Money bags was first to regather his wits about him. He said, "I don't know what is going on, but I believe we can come to a mutual agreement on things here."

John said, "You think so? What about that jet?"

Mr. Money bags said, "You want my Jet?"

John just looked at him. Then John said, "If I wanted to go somewhere but I can't officially leave stateside, can you get me there?" Mr. Money bags began to feel at ease. Then John said, "If I wanted to bring someone to America or a group of someone's, how could I do this?"

Mr. Money bags was starting to see dollar signs so he went on to say, "A couple of people, we can fly. A group of any size, we can ship."

John asked the Chinese driver, "In containers?"

The China man hesitated and Money bags said, "Does it matter how we get them here for you?"

John then asked, "How does Ling-Ling get containers around Port Authority?"

Without thought, Mr. Money bags said, "I give them diplomatic immunity papers."

John said, "Not anymore."

The shot was loud in the small office. Mr. Money bags could not buy his way out of that one. Now the China man was trying to spill the beans on Mr. Money bags. John said, "You may have been a good partner in smuggling young ladies from who knows where, but to be a Chinese spy to boot under the wings of a crooked politician? Well now, we can't have that can we?"

Randy came around by then and was also facing him. The China man now had fear in his eyes. John said, "See Ya, hate to be Ya." At that, a second loud boom resonated in the office. John sat the Mohawks up side by side and put pistols into their dead hands with fingers on the triggers.

"Now." John said, "Keys." They opened the desk and only found receipts of hanger rent, jet fuel, jet fuel charges and other aviation related papers. Then they went into the file cabinet. More papers related to aircraft inspection records and schedules. Then, In the bottom back of the file drawer, John pulled out a small folder and in it was a list of all Ling-Ling owned shipping containers. All nine of them. It showed what port they were last sent to and the serial numbers. John smiled and said, "I bet Mr. Bill would love to get his hands on these." They wiped down the keys after locking the desk and file cabinet back up. The desk pulls and door knobs and any other thing they may have inadvertently touched.

John and Randy walked out of the office and the girls were peeking around each end of the big door, then they came walking toward them. Mary said, "The pilots left as soon as they got that thing shut down."

John glanced around and found what he was looking for. He led the group to the right side of the hanger door and flipped a switch with his elbow. The stack of doors started rolling closed. He had the file in his hand. He held it up to Mary and said, "A gift for Mr. Bill." She smiled at the thought.

Upon seeing the group walk out of the hanger, their ride lurched forward down the way and rolled to a stop beside them. The door opened and they boarded. The jet turned around at the end of the runway and full throttled. They were up and out of there in no time. Next stop, Brookshire, Texas. Or so they thought. It was not until Randy said, "Looks like the Gulf of Mexico."

John said, "We must be coming around air traffic then." He remembered they were not landing at Hobby; they were landing in Brookshire which was nowhere near the coast. He motioned at the young stewardess and asked her what was up. She went to the cockpit to speak to the captain.

The stewardess came back and said, "There has been the matter of a little detour."

John asked, "What detour?"

She said, "Next stop, Ft. Lauderdale, Florida."

John replied, "Do what?"

Mary started patting him on the shoulder and laughing. "Calm down John. Who do you know who owns real estate in South Florida?"

At that, John just said, "Oh!" It was not long and they were descending down over the Everglades. The Ft. Lauderdale airport was an East West runway that started at the side of the freeway and ended at the edge of the Atlantic Ocean.

They landed and taxied over to a line of hangers on the North side of the runway opposite the commercial terminal building. They pulled up to the one on the end, closest to the ocean and sat there for a few minutes. Then the big Limo and all the black suits and flyers sunglasses that came with it, pulled up beside the craft.

The stewardess opened the door and in came Mr. Don T. He said, "I hope you haven't been waiting long. I was finishing the ninth hole just up the road a piece." He then asked John, "How did your day go? I had nothing to do with your targeting. I have been down here playing golf, but my pilots keep me informed, informally of course. The reason you are here is because we are having a meeting on that Belize affair. My pilots picked you up and flew you here for a meeting. You were never on the West Coast today. If you get tracked, it will be to Ft Lauderdale but not that I know of anything going down on the west coast. If something happened out there, it will be a total surprise to me. When you get back to Houston, file your report that you were in Florida today and ask if you should pursue your targets to California. Use that line you told me. What was it, 'the ones that got away.' That should shake some fruit out of the trees back at the commission. Now, more important matters. That package of those smoke-dried slim sausages. I think they can be addictive. I need to know where you got the meat and who processed it." John was caught off guard by that question and he said, "Really?"

Mr. T. said, "Yes John, really."

So, John told him of his surprise hunt out at Pearl and Pegs ranch and that the hired ranch hand took the meat to the country processors. Mr. T thought about it a minute and said, "The powers that be won't let me wonder around in the woods where there are high powered rifles so I can do this. Get me Pearl's information and I can set up a hunt for a wounded warrior and split the meat. That should work out for everyone involved don't you think? What was that animal called again?"

John said, "Nilgai. That should be plenty of meat to split. We still have close to three hundred pounds in the freezer."

"Okay then." Mr. T. took Pearls card from John and said, "Meeting is adjourned." He then exited the aircraft, climbed back into the Beast and they drove off. The fuel tanker then pulled up and hooked a hose to the wing and started pumping JP fuel.

Randy said, "I wonder if any snooping dogs may be over in the terminal wondering what kind of meeting took place on the tarmac."

John laughed and said, "Yea, we were discussing our future grandchildren right."

They all busted out laughing on that one. Soon the tanker unhooked the hose and rolled it up on its spool and the driver gave the pilot the ticket and he then drove away. The pilot boarded and the stewardess pulled the door closed and soon the turbines were whining. By the time they were airborne, darkness was rushing at them. They diligently chased the horizon but the sun out ran them. By the time they got back to Brookshire and their vehicles and unloaded their bags and the file, the jet rolled on out and took to the air headed back to its nest a short hop away at Hobby.

Randy and Rochelle decided to head on out to the Rock from there. Rochelle would file a 'got away' report when they got back to the mini mansion. John and Mary got in old Betsy and headed in the opposite direction back into the city. John called Jay and Kathy and Lloyd and Lacy and asked them to meet them in the morning at the Fifty-Niner Diner on Kirby for breakfast. They all agreed.

After completing the calls, John said "What a day. I did not see this coming at all. First, to attend a funeral and then create a couple of more future funerals in the same day by the same attendees.

Looks like the undertaker, aka Yekun and the Wild Rose aka Rose Smith are going to wake up as lonely business associates."

Finally, back at the cubby hole, Mary sat down to file her 'the one that got away' report. John sat down with his laptop. He pulled some more pictures out of the stack and put in a wanted file, not the abort file. This was the first time he had ever considered a wanted file. After Mary filed her report and said "Done, now we wait."

John added, "To see who falls out of the tree at the commissions office I suppose. Someone grew a set of nuts and somehow managed to put our top targets on an abort list. Now the weaker leakers who protected them will probably show themselves when news breaks after they find an office with strange bed fellows. It might be blamed on the Mohawk heads, who knows."

As John sat in front of his laptop, he decided to do a quick search on Yekun when he pressed enter, he got mixed results. "Seriously." He said to Mary. "Look at this. It says, Yekun was one of the fallen angels. He was the rebel who seduced the sons of angels to descend upon the earth and lead astray men."

Mary said, "I don't know about the angel part, but our Yekun or undertaker has sure led his share of men astray all right."

John said, "Well, when the time comes, he is going to join all those corrupted souls he created."

Mary said, "What are you going to do with that?" She was pointing to the Manilla folder.

John said, "Give it to Bill. Now that you mentioned it, I will send a message to see if he wants to meet with us over at the Fifty-Niner." He sent the invite and a minute later he got a reply from Ranger Bill. 'See you there.' Then John said, "I am ready to call it a day. We only went coast to coast and back. What more can one do in a day?"

Mary grinned and said, "Attend a funeral. If anyone questions your whereabouts today, I am sure Jay and Kathy have photos of you coming out of the service chapel."

John said, "That's a good one. I forgot about that." With that, they headed for the bedroom and shower.

Morning came early and John looked at Mary and said, "Why is the sun in such a hurry?"

Laughing Mary tossed a pillow into his face. She got up and started the coffee pot and said, "We have a little time before we meet the others and I am not waiting that long for my cup of coffee."

John said, "I am with you on that point myself."

Dressed and a cup of coffee down the tube, they armored up and headed out the door for Betsy. Once at the dinner John waited for the end booth away from the door to come available. If need be, they could slide a table up to the end of the booth. Jay and Kathy showed up with a file folder with photos and so did Lloyd and Lacy. It was waffles and eggs all around. After they finished and the table cleared, except for the coffee cups, Ranger Bill strode into the place like he owned it. He spotted the group and grabbed a chair and told the waitress coffee as he sat at the end of the booth table.

Ranger Bill looked over the spread of photos and raised his eyebrow picking one up of Mr. Money bags and his Chinese driver. He said, "Where did you get this picture?"

Jay said, "I took that picture at the funeral chapel yesterday for a man known as the Butcher."

Bill said, "Oh yea? Well, that is interesting. It was just on the news that these same two people must have had some kind of bad deal with a group of Mohawk heads and got killed in some kind of shootout."

"Really?" John said, "Imagine that."

Bill asked, "What do you know about that business then?"

John replied, "Actually, sometime after the funeral and internment over where Howard Hughes was buried, we were summoned to Ft. Lauderdale to meet with the man who presented you with that medal."

"Oh," Bill said.

John asked Bill, "Did you know that the China man driver spy for Miss Politician was also the front man for Ling-Ling Imports for Mr. Money bags the Politician's husband?"

Bill said, "I was kind of working in that direction of thought."

John replied, "You have not been able to trace Ling-Ling on supplying the warm bodies to the Topsail Industries?"

Bill said, "It seems those County Mounty's out there in California could give two hoots for what a man in Texas might ask for."

John asked, "What would you need to just go out there and rattle some of their cages?"

Bill said, "Something to prove that Ling-Ling was smuggling in people."

"Well, in that case." John said, "Do you like to travel?"

Bill looked at John hard. "Just what are you saying John?"

"I found this hanging on a fencepost." John said handing Bill the Ling-Ling file.

Bill opened the file and looked at where all the containers were in port or scheduled to arrive with all the tracking serial numbers on them and he looked up at John. "How the hell?"

John raised his hands palms up shrugging his shoulders. Like I said, "I found it on a fence post. You might want to meet number three on the list at the dock this evening with a set of lock cutters and a County Mounty."

"Oh hell." Bill said, "Now I have to go catch a plane. Not quite what I had in mind this morning." He then looked at the group and asked again, "Just who are you guys?"

John laughed and said, "Don't you remember? Department of Agriculture." He flipped out his I.D.

Ranger Bill said, "Yea, and lead balloons fly." Bill stood up and shook hands with everyone and turned and walked away with a file in his hand.

Lloyd said, "I think that fellow with that Stetson hat likes you." John started laughing and said, "That is probably a good thing because if he didn't like us, what do you think a Texas Ranger could do to interrupt your life?"

"I don't want to even think about that." Lloyd said.

John brought their attention back to the photos. "These go in a wanted file."

Jay replied, "Wanted? I thought Bill said they were dead."

John said, "They were put on the abort list yesterday. So, now we list them as wanted."

"Alrighty." Lloyd responded.

Jay said, "Wanted list huh?"

John said, "That's the official status. If they are dead or alive."

Then Jay said, "What did Bill say about a shootout with Mohawks? Aren't a pair of Mohawks the ones who tried to take you out a couple of months back?"

John replied, "Yes it was and if they are connected, that would explain a little of the mystery of who would like to see me dead. Maybe it was just the China man trying to do some preventative maintenance and his team failed."

"Well." Jay said, "That might make sense. It would look kind of suspicious if another set of mohawk heads came and tried again don't you think?"

They all agreed but John was thinking of the rush he felt as those two were pawing for their weapons. Actually, it was not a rush, it was a sudden fear. A calm but sudden fear and his trained reaction saved his life once more.

Jay broke John's thoughts by saying, "Who is picking up the tab?"

Lloyd said, "I will get it this time." Everyone looked at Lloyd funny as this was a rarity. Not at all normal. Lloyd shrugged his shoulders, "What? You guys think you can do it all the time?" They looked at Lacy and she just shrugged her shoulders and smiled.

John told the group that he did not know anything of those other people at the funeral. Maybe they were local or maybe not. Mary was not getting any help lately from her friend on the recognition thing. She had put in several requests lately, but has received no reply.

Jay said, "Who knows, maybe the Butcher's landlord or a couple of his neighbors or drinking buddies."

Mary then asked, "After we left the service, did anyone happen to see our commission doctor lurking around in the shadows?"

Jay and Kathy said they didn't see him at their post. Lloyd and Lacy said the same. John asked, "Where is our fine doctor if not with his hunting buddies or at the funeral of one them?"

As they walked out of the Fifty-Niner Diner, John looked at his watch and said, "Well now, since we are in the neighborhood, it would be a shame to drive by the House of Pie without picking up a few slices of pie to take home."

Mary laughed and said, "John, just get the whole pie and forget about a slice or so."

He grinned and said, "Why not." So, he did. On the drive back to the cubby hole, he looked over at Mary who was holding his strawberry cheesecake in her lap staring down at it. She looked up at him looking at her and jammed her index finger to the bottom of his pie. He got excited. "I know you didn't just do what my eyes think they saw you do!"

Mary started laughing out loud and stuck her finger in her mouth and cleaned all the cheesecake off of her finger and said, "Yep, sure did." Then John started laughing. Nothing else was said the rest of the way back to Betsy's parking facility

Once back in the cubby hole John made sure his pie was properly placed in the refrigerator without further damage. He then went to the table and started his laptop. He took the new photos of Mr. Money bags and China man driver and filed them in the wanted file. He looked at the new pictures of the Wild Rose and she appeared to really be in mourning. He looked at the Undertaker Mr. Yekun also had on his sad face. John wondered if they have had any bad news today. At that, John got up to turn on the TV to listen and watch the mid-day news.

Finally, there was a picture of an aircraft hangar and a report of gang violence taking the beloved husband and her faithful driver in an unexplained shootout. Eighteen more mohawk heads had been arrested and jailed pending further investigations. John said to Mary, "I wonder where Bill is about now?"

Mary replied, "Probably over Arizona." They both laughed.

John said, "What a mess we got him sucked into."

Mary said, "He may be the only one who doesn't mind doing a little cleanup work."

Later that night, John got a call from Bill. "You were right. I rounded up a couple County Mounty's and we waited for that container to come off of the ship and we followed it to a warehouse controlled by this yoyo's with Mohawk haircuts. City Swat was called in and raided the joint. After opening the container from Ling-Ling Imports and finding about two dozen young ladies in it, about twenty more feather tops got the 'Do not pass go,' go directly to jail card."

"Feather tops. I like that." John replied.

Bill said, "Looks like anyone associated with this group is up on Human trafficking charges plus drugs and weapons charges. The County Mounty's decided they want all the glory now that I had to fly all the way out here and physically show them the light."

John laughed and said, "Typical. They can't have someone from Texas come out and show them how to do their job."

Bill said, "I made copies of that container list and gave one to the port authorities. Gave one to the County Mounty's and I am taking one to the FBI Field office to monitor the others. Can't have a container full of live bodies show up and get forgotten and end up with a bunch of dead bodies now can we. I will be monitoring the remaining containers until they all get back and accounted for with no more people inside of them."

John said, "Good job Ranger Bill." He disconnected.

John turned to Mary and said, "That pretty much puts the brakes on that branch of import smuggling. Gang under arrest tied to Ling-Ling. That's going to go over well. More trash to pile on to Miss Politico from California. Be kind of hard for her to explain about her husband's and driver's involvement in this mess when the dust settles. She is going to be treated like the plague or she has leprosy or something in Washington. No one wants to be associated with trouble."

Mary said, "I wonder if this is starting to drive Rose crazy?"

John said, "Speaking of Rose, I guess I should check in with Moe." He picked up his device and speed dialed. "Hey Moe. What's up?"

Moe said, "Nothing. It's deader than a cemetery the last few nights."

"Well, I think I know why. What I don't know is what the Undertaker is planning to do nowadays. He damn sure is not going to be a door greeter at your local big box store."

Moe laughed at that and said, "No way. Can't buy a good hunt on those wages."

John said, "No. I guess you cannot. I am sure he still has some cartel connections down south. You think he is just laying low for a while?"

Moe replied, "That would be my bet."

John said, "I think I am going out to the Rock in the morning. I need to get with Bobby Sox and get some shooting time in."

Moe said, "You see that stuff on the news about those killings and gangs and all that?"

John said, "Yep. Sure did. Now that was something, wasn't it?"

Moe asked, "Was that the same group that was sending all those girls here by barge?"

John replied, "I do believe it is the same group. Looks like they are out of business now."

Moe said, "Good."

John said, "Later." And then he disconnected.

The next morning over coffee, John asked Mary, "Are you up to going to the Rock?"

Mary said, "Sure. I have a couple of more pillows I want to take out to the Scooby Doo."

John laughed and said, "Good. Let's get packing."

They packed up what all they wanted to take with them including the cheesecake. Upon arrival at the Rock, they put their bags in the Scooby doo and carried the cheesecake to the mini-mansion. Rochelle greeted them and Randy came in behind them. Rochelle said, "What happened to that cheesecake?"

John said, "Don't ask."

Mary started laughing. "Well." Rochelle said, "We know which slice yours will be."

John said, "I am going to go over and see what Bobby is up to."

Mary said, "I will stay here with Rochelle."

So, John went over and found Bobby in the barn. He said, "Just in time John. I just set up. Grab you a six shooter and let's go."

When they went out back, John about fell off of his horse laughing. "What the heck?"

Bobby said, "Well, somebody at a shoot complained that shooting black balloons was a racist thing so they wanted us to shoot the white balloons. I guess we could shoot green ones with alien faces on them. It doesn't really matter. Until I can get a load of green balloons, we get to shoot Mohawk balloons. I cut up pieces of paper and made paper Mohawks."

John was laughing so hard that his side hurt and he said, "I don't think I can shoot at the moment."

Bobby said, "I understand."

After a few minutes, John took a breath and said, "I am ready now." He spurred his mount and shot his way down the fake street. Six shots, six Mohawks down. John reloaded and galloped back. Six more shots, six more Mohawks down. John slid off his mount and retrieved twelve Mohawks and started sticking them on fresh balloons and re-staking them at different heights and places. That was how the morning went. Around lunch time John said, "I feel better now."

Bobby said, "What better therapy than the smell of gun powder in the morning?"

John agreed as he unsaddled his ride and brushed her down and gave her a slice of a square bale to chew on. John said, "Watching her chew is making me hungry. My stomach is growling. I had better head back over to Randy's. You should slide by if you want a slice of cheesecake and bring your other half, we don't bite."

Bobby said, "I'll see what she wants to do."

John said, "That's fine. See you in a bit. Besides, Mary might get a kick out of shooting Mohawks."

Bobby started laughing and said, "We got them to shoot."

During lunch, a vehicle arrived and Randy looked out and said, "That looks like Moe."

John replied, "Moe? What's he doing here?"

Moe approached the mini-mansion with admiration looking it over. When Randy opened the door, Moe said, "Nice." Giving a thumbs up.

"Come on in." Randy said.

"Hey Rochelle, Mary, John." Moe said. "You told me you were heading out this way. Pat called and Pearl said the Undertaker fellow scheduled a hunt. He said same deal as last."

John said, "That's strange. I bet Pearl doesn't even know that the Butcher has been planted yet."

"I don't know." Moe said.

John replied, "Hold on." He walked over to the Scooby Doo and retrieved a GPS tracker. He said, "I don't know why we didn't think of this before. If the Under taker drives his vehicle out to the ranch, stick this up under the back bumper or in the frame somewhere. If he comes in a big four by four with Red driving, that one is already tagged. Just to be safe, take two. You never know who will show up at a gun smuggling, drug hauling meeting."

Moe said, "Thanks. I will see what I can do. Now I have to get back on a day time schedule." He headed back out the door and headed north to Pearl's ranch.

John said, "I was not expecting a hunt after the death of a sidekick now. I am curious as to who this group is."

Mary said, "Maybe the Doctor and Red and that's all."

John replied, "Maybe so, but I suspect something a little different." Then John asked Randy, "Have you been over to Bobby's lately?"

Rand said, "Been kind of busy lately, why?"

John started laughing at the thought and said, "It's all about racist balloons, so now we shoot Mohawks." Randy just looked at

John. John still laughing said, "For real Randy. When I went over there, I about busted a gut and almost fell off of the horse looking at all those feather heads as Bill calls them."

The three of them were all looking at John and all said in unison, "This, I have got to see."

They all went over to Bobby's. By evening sun, they had already shot through a couple hundred rounds of rat shot and then back over at Randy's. They had the fire burning and were all sitting around. Mary said, "I haven't had such fun in a long time."

Rochelle was laughing at a thought and said, "Me either."

Randy looked at John and said, "Feather heads. Would that be their hairstyle or the contents of their brains?"

John cracked up again and said, "I don't know how much more I can take. My sides are sore already."

Mary said, "They say laughter is the best medicine."

John said, "Not an overdose of laughter. It's got to be bad for something."

Mary said, "I am sure you will tell me in the morning."

The following morning John was up at daylight kicking the coals and rekindling the fire. Once he got a blaze going, he sat back in his chair and watched it grow. He was listening to the crackling of the wood, a rooster crowed off in the distance, with a satisfied smile on his face. Randy came out of his mini-mansion with two large cups of coffee ready-made. He said to John as he handed him a cup. "Perks of electricity."

John laughed and touched his ribs. "Not as bad as I thought it would be." Taking the cup and a sip of the hot brew.

Randy then asked, "What kind of a meeting do you think is going to take place today over at the ranch?"

John said, "Well, we know a Mr. Yekun aka the Undertaker is there for sure and that is all until we hear from Moe or Pearl or Pat."

Mary came by and asked Randy, "Is Rochelle up?" He nodded, so Mary went on in to the mini-mansion. After a bit she came out with a platter with egg and cheese on toast sandwiches. Rochelle brought out coffee refills and they all sat around the campfire and silently ate breakfast.

John said, "There is another rock that we did not look under yet. Isn't it amazing how a fire can clear your mind and pull random thoughts to the surface."

Randy said, "What rock?"

John replied, "Who owns the pipe coating company? Is it like the Ling-Ling, a subsidiary of a subsidiary type of a business? That should be easy to check when we get back to the city."

Mary said, "Bill probably has all that stuff checked out. Be easier to ask him than to do double the work if he has already looked into it."

"Your right." John said. "After all, the owners of Topsail Industries went down with the ship being on site when SWAT stepped out of the back of that truck."

Randy said, "I sure wish I could have had a picture of their faces when that back door opened."

John said, "I saw a few bug eyes in my mirror. It was funnier than that deer in the headlights look."

Randy then said, "What about our round-trip ride that was a little out of the norm?"

John said, "Yes, it was. But I hope with Mr. Money bags out of the picture, we will now see if he was the puppet master."

Randy said, "I sure hope so."

John added, "It was a good thing to get our sites on the seemingly untouchables. Makes others think twice about getting involved in the wrong line of work."

Meanwhile, Rochelle had put that picture that John sent of her and Randy into a frame and she asked Mary, "Where do you think?" Holding it up at various places inside the mini mansion. They finally mutually agreed to a spot and called Randy in to place a hanger. He nailed it at the spot directed and hung the picture saying, "Good choice." He then walked back outside again and sat back at the fire with John.

Bobby drove up and walked over to join John and Randy. He said that they were still talking about Mr. Money bags on the news and the gang affiliation. The talking heads having a hard time trying to put some kind of spin on the truth, but it wasn't working. "You can put makeup on a pig, but it's still a pig."

Randy and John laughed. Randy stated, "Good point."

Bobby then said, "Seems that some fellow from Texas intercepted another one of those shipping containers with people in it."

John said, "That would be our pal Texas Ranger Bill Esterling. A good man, that one. Not scared to kick ass and take names. He is the one that made taking down that smuggling operation over at that pipe facility and also set SWAT in the back of that truck I had the pleasure to deliver to Topsail Industries."

Bobby said, "Well, that fellow gets around, doesn't he?"

John said, "You don't know the half of it."

As they were sitting around chatting, Moe suddenly drove up and got out and bee-lined straight to John. He said, "I guess the gang is all there and I have to get back, but that Undertaker is there and so is the Doctor but that is not all. The wild Rose lady also showed up."

John said, "We kind of figured that."

Moe said, "That newly widowed politician is there also."

"No way!" John exclaimed. "They haven't even buried that man yet."

Randy said, "Does that make her the puppet master? She has the power to pull lots of strings."

Moe replied, "I tagged the Undertaker's vehicle on my way out but I have to get back."

John asked, "Is Ms. California in a staff car or a rental?" Moe replied, "I don't know, but it has California plates." John said, "Tag it. We can catch up with it later."

Moe replied, "Will do." Then he left.

Rochelle and Mary came out and Mary asked, "What was that?" She pointed to the dust cloud left behind as Moe hurried off.

John said, "It's a foursome at the ranch." Mary asked, "Foursome?"

John said, "We were right on the first three names, but who would have thought Ms. Politico would be here and not at home mourning her loss."

Mary replied, "Are you serious?"

Randy said, "Yes, he is. Moe just dropped the bomb and left."

Rochelle asked, "You think she is shopping for someone to take over California operations?"

"Now that's a new thing to think about." John said, "If Moe tags her, we will be able to catch her without her bird dogs watching over her."

"How's that?" Randy asked.

John said, "She is at the ranch. Where are her bird dogs? Creeping in the woods? I think not. I think she has a tendency to wave off or sneak around the secret service to pursue her personal business. If that's the case and she pings our screen, we already have an ace up our sleeve."

"Good point." Randy said.

Bobby scratching his head said, "You guys got too much going on. I think I will head back to the barn." He got up and left.

John picked up his device and speed dialed Lloyd. "Hey Lloyd. How's it going at the dock work?"

Lloyd said, "Nothing different that I have seen." John then told Lloyd that Moe was off night watch for now. He was back at the ranch playing green acres. Lloyd laughed and said, "I think he likes it out there."

John said, "No thinking about it. I was just checking on you.

Lloyd said, "All good here." He then disconnected.

Then he called Jay and had the same results. Nothing going on. John sat staring at the fire and he asked himself if this was the calm before the storm. Then the sight of the Mohawk balloons came to mind and he started laughing again. He then asked Mary, "Do you think you can search the link out there in New Mexico around Area 51 and get Bobby stocked up on alien head balloons?"

Mary started laughing, "I will see what I can find. What's the matter? You don't like picking up those Mohawk scalps and sticking them on more balloons?"

John grinned and said, "It's not that. It's the petty whining that black balloons are racist. If we get red ones then the Indians will say that it is racist. Then if we get brown ones the Hispanics will say that it is racist. We get the yellow ones and it's still a racist thing. We can't use blue it will make little boy blue blow his horn. Since when does a race own a color? It's not possible to own an act of nature. I digress."

About that time, Pearl pulled up and motioned for John to go over. Pear said, "Moe told me you were over here."

John said, "What's up?"

Pearl said, "I got a phone call this morning out of the blue. Do you know who called me?" John replied, "The big cheese?"

Pearl started laughing. "I guess you can say that. I suppose you know what he wants to do?"

John said, "Something about a wounded warrior hunt?"

Pearl replied, "That is exactly what he wants."

John said, "Would it be that he wants half a Nilgai made into little Smokey sticks?"

Pearl looked at John and said, "Where and why would he get that idea?"

"Oh." John said, "A little while back we were sitting around that campfire." He pointed to where the others were sitting. "A helicopter landed up at that corner slab, next thing we know the big man comes in out of the dark. He bums a link and liked it so I gave him a whole package. Now he's hooked."

Pearl replied, "Quit pulling my leg."

"Hold on." John said. He waved Mary, Randy, and Rochelle over. John said, "Ask them." Pearl did and they explained it to him. Then John said, if that's not good enough, go talk to Bobby. He was here also."

Pearl said, "Well, I'll be."

John said, "I hear you have a motley crew over at the ranch."

Pearl said, "That is a mix and I think Miss Smith may be the only one who shows an interest into maybe shooting something."

John said, "You know, that's a long drive for Ms. Politico. Especially after her other half was just found dead."

Pearl said, "I thought that was kind of weird myself."

John asked, "Any idea why the meeting? We know it's not about trying to make any kind of funeral arrangements, don't we?"

Pearl shook his head and said, "What kind of plans are going on at the ranch can't be any good. That one fella is not here this time."

"Oh." John said, "You didn't know they planted that other one the other day."

Pearl said, "What happened?"

John said, "He fell off a pyramid down in Guatemala."

Pearl replied, "Ouch. I bet that hurt."

John said, "Not long enough."

Pearl just looked at John and shook his head and said, "I have to go." And he did.

John walked back over to the campfire and sat. After a bit, he got up and told Mary, "I think I am going to go over to Bobby's and take care of a few more Mohawks."

She understood and said, "I will see you later then."

He climbed into Betsy and fired her up. After a few hours of shooting and talking with Bobby, John eased back over to Randy's place. He told Mary, "If no news comes in from anyone this evening, we will head back into the city in the morning."

Randy was painting some window trim and John said, "Hey, you missed a spot."

Randy said, "You want this brush?"

John replied, "Only if it has a pistol grip." That got a good chuckle out of Randy. That's how the evening went.

CHAPTER FIFTEEN

The following morning, John opened his eyes to the sound of that rooster crowing in the distance. He tried to get dressed in Scooby Doo without waking Mary but that was a futile attempt. She looked up smiling and said, "Good morning."

He grinned and said, "Good morning." He kissed her on the cheek and slid out the side door. Feeding the embers, he soon had a little stream of smoke, then combustion, flame on. He grinned and watched the little blaze grow. The rooster crowed a couple of more times before Randy came out with two mugs of brew. "Just what the doctor ordered." He said accepting a mug from Randy. They both sat back and watched the blaze.

After a bit, Mary was up and headed into the mini-mansion and helped Rochelle do some scrambled eggs and hash browns. After breakfast was served up John loaded up Betsy and they said their farewells and headed back to the city. John called Jay to see what was up. Jay said, "Nothing is going on in my neighborhood."

Then John called Lloyd and Lloyd told him, "My man at the weapons store told me they received a triple sized order of AR-15's and thought that a bit strange."

John could already in his mind see the Undertaker trying to get his weapons and drug smuggling going again. He told Lloyd, "Good job. Stay on it. Could be something brewing." They disconnected.

Slapping Betsy's steering wheel he said, "I knew it." Mary asked, "What?"

John said, "I think they are rebooting the weapons run thing again."

Mary said, "A hurst isn't hard to follow."

John said, "I don't think they will try the same trick twice. Look what happened to Ricky and Dicky." Mary said, "Then what?"

John replied, "That's what we need to find out. Poor Moe's going to feel like a yoyo as soon as that ranch party breaks up. We need him back on night watch at the loading dock of those two businesses."

Back at the cubby hole, John was still in thought of the ways and means to deliver caskets full of weapons. "Hell." He said out loud. "Trains, planes, trucks, boats, for that matter but I haven't heard of anyone shipping caskets on a slow boat to anywhere."

Mary said, "Maybe a cruise ship."

John said, "That might work. A direct shot to Cancun or Cozumel. It's the return trip that I don't think will work. Customs checking all passengers and such. Dogs sniffing around. I think it's safe to say a cruise ship is out of the question." Still in thought, John said, "Large orders of caskets go by eighteen-wheel freight trucks. That brings us down to the little bobtail trucks like I hauled SWAT to the kite store in. Now that might work. That's something we need to look into. I need to go to Boston for a couple of more trackers. You want to ride?" He asked Mary.

"Sure." Mary said.

In a matter of minutes Betsy was back out on the road and heading across town. They pulled up in front of Boston's store just as he was stepping out to post a flyer on his window. They greeted and walked back to Boston's office. John told Boston he was in need of a few more trackers and Boston smiled and said, "I just put together a new batch. How many do you need?"

John thought and said, "Three for starters. We should be able to retrieve the others soon, I hope. I think three will do for now."

Boston said, "No problem." He went into his special closet and brought out three more tracking devices. He handed them to John and said grinning, "Hot off the press." Then he asked, "How are things going?"

John said, "It looks like the vicious circle is trying to start back up."

Boston said, "Oh, really. Any way I can help?"

John said, "I'm not sure, but if I think of something I will let you know." He and Mary rose up to leave. They thanked Boston and strolled next door.

J-Lee was happy to see them. J-Lee told John that since the Butcher's funeral, there has been some inquires for some sort of contract drivers of sorts for long-haul and not local. He told John, "You know I ship stuff. Books and paintings and rare objects, but this gig wanted two drivers' full time. I have one driver and she is happy with her present schedule."

John asked, "Who was hiring?"

J-Lee said, "That's just it. They never did get around to who they would be driving for, what they would be hauling or how long of a long-haul. No answers there."

John said, "That could have been any kind of delivery from cases of magazines to cartons of tennis shoes."

J-Lee said, "If that were the case, they would have identified themselves."

John's device buzzed and he answered. "Lloyd, what's up?"

Lloyd said, "Besides the extra weapons I told you about, just now fresh off of the car hauler, two brand new vans. Three-quarter tons, no side windows. You know like a construction worker might drive."

"Really." John said, "To the weapons store?"

"No" Lloyd said, "Front door of the casket factory."

John looked at J-Lee and said, "We got to go. Two vans were delivered just now to the casket store." Then John said to Lloyd, "We are on our way." And he disconnected.

The ride across town didn't take long. Soon Betsy was parked out of sight on a side lot and John got with Lloyd with Mary in tow. The vans had already been decaled over in a wrap that looked like a grave yard scene. Green grass, headstones, trees. "How cute." Mary said as her and John walked behind the vans placing trackers on each one on the frames near the bumper bolt up. They continued walking around the block. That's when they noticed another delivery van dropping off a set of custom ramps by the loading docks.

"That makes easy loading for the vans." John said, "Maybe they used that side-wangled forklift they use to stack all those coffins in the warehouse. I don't know."

John called Jay and said, "You need to pack your boom bag. It looks like another road trip is in the future."

Jay said, 'Good, I was getting bored. All this sitting around."

John laughed and said, "It might be that same long haul out to New Mexico. I don't know yet, but trackers are set."

Jay said, "So soon?"

John said, "Possibly."

Jay said, "Why can't we just fly out there and wait for them?" John said, "Because we don't know if they take a left turn down to Big Bend or a left turn at El Paso. We just don't know. We are going to just have to stick this one out again and see where it leads us."

Jay said, "Well, whatever. There is a boom in for me, right?" John laughed again and said, "The boom is all yours."

On the way back to the cubby hole, John got a call from Moe. "Hey Moe."

Moe said, "The party is breaking up as we speak."

John asked, "Is that so? What do you got?"

Moe said, "I ran into town before they left and two of them went west and two of them went east."

Then John said, "It's starting."

Moe asked, "What's starting?"

John said, "They are starting the cycle again. I guess they didn't get the message. They got two new vans to do their hauling with now and I suspect contract drivers that won't have a clue as to what they are hauling so that's going to throw a kink in things. I'll see you in town." They disconnected.

Now his device buzzed again and it was Lloyd. "What's up Lloyd?"

Lloyd said, "It looked like the gun store just rolled a crate across the docks into the casket store."

"Good catch." John said, "It has begun."

Lloyd asked, "Are you going to need any dancers?"

John chuckled, "You never know. For now, watch those vans and let me know if one catches a casket and leaves."

"I can do that." Lloyd said and with that, they disconnected. Leaving Betsy in her stall, John and Mary headed back into the cubby hole for a quick pack up and then tried to kick back for a nap if they had to hit that long drive again. John was thinking to himself. The only way to stop this is to rid the world of the evil greed that manipulates this. Miss Politico, Miss Rose Smith, Mr Yekun the Undertaker and what's with that Commission Doctor?

It did not take long for John to doze off and it seemed like less time before Mary's device sounded 'ping'. John, rubbing his eyes said, "Now what?

Mary said, "Give me a minute. I just woke up too." After a minute she said, "A philanthropist practicing the wrong kind of philanthropy."

"How's that?" John asked, "I thought giving finances to a cause was a good thing."

"Well, it seems that this young attorney turned Assistant District Attorney can't lose a case. Every case comes before her, but the little petty one's she seems to get outright guilty verdicts even without any incriminating evidence." Mary said.

John asked, "How is that possible?"

Mary said, "In steps, Mr. Philoman bribes out the jury, all or nothing. Twelve thousand dollars a trial. All to keep his spoiled brat happy. Evidently, lots of innocent people are sent to prison on a bribed jury."

John said, "Damn. It doesn't ever stop. Evil breeds greed and good people get sucked into it. Might as well gear up and go."

It didn't take them long to find their target. He was hanging out in the lower level courthouse where the restrooms were. He sat on the hall bench like some kind of hall monitor getting up and meeting people coming out of the restrooms. John walked up to the man and sat next to him. John asked the man, "Do you enjoy taking innocent people's lives away from them by sending them to prison for things they did not do?"

The man looked at John and said, "What does it matter to you?"

John said, "It's not what matters to me, it's what matters to that District Attorney upstairs. Where there is no more spoiling of the brat."

The man huffed at John and said, "Like you are going to stop me."

John said, "Exactly." He hit him on the thigh with a yellow jacket and the last thing the man saw was John's back as he was walking for the stairs to exit the courthouse. "Now, let's see how good of a lawyer you really are." John said. Mary grabbed his hand and they walked back out to Betsy and headed back to the cubby hole.

John was still angered at that man's arrogance of putting innocent people in prison for his spoiled brat's benefit. John said, "I read somewhere that there are thousands of innocent people cast into the prison meat grinder just to become slaves of the state. Big industries man-powered by men in white with no pay. One fellow got a fifty-year aggravated sentence with no possibility of parole with no physical, medical, or DNA evidence to prove his guilt. Just spoken words. Can you imagine being ripped out of your life because somebody just said something? Love, hate, anger, jealousy, money, greed, spite, or plain meanness is all it amounts too and it's sad that the great State of Texas let's it happen."

Mary said, "That is sad. What a waste." The rest of the ride was in silence.

Back at the cubby hole, Mary filed her report. Philanderer has been aborted. She cleared her screen. John looking at the pictures on the table then said, "Well, I guess Miss California and Miss Rose ought to be half way to New Mexico by now if not farther. I would bet the gun run starts tonight, but I may be wrong."

He was wrong for some reason. It was the next morning when the van backed up on the new ramps so they could slide the casket into the back. Lloyd called John and said, "The van is loading now."

John said, "Thanks." He disconnected and speed dialed Jay and Kathy. On the second ring Jay answered, "Yea?"

John said, "Time to roll. We will be waiting in Betsy."

Jay said, "Good deal. We are on our way now." They disconnected.

As they waited, Mary made another report. Suspected gun running has possibly been resumed. She received a reply that said, 'Take all necessary actions to stop them permanently.' Mary typed back, Miss California the widow Politico, Mr. Yekun aka Undertaker and the Miss Wild Rose Smith and possibly the doctor from the commission are driving the train. The reply back said: Miss California, Miss Smith and Mr. Yekun are now authorized to be aborted at first opportunity. No loose ends including checkpoint personal.

"Well, that opens up a whole new ballgame." Mary said. Jay knocked on John's window and said, "Open the trunk."

John had to get out and manually turn the key. This ride was decades ahead of the trunk popper switches and levers. The trunk slammed shut. John, Jay and Kathy climbed into Betsy and he fired her up. Once headed to the freeway, John looked at his GPS tracker and he was ahead of the one going west so he stopped to top off his tank. Then he fell in a safe distance behind the new van. Before crossing Six-Ten west, another blip appeared on the tracker. John said, "Gotcha Mr. Yekun. Hanging out in a private presidential neighborhood. John said to Jay, "You got that tagged?"

Jay said, "Got it."

John smiled and said, "Oh yea. Ballgame?"

"Oh." Mary said, "We no longer have to wait for a face and a satellite blip. It's open season on all involved. California, Smith, Yekun and any other associates that make this thing work, but and this is a big but, no doctor on our list."

John said, "Just what is that man's game? He is always playing in the sandbox. It just doesn't figure."

Mary said, "Look." She showed the text to the others. It just stated the three names and possible checkpoint corruptors.

John looked into his mirror and said, "Jay, did you bring plenty of boom with you?"

Jay smiled and said, "Do you even need to ask?"

It was a long drive and coincidentally the van pulled into the City of Rocks for an overnight rest. John pulled into Faywood and rented a cabin. After a short soak in the Hot Pools, John and Jay were ready for the hike across the desert again. Jay with one of his boom bags on his shoulder. The driver was reclined all the way back with the window open and headphones on. John dug in his goody bag and came out with a retrievable blow dart and loaded a small amount of tranquilizer serum in it. He blow-darted the driver in his neck and before the driver could react, John jerked the dart out by filament and squatted down. The driver scratched his neck and found nothing. Then he went to sleep.

John reached in and pushed the unlock button. The locks clicked. John and Jay crawled into the back of the van and found the casket was sealed. "Crap." John said. Then he and Jay started looking the van over for the turn key. All the obvious places with no luck. Then Jay reached in to the hollow of the back door panel and there it was. Its location was probably unknown to the driver to keep him from being nosey. John inserted the key at the foot end of the casket and turned the key several rotations before it clicked. Jay lifted on the lid and lo and behold there was no body. Stacks and stacks of AR-15's semi-automatic rifles. John said, "Jackpot."

Jay went to work. He stacked about twenty pounds of C-4 on each side of the coffin, wired up a compression switch and closed the lid. Once the lid was next opened, it would no longer stay attached to anything. They put the coffin key back in the door panel and exited the vehicle. John walked back to the front window, reached in and pushed the lock switch. Click, click, click. John turned and high-fived Jay and they headed back across the desert to the Hot Springs.

The following morning, they followed the van into Silver City. It turned North at the Old Fort Road. John said, "We know where he is going, now don't we? While he gets his verification stop, picks up his free pass and drops his deliver off somewhere between here and the border. Let's go see Mr. Coffee before we head south."

The sight of Betsy pulling up to the curb put a smile on ol' Mr. Coffee's face. "Hey." He said, "Welcome back. What'll it be for you?"

They ordered up and sat at the same sidewalk table as before. John said, "So, how's business?"

Mr. Coffee said, "It's picking up a bit now that there really is some work going on over there." He pointed to the old government building.

"That's good." John said.

Mr. Coffee said, "It's starting to bring a little life back into this old town here."

John was watching his tracker. The girls just got back from the little bakery when John noticed movement on his tracker. He told Jay, "Well, that's a good sign. No thunder out of the foothills this morning."

Mr. Coffee looked at him and then up at the clear morning sky. Jay grinned and said, "It's an inside joke."

John asked, "What about those people that worked over there?"

Mr. Coffee said, "You know, that's a strange one. The one went to sleep behind the wheel of that fancy sports car in a mini-storage up the hill there. That red-head, she just up and disappeared."

"Hmm." John said, "Imagine that."

"And that old building, after the fire department found those drugs in there, it didn't take long for a senior official to come over from the temporary annex and get the ball rolling on the restoration. In six-months or so, life might be back to normal around here." Mr. Coffee said.

John looked at his tracker and told Mr. Coffee to have a good day and they would drop in sometime as the group stood and said their thanks and farewells. They all reclaimed their respective seats in Betsy, waved at Mr. Coffee and drove away from there.

Out on the highway, John was catching up with the van when he noticed the other blip on his tracker behind him. "Well now, this could be interesting. If the Rose is following and gets too close, we may have to pass up the van and wait on a side street in Deming to see what's going on." As it turned out, Rose was in no hurry to catch the van so John stayed equidistant in between them. After crossing under interstate Ten and cruising through Deming, it turned out the following blip made a left turn at the Interstate and was soon out of range.

As John followed the van south towards Columbus, New Mexico, he was wondering who Rose was going to see to butter their palm. Did they find a new recruit or are they going to force Mr. Scared Commander of the Guard to do what the powers that be put him there to do. This will be interesting to see he thought to himself. About an hour south of Deming as they neared the little border town, the van slowed and then turned into a gate which was open. There was a barn type of building about a quarter of a mile in with a half a dozen vehicles pulled up around it. As John drove past the gate, a door was swung open and the van disappeared inside. John told Jay, "Now this could be interesting."

Jay grinned and said, "Now to see if that van comes back out of there in one piece or many pieces."

John pulled over about a mile up the road and waited. Soon the dot started moving on his tracker. "I wonder how much of a head start they give that van driver before they open the box? We will soon find out. Don't you agree John?"

John laughed and said, "I think so." He fired up Betsy and took up pursuit of the van that was almost out of range. He turned left and Betsy had no problem closing the gap up somewhat.

Mary said, "It's a shame we could not take out Rose while we had her."

John said, "First things first. First is to destroy this smuggling ring once and for all. Then before they pick up the pieces, take out the force behind it. Right now, we need Rose to lead us through their operation. Once the receiving end is wiped out, then what's the story say? All the king's horses and all the king's men could not put humpty dumpty back together again. That is our goal."

Once across the state line the van pulled into a truck stop so John pulled in, refueled, and slid around to the side and parked. It appeared that the driver was ordering lunch. Then John remembered. If this is like last time, they would have to wait for evening shift to pass the checkpoint station. Might as well do lunch now while we bide our time. As they waited for their order, they observed the driver. He seemed non-concerned so, that means he has not had any negative feedback from his delivery. John stood up and said, "I will be back." He walked outside over to and around the van and then came back in.

He then went over to the van driver and asked him where he got that wrap from. The van driver explained it was not his van that he was just a contract driver. He then said, "It was a strange trip out here to trade out a casket that some client had rejected. So, now I'm taking the reject back to Houston."

John smiled and said, "That does seem strange indeed."

The driver said, "I am not complaining. The pay is excellent."

John said, "Have a safe trip."

Back at the table John told the others, "This driver has no clue what he is really doing. He thinks he just hauled a replacement casket all the way out here to trade off for a reject and take the reject back."

Kathy said, "So, this driver does not have an inquisitive mind. All he thinks about is to get from point A to point B and what's behind him, as in what he is hauling does not matter."

John said, "Yea, something like that."

"It takes all kinds." Mary said.

Then John said, "Remember this is a trial run. You figure the driver would catch on if once a week he had to go fetch a reject."

"That makes sense." Jay said.

After a while, the van driver looked at his watch and then got up and cashed out. He got into his delivery van and drove out of the lot. John and company were not far behind in Betsy. If the driver took his time, he would make the checkpoint just after shift change. John would hang a mile or so back until arrival at the check station. Then he would catch up and slip in behind the delivery van with Jay on handy-cam to see who he interacts with and waves the van through. That's what they did. John said, "Well, well, well. Look who we have here. I guess the message was not clear."

Jay chuckled and said, "Maybe someone made him an offer that he could not refuse."

John said, "Either way, it's a bad deal for him. We have our orders. Wait until Lloyd hears this. He saw the look of pure fear in that fella's eyes when he discovered the Assistant Director D.O.A."

Mary asked, "How are we going to do this one?"

John replied, "I'm not sure. We might have to make a return trip." Soon afterwards John said, "Look at this."

The van was around a mile ahead of them. Then a second blip was a few miles out. I guess old Rose is going to check to make sure her man got past the checkpoint. Once the van past the other blip, John slowed. He did not want Rose to recognize Betsy. He had pulled over and almost stopped when the blip started heading east at a fast clip. John pulled back onto the lane and aired Betsy out for a minute. He kept his distance and watched his tracker and it wasn't long before blip number two overtook and passed blip number one and proceeded to stretch the gap until it was so far ahead that it was out of range.

Jay asked, "Do you think she is going to babysit all the way back or was this just to ensure he made it past the checkpoint?" John grinned and sang these words. 'She just checked in to, so what condition her condition was in.' Mary and Kathy both got a laugh out of that one.

Jay said, "I would be willing to bet she is out of here. She must make things ready in the city."

John asked Jay, "You still got another boom bag?"

Jay grinned and said, "I don't leave home without them."

"How long would it take if we got you a few minutes alone in the back of that van?" John asked.

Jay replied, "Longer to unseal and reseal the casket than to set the charges."

John asked, "So, five minutes' tops?"

Jay replied, "Yea."

"Now all we need is a moment of opportunity." John said, "Make sure everything is ready."

Next stop, Ft. Stockton truck stop. The van pulled in and fueled and pulled over to the rest lot and the driver went inside. John coasted by and let Jay and Kathy out on the blind side of the van. He then circled around to the far opposite fuel pumps and filled Betsy to her fill. Before John could park Betsy, Jay and Kathy came walking up. John said, "What's wrong?"

Jay said, "Nothing."

Kathy held up her slim-jim door un-locker laughing and said, "I guess our driver doesn't think anyone would steal a casket. He didn't even bother to lock the doors."

John said, "No way."

Jay said, "I stepped in the back. The tool was in the door panel. Wham, bam, thank you ma'am.

John laughed and said, "I can't believe the luck. No reject bodies in there I take it?"

Jay said, "Nothing but powder, powder, and more powder. It's going to make a hell of a cloud when they open that lid."

"Good." John said, "Make them call in the hazmat crew to clean up the mess this is going to make."

Jay said, "No weapons to damage so, I just put in a ten-pound pack. Still blow the walls open but then, it can't be hid."

John watched the van drive out the lot headed east. He picked up his device and called Randy. "Hey John." Randy said, "What's up?"

John replied, "You are. In around eight or so hours a delivery van will come through. Pick it up on your tracker and follow it into the city. It will more than likely go to some seemingly empty warehouse, drop its package and leave. When the delivery van leaves, make sure you are at a distance. Jay rigged the package."

"How about a city block?" Randy asked.

John said, "Jay said that should be sufficient." "Got it." Randy said and John disconnected.

John started Betsy and headed out to the freeway and passed his right-hand turn drove under the freeway, then turned left. Next stop El Paso. Jay, Mary, and Kathy looked at him and he said, "Now is as good time as any to take care of that checkpoint boss. He is on our list isn't he?"

Mary replied, "He is."

"Alright then. We do it now and save ourselves a trip back out here." John said.

Mary said, "That makes sense." They all kicked back and watched the barren scenery go by.

Mary was looking for more information on the second shift commander and any hangouts he may use. As they passed by the checkpoint westbound without slowing down. John had his shades on driving into the lowering sun. He said, "Well, how about that?"

Mary asked, "How about what?"

John said, "My glasses picked up our target as I drove by."

Jay said, "You mean like they did down in Guatemala?"

John replied, "Exactly like that."

"That makes things a little easier to find a man driving home in the dark." Jay said.

John replied, "After shift change, we wait on the south of town for our man to drive by and follow him to his demise." That is what they did.

Mary looked around at the crew in the car. It was almost midnight and they all had on their proximity shades. She laughed at the sight and started in on 'I wear my sunglasses at night so I can, so I can. Keep track of the visions flowing before my eyes.'

Everyone cracked up at that looking at each other. Kathy said, "I bet if an alien walked by, we sure would look weird."

"Finally." John said as he turned the key bringing Betsy to life. He put her in gear and they rolled. They pulled up on the freeway and fell in just behind their target. Eventually he pulled off of the freeway and stopped at a twenty-four-hour convenience store, went in and came back out with a six-pack. John was leaning against his car. He told John, "Excuse me." He opened the car door to get in and John let him, but he did not let him close the door.

John said, "I guess I misjudged you."

Mr. Checkpoint replied, "I don't know who you think you are but you better let go of my door sir."

John said, "I gave you a pass, and you blew it."

Mr. Checkpoint was getting agitated and said, "I don't know what the hell you are talking about."

John said, "Okay. Your new position became available thanks to me and you would have been string puller you found sitting in a corner booth that is no longer with us thanks to me." It finally started to register what the future looked like to Mr. Checkpoint. John then said, "You let the red-head sweet talk you, didn't you?" Mr. Checkpoint started breaking into a sweat. John continued, "I got you on film taking envelopes and waving traffic through with no check." John pulled his pistol and said, "Let's have a look at that envelope." Mr. Checkpoint was seriously shaking by now. John said, "Your life is only worth ten grand? Too bad."

Mr. Checkpoint said, "I can fix this."

John asked, "What would Red say about that?" John signaled Jay and then said, "Once you cross a line, you can't uncross it." He stepped back and closed the agent's door. "Have a good day sir."

The agent had a sudden flush of relief and said, "Thank you sir, you won't be sorry." He started his car and about two blocks down the road, his car and him were blown to hell.

John got back into Betsy and said, "Good job, Jay. Now we go home."

It was a long haul back. They tag teamed back non-stop except for fuel and coffee. They actually caught up to the van who was sleeping in a rest area out west of Columbus before heading in to the city. John said, "That fellow must have spent time in over the road driving. They can only drive so many hours a day by a log book."

The van had been stuck in rush hour traffic trying to get across town when he came into tracker range. John said, "Are you happy now, Jay?"

Jay said, "Happy about what?"

John replied, "About maybe witnessing your handiwork in action again."

Jay just put that big grin on and said, "Sure."

John sent Randy and Rochelle back home. No sense for them to be there also. John now called Lloyd and told him if that van comes there and they unload that casket to grab his friend and get away from the building as it could get ugly. Lloyd said that he would and thanked John for the warning. As it turned out, the van went to an old warehouse in Pasadena. The van drove in and in five minutes, the van drove out. "Now we wait." John said. They watched as three other vehicles arrived and went inside of the warehouse and that's when it happened. 'Kawhoooph.' Metal walls bulged and the brick storefront crumbled and then there was the flash fire. "Wow." John said, "I wonder what else they had in there?"

Mary said, "The good news is, the fire prevented a white coke cloud from drifting over the neighborhood."

John started Betsy and busted a U-turn and headed back to the cubby hole. Once back at Betsy's stall, Jay and Kathy grabbed their gear and loaded their vehicle. John gave Jay a big bear hug and said, "That's some work that you do."

Smiling real big Jay said, "Ditto that John." Jay and Kathy then left. John grabbed the bags and walked with Mary to their cubby hole.

Mary put a brew on and sat down to file the successful abortion performed on Mr. Checkpoint. John turned on the TV just in time for the mid-day news. In local news, firefighters were fighting a warehouse fire in Pasadena. John smiled thinking that at least the drugs were destroyed. No identification as of yet to who the victims of the fire were. Moving to national news, there was a mild earthquake in California. Nothing special. Now breaking, the Governor of New Mexico is officially missing in action. His whereabouts are unknown. There is speculation of possible kidnapping or other possibilities. No answers at this time.

John looked at his stack of pictures and pulled the one out of the governor of New Mexico with Ms. Wild Rose and said, "I wonder."

Mary asked, "You wonder what?'

John said, "If he was holding a grand opening ceremony to a new venture yesterday morning?"

"Ooh." Mary said, "It seems all of Ms. Rose's circle of friends is getting smaller and smaller. We have the Undertaker and Ms. Politico left, besides the Wild Rose and their time is drawing near."

"Today we need to rest." John said.

John's device buzzed. It was Lloyd. He told John that the new delivery van made it back and that it must have been empty. The driver parked it front row at the front door to the casket company, got into his personal vehicle and left. John said, "The package has been delivered."

Lloyd said, "Is that what all that fuss is down on the south east side?"

John told him, "It probably was."

Lloyd laughed and said, "Rather there than here."

John asked, "Has that big four by four made it back?"

Lloyd said, "I have not seen it yet."

"Okay, good." John said, "Let me know." He then disconnected.

CHAPTER SIXTEEN

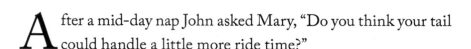

After a mid-day nap John asked Mary, "Do you think your tail could handle a little more ride time?"

Mary replied, "I reckon so. What's the plan?"

John said, "We need to go and scout out Mr. Undertaker's neighborhood. Maybe we can get close enough to retrieve some tracker information so we can make some sort of a plan."

Mary said, "Let's get it done then."

John grabbed their bag and, in a few minutes, Betsy was backing out of her stall. The ride back out to the west loop didn't take long at all. They were ahead of the five o'clock jam. The tracker signal was picked up as they approached the loop and John exited south onto the loop. Then he exited right on Memorial, then left on Post Oak Lane.

John was looking at the six-story black building. "Well." John said, "Do we have an office here Mr. Yekun?" John drove by the building missing the side drive to the multi-level parking facility behind the building. He drove on south towards the Galleria before turning back up Post Oak Lane, this time he spotted the narrow drive on the north side of the building. He turned left and followed the drive into the parking area.

Mary said, "No monster trucks here. The clearance is just under seven-foot."

"That's why that delivery truck was using the front door." John said.

John drove straight up to the roof top parking. "Looks like this level doesn't get much use."

Mary squinting said, "Bright sunlight tends to make hot cars."

John called Moe. "Hey Moe, what kind of a vehicle was that Undertaker fellow driving out at the ranch?"

Moe said, "That would be like a fire engine red Prius Hybrid."

"What?" John exclaimed. "A man doing millions in drugs and weapons dealings wants to do his part to save the world by driving a hybrid?"

Moe said, "Yea. I thought that was weird, unless he was driving his wife's car."

John thought on that for a minute and then said, "I have no information on a wife, girlfriend or roommate so I don't think so. Thanks Moe." He then disconnected.

John looked at Mary and said, "Red Prius."

Mary started laughing and said, "Really?"

John picked up his tracker receiver and said, "Let's take a walk."

They left Betsy on the rooftop lot and began walking back down the ramps by passing the stairs. It was parked at the corner spot on the second level. John downloaded the mapping from the tracker. They continued down to the first level and entered the building and looked at the directory. Nothing to identify Mr. Yekun aka the Undertaker. The building had an open atrium full height to ceiling. A water fountain was in the center on the main floor. Mary jabbed John in the ribs to get his attention. She pointed at a front glass wall. John looked out and coming to a stop in the delivery lane was a big four by four with New Mexico plates.

John and Mary backed into a short hallway leading to the stairs. The wild rose came walking in with a very distraught worried look on her face. She went straight to the elevator and pushed the sixth-floor button. "That narrows it down." John said walking back to the directory. He heard the slight ping of the elevator door open on six. He watched Rose walk around the atrium to an office in front on the street side. "Now that pin-points it." John said.

They made the trip up the stairs and eased around the atrium to the door that Rose entered. Penemu Investments. They could hear muffled unhappy voices as they walked by. "Do you think someone lost some money?" John asked Mary as they made it to the elevator. He pushed one and waited for the door to open and they rode it back down to the lobby. He checked the directory and there was a Penemu Investment Firm.

John and Mary went out to Betsy and boy was she hot. Mary said, "I bet she would fry an egg on that big black hood."

John said, "Well, we won't mess up the paint to find out." He started Betsy up and moved her down two levels to a recently vacated slot. "This will make her feel better." He said patting the steering wheel.

Mary grinned and said, "Me too."

John asked Mary, "Are you in a hurry to go anywhere?"

Mary replied, "Nope."

John got out of Betsy and walked back up to the red Prius shaking his head. "Not what You would think a major drug dealer would drive." He walked back down to Mary and said, "Let's go sit in the lobby until Red finishes venting on her bad investments."

Mary laughed and they sat by the fountain and waited. John said, "How's your stinger?"

Mary said, "Loaded for a bear."

"Good." John said, "I think our fine investor is going to need a shot."

Mary grinned and said, "I am ready."

John looked up in time to see Rose exit the door that said Penemu, walking around the rail towards the elevator. John and Mary walked over to the stairwell hallway and watched Ms. Rose leave the elevator and then head out the front doors. Mary said, "That did not look like a happy camper." They watched as Rose drove out onto Post Oak Lane.

John said, "Her news is only going to get worse." They went out the back door into the parking garage. "All we do now is wait for our Mr. Yekun to show up." And they waited. Most of the parking garage was empty by now. A few random scattered vehicles of after-hours workers remained. Mr. Yekun aka the Undertaker came out of the stairwell. Mary was standing in the middle of the drive looking towards his Prius acting like she was biting her fingernails and grinning big. As he rounded his Prius, John was laying on the ground acting like he was trying to reach for something under the car. John looked up and said, "Oh good, you are here. My lady friend here tossed me the keys and you know how women throw things right?" He started laughing, "Anyhow, I can't quite reach them."

Mary was easing around the back of the car grinning. Mr. Yekun said, "Well, I will be out of your way in a moment." He opened his car door. About the time his butt hit the driver's seat, the yellow jacket stung him on the top meaty part of his leg. She was so fast that he didn't even see it. He pulled the door closed and started the vehicle in one swift move. That was the last of his swift moves. All used up.

John stood up in time to see the lights go out in Mr. Undertakers eyes. He took Mary by the arm and they walked back to Betsy. "Oh." John said as he trotted back to the Prius. He laid down behind it feeling around until he found his tracker. "Thank you, Moe." He said out loud. He trotted back to where Mary was waiting and said, "You were going to let me forget about this."

Mary laughed and said, "I knew you would not leave without it."

John said, "A couple of loose ends is all that is left of this international crime ring. Ms. Politico out in California or where ever and our Ms. Rose here. I need to call our friend Ranger Bill and explain that a certain Penemu Investment company may be tied to his ongoing smuggling investigation and that maybe he should check them out." Mary just grinned.

Back at the cubby hole Mary was filing her report as the man named Yekun also known as the Undertaker has been successfully aborted. John pulled his pictures out of the pile and filed them. Only two pictures to go. He picked up his device and called Randy and asked if they were up for a trip to California.

Randy said, "Sure, why not." Then asking, "Fly, drive, or a little row boat?"

John laughing said, "That was a good one. Little row boat." He then explained that he was not sure Betsy was allowed to cross into California because of the state's pollution standards.

Randy laughed and said, "I forgot Betsy is older than those who wrote the laws."

John said, "As soon as you get here, we will catch a flight out to Los Angeles and find a rental."

Randy said, "All righty then. See you in a couple of hours." They disconnected.

Mary said, "Wow, loose clothes too."

John said, "I want to be out there and back before Ms. Rose sees the door closing on her." So, it was a shower, a change of loose cloths to cover their body armor, bags freshly repacked. They had four more trackers to retrieve. Starting at the farthest and working their way back. They met Randy and Rochelle on the street and hopped into Randy's ride and went to the airport. John and Mary slept. Randy and Rochelle were fresh. It was the wee hours of the morning when they touched down at LAX. Rochelle had already had a rental on standby ordered during the flight. It was waiting for them.

They headed south out of town on the ocean Highway. It was when they were getting near El Toro when the tracker alerted. It was in range as they neared the tracker location. Something seemed not quite right. They arrived at a wrecker winching up a wreck out of a ravine. John went and spoke to the wrecker driver. It seems Ms. Politico lost it on a curve and ended up in the bottom of the ravine. She got ambulanced to the hospital in better shape than the car. John waited until the car rolled up over the edge as the wrecker operator was pulling it into position to load it up. When he stopped, John unhooked his cable for him. As the driver repositioned his truck in line with the wreck, John repositioned the tracking device into his possession. He helped guide the driver back. He then asked for directions to the hospital. The driver thanked him for his help and he left the scene.

Back in the rental, he told the others to find St. Martins Hospital. Mary said, "We passed it coming down here." They busted a U-turn and headed north again. Twenty minutes later they were at the hospital. Ms. Politico was babbling to the doctors that people were dying. The doctors could only agree that yes people are dying, they do so every day. Ms. Politico was yelling, "You don't understand."

The doctor said "I understand that you are not sober." She blew up on that and the doctor said, "I am going to order you a sedative." He turned and walked out.

In the meantime, Rochelle found the nurses changing room and put on a set of flowery scrubs. She came strolling past them and into the room. She had to mix some evergreen in a cup and stir. Then she held the cup up under Ms. Politico's nose. After about the third breath her eyes widened as she realized something was wrong. Rochelle then crumpled and flushed the cup and walked out of the room. Flashing lights and buzzers started going off at the nurse's station. Nurses scrambled in giving CPR to no use. The doctor rushed back in and tried shocking also no use. After almost ten minutes of nothing but flat lines, the doctor shook his head and pulled the sheet up over her cold dead face.

Rochelle came strolling down the hallway dressed normally and said, "Oh, did I miss something?"

Mary high-fived her and the group turned and walked out of the exit. Back at the airport John said, "Home early enough for a late breakfast." They returned the rental and were on the first early bird to Houston. John sat back and smiled. One more tracker to collect. The one that started this whole wild goose chase. It was mid-morning by the time they touched down back at Houston.

Riding in the back of Randy's ride, John called Lloyd. "Anything new going on?" John asked.

Lloyd said, "Red is at the casket factory at this very moment."

John disconnected and tapped Randy's shoulder and said, "Detour."

Randy asked, "Detour?"

"The casket factory." John said.

Mary said, "Look at your tracker. There should be three together and if one leaves, we should probably follow it."

It didn't take Randy long to locate the casket factory. He saw Lloyd and pulled up and stopped at a spot beside him. They got out and asked Lloyd, "Anything new?"

Lloyd replied, "Not yet."

John said, "While we figure this one out, I am going to go collect those two trackers from those two vans." He left at a leisurely stroll. If someone was watching from the inside, you would not have even guessed the man walking behind the two new vans had time to reach and remove the trackers as John did. He thought to himself that he only had the one to go. Ms. Wild Rose. Now the question remained on how to finish this without undue cause for attention. On his stroll back, he downloaded the recent travels of Ms. Rose on his GPS device.

Back at Randy's vehicle, he pulled out his laptop. He booted it up and loaded Ms. Roses stopping points. Finally, he looked up at Lloyd and said, "Are you going to miss this place?"

Lloyd asked, "What do you mean?"

John said, "I do believe this is the final chapter. The end game."

Lloyd said, "Oh. I can still come visit my neighbor."

John said, "Yes you can. He can still let us know of any more of those big orders his boss likes when they happen right?"

Lloyd said, "Hell yes, he will. He doesn't like bad kinds of business deals like he has been seeing. Can't be no good where all those guns go."

John said, "Good. Stay in touch."

John then turned to the others and said, "There are too many loving employees to take out our target here. Looking at my map, there is a favorite restaurant, a gym that she frequents and a home in Kingwood. Let's see which comes first."

"Whatever you do will be sooner than later." Lloyd said pointing in the direction of the casket showroom. In unison all heads turned to see a very distraught looking Wild Rose running down the steps and climbing it to her big four by four. Randy started his vehicle in a reflex action as the rest settled in.

Mary said, "Looks like she just received some very bad news."

"Let's play follow the leader and see where the scared rabbit leads us." John said.

The four by four lurched out into traffic almost causing a collision with horns blowing and fingers raised. Red headed for the freeway and turned west. "Well, we know she is not going home at this moment." Mary said. "Maybe she is going over to Penemu Investments for advice like she did yesterday."

John said, "That would be interesting."

Mary said, "It would be more interesting to see if that red Prius is starting and stopping and starting yet."

Rochelle asked, "What are you guys talking about?"

John laughed out and said, "Who would think an international smuggler of weapons and drugs and warm bodies would be environmentally inclined to drive a hybrid Prius?"

Randy said, "For real?"

Who knows if anyone has gotten curious yet and Rose led them straight back to the six-story black glass building and she pulled up into the delivery drop off lane. As she entered the building, John showed Randy the narrow drive and in they went. As they rounded the corner John said, "This is going to be good."

Randy asked, "What?"

John pointed at the Prius still sitting where it was cycling on and off from gas power to battery to gas. He must have had a full tank. Randy pulled into an empty spot as John was looking up Penemu Investments. What caught his eye was the hit on (Penemu). John said, "What's with these people? Penemu was the name of another of the two hundred watchers in pre-biblical days who went bad and was cast into the darkness. He taught early man (bitterness and sweetness, some secrets of wisdom and writing. Ink and paper.)"

"Weird." Randy said.

John closed his laptop and got out of the vehicle. The others followed his lead. John said to Mary, "I will wait with the Prius and you two go hang back by the stair well."

Finally, Rose came out the back of the office building heading for the red Prius as it cycled to gas and started running. Relief went across her face. Then she looked at John and Mary. Mary looked in some way familiar, she just could not place it. John said, "Hello, Rose. We have been waiting for you."

She stopped in her tracks and digging into her hand bag, she pulled out a little twenty-five caliber pistol. She said, "Who are you?"

John said, "Your circle of friends are all gone. That's who we are."

Rose said, "You don't know who you are dealing with here." John said, "Let me see. A really expensive sports car driving clerk. That one, plus a set of identical triplets, that's four. Plus, an assistant director makes five. Two second shift commanders of the checkpoint, that makes seven." Rose flinched at that last statement. "Let's see." John continued, "A boost over the edge of a pyramid. That's eight. Shall I keep going? I do believe that your pal the governor in New Mexico was so proud of his new venture out there, he attended the grand opening ceremonies with the leaders of multiple gangs and they all got blown to hell." This visibly shook Rose. "Same deal in Pasadena. Oh yea, if you have not heard yet, your lady friend in California is no longer with us. She drove her car off the road. It didn't turn out well for her when we had a meeting with her at the hospital last night. And this fellow right here, has been waiting all night for you to join him." John pointed at the driver's seat of the Prius.

Rose snapped and screamed and started firing that little twenty-five at John and Mary. John stepped away from Mary drawing the fire as Mary let the stinger fly. It sunk into Rose's upper left breast. Rose screamed in rage again as loss of body controls soon enveloped her. Mary said, "That hurt bitch." John and Mary caught Rose's falling body and Randy used his shirt tail to pop open the passenger door and they sat Rose in beside Mr. Yekun. They turned the air-conditioning up and closed the door. It still had plenty of gas to sit for a while.

Mary said, "The bitch winged me." She held up her arm looking at a narrow cut inside her upper arm.

John looked at it and grinned. "Aww. That's just a scratch."

Mary slapped his hand away and added, "I guess I will take that off the bucket list.

John said laughing, "Are you going to claim that?"

Mary raised her shirt. Three more flattened rounds stuck on her body armor. She said, "No. I'm claiming these."

"Oh." John said in a change of tone. "Yes, I would say that counts."

They picked up the casings and got into Randy's vehicle and drove out of the exit. John told Randy to circle through the front half-moon drive and stop by that big four by four. John stepped out and retrieved the tracker from under her bumper and said, "Our work is almost done. Home James." John said with a grin. Randy said laughing, "Watch it now." They drove out of there.

CHAPTER SEVENTEEN

Randy and Rochelle dropped John and Mary off at the end of the alley and headed out for the Rock. As John and Mary approached the cubby hole, there was a young couple sitting on a set of duffel bags. Mary said, "Can we help you?"

The young man stood up and asked, "Do you live at this address?" Mary said, "Yes we do."

"Oh good." He said and handed John a big brown envelope. It was from the commission. John opened the door and turned off the alarm and invited the young couple in.

John said, "You can set your bags over by the TV."

Mary put on a pot of coffee. John turned on the TV and told the young couple they had a couple of business things to close out, to make themselves comfortable. They sat looking around curiously. John got on the phone with Ranger Bill. He told Bill that it may behoove him to check Penemu Investments with all the other businesses already being looked into. The ranger told John that he had already

retrieved and released another can of girls. Only a couple of stray containers left floating around out there, but he was determined to collect every last one of them. John looked at the table and picked the remaining photos up and filed them away in the mission accomplished file. He just grinned at the file of the one's who got away. Still on the phone Ranger Bill said, "Oh yea. It seems one of California's fruits and nuts finally fell out of the tree."

John chuckled and said, "Meaning?"

"The political arm of your problems are over." Bill said. John replied, "How so?"

Bill said, "A car accident, then a fowl up on medication or something at the hospital is all they say on the local news out here."

John said, "Well Mr. Bill, you keep up the good work and have a good day." He then disconnected.

Mary was typing in her reports the final three abortions successful. Mr. Yekun also known as the Undertaker; abortion successful. Ms. California Politico, money bags financer; abortion successful. Rose smith also known as the Wild Rose the manipulator and fixer of trafficking operations; abortion successful. She pushed the send button and turned to John and said, "Reports sent."

John was reading the contents of the big envelope and turned to Mary and said, "Well now. It looks like we have been directed to take a couple of interns under our wings."

Mary said, "Oh, how fun." She turned to them and asked, "Do you two drink coffee?"

They both stood up and said, "Sure." Mary poured four cups.

John directed them to some chairs at the table and said, "You two come highly recommended. Meaning you have caught someone's attention and they were impressed with your abilities. My name is John Myers and this lovely lady is Mary, and you are?"

They stood stiff and straight with that military air about them. He said, "My name is Devin and this is Lupe." They all shook hands. They were starting into some background history about themselves when there was a knock at the door. John got up in mid conversation and opened the door. You could have heard a pin drop.

The commission doctor said, "John. I need to talk to you."

ABORT: Terminate Prematurely

Book II Preview Chapter 1

John stood there watching as the front door closed. The gears in his head were spinning. What the company doctor told him had answered some of the questions that he and Mary raised, but more importantly, many new questions were floating to the top like cheerios in a bowl of milk.

He still did not understand the full scope of the doctor's involvement with such characters that him and his team had successfully taken out of the picture. Now the realization was sinking in. He looked over at the two interns and then at Mary. "What that man just said means we are going full on global."

"Oh cool! I like to travel." Mary said.

John replied, "Yes, but this won't quite be like going to a couple of tourist spots to take out our assigned targets. It could range from high rises to sewers, rice paddies to jungles, paved roads to burro trails. This is going to be a whole new ball game."

"Good!" Mary said. "Let's get the gang together to meet out at the Rock. We can introduce our new interns to them as well."

John looked at Devin and Lupe and said, "How are you at shooting from horseback?"

They were kind of looking at John as a deer looks into the headlights of a rapidly approaching vehicle.

Mary said, "Oh this is going to be fun. I will start making the calls now."

Devin and Lupe were looking at each other thinking what on earth did we just sign up for.

"How do you two feel about camping out?" John asked.

Lupe said, "How's the ground? We have slept our share of nights on lumpy rocks in the middle east."

"Oh, you will love this. Lots of carpet grass and shade trees. If you don't have a tent, you can use ours. We recently graduated to a Scooby doo van."

"A what?" Devin asked.

"It will be self-explanatory when we get there. That gives us a few days to familiarize ourselves with each other and teach you the guidelines and methods of our chosen field of employment. You will need to also get yourselves fitted with body armor such as this." John showed them his essential set-up. They took note of what they would need to start on a new career in the cleaning up of societies trash that has begun to take over the world.

After a few hours of discussing the ins and outs, what to do and not do of their new line of work, Devin and Lupe began to relax a little. The main questions having been answered. Lupe got up to help Mary throw some sandwiches and a salad together and they all enjoyed their first of many meals together.

As evening came and went, it came to the point of how Devin and Lupe were going to work out their sleeping arrangement over in the corner of the living room by the window. At this point John decided that this little cubby hole was getting too small.

That night, he and Mary made up their minds to find a bigger house to live in. At least a two bedroom for sure. The commission would foot the bill, but John did not want an apartment, condo, or trailer. Maybe they could find a house with a decent yard in an older neighborhood. So began the search.

The next morning after a meal of bacon, eggs, toast and orange juice, John and Mary lead Devin and Lupe over to the parking garage and introduced them to "Betsy" the shiny jet black sixty-three Impala with lots of leg room and big seats.

"Nice." Devin said as he walked around checking her out.

They headed over to the local commission facility to pick up the issue of armored clothing and check out all the different types of tools available to them to ensure they had no problem in finalizing the mission assigned to them.

Lupe was checking out the up close and personal tools like the stinger, assorted blades and chemical types of weapons. Devin was the sniper type as he was looking at the long-range tools of death. John pointed Devin to a little black box.

"What is this?" Devin asked.

John opened the lid and showed Devin assorted bullet molds.

"Oh, I see." Devin said.

John said, "These molds are for ice bullets. Either pure water or you can add a chemical soup to it and it does the job. No copper and lead to trace as the ice melts in the body. Dead is dead. No trail to follow."

"I like that." Devin said as he headed to the agent in charge to sign that tool out.

After Devin and Lupe had finished their selections of all their own personal tools of the trade and collected their new body armor clothing, everyone headed back to Betsy.

Authors Comment: Sticks and Stones

The old saying goes, Sticks and Stones may break my bones but words will never hurt me. Not so in Texas, more specifically in Austin County, and even more specific in the Bellville Courthouse. With both the District Judge and the District Attorney absent, the Assistant District Attorney and a retired Judge along with an intimidated Jury, convicted me to a fifty year flat, no parole, aggravated sentence with no medical, physical, or DNA evidence. I was convicted of a crime I did not commit by adult words put into a child's mouth. The Investigative Sheriff detective lied on the stand. Ninety percent of the audio was deleted or muted from my recorded interview. The Assistant D.A. lied in the closing statements and also yelled and screamed next to the Jury Closet while deliberations were ongoing as many witnesses heard this out in the public hallway. With sticks and stones, I could have walked home. Let's not forget the clerk photographing me with a cell phone in the courtroom to show my accusers who to point at in the courtroom. I was never mirandized upon being arrested and cuffed. I was told not to give those jailers a hard time. It was just a piece of paper. Now I make license plates for the state. I never thought I would write a book, so give me a break on the first one. The second only gets better.

About The Author

Randy Hudson was born and raised in Colorado County, South Texas about halfway between Houston and San Antonio. He is a Vietnam era United States Marine Corps Sergeant upon honorable discharge. He spent most of his life hanging iron and raising a family of five kids. He is now a grandfather and great grandfather. He also spent a few years in the oilfield as a roughneck in the eighties. He is an avid reader of books, likes to travel when he can and enjoys just being alive. Writing a book was a wonderful challenge at his old age. He never saw it coming.

Milton Keynes UK
Ingram Content Group UK Ltd.
UKHW022000241123
433237UK00004B/85